BERKLEY TITLES BY RACHEL LINDEN

The Magic of Lemon Drop Pie

Recipe for a Charmed Life

The Secret of Orange Blossom Cake

A Sprinkle of Sweet Serendipity

Praise for the Novels of Rachel Linden

"Heartfelt, heartwarming, joyful, and uplifting. You can't go wrong with a Rachel Linden book."

—Debbie Macomber,
#1 *New York Times* bestselling author of *One Night*

"A poignant, hopeful must read for anyone who has ever wondered about a different path. Rachel Linden creates unforgettable characters that will work their way into your heart and a compulsively readable story that will keep the pages turning late into the night. Five huge stars!"

—Kristy Woodson Harvey,
New York Times bestselling author of *The Summer of Songbirds*

"A magical novel about second chances! Warm, witty, and wise, I loved it! Linden is a master at creating lovable characters! *The Magic of Lemon Drop Pie* is escapist reading at its best!"

—Jill Shalvis,
New York Times bestselling author of *The Summer Deal*

"An enchanting tale about the one thing we've all imagined: a magical second chance. Rachel Linden expertly mixes romance, mystery, and family drama into a delicious recipe of a story. . . . With her trademark warmth, Linden delivers a captivating story with a magical heartbeat at its center."

—Patti Callahan,
New York Times bestselling author of *Surviving Savannah*

"Magic, sweet treats, heartfelt charm . . . this dreamy tale has it all!"

—Woman's World

"*Recipe for a Charmed Life* is actually a recipe for a magically marvelous read about expectations, second chances, and following your heart. Rachel Linden writes complicated and compelling characters that are as relatable as they are likable. I enjoyed every bit of this delightful novel."

—Jenn McKinlay,
New York Times bestselling author of *Summer Reading*

"The perfect mix of delicious backdrop details, family secrets, and the quest for purpose and lasting love. Enchantingly delightful from first page to last."

—Susan Meissner, *USA Today* bestselling author of *Only the Beautiful*

"Rachel Linden whips up an irresistible family drama oozing with charm and magic! *The Magic of Lemon Drop Pie* is a must read for anyone who longs for second chances. A gem of a novel that charmed me from [the] get-go, perfect for fans of Sarah Addison Allen and Alice Hoffman."

—Lori Nelson Spielman,
New York Times bestselling author of *The Star-Crossed Sisters of Tuscany*

"A delicious read, down to the very last lemon drop! Rachel Linden delivers a delightful escape, wonderful characters, and a magical experience that will leave readers hungry for her next book."

—Julie Cantrell,
New York Times and *USA Today* bestselling author of *Perennials*

"A delightful tale of food, family, and sweet romance. . . . This story is an absolute feast!"

—Lauren K. Denton,
USA Today bestselling author of *The Summer House*

"Completely charming! Take a spunky heroine, add a swoonworthy, orange-rubber-overall-wearing oyster farmer, throw in a dash of the real-life messiness we all understand, and sprinkle a dusting of Linden's signature magical realism, and you've got the recipe for a delightful story you can't put down."

—Katherine Reay,
bestselling author of *A Shadow in Moscow*

"A deliciously sweet tale about refusing to give up on your dreams and finding your bliss against all odds. Linden gives readers so much to enjoy—romance, family drama, and bittersweet second chances—all served up with the perfect dash of magic."

—Kate Bromley,
author of *Here for the Drama* and *Talk Bookish to Me*

A Sprinkle of Sweet Serendipity

RACHEL LINDEN

Berkley
New York

BERKLEY
An imprint of Penguin Random House LLC
1745 Broadway, New York, NY 10019
penguinrandomhouse.com

Library of Congress Cataloging-in-Publication Data

Names: Linden, Rachel author
Title: A sprinkle of sweet serendipity / Rachel Linden.
Description: First edition. | New York: Berkley, 2026.
Identifiers: LCCN 2025049323 (print) | LCCN 2025049324 (ebook) |
ISBN 9780593816660 trade paperback | ISBN 9780593816653 ebook
Subjects: LCGFT: Romance fiction | Magic realist fiction | Fiction | Novels
Classification: LCC PS3612.I5327426 S67 2026 (print) |
LCC PS3612.I5327426 (ebook)
LC record available at https://lccn.loc.gov/2025049323
LC ebook record available at https://lccn.loc.gov/2025049324

First Edition: May 2026

Printed in the United States of America
1st Printing

The authorized representative in the EU for product safety and compliance is Penguin Random House Ireland, Morrison Chambers, 32 Nassau Street, Dublin D02 YH68, Ireland, https://eu-contact.penguin.ie.

To all the sandwich generation mamas
who juggle caregiving, children, careers,
and keep the world turning.

This one's for you
and for A + B.
You have my whole heart.

A Sprinkle of Sweet Serendipity

Chapter 1

"Emmie, why does our candy shop smell like burning eyebrows?" My mother's puzzled voice floats from the front of the store as she comes in the door with a jingle of the bell.

With a start, I snap back to reality. I'm standing in the commercial kitchen of the Happy Viking, our family's candy and fudge shop, lost in thought while acrid smoke curls up from a large copper kettle in front of me. I've scorched the peanut butter fudge. Again.

"Oh, sugar!" I cry, snatching the smoking kettle off the gas burner and rushing to the back door of the kitchen. I'm careful to not say a stronger word, so I don't have to put a quarter in the naughty-word jar. I'm trying to avoid filling the jar because when I do, I promised to buy my six-year-old space-obsessed son a pricey working model of the solar system. However, this morning is testing my patience to the limit. At this rate, Gus may be earning his model sooner than anticipated.

Carefully, I set the overheated kettle on the concrete stoop and pause to draw a deep breath of the cool, salty breeze blowing across Liberty Bay. It's a relief to be out of the smoky stench. The bay laps gently at the shore just a hundred yards beyond the kitchen door, silvery and rippling in the morning light. It's late June in the Pacific Northwest, which means long days, soft breezes, and lots of our rarest commodity, sunshine. It would be a perfect summer day if I wasn't feeling so anxious. And forgetful. This is the second batch of fudge I've ruined this morning. I don't know what's wrong with me. Scratch that. I know exactly what's wrong with me, I just can't do anything about it. It's my thirty-fourth birthday, and the nerves and anticipation are making me uncharacteristically absent-minded. Maybe this year my wish will finally come true. I make the same wish every year though, and so far I've been disappointed every time.

With a sigh, I head back inside to deal with my mess. I grab a dish towel and wave it vigorously through the air. I don't want to set off the fire alarm and the sprinklers. I wrinkle my nose. There's nothing on earth quite as acrid as the smell of scorched butter and sugar and cream. It smells like all the good and cozy things in the world gone wrong.

"Come on, Emmie. Chin up," I whisper hopefully. "Maybe this year will be different."

The smoke is dissipating, whisked out the open door by a lively breeze, but the smell lingers, the unpleasant fug of scorched candy hanging low and heavy in the kitchen. It reminds me of the time I bent too far over the candles on Ava Jorgensen's ninth birthday cake and singed my right eyebrow almost completely off. You never forget the smell of your own burning hair.

Mom comes into the kitchen, moving slowly and leaning on her cane, her handbag slung over her arm. "Honey, are you okay? What happened?" She's accompanied, as always, by her pudgy

French bulldog Mr. Butters, who wags his little stub of a tail when he sees me. He's wearing a bow tie today that is festooned with lilac satin stripes. They contrast nicely with his pale gold and cream coloring. Mom spends an almost embarrassing amount of time and money planning daily outfits and accessories for Mr. Butters, which he submits to wearing with an air of good-natured resignation.

"All good," I reassure her brightly. I don't like her to worry, so I try to put the best spin I can on everything. She has enough to worry about. I stoop to give Mr. Butters a scratch behind his huge batwing ears, and he grunts enthusiastically, his entire backside wriggling with pleasure.

I'm annoyed with myself. Burnt fudge means more work, less profit, and a slow start to the day. I give Mr. Butters one final scratch, then lug the cooling kettle back inside and carefully scrape the ruined goopy mess of the fudge into the trash with the big wooden fudge-stirring spoon. "I messed up. The burner was acting up again and I got distracted," I admit.

Mom's expression of concern softens in understanding. "It's a big day for you," she says gently, wincing as she slowly makes her way around the marble slab table in the center of the kitchen. It's where we handcraft all our fudge. At sixty, she's slender and lovely with a neat puff of soft gray-blond curls and a touch of pink lipstick that matches her sweater. Her face looks younger than her years, but her body is bent into a slight question mark and she walks with a pained effort she tries hard to conceal. I see it though, and it gives me a pang of worry straight through my heart. I should be used to those pangs by now, but I'm not. I don't think I'll ever be. I blink hard and poke at the scorched brown mess glued to the bottom of the kettle.

"I'm really hoping today is the day," I admit softly. I give up on the kettle. I'm going to have to let it soak in boiling water and then use salt and lemon to scrub it clean. I'm feeling off-kilter today, not my usual glass-half-full, can-do self. It's hard to want something, wish for something, year after year, and be disappointed each time. I'm feeling the rising anxiety as my birthday rolls around once more—the hope mixed with apprehension. I want it so badly, but I'm worried I'll just be disappointed again.

"Emmie." Mom's voice is a warm reprimand. "Every birthday we get on this earth is a special day, regardless of what happens on it."

"You're right," I sigh, and set the kettle in the sink, then lean back tiredly, swiping a wisp of pale blond hair from my forehead and tucking it behind my ear. I need more coffee, but I've already had three cups. I feel like I'm always tired, like tired is my default setting. I can't remember the last time I didn't feel the dull tug of exhaustion. I'm tired from the moment I open my eyes each morning as Gus clambers into bed next to me at the crack of dawn, blinking solemnly at me like an owl from behind his round glasses with electric blue frames. He's usually holding a science book from the library, eager to share a new and alarming fact about the universe. A fact I'm pretty sure no first grader should know. And I'm tired each night I stay up late poring over accounts and spreadsheets until the numbers swim in front of my eyes. Tired from juggling everything at once—single parenthood; medical bills and appointments for Mom; trying to keep the shop afloat; trying not to drop anything important; trying to be a good friend, neighbor, small-business owner; trying to eat enough fiber and stay hydrated and floss my teeth; trying to remember to just breathe . . .

Sometimes—often—it feels like too much, like I'm drowning in a sea of responsibilities. But I can't let anything sink. Everyone is depending on me. I fill a glass with lukewarm water and chug it in lieu of another cup of coffee. It helps a little. Maybe.

"You should take some time for yourself today," Mom urges, eyeing me with a soft expression of concern. "You could get a massage or get your nails done? I bet Mary Beth could squeeze you in over at the Nail Boat. My treat."

I picture the only nail salon in town, decorated to look like a Viking longboat. In keeping with our town's nickname, "Little Norway," all the staff at the Nail Boat wear fake blond braids and plastic helmets with horns on Halloween. The residents of Poulsbo, Washington, are proud of their strong Viking heritage, and take every opportunity to celebrate it. They've turned our quaint little town nestled on the shore of Puget Sound into a tourist destination, with festivals, annual events, and a charming downtown dotted with brightly painted wooden buildings that look like they've been lifted straight from the banks of a Norwegian fjord.

I shake my head. "Thanks, Mom. I'm okay. I've got too much to do to leave right now. Besides, I think Dani's going to swing by with coffee soon."

Caffeine and Dani Diaz are my two best friends. Together they help keep me sane and vertical. I run hot water into the copper kettle and leave it to soften the burnt remains of the fudge. "If anyone is getting a massage, it should be you." I glance pointedly at Mom's hands. She's covertly massaging the joints of her right thumb and snatches her hand away guiltily. "Is it bad this morning?" I ask softly.

She waves away my concern. "About like always."

Her hands are so gnarled that her fingers are bent and twisted sideways like the roots of a tree. I watch her put on a brave face as usual, but I'm concerned. Despite what she says, I can tell her pain has been worsening. She's using her cane almost every day now. Her rheumatoid arthritis is steadily growing worse. It's why she's now unable to make the fudge she and my dad crafted together and sold here in our family's candy shop for almost four decades before he passed away after a long battle with cancer. It's why I came home from Paris after years living abroad.

The call came a little more than seven years ago. Faced with Mom's gradually deteriorating health and Dad's grim diagnosis, they needed help. As their only child, I was the one they turned to. At first I thought it would be temporary, a few months or a year at most. But a few weeks after I arrived home, I found out I was pregnant. Gus is six going on eighty-five now, a little old soul and the brightest spot in my life, but when I realized that the nasty flu I couldn't quite seem to shake was actually morning sickness, it threw me for the biggest loop of my life.

"Oh golly, five minutes till we open," I tell Mom in surprise after a glance at the clock. I grab a tray of maple pecan fudge slices sitting on the counter and head toward the storefront. Mom follows slowly behind me, hands empty except for her cane. She can't carry the heavy trays of fudge anymore. Her joints won't take the strain. Mr. Butters waddles behind her. He pauses in the doorway leading from the kitchen to the storefront and tries to wriggle out of his bow tie by scraping it against the doorframe, but it won't budge. With a resigned grunt he trots into the store and settles onto his bed below the cash register. Anytime Mom is in the shop, this is where he naps, waiting like a little sultan to receive pats and adoration throughout the day from customers. He's a local celebrity in Poulsbo. Everyone knows and loves Mr. Butters. Someone even wrote him in as a candidate for mayor in the last election.

I open the case below the register and slide the tray of fudge onto the shelf, mentally taking inventory of the flavors left this morning. No peanut butter fudge today due to this morning's mishaps. Oh well. There are still fourteen other flavors customers can choose from. We are running low on chocolate cherry though. I'll have to whip up another batch today or tomorrow. And I promised to donate five pounds of fudge for a silent auction to raise funds for a new local women and children's shelter. I'm going to need to make at least a couple more batches today. I resign myself to the task. Making fudge lost its novelty a long time ago. Now it's just another chore in a seemingly endless list of them.

With a soft sigh, Mom shuffles to the front door and peers out. "Looks like it might be a busy day with all the tourists heading to that music festival over on Bainbridge Island," she comments. Already the sidewalk is starting to fill with passersby. It's a sunny weekend in June. The town will be packed by noon. Fingers crossed business will be good.

"Can you open the till while I do the morning walk-through?" I ask Mom.

As she gets the register ready for business, I take a brisk little walk around the store to make sure everything is in order before we open. Every nook and cranny of this space is as familiar to me as the palm of my hand. I grew up in this store. I spent countless hours here finishing homework after school, nestled in a nest of blankets squashed in the corner by the bubble gum section. I learned to read by sounding out the names of lemon drops, butterscotch buttons, root beer barrels, and horehound lozenges on the rack of old-fashioned candies, and I practiced math by working the cash register and helping out in the kitchen measuring ingredients for fudge. How many ounces in a quart of cream? How many cups of sugar in a twenty-pound bag?

Not much has changed since I was a kid. The store has a small footprint, but my parents maximized every inch of space. The aisles are cluttered with racks holding packaged candies from bygone eras, a section of British sweets like Wine Gums and Jelly Babies, an endcap of stick candy and rock candy in every imaginable flavor and color, and a wall of bubble gum. While the store has grown slowly shabbier over the years, the brightly colored packages of sugar distract from the worn, dingy gray carpet and the sagging display racks.

The Happy Viking has been Poulsbo's candy shop for decades, but its age is really starting to show. I heave a sigh as I look around. Some days I wonder how long we can hang on. Some days I wonder what it would feel like to be free of this constant stress and worry, the responsibility and the slow decline. For years I've dreamed of opening my own shop. It would be a bespoke chocolate boutique where I could dream and play with flavors and textures, offering people a little taste of happiness, a sliver of delight. Crafting handmade chocolates is my passion in life. It's why after high school I left Poulsbo to train at a prestigious chocolatier program in Switzerland and then apprenticed with Jacques Genin, a premier chocolate maker in Paris. I'd always planned to turn that passion into a business and open my own storefront somewhere far away from Poulsbo. Someday, maybe I will. But increasingly that day feels far off.

"Hey!" Someone raps firmly on the glass door, making Mom and me both jump. Mr. Butters raises his head and gives a single lazy whuff of alert.

"Dot, you scared the daylights out of us," Mom scolds, unlocking the door and letting in her best friend of many years. She flips the sign on the door to **OPEN**.

"Where's our birthday girl?" Dot booms, glancing around until she sees me. At almost six feet tall, Dot is broad-shouldered and larger than life, with a chopped pixie cut dyed a shade of burgundy usually reserved for red velvet wedding cake and a gravelly voice that sounds like bottom-shelf whiskey on the rocks. She's loud, opinionated, and unapologetically herself.

Today Dot is wearing a tight T-shirt that proudly proclaims "Part-Time Mermaid." People tend to assume the shirt is a joke since Dot owns the Salty Mermaid, the boutique next door where she sells all sorts of seaside-themed home décor and personal apparel. However, Dot is quick to whip out a business card for her side business, Mermaid Tales. A two-hour session costs two hundred and fifty dollars, and Dot will come to your chosen location dressed as her alter ego, a mermaid named Serene, and entertain guests with clean or bawdy (your choice) stories from the sea. Or if you have a pool, she also offers a one-woman aquatic show. If it's an adult party, she can also bartend, either in the water or on land.

When Dot turned fifty, she had a mermaid tail custom made for her by a woman in California, bought a long tangerine-and-teal-colored wig from Etsy, and somehow mustered the breezy and brash self-confidence to pull the whole ensemble off. Serene is especially popular with bachelorette parties, or so I'm told.

"Happy birthday, baby girl," Dot announces, holding out a package wrapped in the starfish paper from her shop. I tear the paper off carefully, revealing a silicone spatula with the words "Getting older is a beach" printed on the handle, below a row of starfish whose arms are embedded with crystals.

"To replace that ratty old one you have in your mom's kitchen," Dot explains. "Figured you could use a new one. This one's good quality. Plus, you know I love a naughty pun and a little sparkle."

I'm touched that Dot noticed my spatula, which is old and falling apart. It's also one of the only things I brought back with me from France. It holds so many good memories from my training days in Switzerland and bittersweet recollections of long-ago evenings with Romaine in the Jacques Genin workshop kitchen in Paris, talking and working side by side, gradually falling in love. I can't bear to part with that old spatula, even though the handle tends to fall off every now and then at inconvenient times. It reminds me of a time of life that is now gone.

"Thank you. I love it," I tell her, pressing a quick kiss to Dot's leathery cheek. "I have to hide it from Gus though. He gets puns now."

Dot chortles. "Glad you like it, baby girl. You know I love you like you're my own." I squeeze her hand. Dot and her partner Jude never had children, and after Jude passed away almost a decade ago, Dot was left with just us and her brother Walt as her family. She's like an aunt to me, and she has always loved me to bits.

"Any news from around town this morning, Dot?" Mom asks as she opens the till. Dot manages to know everything that goes on in Poulsbo, a mysterious talent that often comes in handy.

Dot shrugs. "Same old, same old. Nothing much to report today. Although I noticed your doorknob is loose. Felt like it might come off in my hand when I came in just now."

"I'll take a look. Probably just the screws are loose again." I grab my little tool kit from its place on the shelf below the cash register. As I tighten the screws on the doorknob, I try not to think about the long list of old and worn items that need to be replaced around here, starting with the gas burner for heating the fudge. A new, modern system costs thousands of dollars, so I've been making do with the finicky burner, watching it like a hawk in case it acts up. Today's burnt fudge is a stinky reminder that we need more reliable equipment. We need a lot of things.

Every time I turn around something is going wrong in this

tired place. A leaky faucet, a wobbly shelf. I always try to fix small problems by watching YouTube videos. I give it my best shot, and I've learned to do more than I thought I could. And sometimes I swear things seem to repair themselves in the night. More than once I've come in after something breaks to find it seemingly miraculously working again, like we have elves helping us as we sleep. I wish that were true. I want it to be true. But those little repairs—my own and the inexplicable ones—do not even begin to touch the renovations this old place needs. Those are going to require far more than YouTube and elbow grease or handy elves.

I shudder to think of the cost we could be facing eventually. So far we've avoided having to make the more major repairs, but word around town is that new county standards are going to be enforced soon, and that all businesses are going to have to bring their plumbing and electrical systems up to code. At least that's the scuttlebutt Dot has heard. I try not to think about what that might entail, not just for us but for many of the small businesses that surround us downtown. I think we're all just trying not to worry until we have to. As Dad used to say, "No use borrowing trouble. It'll come knocking soon enough."

I stash my toolbox back in its spot and grab the last tray of fudge from the kitchen. I'm just coming back with a tray of orange dreamsicle slices in hand when the bell on the door jingles.

"Freeze! Police!" A petite woman with a cascade of dark curls, wearing a navy blue uniform and a shiny gold Poulsbo Police badge, pops into the shop. She spots me and says with mock sternness, "Ma'am, I'm going to have to ask you to step out from behind the counter and come with me."

I grin and quickly slip the tray of fudge into the case. "Why, Officer Diaz, have I done something wrong?" I blink in faux innocence, playing along.

My best friend shakes the handcuffs at her waist and frowns. "Failure to comply will result in police action," she announces, trying to look stern and failing. She beams at Mom and Dot, her smile such high wattage it looks as though it could power the sun. "I'm afraid I'm going to have to take this suspect in for questioning," she tells them. To me she says, "Come on, birthday girl. Let's hit the bakery before they run out of raisin buns." Then she notices Mr. Butters, who has left his dog bed and waddled up to her, wriggling his stump of a tail so enthusiastically that his whole body shakes. He's standing beside her, making whining noises, trying to get her attention. He adores Dani because she breaks the rules for him every time she thinks we aren't looking.

"Ooh, Mr. Butters, you handsome devil." She pauses and fishes a doggy pot pie out of her pocket, feeding it to him on the sly. He swallows the pot pie whole, then licks her hand, grinning happily. He's supposed to be on a diet, since he's gotten a little pudgy and looks like a Twinkie or a Tater Tot. But Dani indulges him. She's also been known to pocket more than one of his more humiliating accessories (here's looking at you, twinkling Christmas light doggy headband), for which I think Mr. Butters is eternally grateful.

She looks at the bow tie. "It's not that bad," she whispers to him, scratching him affectionately under the chin. He pants and grins happily.

"Ready to go?" she asks me.

I glance at Mom, who makes a shooing motion.

"Go," she urges. "Enjoy your birthday treat. It's tradition."

It is tradition, but I thought Dani would bring something yummy to the shop. I don't like to leave Mom to manage the store by herself. What if someone needs help reaching a high shelf or buys something heavy? What if the shop is suddenly overrun with customers?

"I'll help keep an eye on things here," Dot promises. "You go celebrate. Bring back a bear claw for me."

I hesitate a moment longer, torn between a feeling of responsibility and the desire to sink my teeth into a delicious fresh Scandinavian pastry. It's my birthday so the pastry wins out. Barely.

"I'll be back in half an hour," I promise, heading out the door after Dani. "Don't do anything crazy while I'm gone."

"Sorry, we can't hear you," Dot shouts as the door swings closed. "We're too busy planning all the crazy things we're going to do while you're gone."

Chapter 2

"Thanks for taking me into custody, Officer Diaz." I trot briskly to catch up to Dani as we spill out the door onto Front Street. Away from the shop, my guilt at leaving and my lingering anxiety about my birthday start to ease, replaced by a sense of enjoyment. It's a beautiful day and I turn my face to the sun, enjoying the rarity of being out and about on a lovely summer morning.

"I knew you could spare a few minutes on your birthday to get a raisin bun," Dani says, walking at a fast clip. Even though she tops out at barely over five feet, meaning she's a good two inches shorter than me, Dani somehow manages to always outpace me by a decent margin. Speed walking must be something she perfected at the police academy.

"You mean a raspberry Danish?" I remind her. "Which is absolutely the best pastry in the world."

"Blasphemy." Dani sticks her tongue out at me as we continue the argument we've been having since kindergarten.

We've been best friends since the first day of school when the teacher seated Dani next to me. A tiny, quiet new girl with huge, dark eyes, Dani was still learning English and had been in the States only a few months after her parents and grandmother emigrated from Mexico. Feeling sorry for her, Mrs. Thomas paired her with me. She thought my friendliness and helpfulness would be good for Dani, whom she labeled as painfully shy. How very wrong she'd been about that! It took Dani about a month to warm up, but by the end of the year, Mrs. Thomas had come to rue the day she'd seated us next to each other. We simply could not stop talking and laughing once we got going. Twenty-eight years later, it's still true.

For most of our twenties we went our separate ways. Dani spent several years in New York, and I moved to France. But then we both found ourselves unexpectedly back home and picked up our friendship as though the years apart never happened. Dani is my polar opposite—brash to my gentle, loud to my soft-spoken, a little wild to my levelheaded. She is the most loyal, exasperating live wire of a best friend a girl could wish for. I absolutely adore her and could not have made it through these past few hard years without her.

"We're headed to Sluys, right?" I ask, turning in the direction of the most iconic Scandinavian bakery in town. She grabs my hand and drags me in the opposite direction.

"No, Kristensen's. I have to show you something. You're not going to want to miss this, I promise."

Curious, I follow her. Our candy shop is located in the heart of downtown Poulsbo on Front Street, the main street in the historic district. Downtown is just a few blocks long, with rows of brightly painted wooden buildings, some decorated with fanciful gingerbread and pointed eaves, others with a retro chalet vibe.

Combined, they give the town a charmingly European feel. Poulsbo is tiny and postcard perfect, with local shops and bakeries and several Viking- and Norwegian-themed murals by local artists.

"Got any hot birthday plans yet?" Dani asks as we walk down Front Street toward Kristensen's Bakery.

"Just the usual—birthday dinner at the Longboat, which you know about since you're coming to it. And then probably home to try to put Gus to bed on time for once. If I'm lucky, I'll get through at least one episode of *Savor* before I fall asleep." I wince at how lame that sounds. I can't recall how many episodes of my favorite show I've drifted off halfway through. It's a lot.

I don't mention what's eating at me today, the question that swirls around every birthday for me. Dani knows about it, but there's nothing she can do. There's nothing any of us can do. I feel a flutter of anxiety again at the thought of the birthday cake, of blowing out the candle once more and making a wish and . . . I'll have to just wait and see what happens. Maybe this will finally be the year my wish comes true.

"That is a super-boring birthday plan," Dani announces, pulling a face. "We need to get you a hot date with a real man, not a hot date with your couch, drinking wine in your pajamas and drooling over your celebrity TV crush."

"I don't drool over Henry Summers," I protest. This is a lie and Dani knows it. She throws me a disbelieving look.

"What?" I lift my hands. "I *admire* Henry Summers. His whole goal is to celebrate inspiring stories of food and family across the globe. I love to see all the unique places he finds in out-of-the-way corners of the world. That episode he did on the pub in the Yorkshire Dales that's been in the same family for two hundred years? Amazing. Mom thinks he should come here and do a show about the fudge shop." It doesn't hurt that Henry has the plummiest English accent and rocks a sweater blazer—"swazer," as they're called—better than any man on the planet.

"Mm-hmm, well, you need to 'admire' someone who isn't on the other side of a TV screen," Dani says, looking skeptical. "Henry Summers is dreamy, no argument there. That English accent—yes, please! But is he going to keep your bed warm at night? You need a real man, Emmie. A big, hairy man . . . in the flesh."

She confidently steps off the curb and jaywalks across the street. I trot behind her.

"I'm not the biggest fan of hairy men. I like my men a little . . . smoother," I tell her. "You can have the hairy lumberjack types." But she's right about one thing. Henry Summers might be my dream man, but he is also completely unattainable. It would be nice to have a crush on someone real, not someone I see only through a TV screen.

Golly, that makes my life sound sad. It's not. It's really not. I adore my mom and my son. I have a lot to be thankful for. But yes, there are a few things I wish I could have. Like a chance to make a life somewhere other than the tiny town where I grew up. Or a real boyfriend. Heck, I'd even settle for a nice dinner with a man who didn't text me beforehand asking for pictures of my earlobes. That happened, by the way, and it wasn't even the strangest text I've gotten before a first date.

"Besides, I don't have time to date right now," I counter when we reach the far curb. "And I feel like I know every available bachelor in Poulsbo. It's pretty slim pickings." I roll my eyes.

I've tried dating off and on over the past couple of years, mostly because I give in to Dani's badgering and try online dating for a few weeks or a month or two. The whole dating app situation has been quite disappointing. Dani rocks the apps, chatting with like ten guys at once, going out to Bremerton or Tacoma every weekend with someone new. She doesn't want a serious relationship, just some companionship and fun. For me, it's been really underwhelming. One guy canceled our coffee date an hour before we were to meet for the first time because he decided I looked too short in my photo. Another asked me to text him a picture of my boobs after we had lunch once. It's a weird world, online dating. I don't think it's for me. Which leaves my chances for romance in real life at about a zero. Unless a guy wanders into the fudge shop or works at the elementary school, I'm not likely to cross paths with him.

"You need to keep getting out there," Dani encourages me. "Any guy would be lucky to have you. You just haven't met the right one yet." She heads toward the red Kristensen's Bakery storefront.

"I think I scare guys off," I tell her, breaking into a weird little hybrid hop/walk to keep up with her pace. "Let's be honest. I'm not a great catch. I'm a tired single mom. I live with my disabled mother and a six-year-old who likes to wear sweater-vests and is obsessed with space disasters, and I'm tied to a family business that's slowly failing. That's a little bit of a hard sell."

Dani halts in the middle of the sidewalk and holds up her hand. Her tone is stern. "Stop right there. Emmaline Gwendoline Wynne. You are a young, hot single mother. You look like Reese Witherspoon in her *Legally Blonde* era, and you are a small-business owner, an excellent mother, and selflessly devoted to your family. You are the kindest, most generous person I know. You make casseroles for anyone who's sick, and cards for the nursing home on Valentine's Day. You are a pillar of your community, and you always smell like candy. What's not to love?" She wags her finger in my face. "Stop selling yourself short, reinita." She loves to call me that, her pet nickname for me, her little queen.

Dani stops lecturing me as we halt in front of the big plate glass front window of Kristensen's Bakery, which has been in the Kristensen family since the 1930s. I can't remember the last time I visited this bakery. We always go to Sluys down the street. Warm light spills from inside, and the windows are crowded with trays holding a wide assortment of Danishes and sweet buns, cream buns, donuts, cardamom braids, butter cookies, gingerbread men, spicy pepparkakor cookies, and piles of freshly baked loaves of bread. My stomach rumbles. It's been a while since my three cups of coffee. I scan the trays in the window, trying to decide what I want to splurge on today.

"Emmie," Dani hisses out of the corner of her mouth. "Look. Up."

I glance up and my heart misses a beat and lands with a thud in the bottom of my stomach. There behind the counter, wearing an apron and dusted in flour, stands a Norse demigod of a man. Tall and broad-shouldered and built like an inverted triangle, he has blond hair pulled back in a stubby ponytail and is wielding a rolling pin like he means business. The sleeves of his tight T-shirt are rolled up, revealing tattoos snaking around each bulging bicep. I swallow hard. Why is my mouth suddenly so dry?

"Is it my imagination or did hot Thor just show up in our town and start baking cookies?" Dani asks in a hushed, reverent tone. The man seems unaware of our hungry eyes on him. He's concentrating on rolling out the dough, his back mostly toward us. I can't see his face, but there's something strangely familiar about him.

"Where's Gunnar?" I whisper. Why am I whispering? Gunnar Kristensen, the patriarch of the Kristensen clan, has been baking pastries in this shop in taciturn silence for almost forty years. To find someone new in his place is jarring. Especially if that someone does indeed look like a lost Hemsworth brother.

"Gunnar says he's retiring now that Jakob's back," Dani replies, her tone nonchalant as the man expertly shapes the dough into a long roll.

"Jakob?" My jaw drops. No, it can't be. I squint at the man behind the counter, trying to superimpose him on the scrawny, earnest boy who was my debate partner in high school and one of my best friends. Until he wasn't. Just then the demigod turns and glances up and for a moment the world slams to a halt.

It's him. Same intelligent, piercing blue eyes. Same amused, questioning tilt to his mouth. Oh good heavens, why am I staring at his mouth? My gaze snaps up to meet his, and he arches one blond brow quizzically. I realize my mouth is hanging open slightly. Also, I suddenly remember that I have a smear of scorched fudge down the front of my shirt. Why oh why did I decide today was the day to skip makeup and a shower and just pull my hair back in a ponytail? All I'm wearing is Burt's Bees lip balm. I duck my head and concentrate hard on the pastries in the case. Ugh, this could not be more embarrassing. We haven't seen each other in sixteen years and Jakob Kristensen just caught me ogling him.

"Come on, you have to try his sticky buns," Dani orders, grabbing my arm and pulling me into the bakery. I pull back, but resistance is futile with Dani. The bell on the door jingles and we are instantly enveloped in a warm, welcoming embrace of cinnamon, butter, and melted sugar.

"Hi, Jakob." Dani saunters to the counter and greets him brightly. We are the only ones in the shop. "Welcome back to Poulsbo. I don't know if you remember us, but we went to school together. Dani Diaz and Emmie Wynne?" She waves her hand at me as though she is a game show host presenting a new prize—a set of matching rolling luggage or a Jacuzzi tub. I am the Jacuzzi tub. I want to sink through the floor.

Jakob wipes his hands on a towel, looking from Dani to me with a neutral expression. "I remember you, Dani," he says finally, then turns to me. Something pained and surprised flickers in his eyes for a brief instant. "Hey, Emmie."

His voice is deep and a little rumbly sounding. I feel the vibration of it in my stomach. I can feel his gaze on me and I flush pink. Be cool, Emmie. Be cool. I raise my chin and try to smile confidently. "Hey, Jakob."

"Are you back home for good?" Dani asks, shamelessly prying for information.

Jakob hesitates and shoots her a small, noncommittal smile. "Back for now," he says finally. He watches us both evenly, giving nothing away. Whatever emotion I saw in the first split second is gone now, replaced by a cool self-containment.

"Well, it's this lovely lady's birthday, and since she's currently single and not getting any bedroom action, I want you to give her whatever you make here that's better than sex," Dani announces.

"Dani!" I hiss, scandalized. I thought Jakob catching me ogling him was the low point of this interaction, but I was wrong. This definitely just got more embarrassing. In fact, this now ranks as the most embarrassing moment of my life. I can feel my cheeks flushing scarlet. To his credit, Jakob doesn't bat an eye.

"That sounds like a tall order," he says slowly, glancing at me and then over the pastries. "But I'll do my best." I see a small smile quirk up the corner of his mouth. There's a faint trace of irony in his tone. "You like raspberry, right, Emmie?" He's looking at me. I think he finds my discomfort amusing.

I nod, trying to gather my dignity. I'm surprised he remembers I like raspberry. It's been years. The first time I went to the Kristensens' house to study with Jakob for a debate, we polished off an entire box of leftover Danishes. I quickly grew to love studying at their house because they always had boxes full of day-old baked goods on their counter and we could eat our fill. Jakob would always opt for the sweet cheese Danishes and leave the raspberry for me, since I'd confessed that first day that raspberry was my favorite. I found out years later that he actually didn't care for the cheese flavor. His favorite was also raspberry. He was always like that, thoughtful to a fault.

Jakob pauses and then selects the most decadent-looking raspberry-filled Danish and slips it into a small waxed paper bag. He moves confidently for such a large man, with an economy of motion that is almost elegant. He seems to be perfectly in command of himself. He reminds me of a wolf somehow, lean muscle and power and quiet, keen observation. He's always been tall, but he was gangly and awkward in adolescence, all acne and elbows and the same buzz cut his mom Astrid gave all three of her sons. He's certainly filled out nicely since then. I clear my throat and glance away. This day is taking an uncomfortable turn, and it isn't even midmorning.

"Happy birthday, Emmie." Jakob hands the bag to me, our fingers brushing. "On the house." The light hairs on his forearms are dusted with flour, I notice. Suddenly I forget how to draw a breath. I clear my throat and lift my chin to meet his eyes. No use trying to hide the fact that I look washed-out and tired. Might as well own it. I read somewhere that a woman's sexiest attribute is confidence. That appears to be the only attribute I have at the moment, so I lean into it. "I'm surprised you remember I like raspberry. That was a long time ago," I say lightly.

"I remember a lot of things," he says, meeting my eyes and holding my gaze without blinking. His eyes are a pale bright blue, the irises shot through with silver, like the Arctic, like a glacial milk Alpine lake. In a flash I remember what he's talking about, the things he might remember. The questions I was left with, and the regret. It all hits me in the stomach like a well-aimed kick. I flush, drop my gaze, and mumble a thank-you, then hurry from the shop, not waiting for Dani. So much for rocking cool confidence.

I duck around the corner and lean against the yellow wooden storefront of a boutique that sells bespoke Norwegian-inspired baby items. I press my hand to my chest, trying to still my erratic heartbeat. What in the world just happened?

Once, Jakob and I were as comfortable together as a pair of old shoes. We'd share packets of Twizzlers and cans of Coke at my parents' store as we studied for debates. Slowly we learned how to read each other's nonverbal cues, grew familiar with each other's moods, and shared our worries and hopes and dreams. We laughed at the same bad '80s movies and suffer through the assigned reading in Mrs. Fitz's AP English class by reading aloud to each other while we ate snacks in the Kristensens' den. Jakob and I were almost as close as Dani and I were. Maybe closer. He was my best guy friend, and the standard by which I've measured all other guys since.

But that was years ago. Before high school graduation and the horrible moment I ruined our friendship forever. Before Jakob abruptly left town and shocked everyone by joining the Marines. Before I left for Switzerland and Gus came into the world and my dad left it. And now here is Jakob, standing a scant few yards away, confident and beautiful and strangely familiar in a way that makes me feel like I want to crawl out of my skin. I clutch the bag with the raspberry Danish. He made this Danish with his own hands. And then he remembered what I liked and gifted it to me. What does that mean?

I remember a lot of things.

Did I imagine it or had his tone held an edge of challenge? It's been years since that day, but the regret and the questions still burn like a hot coal in my throat. I didn't mean to hurt him, and I never got to apologize. I never got to explain. I wonder if he even thinks about what happened.

I open the bag and peer down at the Danish, my mouth watering. One thing is for certain. No matter what else happens today, this is not going to be a birthday like every other birthday, because out of the blue, Jakob Kristensen has come home.

CHAPTER 3

"Happy birthday, darlin'!" Dot leans across the table at the Longboat, Poulsbo's iconic waterfront Scandinavian restaurant, and clinks her glass of beer against my chilled chardonnay.

"Thanks for coming to celebrate with me," I reply. Beside Dot in the booth, Mom is sipping sparkling water, and next to me Gus is sketching a black hole swallowing the Milky Way on the back of his kids' menu. After we closed the shop for the day, we dropped Mr. Butters off at home to enjoy his carefully portioned-out kibble for senior dogs and then met Dot here. Dani is on her way.

I sip my wine and gaze out the huge plate glass window at the harbor. The Longboat is located on the second floor of a building built on a pier over the bay just a couple of blocks from our store. We've been celebrating birthday dinners here since I was a kid, and the menu and décor haven't changed at all since then. It's five thirty and the place is almost empty, just us and a few senior citizens here for the early bird special. I'm feeling increasingly nervous and off-kilter despite the tranquil setting. It's almost time to see if this will be the year I finally get my wish . . .

Outside the window, the light is golden on the water and seagulls wheel and cry. The longest day of the year is right around the corner, so we have hours of daylight left. It stays light now well past ten thirty at night—a fact Gus likes to mention when he's pressing me for another half hour of reading.

"You shouldn't fight circadian rhythm, Mom," he told me gravely last night. "It's not good for my nervous system."

Mean mommy that I am, I made him go to bed anyway, because circadian rhythm or not, he's still six years old and needs to sleep or he's a grouch monster in the morning.

"Hey, birthday girl!" Dani calls loudly across the restaurant as she rushes in the door, late as usual. She's off duty and out of uniform now. She worked a night shift last night, and after taking me for our humiliating little pastry outing this morning, she went home, slept for a few hours, and is back for dinner looking refreshed and mischievous in a cherry-red romper and espadrilles. She's also carrying a big sign that screams in huge red letters: **SLAY, QUEEN! CONGRATS ON ROCKING 34 TRIPS AROUND THE SUN!** And below the words she's pasted a hideous, grainy black-and-white photo of me. I recognize it as a terrible school photo from one of our middle school yearbooks. I'm grinning, all braces and straight blond hair and dark eyeliner, channeling Avril Lavigne. She's written *"Reinita!!!!!!!"* in red Sharpie across the bottom of the poster with seven exclamation points.

I shake my head and roll my eyes at her. She's carried that all the way through town from her apartment, no doubt. Everyone has seen it. She chortles when she sees my embarrassment and sticks it to our booth with a roll of duct tape she pulls from her giant, slouchy purse. She carries everything in that purse—Band-Aids, airplane-sized bottles of booze, bear spray, gum, a pair of handcuffs—you name it, she's probably got it in there. It's like blue-collar Mary Poppins bag.

"Scoot over," she orders, sliding into the bench next to me. "Hey, Gusto, how's my favorite guy?" She leans across me and ruffles Gus's hair. If I tried to do that, or used that nickname, he'd roll his eyes and give me a long-suffering sigh, but he lets Dani get away with anything. They have a mutual admiration society that's endearing.

"Hey, I've got a joke for you," she tells him, leaning so far across me that her ample boobs are perched in my lap. "How do you organize a party in space?"

Gus pauses and frowns, a little crease appearing between his brows. "I don't know," he says after a moment. "How?"

"You planet!" Dani cackles and sits upright as our waitress Freya comes to the table with an appetizer of gravlaks, dry-cured Norwegian smoked salmon served on long, skinny rye crisp crackers. Her eyes widen when she sees Dani's sign.

"Happy birthday, Emmie," she says, eyeing the sign.

"It was my emo era," I tell her, pointing to my photo on the sign.

"I remember." She purses her lips knowingly. Freya was a couple of years ahead of us in high school. "We've got your special cake all ready in the back," she tells me. "In the meantime"—she pulls out her notebook—"what can I get you?"

We give her our orders. Dani orders vafler, heart-shaped Norwegian waffles served with cloudberry jam.

"Me too," Gus pipes up.

I shake my head. "Too much sugar for dinner," I tell him.

He nods sadly and looks down at his menu, slowly trying to

pronounce the Norwegian names of dishes. He looks so disappointed.

"I'll share my waffles with you," Dani whispers to him across me, loud enough that I can clearly hear her. I give her a side-eye but she just grins, completely unrepentant.

"What?" she says. "It's your birthday. Let the boy have waffles."

I hesitate for a minute and then cave and let Gus order the vafler.

As a single parent, I sometimes really want to get to spoil Gus more. I'm the only disciplinarian, the only one making the hard decisions. Sometimes I wish I could be the fun, irresponsible one. Every now and then, it feels good to let myself be. Tonight is one of those nights.

"Did you know that the sun is so big that one million earths could fit inside it?" Gus asks us as Freya walks away to turn in our order.

"I did not," Dani tells him, looking impressed. Gus is constantly sharing strange facts he's learned about the universe. It's a little unnerving sometimes, the things he's learned. Usually I think we humans would prefer to forget about the vastness of the universe; life on earth can feel overwhelming enough. But I adore my son, despite his slightly odd space fixation. Right now he looks so much like his father it's uncanny. I brush the thought away. It's rare these days that I think of my life in France or of Romaine, the man I once loved, the man who gave me Gus by accident. He lives in Belgium now and is married with a child. He does not want to be involved in our lives. He made that perfectly clear when I contacted him after the positive pregnancy test. We were colleagues in Paris, then lovers for a time, and now we are strangers, which is fine by both of us.

"Emmie." Dani turns to me with a naughty look in her eye.

"So tell me. How *was* that Danish from Kristensen's? Was it really better than . . ." She wiggles her eyebrows suggestively.

Dot and Mom look mystified.

"Better than what?" Mom asks innocently. She pushes the appetizer plate in my direction. I take a rye crisp cracker layered with thin slices of bright orange smoked salmon and stuff it in my mouth.

"The Danish was delicious," I say firmly. I glare warningly at Dani. Gus is busy filling in the black hole with black crayon and doesn't seem to be paying attention to our conversation.

"Did you try one of those bear claws you brought me?" Dot asks. "That was the best bear claw I've had in years."

Dani pins me with a wicked little grin. "That's because Gunnar didn't make it," she says slowly. I shake my head at her, and she looks gleeful.

"But who's baking at Kristensen's if it isn't Gunnar?" asks Mom. She takes a sip of her sparkling water. Alcohol aggravates her symptoms, so she doesn't drink.

"Who indeed?" Dani wiggles her eyebrows again. I wish she'd knock it off. In that red romper she looks like a petite evil supervillain. "Who made the bear claw, Emmie?"

I sigh. There is no getting around this. "It's Jakob," I say. "Jakob is back."

"Oh!" Mom claps her hands, looking delighted. "I heard he was coming home. Such a good man to help his family like this. And such a distinguished career in the Marines. I heard he was awarded a medal by the president . . . for bravery."

"Hear that, Emmie? For bravery," Dani repeats, giving me a meaningful look. "And he can bake Danishes that are better than you-know-what . . ." She winks at me suggestively. I ignore her. Sometimes Dani acts like a horny sixteen-year-old boy. Nothing is going to happen between Jakob Kristensen and me. I unintentionally made sure of that years ago, and I've regretted it ever since.

Mom looks from Dani to me in puzzlement. I ignore Dani and finish my rye crisp. Our meals come, and Gus peers down at his waffles. They're so pretty—golden, and the hearts are arranged in a pattern that looks like a flower.

"Mommy," Gus whispers, leaning into me. "Can I have courage sprinkles on these? Please?" I hesitate, thinking about the sugar content of those waffles, but then I relent.

"Sure, honey." I reach for my purse. I always carry a little plastic shaker of sprinkles in the back pocket of my purse nestled next to the wet wipes and an airsickness bag I swiped from a flight years ago, just in case of sudden vomit. As a mom, you can never be too prepared for . . . well, everything, really. The sprinkles are a big part of my mom kit, an essential I always have with me. We are BIG fans of sprinkles.

It's something Gus and I started when my dad was in the hospital during his long, slow, last decline. I'd take Gus every few days to visit Dad, and we'd stop and get frozen yogurt before going to the hospital, a way to gird ourselves for the hard task of watching Dad slowly slip away from us. Gus would always ask for sprinkles on his vanilla swirl yogurt. Somehow—I don't even remember who started it—we began calling them courage sprinkles, pretending that they gave us special powers to do hard things. It was a silly little tradition, but it helped us both. It made the hard stuff a little easier. Bolstered by the courage sprinkles, Gus would walk bravely into the hospital to see his favorite person on earth, my dad, as he grew ever more frail and wasted. Now we use courage sprinkles for all sorts of potentially scary things—first day of school, standardized testing days, jujitsu competitions, trips to the dentist—you name it, we put sprinkles on it so we can have courage to face the hard things in life.

"Are you feeling like you need some courage sprinkles, buddy?" I whisper to Gus. He peers at me through his round blue glasses, then nods.

"What's bothering you?" I ask.

"The vastness of the universe is a little scary," he says solemnly.

Can't argue with that. I fish the container of sprinkles out of my purse and shake some over his waffles, which are already smeared with cloudberry jam.

"There." I press a kiss on the top of his head. "Now you can face the vastness of the universe."

He tucks into his extra-sugary waffles happily.

We eat our meal leisurely. A few more customers trickle in, and the golden light sinks lower on the horizon. Finally I push away my plate of meatballs, unable to eat more. I'm too nervous. It's almost time for dessert. This is the moment I've been waiting for with half dread, half hope all year. I was so disappointed last year, and the year before that. But maybe this year it will finally happen for me.

"How are you doing, sweetie?" Mom reaches across the table and squeezes my hand as though sensing my conflicted feelings. Dot and Dani are engrossed in exchanging small-town gossip, and Gus is listening in on their conversation and embellishing his black hole picture with fireball comets streaking across the paper.

I just shake my head, not even sure what to say. "I'm afraid to hope," I admit finally.

"Don't worry, Emmie," Mom says softly. "It will happen when it's supposed to happen. Just because the women in our family usually get their visions before the age of thirty doesn't mean that all of us will. My aunt Eileen didn't get hers until she was almost fifty. You've got plenty of time. You can't rush your peek at destiny, no matter how much you may want to. And you know the rules. It always happens. And it's always right. Just you wait and see."

I nod reluctantly. "It's getting harder to wait each year. I just want it so much."

I know Mom is right, but it's tough to be disappointed year after year as I wait for my one chance to finally catch a glimpse of my purpose in life. It's a special gift given to every woman in our family. We each get the chance, just once in our lives, to see a vision of the future that shows us our true destiny.

I've grown up listening to the stories of past visions. At nineteen, my great-grandmother Signe, who was the first one of us to see a vision, glimpsed herself surrounded by children in an apple orchard. She later met and married her husband Joseph, who had inherited his family's apple orchard. They welcomed five strong sons and adopted the orphaned children of a neighboring farmer, ending up with nine children in all. And they tended the apple orchards of Joseph's family until they both passed away within a week of each other at the age of ninety-three.

Signe told my mother that she never doubted her purpose in life after seeing her vision. She knew why she was on this earth, and she never wavered from that single-minded goal. At twenty-two, Mom saw a vision of herself and Dad opening their fudge shop on the main street in Poulsbo. When he proposed to her, she said yes, with the caveat that they stay in Poulsbo and open the shop, just like she saw in her vision. It's been the same with all the women in our family. Each one of us waits to see the vision and then spends her life bringing it to fruition. It's our destiny.

The visions are a gift, much anticipated by each of us. But I'm still waiting for mine. Year after year I blow out the special Norwegian birthday candle that Signe handcrafted long ago, make a wish to see my true purpose in life, and see . . . absolutely nothing. After so many years, I'm so tired of being patient, of waiting every birthday, hoping and praying that this will be the year. I want to finally see where my life is headed, to have all the disconnected pieces at last make sense.

I long to see my true path, to see my purpose, to not just feel stuck in the day-to-day toil of keeping a business going, caring for a parent in failing health, trying to be a good mommy to a small, worry-prone human. More than anything, I want to know that there is some overarching, grand unifying purpose for my life, to finally see why I'm here and to know in what direction I should go. It's the only thing I want every year for my birthday.

"Please let this be the year," I murmur, squeezing my eyes shut and saying a little prayer for it to come true.

Chapter 4

"Here's your cake, Emmie." I open my eyes to see Freya sliding my special-order birthday cake in front of me. It's a prinsesstårta, a gorgeous layered cake covered in a smooth pale pink dome of marzipan and decorated with little rosettes. The Longboat has been offering these cakes made by a local baker for years, and Mom has ordered this cake for my birthday every year since I was a child. Freya hands around the plates, then slices the cake, revealing the layers of soft sponge, raspberry jam, and pastry cream mixed with whipped cream beneath the marzipan topping.

"Ooh, it always looks so elegant," Mom sighs happily.

"Maybe this will be your lucky year, Emmie," Dot says, giving me a hopeful wink. Dot and Dani know about the visions. Not many outside our family do. We tend to keep the birthday visions a secret, but Dot is Mom's best friend and Dani is mine, so they're in the circle of trust but sworn to secrecy.

"I hope so." I glance down at my generously portioned slice of cake. I've been disappointed too many times but still I'm hopeful.

"Baby girl, we'll cheer you on if it works this year and cheer you up if it doesn't," Dot tells me, reaching across the table and squeezing my hand. I squeeze back, grateful for the solidarity.

"Here's the candle." Mom takes a small wooden box from her purse, opens it, and carefully unwraps the length of muslin that enshrouds what is inside. She sets the object on the table and we gaze at it for a moment. A beeswax candle about five inches tall and two inches wide, it is decorated on every side with beautiful gold swirls and starbursts. I reach out and carefully run my fingers lightly over the pretty patterns embossed on the deep golden surface.

This candle has been used for generations. Signe brought it with her all the way to Poulsbo when she emigrated from Norway. And ever since, each woman in our family has used the candle on their birthday until they are given their vision; then they pack it away and pass it along to the next woman in line. It is more than a century old, but only an inch or so has been burned. We only light it for a few seconds each year.

Mom gently presses the candle into the smooth pale pink marzipan rind on my slice of prinsesstårta. The kind of birthday dessert you choose doesn't seem to matter. My great-aunt Tilda is diabetic and she chose a big slice of triple cream Brie as her birthday treat the year she saw her vision. It's the candle that holds the magic, not the food.

"Ready?" Mom asks. She shoots me a sympathetic look. I take a deep breath and nod. It's time. Freya appears with a box of matches with the Longboat logo on the cover. She lights the candle and steps back. Everyone at the table sings a slightly off-key rendition of "Happy Birthday" to me, a few of the other patrons joining in. I shiver a little, eyeing the candle flame, heart beating fast. *Please please please let this be the year*, I murmur silently. I shut my eyes and make the same wish I do every year.

Please let me see my purpose in life. Please show me what is true and real and good.

Then I open my eyes and snuff out the candle with a quick little puff of air. All eyes are on me. I bite my lip and wait, heart beating hard. For a second nothing happens. And then everything changes.

It starts gradually, at first a faint glimmer around the edges of my vision, little pops of shimmering gold shooting bright across my field of sight. My breath catches in my throat as the realization dawns on me. I think this is it. It's finally happening! My heartbeat quickens.

"Emmie?" I hear Mom's voice from far away.

"Mom?" My voice sounds even more distant.

The colors are getting more intense. The gold shimmers are glowing like sparklers crackling along the edges of my eyesight, growing brighter and brighter. It's like shooting stars, like fireworks on the Fourth of July. I blink, and when I open my eyes, I do not see Dot or Mom or Gus or Dani. I do not see the heavy wooden beams of the Longboat dining room or the sailboats bobbing on the silver waters of Liberty Bay.

What I see is something else entirely.

I don't know how long the vision lasts. It feels like only a few seconds, barely enough time to register the scene in front of me, but it feels so real. I don't just see the image. I taste and touch and smell the moment too. I am living it.

Then from far away I hear someone saying my name, and it feels as though I am being forced backward down a tunnel, back down into my real life once more. I plop back into the present with a jolt. When I glance around the booth, Dot, Mom, and Dani are all watching me, silent and wide-eyed.

I catch Mom's eye and stare at her wordlessly, then nod. She instantly starts to tear up. "Oh, honey," she whispers, reaching out and grabbing my hand. "See? You didn't miss it."

"Wait," Dot interrupts. "Was that it? Did something happen? Did you see something?"

I nod again, still stunned. Not sure how to even explain what I saw. There must be some mistake. "It's impossible." My voice sounds dazed. I take a sip of water, trying to clear my head.

"Why? What did you see?" Dani asks eagerly. Gus is peering up at me curiously, looking a little worried. His mouth is ringed with raspberry jam and whipped cream. He has somehow eaten almost all of his slice of cake already.

"Are you okay, Mommy?" Gus asks nervously, eyeing me. He slips his small, sticky hand into mine.

I look down at my slice of prinsesstårta with the candle stuck in it, the wick blackened, flame snuffed out. "I saw a vision." I find my voice at last, small and disappointed. "But there's no way it could be true. I think something went wrong."

"Why, honey? What did you see?" Mom asks. They all lean forward eagerly.

I shake my head at the absurdity of the situation. I feel so disappointed. I waited all my life for this? For something that is so outside the realm of possibility it's clear I dreamed it up? It must have been my own wishful thinking. What else could it possibly be? I blink back a prickle of tears behind my eyes, then take a deep breath and tell them what I glimpsed.

"I saw Henry Summers proposing to me."

There is a long beat of silence. Then Dani pipes up, "Wait, like Henry Summers the TV star? Your celebrity crush?"

"Is he that darling British man who hosts that travel show you like?" Mom asks, puzzled. "The one who goes around the world and finds little family food spots and interviews the owners and explores the history? What's it called?"

"*Savor*," I say miserably. Now I'm feeling embarrassed. I want to sink straight through the floor into the bay. Figures that I'd wait all these years and then my mind would make up an absolutely absurd fantasy in place of my real purpose in life. Ugh. I lean down and rest my forehead on the table. I give up. I'm just going to go through life purposeless. Maybe that's my destiny.

"Hold on, Emmie," Mom interrupts. "Can you tell us what you saw?"

I raise my head slightly. Gus scoots near me. He looks worried, his big brown eyes magnified through the thick lenses of his glasses. He squeezes my hand.

"What's wrong, Mommy?" he whispers in concern. "Do you not like your cake? Can I have your piece?"

I pull him to me and press a kiss to his head, to the soft little pulse point on his temple. I hold him close for a moment, inhaling him. He smells like raspberry jam and crayons. Already he is wiggling away. I release him, wondering why it is that motherly love feels just a little like heartbreak.

"I'm fine. Nothing's wrong, sweet boy." I force a smile. "And it looks like you've already had cake. Do you want to read your book now? Can you find a really crazy space fact for us?" He nods and leans away from me to grab his *Weird but True* book of facts about the universe from his backpack.

"We need booze," Dot announces. She waves Freya over and orders us all shot glasses of aquavit. When it comes, she throws hers back without hesitation. I sip mine and grimace. The iconic Norwegian liquor tastes like vodka heavily spiced with botanicals, chief among them caraway. I slide my glass over to Dot, who downs that one too. She can drink anyone under the table and never seems to feel it.

Dani takes a sip of her shot and whistles. "That will put hair on your chest," she announces to no one in particular. "No thank you." She slides her shot over to Dot too. "So, Emmie, tell us what you saw."

Then Dot, Mom, and Dani all turn their eyes on me, waiting for an explanation.

I tell them about the sparklers, about the pops of brilliant gold color, about opening my eyes and being somewhere else entirely, like I was stepping into another time and place. It felt so real, like I was an invisible observer, standing there watching a few seconds of my life unfold somewhere else entirely.

"I was standing in my own boutique chocolate shop," I explain. "It was exactly as I've imagined it for years." I shoot a nervous glance at Mom, who smiles encouragingly. "Like the one I used to talk about having someday."

Like the one I've been secretly dreaming about. The shop looked like I'd always imagined it would—big windows, dark wood floors, gleaming glass-and-wood display cases, a few whimsical decorations. There was a tree with chocolate ornaments, a bird's nest of spun chocolate with colorful chocolate eggs decorated with fancy sprinkles perched in the branches. It was cozy and tasteful and fanciful and lovely.

"You were all there, standing around me in the shop."

They'd been gathered close to me—Mom, Dot, Dani, and Gus, who was clutching a glass bottle of fancy soda, and a few other folks I recognized, fellow shop owners from town . . . and Jakob Kristensen was standing next to me too. Weird. I don't let myself dwell on that one too long.

"Everyone was holding champagne coupes, and I was wearing the prettiest yellow dress that looked like sunshine. I think it was chiffon. And Henry Summers was . . ." I hesitate, not sure how to say this. "Well, he was proposing to me."

There was no mistaking that famous face—the warm hazel of his eyes, the swoop of wavy hair across his brow, the touch of scruff along his strong jaw. The posh UK accent, the Breton striped shirt and his signature swazer. In my vision, Henry Summers of the melting eyes and dreamy accent was down on one knee, holding up a little red box to me. An engagement ring–sized box.

I had my hand over my heart and happy tears were streaming down my face. Not ugly crying. Pretty crying. Which is also how I know this can't really be my future. I don't think I know how to pretty cry. In the vision, I reached out to accept the little box, and then Henry got up and embraced me, brushing a kiss against my cheek. The look on my face . . . I've never looked more joyful. I was as radiant as sunshine, even through the happy tears. Which is why it hurts so much to realize this is all clearly just a figment of my imagination.

When I finish telling them the vision, no one says anything for a full minute. Then Dot clears her throat. "Well hot dang," she says. "I got nothin'. Gwen?"

Mom looks puzzled and a little troubled. She takes a small sip of her aquavit and shudders, pushing it gently away.

"Tell me again how it starts," she says. I describe the gold sparklers, the clear and precise sensation of being somewhere else entirely. She *hmms* when I'm done.

"It sounds right, Emmie, like you really saw your vision. You don't think there's any way it could be true?" she asks me cautiously.

"Mom, come on." It's like a mash-up of all my daydreams in one five-second clip. My own boutique chocolate shop. Everyone I love gathered around. Henry Summers proposing to me. Me, elegant and beautiful in a floaty dress. "None of it can possibly be true. It's all just wishful thinking," I conclude glumly.

No one disagrees. Silently we finish our drinks and cake. I'm so disappointed I just want to go home and have a good cry. Even though the sun is still shining, the evening feels faded and already over. Dani asks Freya to bring the check, and Mom carefully wipes off the candle and wraps it back up. Freya boxes up the remainder of the prinsesstårta. No one speaks.

Inside I feel the hollow throb of bitter disappointment jumbled up with a hopeless sense of longing. I know it can't possibly be true, that what I saw must be just a product of all my secret wishes smashed together in one perfect fantasy scenario. I know there's no way it's actually my future, but if it could be . . . if it were . . . it would be everything I've ever wanted right there in one beautiful, impossible moment. I'd give anything to really live that moment. It crushes me that there is no way it could ever really come true. With a wistful sigh I take my uneaten birthday cake and prepare to return to my normal life.

So much for thirty-four.

Chapter 5

"Moe, this loco moco is the best I've ever tasted. Tell us about this recipe and what it means to your family. You learnt it from your grandmother, is that right?"

It's midnight and I'm standing at the stove in the homey warmth of my kitchen, stirring dried lavender buds into a Le Creuset Dutch Oven of honey sea salt caramels and trying to forget the disappointing vision from earlier this evening. It's a little difficult to do though, because as I stir, I'm half concentrating on an episode of *Savor*. Onscreen, my TV heartthrob Henry Summers is in Los Angeles, eating at a diner tucked into a bowling alley. He's sampling their Hawaiian fusion food and chatting with the owner, who is a double amputee. Henry really does have the plummiest accent. It makes me think of armchairs in wood-paneled libraries and polo parties on manicured lawns. It makes me think of Henry down on one knee with a red box in his hand . . .

I shake my head, trying to dispel the feeling of longing and disappointment. Here in the shabby little kitchen of my childhood home, under the bright overhead lights, the delicious aroma of melted butter with honey, vanilla, and lavender perfumes the air and soothes me with the familiar scent. It's been years since I made these caramels—or anything from my life in Europe, as a matter of fact. Tonight I was inspired by my vision, impossible though it may be. As soon as I tucked Gus into bed and bid good night to Mom, I came down here and started making these from memory. I can't recall the last time I made something that wasn't fudge or a simple dinner whipped up quickly between the shop closing and Gus's bedtime.

Today was a disappointment, but it wasn't all a loss. I may not have seen my true purpose in life, but glimpsing the chocolate shop in my vision, the shop I've dreamed of for so long, inspired me to try my hand at something from my past, a recipe I learned in France. It's a far cry from actually opening my own shop, but it's a step toward reclaiming an important part of myself. I may not be able to make my vision come true, but still I was reminded tonight of who I was, who I always dreamed I'd be. These caramels are helping me reclaim a part of myself I'd tucked away and almost forgotten.

"What do you think this diner has meant to your community all these years, Moe?" Henry asks the owner, a large, bald Hawaiian man. "What would you say is the legacy of this place?"

Moe scratches his chin and thinks. "Legacy? Probably the community that comes here, that's always been here," he says. "This place is like the beating heart of our neighborhood."

I slowly stir the butter and cream and sugar mixture as it melts, watching Henry onscreen. This is why I have a crush on Henry Summers. Because he asks questions like this. He cares about the history of places, about the people. He doesn't just produce a glossy reality show with manufactured drama and scripted tension. He really seems to be interested in people's personal stories, in real life. He is thoughtful and curious and kind. And who doesn't love a man wearing leather elbow patches?

The caramel mixture in the saucepan reaches a rolling boil, and I pour in another cup of heavy whipping cream and stir. Now I just need to keep stirring and wait for it to come up to temperature. I eyeball the color as it changes, then check my digital thermometer just to be sure. It reads 180 degrees. Still a ways off. We need to reach the soft ball stage at 250 degrees. I keep stirring.

It feels good to do something I understand, to control an outcome and make something delicious from this familiar process. If only I could do that with my life. The truth is that increasingly I feel stuck. I love my mom dearly, and Gus has my whole heart. I love our Poulsbo community too, and Dot and Dani. But my responsibilities are a heavy weight that feels like it presses out most of the energy and creativity I once had. I would never neglect caring for my mom or Gus. They're the ones I love most in the world, but sometimes . . . sometimes . . . I just wish there was a little more of me left over at the end of the day. After I dole out my time and energy to everyone who needs me, what remains often feels scanty, like too little butter spread over too much toast. There's not enough of me to go around. Tonight is a perfect example. All I have left over for myself is a little sliver of time when I should be sleeping. Instead, I'm making caramels in my pajamas at midnight and mooning over a guy who doesn't know I exist.

Onscreen, Henry is tasting the diner's famous butter mochi. His hair is a little longer, down past his ears, and wavy. I want to run my fingers through it. I recall my vision from earlier, Henry rising and embracing me as I cry prettily, and I find myself wishing that somehow it could be true.

"Bergamot," I say aloud in the empty kitchen as I stir. "Henry Summers smells like bergamot."

I am officially losing it.

I check the color of the caramels, which are turning a rich butterscotch shade somewhere between yellow and brown. Almost there. For the last degree or two, I use the thermometer to get it exactly right. Candy is finicky. A degree can make a difference. At 250 degrees exactly, I carefully pour the hot liquid caramel into a buttered glass dish. Then, before the mixture can cool, I sprinkle sea salt from nearby San Juan Island over the top and a pinch of dried lavender buds. It's hard to beat a good caramel, but adding sea salt and lavender bumps it up a notch to a whole other level. As a last step, I scrape out the darker brown leftovers at the bottom of the Dutch oven and drizzle the hot caramel onto a little dessert plate, sprinkle on salt and lavender, and leave it to cool.

"Something smells good."

I whirl in surprise. Mom is standing in the doorway in her floral cotton nightgown, leaning on her cane. Mr. Butters is at her heels. Her face is bare of makeup, her usually perfect coiffure a little mussed. She looks smaller somehow, and more tired. I take in her bent form with a sharp pang, a familiar mixture of love and worry squeezing my heart.

"They're honey sea salt lavender caramels," I tell her. "Want a taste?"

"I'd love one." She comes into the kitchen, Mr. Butters shuffling along right behind her like a snuffly, asthmatic shadow. He was a gift from my dad, the last big gift he ever gave Mom, and while she's always doted on the dog, they've been inseparable since Dad's passing. We tease her about it, but I think somehow Mr. Butters makes her feel closer to Dad. Now she pours all the love and care and attention she gave to Dad for so long into the dog. I'm not sure it's good for either of them. Mom needs something more to focus on than what sweater-vest Mr. Butters will wear today.

I run warm water and a squirt of dish soap into the Dutch oven. "What are you doing still up? Is the pain bad tonight?"

"About like normal," Mom says, waving away my concern. "I just came down for a glass of water."

She reaches into the cabinet, wincing, and I spring to grab a glass, running cold water from the tap and handing it to her. Her fingers close painfully around the glass and she drinks.

"Thanks, honey. I don't know what I'd do without you." She sets the glass down and gives me a grateful smile.

When I came back from France, I moved back into my old room upstairs temporarily, intending to find an apartment as soon as Dad was on the mend. But then I found out I was pregnant, which changed the timeline for me to get my own place. I was still planning on moving out at some point after the baby was born, but then Gus arrived and turned my world inside out. I don't know how he and I would have survived if it had just been me and this tiny, squalling human I had to keep alive. Mom was a rock star grandma, taking a few night shifts a week so I could sleep, rocking Gus for hours when he was fussy. Dad was great with him too. Somehow we got through the first hard year together, and then soon after Gus's first birthday it became obvious that Dad was in a slow decline from which there was no recovery. So I stayed.

It was good for all of us. My parents helped watch Gus, and I helped drive and organize medical appointments and cook and keep the household and the candy shop running during Dad's long deterioration. After he died, the thought of moving out never even crossed my mind. By that point, Mom's condition was taking a turn for the worse too. There was no way I could leave her. Nor did I want to.

Now it isn't practical for Mom to live alone anymore, as she can't do things like drive a car or open jar lids. Sometimes she even has trouble with doorknobs. So we are a multigenerational family of three under one roof, and I can't imagine us any other way. What would she do without us? What would we do without her? And yet sometimes I still secretly dream of another life, one where I get a starring role, where I still live in France, where I open my chocolate shop, where my days revolve a little less around others and a little more around what I always hoped my life might look like. But that isn't now. That isn't real. So I tuck those thoughts away and get on with life as it is.

Mom sits down carefully at the little round kitchen table where we eat all our meals at home. Mr. Butters parks his squat body next to her chair leg in the hopes that she will drop something tasty. I slide the dessert plate into the center of the table and sit across from her. Carefully I twist off a bit of caramel and hand it to her. It's greasy with butter and still warm in my hands.

"It's been a long time since you made something like this. Did you learn to make these in France?" Mom asks, taking the caramel from me.

"Romaine's mother taught me," I confirm. "His family owned a property in Provence, nestled in the lavender fields. He took me there once for a weekend, and his mom taught me how to make these." Although my relationship with Romaine didn't last, I walked away with Gus and a handful of really excellent recipes.

"Mmm, that's delicious." She nods approvingly, chewing the candy. "Your creativity is such a gift, Emmie."

"Thanks." I'm pleased by the compliment. I twist off a long ribbon of the caramel for myself. The candy itself is rich and buttery, and the sea salt and lavender give a nice bite at the end. It really is decadent.

"How are you doing, sweetie?" Mom eyes me carefully. "After what happened at dinner."

I blow out a breath. "I'm disappointed," I admit. "I really felt like this was going to be the year I'd finally get answers and figure out what I'm supposed to do with my life." I look down and pick little sticky flecks of caramel from my nails. "Now I feel more confused than ever." I don't say it, but I also feel a little embarrassed to have made up this ridiculous fantasy of a future for myself.

"You know what's strange about what you saw," says Mom slowly. I glance up. Her brow furrows in a confused frown. "I saw the same things when I got my vision. The same gold sparkles and shimmers and fireworks. It's exactly what every one of us has seen when we've been given our visions. I know you think there's no way what you saw could be true, but what you're describing feels like the visions we've all had. Exactly the same. And every one of those visions has come true."

I shake my head. "Well, I guess there's a first time for everything." I twist off another bit of slightly too-dark caramel and pop it into my mouth. "Because there is no way what I saw is anything but a pipe dream."

Mom cocks her head and considers me thoughtfully. "Or maybe there's something we just don't understand yet," she says, arching a thin, plucked eyebrow and looking at me expectantly. "I have a feeling, my sweet birthday girl, that you just may be in for a surprise."

Chapter 6

Early the next week I'm tending the shop alone with Mr. Butters. Mom is at her monthly Social Ladies' Tea Time at the senior center, and Gus is at jujitsu. It's almost closing time on a wet, gray Monday. Foot traffic has been slow all day and the shop is empty. The weekend was sunny and business was good, but now the rush has petered out. Apparently no one wants fudge on a drizzly Monday. I'm taking the opportunity to set up my new side project.

At least one good thing has come from my disappointing birthday. After my spontaneous caramel-creating session that night, I decided to see if my caramels would sell at the shop. Of course I can't do anything large scale yet, but I've decided to start making some of my own chocolates on the side too. Just for fun, in my nonexistent spare time. I've started to fill a notebook with ideas for chocolates I want to try to make. I can't produce chocolates at the scale or, frankly, the quality I aspire to. That takes professional equipment I have no money to invest in right now.

But these caramels are at least a start. When I told Mom my idea, she agreed immediately. Since then, I've been staying up late every night to research and brainstorm while I watch reruns of *Savor.* I'm even more tired than normal today after another late night getting my first inventory ready to sell, but I'm strangely energized too. It feels amazing to finally be exercising my creativity once more.

Since the shop is empty, I seize the opportunity and empty out a glass case on the counter near the register. We've been using it to display novelty candy items like licorice pipes and candy cigarettes (high time to retire those bad boys—it isn't the '80s anymore!) and those rolls of colored sugar buttons that taste like the white paper you can never quite fully peel off the back. Now I box up the dubious novelty candy and replace it with a selection of my own caramels. It is a far cry from my dream shop, with wooden floors and a tree full of candy whimsy, but it's a start. Seeing the neat rows of caramels I created with my own hands is gratifying. It reminds me of my years in Switzerland and France, of Jacques and the crew who mentored me, of Romaine and those heady, giddy days in Paris. Those memories are bittersweet. I know I won't go back to live in Paris, but it feels good to bring a little more of Paris into my life here and now. It feels like a step in the right direction.

The doorbell jingles just as I finish up arranging the caramels on pretty silver trays and place them in the case. I glance up and stop dead. There, standing in the doorway, is Henry Summers. I blink hard, but he is not a mirage. Henry Summers is standing in our candy shop. What. Is. Happening? Henry looks around with a slight frown, sees Mr. Butters in his tweed doggy newsies cap and does a double take, then starts to back out the door.

"Hello, can I help you?" I blurt out, too stunned to think of something smooth to say. I can't let him leave. He just can't go yet, not when he's here, in the flesh. What is he doing here? My palms have gone clammy. My heart is beating so hard I feel as though it may fly straight out of me, and I'm light headed. Henry hesitates in the doorway, then steps inside. It's definitely him. He's dressed in butterscotch-colored chinos, boat shoes, and a navy-and-white Breton striped shirt with a navy blazer over it. He looks like an ad for some expensive European cologne.

"Um, hello, yes. Good afternoon."

Ooh, that posh English accent! I force myself to act normally although my hands are shaking, and I feel like I've forgotten how to breathe. Thank goodness I showered this morning and let my hair dry naturally in soft waves. I even put on a flick of mascara and some tinted lip balm. And deodorant. Did I remember deodorant? No time for the sniff test. Henry Summers is coming over to the counter. He. IS. COMING. OVER. TO. ME. My mouth goes dry.

He's a little scruffier than on TV, and it looks good on him. Really good. His hair is damp with rain, and he meets my eyes and smiles, a genuine smile. He has a little gap between his two front teeth. I've never noticed. It's adorable. Mr. Butters heaves himself to his feet and wags his stumpy tail in welcome.

"Hello," Henry says again, nodding to Mr. Butters and to me. He eyes Mr. Butters's hat with a look of curiosity. "Sorry to bother you. I was trying to find my way to Sluys. It's an iconic local bakery, I believe? Somewhere around here, is it?" He leans down and lets Mr. Butters sniff his hand. The dog gives him an approving lick on the palm, and Henry scratches under his chin. Mr. Butters grins happily.

I force my mouth into a smile, trying to radiate helpfulness, competence, and approachability. No man has ever had this effect on me. I feel completely twitterpated. "That's Mr. Butters, our shop Frenchie," I tell him in what I hope is a casual tone of voice. "And Sluys is just down the street, but it's closed now. You have to get there as soon as it opens, when everything is fresh. Since you're here, welcome to the Happy Viking Fudge and Candy Shoppe." I beam. And because it's Henry Summers, I can't seem to stop myself from babbling. "My family's been serving the best fudge in Western Washington since 1986. Want to try a free sample?"

"Oh, thank you. How kind." He pauses to consider the rows of assorted fudge flavors. "So this is a family-owned local establishment then?" In a flash I see the opening and take it.

"Yes." I nod enthusiastically. "For almost forty years. We're proud to serve our community. All our fudge is handmade the old-fashioned way. With these." I hold up my hands and wiggle my fingers, then feel dumb and drop them. Smooth, Emmie. Really smooth.

Henry glances around, taking in the cluttered aisles and wall of dozens of types of bubble gum. "It's very retro, very Americana, isn't it?" he muses, glancing down at Mr. Butters, who is both farting and panting simultaneously. "Have you worked here long, um"—he glances at my name tag—"Emmie?"

"I grew up here," I tell him. "My parents opened this shop before I was born, but my dad passed away about two years ago and now I run the business. With my mom." Talking to him feels surprisingly normal. I'm still short of breath and my heart is beating hard, but I feel like I can at least carry on a reasonable conversation.

"Oh, I see. A true family business then." Henry's gaze is warm and sympathetic. "I'm sorry about your dad. I lost mine too, a few years back."

His eye catches on my little display case of caramels. “Hello, what are these?” He reads one of the cards I handwrote this morning and just finished placing in the case by each type of confection. “Honey sea salt lavender caramels. Are these locally sourced?”

“They’re from my kitchen,” I tell him, mustering my courage. “I make them myself.”

He looks surprised. “You made these?”

“Here, take one. On the house.” I slide open the case and with a pair of tiny silver tongs carefully select a caramel wrapped in waxed paper. I’m proud of how they turned out. I wonder if he’ll like them.

Henry takes the caramel from me and hesitates, “Do you mind if I try it now?” he asks. I gesture an invitation. He unwraps it and bites into it. It’s very pretty, dotted with lavender buds and sparkling with crystals of sea salt. I clasp my hands in front of me and hold my breath. His eyelids flutter closed and he makes a sound deep in his throat. It’s a groan. Henry Summers is groaning over my caramel. Pinch me, I must be dreaming. Dani is not going to believe this.

“That is . . . astonishingly good,” he says with his mouth full. When he opens his eyes, there’s something stirring in their depths. Admiration perhaps? Curiosity. I think he’s intrigued. I am flustered by his presence just across the counter from me. This entire interaction feels surreal. My hands are still shaking a little, but I am managing to keep calm in front of Henry Summers. WHO IS STANDING A FEW FEET FROM ME. For just a second I start to lean in, to see if he really does smell like bergamot, but then I catch myself and pull back quickly. I don’t want him to think I’m some sort of weirdo. Like a girl who has had a vision of him proposing to me in a dress that looks like sunshine. Inwardly, I roll my eyes at myself. Get it together, Emmie. This is your big chance.

"The lavender adds a unique complexity of flavor," Henry observes around a mouthful of caramel. "I've never tasted anything quite like it." He looks pleasantly surprised.

"I make them with local Pacific Northwest ingredients," I tell him, beaming at the compliment. Henry Summers likes my caramels! Other than when Gus was born, this might be the best day of my life. "The sea salt is from the San Juan Islands a little north of here, and the lavender is from an organic farm near Sequim."

"It's lovely." Henry nods approvingly and pops the rest of the caramel in his mouth. "How much do I owe you?" He pulls out a sleek leather wallet.

"Consider it a welcome gift to Poulsbo." I wave away the five dollars he tries to hand me and instead press another caramel into his palm, this one flavored like orange blossoms and almond. "Take one for later."

"That's very kind. Thank you, Emmie." He hesitates, then pockets the caramel and lingers for a moment, seeming in no hurry to leave. He glances at me and opens his mouth. At that exact moment, the doorbell jingles as Dani rushes into the shop. She's in uniform and is already launching into a story as she flies through the door, shaking off the rain.

"You will not *believe* the call I just responded to," she says without preamble or a pause to exchange pleasantries. "We got a request to do a wellness check on a ninety-eight-year-old man, and it turns out he is a nudist! You cannot unsee that wrinkly . . ." She groans dramatically, then realizes I'm not alone. She does a double take when she sees Henry standing at the counter. He nods politely to her.

"Hello," he says. He looks pleasantly bemused. Dani looks like she's been hit in the head with a heavy object.

"You're . . . you're Henry Summers." Dani gapes at him in shock, approaching slowly. So much for playing it cool. She looks like a goldfish out of water, her mouth opening and closing but no sound coming out. Behind Henry's head I pantomime for Dani to cut it out, but she doesn't see me. She's too busy staring at Henry in wide-eyed wonder. For once she seems to have lost all her words.

"Ah, yes. Yes, I am." Henry sticks his hand out and Dani mutely shakes it. "And you are?" he asks politely. His manners are very genteel.

"Officer Dani Diaz," she murmurs. She cuts a glance in my direction, her eyebrows raised almost to her hairline. I shrug, just as baffled as she is that Henry Summers is standing in our shop.

Seeing one of his favorite people on earth and the source of all his contraband treats, Mr. Butters waddles over to Dani and puts his paw on her knee, waiting for a doggy pot pie.

"What brings you to our little town?" Dani asks, recovering a little. "Are you doing a segment on the best small towns in America? Because you totally should feature Poulsbo." Without looking down, she takes a doggy pot pie from her pocket and drops it straight down into Mr. Butters's waiting open mouth. Then she glances down and sees the cap. "He looks like an extra from *Newsies*," she observes. Mr. Butters is unperturbed. He chomps his treat with relish and waddles back to his bed to curl up and nap.

Henry chuckles. He has a nice laugh. "This town *is* very charming, but no, I'm not filming here. I'm here for personal reasons." He glances in my direction, thoughtfully including me in the conversation. "I'm renting a beach cottage just outside of town. I'm taking the summer here to try and finish a long-overdue food memoir." He looks a little rueful at the admission.

I think Dani is going to swoon, but she recovers enough to offer a squeaky "Is that so?" She cuts her eyes to me.

"We'll see how much writing I actually get done," Henry says with a self-deprecating grimace. "You'll probably see quite a bit of me around town this summer. I'm very good at procrastinating."

"Emmie should show you around, since you're going to be in town for a while," Dani says in the most unsmooth segue I've ever heard. "She knows everyone here—all the good places to go, and which ones to avoid."

I open my mouth to protest, but instead squeak out a high-pitched "Happy to be of service!" And then I just stand there grinning like a ninny.

Henry shoots me a polite smile. "That's a generous offer," he says. "I might take you up on it, once I'm settled. Thank you, Emmie."

I like how my name sounds in his mouth. All crisp vowels, like a forkful of lemon tart.

"Of course. Anytime," I tell him, smiling in what I hope is a casual, friendly way. I'm trying to play it cool, as though I'm unaffected by this gorgeous, famous man who has just shown up in real life after appearing in my vision with a ring box in his hand. Am I looking at my future husband? I give a jaunty little wave as he turns to the door. My hand is shaking. I tuck it behind my back.

"Good to meet you both," Henry says over his shoulder. "Thank you for the delicious caramels, Emmie."

And then he is gone. I place my trembling hands on the counter and try to remember how to draw a full breath. I feel like I've just run a marathon. My legs are as wobbly as cooked noodles.

"Henry Summers was just standing right there," I say faintly as soon as the door shuts behind him. I stare at the spot on the carpet where Henry was a moment ago. I feel dazed.

Dani rushes around the counter to where I'm standing behind the register and grabs me by the shoulders so hard she pinches a nerve in my neck. "Henry Summers is here IN REAL LIFE," she shrieks, giving me a little shake.

I nod. "I know. I gave him one of my caramels and he tried it and groaned. A good groan," I add quickly. It may be the highlight of my life, that groan. I'm going to be replaying it in my head for the next . . . oh, decade, probably. Maybe more.

Dani is staring at me, eyes wide in wonder. "Emmie, Henry Summers is going to be here *all summer*."

I nod, too amazed to really know what to say.

"You know what this means, don't you?" Dani asks portentously.

"What?" I shake my head. I'm still reeling from this unexpected encounter with my celebrity crush.

"Your vision might actually be real," Dani whispers urgently. "Think about it. What if what you saw wasn't just wishful thinking?" Her voice drops to an awed hush. "What if it could really come true?" She clasps her hands in front of her in anticipation.

I close my eyes and replay the vision once more—the dress like sunshine, my happy tears, Henry on one knee with the red box in his outstretched hand. I feel again the brush of his lips against my cheek, the tantalizing hint of bergamot. When I open my eyes, I wonder if I was too hasty to dismiss what I saw the night of my birthday. I thought that vision was nothing more than wishful thinking, but what if I was wrong? What if I saw something that could actually, improbably, come true? My heart swells with hope like a helium balloon, getting bigger and bigger. It almost makes me afraid how suddenly full of anticipation I am.

“What if it wasn’t a mistake?” I whisper, staring after Henry and hardly daring to hope. Could it be that the vision I saw might actually be possible after all?

“Call Dot and Gwen,” Dani demands. “We need to have an emergency meeting. This changes everything.”

CHAPTER 7

"What's all the fuss about?" Dot demands as Dani, Mom, Gus, and I pile through the front door of the Salty Mermaid thirty minutes later, Mr. Butters in tow. "Dani texted me and said it was an emergency. Did somebody die?" Dot looks at all of us, alarmed.

"Everyone's fine," Mom hastens to reassure her. "But Emmie says she has some exciting news." She glances at me questioningly.

As soon as Henry left, Dani volunteered to pick up Mom and Gus and bring them to Dot's shop while I closed up the store a little early. We haven't breathed a word about Henry being in town. We figured it was best to tell Dot and Mom at the same time.

"You won't believe it," Dani hisses dramatically, "but I saw it with my own eyes."

"Oh?" Dot's penciled eyebrows arch in curiosity. "Just a minute." She turns the **OPEN** sign around to **CLOSED** on the front door. It's a few minutes early to close, but the store was empty anyway. I did the same thing.

"Head on back to the table and make yourselves comfortable." She points us to a small area at the back of the store where she hosts weekly mermaid- and nautical-themed craft nights. I set Gus up behind the cash register with a cartoon on my phone and a bag of Pirate's Booty. He never gets to watch TV after school, so this is a rare treat. Mr. Butters stays with Gus, sitting with his turgid little body pressed against Gus's side, hoping to get lucky and snag some dropped snacks.

I gingerly navigate the crowded aisle of merchandise and head to the back of the store, careful not to topple any of the tchotchkes piled around. Dot subscribes to the more-is-more method of decorating, and the store is stuffed with mounds of decorative pillows with slogans like "Beach hair, don't care," along with cable-knit lap blankets, soap dishes in the shape of seashells, glass vases filled with sand dollars, and all manner of mermaid-themed apparel. It smells salty from the bay out back and like the candle Dot keeps burning during open hours, Sea Dreams. Apparently sea dreams smell a little like a fabric softener sheet. We cluster around a table that Dot repurposed from driftwood.

"Okay, spill the beans. What's going on?" Dot asks impatiently. Dot and Mom both look at us expectantly.

"Emmie?" Dani invites me with a dramatic swoop of her hand.

"Henry Summers just walked into the fudge shop," I blurt out. "He's here for the summer." I still can't believe it.

Mom gasps.

"Oh my stars." Dot looks amazed. "Start from the beginning," she instructs. "Don't leave anything out."

I describe our meeting in detail, how Henry told us he's in

town for the summer finishing up a food memoir, how he groaned when he tasted my caramel. I don't tell them how I wanted to sniff him to see if he smells like bergamot. When I'm done, I'm trembling all over again from excitement and nerves.

"Does this mean your vision was the real deal then?" Dot demands when I'm finished.

"I don't know. Maybe?" I glance at Mom, who is beaming.

"Oh my goodness!" Mom whispers. "I knew it! I knew it wasn't just wishful thinking. Oh, Emmie!" She hugs me tightly, elated.

I hug her back, feeling a flutter of apprehension and excitement. "I can't believe he's actually here," I say aloud. It still seems like a dream. I keep wanting to pinch myself. Mom lets me go, but her eyes are shiny. I have a feeling she's picturing me in a wedding dress already.

"So what now?" Dot asks. "I mean, there's a long way between this guy stopping in to the shop and him proposing marriage."

"We need to help Emmie make her dream a reality," Dani announces. "We need a plan."

She finds a piece of junk mail in her giant purse and pulls a pen from her bun. Apparently it was the only thing holding up her hair because it tumbles around her in a cloud of dark curls. She taps her pen to her lips and narrows her eyes. "Where do we start?"

"If it's destiny, won't it just come true?" Dot asks.

"It can't hurt to help it along a little, right?" Dani looks at Mom. "What do you think, Gwen?"

Mom clears her throat. "The visions show us our purpose in life, but that doesn't mean we can just sit there and wait for the future to come to us. We still have to pursue it. We have to act to bring it about. When I saw my vision with Bert, with us running our shop, I knew it was our destiny, but we still had to do all the hard work to turn it into reality. Now it's Emmie's turn to help her dream come true. So yes, a plan would be good."

They all three turn and look at me. I stare back at them blankly. I have no idea what to do.

"Um, anyone have any bright ideas?" I ask.

"Emmie, can you tell us your vision again? Give us as much detail as possible," Mom instructs. Slowly, I do, closing my eyes and trying to picture it all clearly as I describe it to them. Dani scribbles down the details on the junk mail as Mom and Dot listen intently.

"Is that all?" Dani asks when I finish talking. We all stare at the paper. She's written down every detail I can remember.

"That's all I can think of."

"Okay, we need a plan of action." Dani fishes around for more paper in her bag and finds a napkin from Byrdie's Coffee, my all-time favorite local coffee place in Poulsbo. "What are the steps Emmie needs to get from here to seeing her vision come true?" Dani loves a good plan. She makes detailed goals for herself every year and keeps lists for everything.

"It sounds like she needs that chocolate shop she's been talking about for years," Dot says practically. Dani writes it down.

"And Emmie and Henry will have to fall in love," Mom says softly. Her eyes are bright with anticipation.

"I need to find that floaty yellow dress," I pipe up. That sounds like an enjoyable challenge. I can't remember the last time I splurged on something that wasn't practical. Replacing my floral cotton underwear and a new three-pack of black leggings from Amazon is as luxe as I've gotten in recent years. The thought of a little glamour is exciting. My life in Paris feels far away.

"And you'll need Henry to give you an engagement ring and propose." Dani nods, satisfied. She sits back.

We all crowd around to look at the list.

To-Do List

- Henry + Emmie fall in love
- Chocolate shop
- Yellow dress
- Engagement ring + proposal

It's crazy to see it written out in her big, loopy handwriting. This is the list of steps to make my vision come true. Are we really just going to make it happen? How?

"Also, Emmie, you need to pamper yourself," Dani announces. "Trust me, reinita. Manicure, pedicure, new haircut, new lingerie . . . A full glow-up."

"Hey," I protest. "That isn't part of the vision. I'm fine as I am."

They all turn and survey me. I glance down at my jean cutoffs and fitted pale blue tee. At least when Henry came in I was wearing lip gloss and my hair was clean. It could have been way worse. It's often worse. "Last week you told me I look like a young Reese Witherspoon and any man would be lucky to have me," I remind Dani. "What changed?"

She waffles. "Well . . . I was being nice."

"Baby girl," Dot interrupts, laying her large, calloused hand on my shoulder. "You are beautiful and kind and sweet as sugar, and any man would be lucky to have you. You don't need to change a thing. But you're talking about trying to catch the eye of a famous TV star, a man who's surrounded by actresses and

Hollywood types. If you want Henry to fall in love with you, maybe a little help wouldn't be a bad idea."

"A little freshening up," Mom offers gently. "To highlight your natural beauty."

"Start with a new bra," Dani interjects, eyeing my chest in concern.

"I'm fine," I tell them stubbornly, crossing my arms over my breasts self-consciously. "I'm not going to twist myself into a pretzel to try to compete with Hollywood actresses. That's ridiculous."

As if I even could. I'm a thirty-four-year-old woman, a mom. I have a little soft, rounded jiggle of a belly from carrying Gus, and my breasts aren't as perky as they were before breastfeeding that little guzzler. I have some split ends because I keep forgetting to make a hair appointment. I'm pretty, but in a slightly tired, girl-next-door way, not Hollywood glamour and sex appeal. I know this is just who I am, and I refuse to try to make myself into a glossy magazine version of Emmie. Either Henry will like the real me or he won't.

Then I glance at my dingy gray bra strap peeking out of my shirt, catch a glimpse of my chewed nails, brush back my slightly too-long bangs, and sigh. Okay, I get it. I don't need to change anything for Henry, but maybe I want to change a few things for me, small things that could help me feel like the shiniest and best version of myself—still me, but a slightly less worn-out, tired me. It's been many years since Paris. It would be nice to regain some of my joie de vivre. I make a mental note to buy some new, pretty matching bras and underwear, because saggy gray is not a good look on *anyone*. And I guess a bang trim wouldn't hurt. And a manicure.

"I'll make a hair appointment with Candace," I agree reluctantly. "And another for a mani-pedi at the Nail Boat."

Dani nods approvingly. "And don't forget the bra. Go for maximum push-up," she urges, making a lifting motion to illustrate.

"So where do we start on the list?" Dot asks with a frown. "That's a lot to tackle."

Mom clears her throat and shifts uncomfortably in the hard folding chair. Sitting for any length of time gets painful on her joints. "Emmie needs to find a way to spend time with Henry," she muses. "Everything else will come later, but they need a chance to get to know each other. Falling in love takes time."

"Good idea," Dani says. She purses her lips, thinking. "Emmie, did he tell you where he's staying?"

"I know where he is," Dot interjects. "Mary Beth Douglas told me last week that she'd rented her little beach cabin out to some cute British guy. It has to be him."

Mom claps her hands in delight. "Oh, this is good news!" she exclaims. "Now we need to figure out a way for Emmie to see Henry as soon as possible."

I swallow nervously. Are we really doing this?

"Okay, we have the first action point in our plan," Dani says, handing me the napkin with the bullet-point list on it. "Step one, give Emmie and Henry a chance to fall in love."

Chapter 8

Which is how I find myself standing on the doorstep of Henry Summers's rented beach cottage at eight a.m. two days later. I'm sporting freshly trimmed bangs and a new lilac-colored lace bra (with just a little bit of push-up). I'm also holding our biggest sampler box of fudge. I knock timidly, heart pounding in my throat. What if he's still asleep? Is he going to think it's creepy that I'm on his doorstep? Probably. This suddenly seems like a terrible idea. Is it too late to back out and leave? I glance toward the car where Dot and Mom are giving me a big thumbs-up. They insisted on coming along.

"To make sure he's not a perv," in Dot's words. I think they secretly want in on the action though. They're hopeless romantics, and I suspect they want to see Henry in the flesh for themselves. I finally gave in to their constant badgering and said they could come if they promised to stay in the car and not cause trouble. They solemnly promised, but I'm not sure I entirely trust them. Mr. Butters is sitting in the back seat with Dot, grinning happily and panting. He seems to be thoroughly enjoying the adventure. I smooth my hands down my cute summer dress, a sprigged spring-green cotton with ruffled pockets.

"Hello?" Henry opens the door, looking confused and adorably rumpled in a soft navy T-shirt and a pair of worn jeans. Too late to change my mind now! I take a fortifying breath and paste on a smile.

"Good morning," I say cheerfully.

Henry's hair is mussed and he's wearing round tortoiseshell glasses and a hint of a five-o'clock shadow. He looks delicious. "Oh." He peers at me and recognition lights his eyes. "Emmie, is it?" He glances around, puzzled. "Can I help you?"

I think he actually means "How did you find me?"

"It's a small town," I say by way of explanation. "And to the best of my knowledge, you're the only British guy in Poulsbo. I swear I'm not a crazy psycho stalker. I just came to bring you this." I shove the box of fudge at him. "Welcome to Poulsbo."

Ugh, smooth, Emmie, real smooth. I'm rusty at this flirting thing, and it's obvious. "The fudge is from my mom," I explain. "She's a big fan of *Savor.*"

Which is true. I don't tell him I am too. I swallow nervously and purposefully don't glance behind me where I am absolutely sure Mom and Dot are glued to the windows of the car, watching us. My palms are sweating. Henry makes me feel fluttery and nervous, like I just swallowed an entire kaleidoscope of butterflies.

"Ah, how thoughtful." Henry smiles as though I've cleared up the mystery for him. "That's very kind of her. Please thank her for me." He takes the box of fudge.

We stand there awkwardly for a moment. He musses his hair with one hand. I hesitate. I don't want to leave, but I'm not sure where to go from here. It's been a long time since I liked a guy this much, and I'm super nervous.

"How's the writing going?" I ask him.

He winces. "Not that well, actually." A pause, then he confesses. "Truth be told, your delicious caramel got me through revising one whole chapter. Now I'm stuck again though, I'm afraid. Maybe this fudge will do the trick." He quirks a brow in an adorably self-deprecating way, then pauses a beat and looks at me. "Actually, would you like to come in for a cup of tea? I was just about to put the kettle on."

I hesitate, thinking of Dot and Mom sitting in the car, but I know they'd insist I accept. This is a once-in-a-lifetime chance to spend time with Henry. "Sure, a cup of tea would be great."

I don't like tea, but I like the thought of Henry Summers brewing a cup for me. I glance back at the car just in time to see Dot and Mom waving cheerfully. Henry spots them too and frowns in a bemused way.

"Are there . . . two elderly women in your car?" he asks quizzically.

I groan. "It's my mom and her best friend. They insisted on coming along to make sure you weren't secretly an axe murderer."

"Right." Henry pauses, then grins sheepishly. "Well then, um . . . would they like to join us?"

"You bet your sweet bippy we would!" Dot yells from the car. "Can we bring Mr. Butters too?"

Apparently she's had the back seat passenger window of my old Honda rolled down to eavesdrop this whole time and I didn't notice. She and Mom scramble from the car with surprising speed, Mr. Butters at their heels. Henry steps forward as they come up onto the porch and extends his hand.

"Good morning, ladies. I'm Henry," he says, clearing his throat.

"Oh, we know who you are," Dot tells him knowingly. She pats him on the shoulder and breezes past him into the house. Mom clasps Henry's hand, leaning on her cane.

"Hello, Henry. I'm Gwen, Emmie's mother."

"A pleasure to meet you, Gwen." He smiles and I see Mom melt. "Thank you for the fudge. Very thoughtful of you." He sounds sincere, and he appears to be taking our unexpected visit in stride. He leans down and scratches Mr. Butters under the chin. "Hello again, old chap."

Mr. Butters wags his stub of a tail.

"I've never seen a dog in a top hat before," Henry observes in a slightly baffled tone, straightening.

"It's . . . a whole thing," I mutter, rolling my eyes. "Don't get me started."

"Can I help you into the house?" Henry asks Mom, offering her his arm. She tucks her cane under her other arm and happily accepts. Mr. Butters trots along behind them.

I follow them inside. I'm trying to act calm although my heart is hammering in my throat. This. Is. Happening!!! I'm having tea with the man I've been hopelessly pining over for years. I pinch myself, right in the tender part of my inner arm by my elbow, just to be sure I'm not dreaming.

The inside of the beach cottage is spare and quaint. White shiplap walls and worn pine floors. The décor is nautical and beachy—an old sea chest against one wall, a fluffy white couch with a sand-colored throw. There are few signs of life. A pair of brogues by the door, a canvas jacket and scarf on a hook on the wall. Henry is neat and tidy, I notice. He leaves little trace of himself.

“I like a tidy man,” Dot announces to no one. “You know you can trust a man who knows how to pick up after himself.”

We follow Henry into the back of the house where an open-concept kitchen / dining area offers a stunning view of the bay. I lag behind a second and send a quick, covert, elated text to Dani, who is covering a day shift today.

HAVING TEA WITH HENRY AT HIS HOUSE!!!

Despite the fact that she’s on duty, she texts back instantly.

GO GET ’EM, TIGER!

I find Mom and Dot seated at the table in the dining area and Henry at the sink in the compact but functional kitchen, filling an electric kettle with water. The back of the house is all windows looking out at the bay, and a pair of sliding glass doors leads out onto a big deck that juts out over the water. At high tide the house must feel like it’s floating, like you’re on a houseboat. One door is open to the sea breeze, and Mr. Butters wanders outside onto the deck. He likes to watch for seals.

Henry putters around, switching the kettle on and getting mugs out of the cabinet.

“How do you like your tea?” he asks us. “Milk, sugar?”

“Plain for me,” Dot tells him.

Mom, the only one of us who actually likes tea, takes hers with milk and sugar. Henry takes his with a splash of milk. I’m not a tea drinker, so I ask him for both milk and sugar. Maybe it will make the taste of tea a little more palatable.

"Shall we take our tea on the deck? It's a fine morning," Henry offers, handing around the mugs when the tea is ready. I gaze into mine, wishing it was a hometown honey latte from Byrdie's, but oh well. I suppose if Henry and I are meant to be, I'd better get used to tea.

"Sure," I agree.

Mom and Dot don't follow us. Dot asks to use the bathroom and Mom demurs and opts to move to an armchair in the living room to drink her tea.

"Easier on my hips," she tells us. "You two go ahead."

I follow Henry out onto the deck. We lean over the deck railing and gaze out across Liberty Bay. Mr. Butters parks himself beside us, enjoying the sunshine, tongue lolling as he smiles out at the view. The sunlight on the water sparkles like diamonds, and there's a fresh breeze. I inhale deeply. I never tire of it, the briny smell of the bay—seaweed and salt water and something a little sweet. I missed it all those years I lived in Europe.

"This place is really quite remarkable," Henry says with a note of wonder in his voice. "There was a seal out here earlier, bobbing about, and yesterday I saw a bald eagle catch a fish and fly away."

"It's magical here," I agree. "Did you grow up by the water?" I'm curious to know more about him.

"Yes, I was raised on the coast of England in Cornwall," Henry tells me, sipping his tea. "I never feel more at home than when I'm by the sea. I miss it when I'm landlocked."

"I feel the same. When I'm away from the water, I'm homesick for it. It feels like a longing nothing else can really satisfy. At least I haven't found anything that does yet." I take a tentative sip from my mug. It's hot and sweet at first, with a bitter bite at the end. Nope, I still don't care for tea.

Henry looks at me as though surprised to find we share this feeling. "Exactly," he says. I wonder if he's not used to being understood. I wonder if he leads a lonely life.

"Do you get to go home much?" I ask.

I'm trying to be casual, to have a normal conversation, but my pulse is fluttering with nerves. I'm hyperaware of every word and movement—his and mine. Everything feels heightened. I keep seeing flashes of the vision when I look at Henry. Our entire interaction feels weighty with potential, with the future.

"I don't get back to England as much as I'd like," Henry admits with a touch of regret. "I try to go back every year for my mum's birthday or for Christmas, but it's hard with the show schedule. I travel quite a lot for work, upwards of nine months of the year. I'm seldom in one place for long." He leans his elbows on the railing and glances sideways at me. "This summer will be the longest I've stayed in one place and not traveled anywhere in years, actually. I'm not quite sure what to do with myself. I'm so used to rambling about. I'm a bit of a wandering soul, I'm afraid." He seems a little bashful at the admission.

I'm taken aback by the reality of his travel schedule. Nine months a year? How can he have a life outside of work? "That's a lot of travel," I observe, sipping my tea. "Does it get lonely?"

Henry nods. "At times. It can get taxing to always be someplace new. But it's fascinating too. I love what I do, despite the grueling schedule." He grins at me, his smile carefree and genuine. "What about you?" he asks. "Were you lucky enough to grow up here?"

"All my life," I tell him, gazing out at the bay. "The Wynne roots run deep in Poulsbo."

"Did you ever want to leave and go somewhere else?" he asks curiously.

"I left after high school," I tell him. "I lived in Europe for eight years. When I was eighteen I enrolled in a chocolatier program in Switzerland, and after I graduated I took a job as an apprentice for Jacques Genin in Paris. I was there for years."

Henry whistles low. "Genin? That's quite impressive." He looks at me with a touch of admiration. I can see him reassessing his initial impression of me, putting the different pieces in place. "That explains the caramel you gave me yesterday. It was . . . utterly delicious. Where can I find more of your creations? I'd love to try some of your chocolates."

I blush, embarrassed. "I don't actually make chocolates anymore."

It feels like a failure somehow to admit that to him. I can't quite believe that it's been so many years since I tried my hand at what was once the center of my whole life. Henry wraps his long fingers around his mug and gazes at me intently. "Forgive me if this is too forward, but is there a reason you quit? You're obviously very talented, at least from what I tasted."

I open my mouth and then hesitate. How can I explain? Any way I slice it, it sounds pathetic.

"My life has been . . . a little complicated for the past few years," I tell him, trying to sound optimistic, skimming over the hard parts. "Family stuff mostly. But I'm hoping to start making chocolates again soon. This summer, actually."

"I hope you do. For all our sakes." Henry gives me a lopsided smile. His eyes on me are kind and curious. I feel like he sees me, like I have his whole attention. It feels like he has all the time in the world to chat with me, which is why I uncharacteristically keep talking.

"Thank you," I blurt out, then blush. "I'd love to do more with chocolate again someday. I've always wanted to open my own shop."

"You should," Henry says promptly. "But why only someday? Why not now?"

I toy with the handle of my mug. "A lot of reasons, actually. After my dad died, my mom needed help. She has a health condition that means she can't make fudge anymore or run the candy store by herself. I'm an only child, so there wasn't anyone else to take over the family business." I think of all the evenings I sit down to work on urgent bills and business paperwork and fall asleep listening to Henry's soothing voice coming from the TV. Now I'm here with him in real life. I can't quite wrap my mind around it. He's a little shorter and leaner than he looks on TV, but just as cute and somehow even more approachable. I hesitate, then add, "And I have a son, Gus. He's six. So I wear a lot of hats. Sometimes too many hats. There hasn't been room in my life to add one more thing."

Henry nods, absorbing this information. "That is a lot," he agrees. "Do you miss making chocolate?"

"I do," I admit readily. "If there was a way to do it full-time, to have my own shop, that would be a dream come true, but the store is struggling and my mom's health is not going to improve. Things are tough right now. I don't see how I can. I don't have the time, and we can't take the financial risk to have me go out on my own. Maybe one day." I shrug, instantly embarrassed by my oversharing.

Henry looks steadily at me, his brow furrowed a little in thought. His eyes are a beautiful clear hazel, I notice, with flecks of green. They're warm eyes, magnetic. I feel like the center of the universe when he's looking at me. It's a giddy sensation. "That sounds like quite a lot for one person to carry," he observes.

I glance away. "Sometimes," I say lightly. What I mean is, always. What I mean is, sometimes I feel as though it's crushing me and I can't breathe with the weight of everything I'm carrying.

He considers me for a moment, then says thoughtfully, "Emmie, you have a real talent. I hope someday soon you can find a way to share it with the world again. If I can help in any way . . ."

"Thank you." I fiddle with the handle of my mug, touched by his offer. "Unfortunately, fudge pays the bills right now, but maybe someday . . ." I lick my lips and gaze out at the bay. I feel ashamed admitting this to him, but it's the truth. I can't justify the risk to do something else. Everyone is depending on me. And there just isn't enough of me to go around. What I want doesn't really factor into the equation. Not now, not when I'm the center around which our world continues to turn. If I tilt, if I drop something, if I falter, my family, our livelihood, our life, will go careening into space.

My phone buzzes in my pocket and it brings me back to the present. I check the time. "We should go," I tell Henry regretfully. "I need to open the store soon. Dot too. Thanks for letting us barge in on your morning uninvited."

"I'm not sorry at all," Henry replies promptly. "It was a delightful reprieve." He shoots me a rueful smile. "But I suppose I really should get back to the grindstone."

Back inside, I place my almost-full mug of tea by the sink and gather Dot and Mom. Mr. Butters trots along behind me. Henry walks us out, offering his arm to Mom again.

"Thank you again for the fudge, Gwen," he says sincerely, pressing Mom's hand gently when we reach the car. "Fingers crossed it will help me churn out another chapter or two."

"I hope we'll see a lot more of you, Henry," Mom tells him, beaming up at him expectantly.

"I'd like that very much." Henry glances at me as he says it.

"Don't be a stranger," Dot tells him, clapping him on the back heartily as though they are old friends.

"I won't, Dot. You have my word. Thank you for the lovely surprise visit this morning."

Henry helps Mom into the car and Dot boosts Mr. Butters into the back seat, since his legs are too short to get in without help. Then Henry and I linger for a moment before I get in. In an uncharacteristic fit of boldness, I fish around in my purse for a scrap of paper, find a receipt, and scrawl my phone number on it. "In case you have questions or need someone to show you around, I can tell you which restaurants are good in town and who has the best Danishes," I say, handing it to him. Too late, I realize it is the receipt for my new push-up bra. Mortified, I consider trying to take it back, but he's already tucking it into his pocket.

"Thank you, Emmie. I appreciate the offer. It's nice to have a friendly face in a new place."

"Call her," Dot yells from the car. She's not even remotely subtle. I shoot her a quelling look, which does nothing.

"See you around, Henry." I try to sound breezy and confident. "Thanks for the tea."

He smiles, his eyes creasing at the corners. "My pleasure. Goodbye, Emmie, it was good to see you again." He starts to put out his hand just as I go in for a hug. We both freeze, then laugh. We hug anyway. It's brief, but I like the feel of his arms around me. It's been a long time since a handsome man hugged me, and he's surprisingly toned under the soft cotton of his T-shirt. I sniff him covertly, just a tiny bit, and am delighted to find he smells deliciously of Earl Grey tea. I was right. Bergamot. His scent is lovely and expensive.

As I get into the car and shut the door, Mom sighs. "Oh, what a darling man. With that accent. And those eyes!"

Dot chuckles. "I've got a good feeling about this," she predicts.

"Shh . . . he can probably hear you," I scold, turning the key in the ignition and checking to make sure all the windows are rolled up. They both grin at me, totally unrepentant.

"I am not taking you anywhere ever again," I grouse at them, but they ignore me, chatting about what color eyes Henry's and my babies might have as we head back down the drive. I hazard a glance in the rearview mirror and my heart gives a little flip. Henry is standing on the front porch, sipping his tea, watching me drive away. He raises a hand in farewell. Maybe he's just procrastinating a minute more, but it really does feel like destiny.

I drive back to town basking in the glow of the morning. Henry is exactly what I hoped he'd be—not pretentious, warm and genuine, thoughtful and kind. I worried I'd be disappointed by the real thing, but he's even better than he seems on TV. I like him a lot, and I think he may like me, or at least he's intrigued by me. It's a good place to start.

I don't know what happens next, but this morning felt like the beginning of something special.

Chapter 9

"How do we go back to our normal life after starting the day drinking tea with Henry Summers?" Mom sighs as we arrive at the shop a few minutes after we're supposed to be open. I hear Dot next door, getting ready to open the Salty Mermaid for the day.

"I know, but we still have to sell fudge," I tell her as we unlock the front door. "I'll grab the new trays." I head back to the kitchen, flicking on the lights. As I go to grab the tray of fudge, I notice a package sitting on the marble slab fudge-making table in the middle of the room. It is small and cylindrical and wrapped in the fanciest gold polka-dotted paper I've ever seen. It looks expensive. And it wasn't there last night when I locked up.

"Hello, what are you?" I ask curiously, picking up the package. There's a little card attached. In gold script it says simply:

Emmie

"Ooh, what is that?" Mom asks, coming into the kitchen. "It looks special." Mr. Butters eyes the package curiously.

"I have no idea. I just found it here. It's addressed to me. Do you know anything about it?"

Mom shakes her head. "Open it," she urges. "It looks like a gift."

Inside the thick paper is a narrow glass container about five inches tall with gold swirls and starbursts etched into the glass. The container is filled with the fanciest gold sprinkles I've ever seen. The sprinkles echo the designs on the jar: tiny shiny gold swirls and starbursts. They're so delicate and pretty. Mystified, I open the card. Inside, in the same elegant script, are two words:

For courage

"That's strange." I show Mom the card, puzzled by who the gift is from and how it came to be sitting in our kitchen. The doors to the shop were locked, Mom was with me at Henry's, and we are the only ones who have keys. Curiouser and curiouser. Gingerly, I unscrew the gold cap on the glass container and shake a few of the golden sprinkles into my hand. They seem to shimmer against my skin, tantalizing. I place one on the tip of my tongue and shiver with pleasure. The taste is subtle, sweet as sprinkles always are, but there's something almost floral, a hint of violets and vanilla. They're delicious, but there's something odd about them too, a faint tingling sensation, a little buzz of energy that zips from the tip of my tongue down to my toes. Like a little jolt of static electricity. I glance at the jar in surprise. It's the same feeling I got when I started to see my vision, when I made the wish and blew out the candle and saw the first gold sparkles burst across my field of sight. I drop the remaining sprinkles into the jar and take a step back. There's something strange about these sprinkles.

"What is it, Emmie?" Mom asks anxiously. "What's the matter?"

I shake my head. "Nothing's . . . wrong. It's just . . . Here." I hold out the container. Cautiously, Mom tries a sprinkle.

"My goodness," Mom breathes a moment later, glancing at me in astonishment. "What in heaven's name are those? They make me feel sort of . . . buzzy." Mom picks up the note and reads it aloud again. "For courage." She glances at me, and then together we stare at the glass jar of sprinkles in bewilderment.

"Any idea where they came from?" I ask a little nervously.

Mom narrows her eyes. "I wonder . . ." she murmurs.

I look at her expectantly. Mr. Butters looks at each of us in turn and wags his tail stub uncertainly.

"Sometimes the women in our family get a little . . . help . . . to make their visions come true," Mom explains. "Help you can't quite explain. The day I met your father, I wasn't supposed to be working at the diner. I didn't have a shift scheduled. But I got a call from my manager, asking me to cover for a colleague who couldn't come in for the breakfast shift. When I got to work, everyone was surprised to see me. I found out that my manager had not made that call. No one at the diner had. But they were shorthanded that morning and grateful for the help, so I stayed on for the shift, and that's when I met your father." Her mouth curves into a soft smile at the memory.

"When I saw him for the first time, sitting there stirring cream into his coffee, I knew instantly who he was, and I knew I was staring at my future." She stops, a little choked up. "We never did figure out who made that call, but it changed my life. It helped my vision come true. And then later, when we started talking seriously about opening the store, I received a letter in the mail one day. No return address. It just showed up on our doorstep. The only thing inside was a handwritten recipe for fudge." She nods to a framed piece of yellowed and butter-spotted paper on the wall beside the door. It's been there for as long as I can remember.

"Our family fudge recipe?" I ask in surprise.

She smiles in a conspiratorial way. "Someone's fudge recipe," she admits. "But wherever it came from, it's the best fudge I've ever had in my life. We've been using that recipe for forty years now." She glances at the framed letter and back to the jar of sprinkles. "I wonder if it is the same for you. I wonder if those sprinkles are going to help you somehow."

"Are you saying you think these sprinkles are . . . magical?" I stare at her, astonished.

She shrugs. "Stranger things have happened, Emmie. What if they are? What if they can give you courage to pursue what feels to you like an impossible vision?"

I am tempted to dismiss her speculation as ridiculous, but then I remember the utter astonishment I felt at watching Henry Summers walk into our family fudge shop. Maybe it's not so strange after all. Maybe I should expand my understanding of what could be possible. Maybe these little gold sprinkles will somehow give me courage to do what seems impossible. My own version of Gus's courage sprinkles but infused with a touch of magic. Wouldn't that be amazing?

The bell on the front door jingles, and Mom heads out front to greet our first customers of the day. Still feeling a little tingly, I set the glass container carefully on a shelf and square my shoulders. Somehow, I do feel more courageous. The impossible feels possible in a way I can't explain. Maybe it's the sprinkles. I can still taste the delicate flavor on my tongue. I think of the sprinkles and imagine them atop a Rainier cherry truffle, and my mouth waters. Tonight I'm going to try my hand at a new chocolate idea and see what happens.

Buoyed by a newfound sense of anticipation, I head into the front of the shop to help Mom out, a spring in my step. Whatever the cause of this sudden burst of courage, I'm excited to see where it leads me.

"Henry went to college at a place called Exeter," Dani tells me, giving the stool where she is perched a little twirl with her foot. "And his mom's name is Edith."

It's early morning a few days after our tea with Henry. It's still an hour before the shop opens, and Dani is fresh off a night shift and keeping me company. She's brought me a hometown honey latte from Byrdie's and is currently amusing herself googling Henry and relaying all the tidbits of information she finds while I finish up my last batch of fudge. It's been three days and Henry hasn't reached out. I'm beginning to get the sinking feeling he isn't really interested. I must have misread his politeness as something more. It's very disappointing, and I'm not sure what to do about it.

On a positive note, I've been working on my new Rainier cherry and vanilla buttercream truffle recipe every night after Gus is tucked into bed, and I'm finally satisfied with the results. I'm yawning my head off from the series of late nights, but happy. Creating a new chocolate flavor is a painstaking process of experimentation and repetition, trial and error. Taste testing, tweaking, trying it again. But the results are finally as delicious as I imagined them to be.

"His last girlfriend was a television producer. See, he likes blondes." Dani holds the phone out to show me a photo from some charity gala. Henry has his arm wrapped around the waist of a curvy woman with a severe blond bob. She looks cool and professional. I swipe at my newly trimmed bangs, feeling intimidated.

"Even if he does like blondes, he hasn't called," I mutter distractedly as I stir a batch of rocky road fudge with a huge wooden paddle. I have to keep a close eye on the temperature of the copper kettle. No more scorched batches for me. I watch as the temperature reading on the thermometer climbs higher, stirring steadily. The constant stirring makes the fudge creamier. The mouthwatering aroma of melted chocolate and butter and cream wafts from the kettle. Making fudge doesn't take a huge amount of creativity, just concentration and some strong biceps.

"His birthday is March fifteenth," Dani says. "He's thirty-seven years old."

"You would make an excellent stalker if you weren't an officer of the law," I observe wryly.

Dani smirks at me. "Who says I can't be both?" She breezily goes back to her Google search results about Henry.

At exactly 235 degrees, I snatch the kettle off the burner and carefully pour the liquid fudge onto the thick counter-height marble slab table in the middle of our kitchen.

"That smells good," Mom says, coming through the kitchen door with Mr. Butters. She shakes the raindrops off her jacket and peels it off her slim form, then helps Mr. Butters out of his yellow doggy rain slicker. He has a matching yellow hat, but he hates it and has managed to scrape it off his blocky head so many times that Mom has given up on it. He squeezes out of the rain slicker like a sausage popping out of a cellophane wrapper and trots off to his doggy bed in the storefront with a visible air of relief.

Dani and I exchange a look. "Your mom needs a hobby," she mutters, and I nod in agreement. Dressing a dog can't be the highlight of a satisfying life. It just can't. Mom needs something more to nurture.

"Everything go okay at drop-off?" I ask, grunting a little at the weight of the kettle as I set it in the sink. "Gus was saying his stomach hurt again this morning."

I came in early today to make fudge, so Dot picked up Mom and Gus. Mom stopped driving a few years ago due to her condition, so Dot often drops Gus off for me and gives Mom a ride to the store if I have to come in early. Gus has been reluctant about school this year, often saying his stomach hurts and coming up with increasingly far-fetched disaster scenarios that might befall him at school. I'm pretty sure it's anxiety, but I'm not quite sure how to help him.

"What if an asteroid hits our school during lunch? What if a black hole opens up in the middle of the gym?" he asked me this morning as he picked at his oatmeal. I shook some of his favorite colorful sprinkles into his oatmeal for courage, and that seemed to help a little.

"He was quiet, but he seemed to be feeling better." Mom peers over my shoulder at the large rectangular frame of narrow stainless steel bars sitting on the marble slab. The fudge is pooling within the frame of the bars, cooling slowly on the marble. The bars fit together to contain the liquid fudge as it cools, like a picture frame. I check the temperature again. It needs to cool more before it's ready to be worked.

"Any news from Henry?" Mom asks hopefully. I shake my head. Mom looks disappointed. I am too. I thought he might drop by or at least text. So far, nothing. I keep thinking of our conversation, replaying it over and over. Aside from wondering if I misread his interest, the part that keeps sticking out to me is his comment about my chocolate making.

Emmie, you have a real talent. I hope someday soon you can find a way to share it with the world again.

Every time I think of those words, I feel a strange twist in my stomach, longing mixed with both hope and despair. I want so badly to be able to share my gift with the world, but I don't know how to make it happen. Yet in my vision, I am standing in my own chocolate shop. How in the world do I get from here to there? I don't have money to rent a storefront, or the funds to renovate it to look like what I've imagined for years, much less buy the expensive equipment I'd need. And what about the Happy Viking? Mom can't run it, and I can't juggle two stores at once. It feels impossible. An impossible dream. And yet I saw it in my vision. Surely there must be a way for me to make it happen? And soon. Henry is only here for the summer. If I don't get my store up and running quickly, how will my vision come true?

Chapter 10

Feeling stymied by the conundrum and stressed by the time crunch, I grab a bag of mini marshmallows and throw them unevenly over the fudge. I should slow down, be more careful. This flavor is one of our top sellers. Milk chocolate fudge, marshmallows, and toasted walnuts is a classic for a reason. It's pure, sweet nostalgia. But today I just want to be done with it. I'm feeling itchy and thwarted. I check the fudge's consistency on the marble slab. It's cooled enough that I know it's time to go to the next step—creaming. It's the most labor-intensive part of the process, but it's what makes the fudge so smooth.

"What's on your mind, honey?" Mom asks gently, eyeing me. "Are you worried about something?"

"What do you mean?" I take a blunt metal scraper and run it along the sides of the bars, smoothly separating the fudge from the metal.

"You're racing around the kitchen like a squirrel on speed,"

Dani observes from her perch on the stool. "I can hear you spinning out from here." She doesn't look up from her phone.

"Just trying to figure out how we can possibly make one of the items on the list come true," I mutter, removing the bars and setting them aside to wash later. The fudge oozes a little, spreading out slightly on the marble slab, but it mostly stays in place now that it's cool enough.

"Which item on the list?" Mom asks.

I sigh. "The chocolate shop." I glance at Mom, letting my frustration leak a little. "I saw it so clearly. It was exactly as I've always dreamed it would be. But I have no earthly idea how we get from this"—I gesture around the kitchen and toward the storefront—"to that. It feels impossible." My shoulders slump in discouragement.

"In your vision," Mom says slowly, frowning a little like she's concentrating on something. "Can you describe the shop to me again?"

I grab a long-handled wooden paddle and start to cream the fudge, walking around and around the marble slab, scraping up long ribbons of fudge and turning them over on themselves, churning and folding as I walk, over and over. It's tedious, and I start sweating a little with the effort. As I cream, I describe what I saw in my vision again, the shop I've always dreamed about. When I finish my description, Mom doesn't say anything, just presses her lips together and stays quiet. She has her thinking face on. I keep creaming. It always feels like it takes an eternity for the fudge to achieve the right consistency.

After a few minutes she nods once, as though deciding something. "Emmie," she says, "I think it's time."

"Time for what?" I keep walking around the slab, creaming

and getting a little dizzy from going round and round. Dani glances up from her phone as though sensing a shift in the conversation.

Mom gives me a tired sigh. "Honey, it's no secret that the store isn't doing well. We've been going downhill little by little for years. I know we keep hoping things will pick up, but so far they haven't." She looks saddened as she states what is obvious to see but hard to admit. "Maybe it's time to not just have all our eggs in one basket. I want you to be able to do what you love. I've been thinking about it for a while now. And when you described your vision, it felt like a confirmation."

I go still. Long, lazy rivulets of fudge fold down on themselves as they fall from my paddle onto the slab. "What are you saying?"

Mom purses her lips, which are a very pale shell-pink shade today. "I'm saying maybe it's time to pivot, Emmie. I know you've always dreamed of having your own shop one day, a place where you can make the chocolates you love to create. Maybe the time is now. You saw it in your vision, and that means it's important that we help make it a reality. I think it's time for you to have your own shop."

"What?" I just stare at her, astonished. I can't believe I'm hearing her right. A thousand questions race through my head, along with any number of good reasons why this won't work. "But who would run this place then?" I protest. I can't possibly be in two places at once, and keeping one small business running is a full-time job already.

"We'd have to hire someone to help here in the shop," Mom acknowledges. "But I could take on more of the administration. We could make it work. I'm sure we could figure it out."

I'm stunned. "I . . . I don't know what to say," I stammer. My thoughts are racing. "I mean, the logistics of running two businesses is really tricky, Mom. And it takes a lot of money to get a chocolate shop established." Money we don't have. How would I even afford to set up a new space? Not to mention first and last month's rent and a damage deposit. It would be thousands of dollars, and we're barely making ends meet as it is. Every month is a white-knuckle race to keep ahead of the medical bills and pediatrician visits, grocery receipts and property taxes. There's precious little left over at the end of the month to do anything else. And starting a new business is a risky venture. What if it fails? What then?

"That's really generous of you," I say quietly, "but I don't see how it will be possible."

"Emmie." Mom comes over and stands next to me, so close I can smell the Ivory soap she uses. She winces a little, clearly in pain, but her eyes are shining with suppressed excitement. "I have a secret," she tells me. "I've been waiting for the right time to tell you."

"A secret?" Dani and I exchange a glance.

"There's a little nest egg I set aside for you," Mom explains. "It's what's left of your dad's life insurance policy. I've been holding onto it for a rainy day since he passed, but I think that the best time to use it is now. I want to give it to you to start your own shop. What can you do with ten thousand dollars?"

Dani looks up from her phone and whistles.

I am gobsmacked by her offer. "Are you serious?" I had no idea she had money tucked away.

She nods once, firmly. "I am."

I run a few quick calculations in my head. The truth is that ten thousand dollars is an enormous gift and at the same time not nearly enough if we're talking about a full renovation and opening a state-of-the-art chocolate shop, but I am so touched by her generosity, I don't want to throw cold water on the idea.

"That's really sweet, Mom, but maybe you *should* save it for a rainy day," I say gently.

She shakes her head, a stubborn little V appearing between her brows. "You have to move toward what you want, sweetie, even when it feels like a risk." She tips her head toward the jar of sprinkles sitting on the shelf. "Remember your courage, Emmie. It's time. The vision confirmed it. It's the right time for you to realize your dream. You are so good at putting everyone else first, of taking care of everyone but yourself, me included. It's okay to want something for you. It's a good idea to leave a little bit of space for yourself in your own life. Let me help you do this. I want to."

"Listen to Gwen," Dani pipes up. "Take the money."

I hesitate. The offer is so tempting. What would it look like to make that part of my vision a reality, to have my own shop, to get to be creative with chocolate instead of walking around this big marble slab like a mule around a grindstone day after day? But am I ready? It's a big change, albeit one I've been dreaming about for years. Mom has given me an amazing opportunity. Am I brave enough to take it?

I glance at Mom, who smiles encouragingly. "It's your decision, sweetie," she says.

I think of Henry's words and of the shop from my vision. How will it happen if I don't make space for it in my life? No fairy godmother is going to miraculously pop into my world one day, wave her wand, and give me a chocolate shop with glass display cases and gleaming walnut hardwood floors. In life we have to make our own magic, Dot likes to say. I think she may be right. Mom has given me a chance, if I am bold enough to try. Maybe it's time for me to be my own fairy godmother.

I glance at the little glass cylinder of sprinkles sitting on the shelf, remembering the words written on the card. *For courage.* I sneak a look at Dani, who has gone back to googling facts about Henry and isn't paying attention. Quietly, I reach up and pull down the container, unscrewing the cap and shaking a few sprinkles into my hand, careful not to draw attention to what I'm doing. Mom and I agreed to keep the sprinkles a secret for now. I place a sprinkle on my tongue, then another and another. The delicate floral sweetness melts slowly in my mouth, and as it does, I feel the familiar zing of anticipation, almost electric. I feel it right down to my toes. For courage indeed.

"Okay," I blurt out, surprised by my sudden resolve. "Let's do it."

I am usually cautious before I make a big change. I like to consult spreadsheets and crunch numbers and weigh pros and cons before making a weighty decision like this. Truth be told, I'm itching to do just that. What if this goes sideways? What if my shop fails and we are left with nothing? It's a terrifying thought. But even worse is the thought of waiting and waiting, of letting my vision slip away day by day. I have to act.

Mom is watching me closely. "It's time, Emmie," she says quietly.

She's right.

I keep creaming. The fudge is now viscous and shiny. It's ready for the final stage, forming it into a long loaf shape so we can slice it. I switch to a short-handled metal scraper that resembles a wide putty knife and keep working the fudge.

"Where do I start?" I ask a touch nervously.

"You take it step by step," Mom says.

"We need a list," Dani says, holding up her phone and looking at me expectantly. She loves getting to start a new list. "We can brainstorm a list of what you're looking for in a space. Starting with location—what are you thinking? Somewhere here in downtown Poulsbo?"

I hesitate. Suddenly this is feeling very real. I've always dreamed of Paris, or New York, even toyed with the idea of Portland or Seattle. But here in Poulsbo? That's never been the dream. Thinking about opening my shop anywhere else presents a huge problem, however. Gus and I would have to move. We'd have to leave Mom, and I wouldn't be able to help out with the Happy Viking at all anymore. I imagine Mom struggling to cope with the demands of managing the store, even if we hired good help. And what about her living alone? Picturing her trying to open a can of soup with her gnarled fingers brings a pang to my heart. I can't relocate to another town. It's just not going to work with the realities of our life right now. Mom needs us, and our family business is here. We can't leave Poulsbo. And yet I really want a fresh start for my shop, somewhere I can create a business entirely on my own terms, the way I've always dreamed. I worry my lip, thinking.

"I guess I picture it somewhere else other than Poulsbo," I admit. "But I know we can't move, so what are my options?"

Dani considers my question. "What about Winslow?" she suggests, tapping one nail against her red lipstick. Winslow is a picture-perfect harbor town on neighboring Bainbridge Island. "The downtown gets great tourist traffic with the ferry terminal to Seattle right there."

I entertain the idea for a minute. It would be a twenty-five-minute commute, but that feels doable. "Winslow could work . . ."

"Or Kingston?" Mom pipes up. Another adorable town close by with a ferry terminal.

"Also a good option," I agree. "Let's see what's available for rent in both those towns." It's not Paris or New York, but maybe it will be good enough, far enough away that I can create my own thing out from under the shadow of my family's legacy here.

As I work the fudge, we talk about the possibilities and brainstorm together. I'm growing more excited by the minute. Dani is on Pinterest, pinning inspiring images from French chocolate shops. Mom is making a list of requirements for a space for the shop on a legal pad in her slightly wavering handwriting. Dark wood floors. Big windows. She writes down all the details I can think of.

I start another batch of fudge, almost afraid to hope. Is this really happening? I have no idea what I'm getting myself into. There are so many things I have to plan for—finding an affordable space to rent, setting up and advertising the shop, handling making chocolates in the quantities needed to keep the business afloat. And I have to find someone to help out here at the fudge shop, and I'll need to walk Mom through taking over more of the responsibilities of running this place. Dad always handled the business side of things, and after he got sick, I filled both of their shoes while Mom took on the role of caregiver for him.

It's more than a little daunting to consider everything we need to do to make this happen, but still I feel a swell of anticipation. I am doing this. I am making my chocolate shop a reality. I'll deal with the practicalities later. I think of the list we made on the napkin tucked in my purse.

To-Do List

- Henry + Emmie fall in love
- Chocolate shop
- Yellow dress
- Engagement ring + proposal

I can't force Henry Summers to fall in love with me, or buy an engagement ring, or propose. Our relationship will have to unfold at its own pace. And I haven't even started looking for a yellow dress yet. But this is something I can move forward on. With my mother's blessing and her little nest egg, I can finally open the chocolate shop of my dreams.

I can't wait to get started.

CHAPTER 11

Three days later, we hit a major snag.

"Emmie, I think you'd better see this." Mom comes hurrying into the commercial kitchen where I'm just starting to get ready for the day, Mr. Butters trotting along at her heels. "We have a problem!"

"What's wrong?" I glance up in alarm from slicing a tray of butter pecan fudge. We dropped Gus off at school and headed into the store together this morning. While I finished restocking the fudge trays in the kitchen, Mom volunteered to do a walk-through of the store before opening time. What in the world has happened?

"There's a leak in the bathroom! The carpet around the bathroom door is soaked." Mom looks distraught, wringing her hands.

It's a bad leak. When I approach the bathroom door, situated next to the office tucked behind the register, my shoes squelch on the soggy carpet. Over a quarter of the carpet in the shop is wet, and the bathroom is completely flooded with a half inch of water. It looks like a pipe burst under the sink. I manage to turn off the water, but the damage is done. We stand in the shop surveying the situation in dismay.

"There's no way we can open for business until we dry things out," I tell Mom. And I suspect we are going to need to replace the carpet at the very least.

"Oh dear," Mom sighs. "How long do you think we'll need to be closed?"

We both know we can't afford to lose the daily business we rely on, not to mention we'll need to cover the cost of the repair bill. I think of the ten thousand dollars Mom has set aside, and my heart falls. Looks like we may need to use some of it to get this place back up and running, but we have no choice. We need to get the store open again as soon as possible.

Mom texts Dot, who comes over to see the damage for herself. Then we start making calls to everyone we can think of who might be able to help us with the repairs. Unfortunately, we come up empty.

"No one wants to take on a project this small," Mom reports, her mouth pursed in a worried little pucker when we compare notes after calling around. Mr. Butters sits on her foot and gazes up at her in adoration.

"And even if they do handle small projects, most of them are booked out a couple of months at least." Dot frowns, helping herself to a sample of Oreo fudge from the little clear-plastic-domed sample platter sitting by the register. She's leaning against the counter by the samples, keeping an eye on her front door in case someone comes into her shop. Business is slow today.

"What are we going to do?" I ask anxiously. "We can't afford to close the shop for any longer than we have to."

Correction: We can't afford to close the shop at all, but it looks like we have no choice. I think regretfully of my chocolate shop plan. It's going to have to wait until I can get this sorted out. I blow out a breath and try to think of a creative solution. "I guess there's always YouTube?" I offer. "Maybe we could do it ourselves? How hard do you think it would be to learn to install carpet?"

"Oh, hon, you're not that desperate," Dot says. She snaps her fingers. "Wait, I think I might just have a solution. What about Walt?"

The silence is deafening.

"Walt?" I ask skeptically. "As in your brother?"

At the same time, Mom says, "Oh no. I don't think that's a good idea."

Mom always gets uptight at the mention of Dot's brother Walt. He and Mom don't get along for reasons that are not clear to me. Walt is a gruff, grizzled character who pops into the shop every month or so to buy a pound of fudge. He always comes when Mom isn't at the till, a move I've started to suspect might be deliberate. I've never understood what Mom has against him, but there is some bad blood there. I've always been curious why.

"What's wrong with Walt?" Dot says, a touch defensively.

Dani comes into the store just in time to hear Dot's last question. "Are you talking about that argumentative, belligerent old codger of a brother of yours?" Dani says cheerfully as she feeds Mr. Butters a doggy pot pie from her pocket. "Fully one-third of my disorderly conduct calls in this town are about your brother. Last week he was arguing baseball stats with some tourists from Utah down at the Four Corners Tavern. I got a call that he'd threatened to brain one of them with a pool cue for bad-mouthing the Chicago Cubs." She rolls her eyes and helps herself to a sample of the Oreo fudge too.

"Walt can be a handful," Dot concedes. "And he does love the Cubs. He just needs a good woman to straighten him out, and something to keep him busy so he doesn't get into trouble. But he's got to be better than YouTube." She looks pointedly at me. I waver. I've known Walt all my life. It's true that he's a crusty old coot, but he's handy and he'll probably work for cheap.

"Ask him what he'll charge," I say reluctantly. Dot texts him and a minute later gets a reply.

She reads his response aloud. "'Thirty dollars an hour and a free quarter pound of fudge per day. And I get to choose the flavor.'"

Beside me, Mom makes a *hmph* of displeasure. I cast my eyes around, looking for another option. Walt seems to be our only one unless we want to do it ourselves or wait until September, which is impossible. We need to get started on this right away.

"He says he can meet you here at nine a.m. tomorrow," Dot adds.

"Tell him yes," I agree, feeling relief that at least we have someone who can help us, even if Mom's not a fan of Walt. The thought of trying to learn plumbing repairs on YouTube and doing the work myself is just too much.

We lock up since we can't welcome customers with part of the store flooded. There's not much else to do. I'll work on bills and accounts today at home. Tonight I have to deliver a meal to a family in Gus's class who just had twins, and I'll drop Mom off at her weekly puzzle club, the highlight of her social calendar. I wish she had more to occupy her time, but she does love meeting with the ladies and puzzling. At least she's doing something one evening a week. While she puzzles, I promised Gus we'd build a LEGO spaceship and watch a National Geographic Kids documentary on outer space. Hopefully all of this will keep me from worrying about the cost of flood repairs. As we walk out the door, Mom sighs in resignation. "We're depending on Walt Perkins," she says with a grimace, glancing back at the corner of the shop with the soggy carpet. "I really hope we don't regret this, Emmie."

At nine sharp the next morning, Walt saunters up the sidewalk to the candy shop just as I unlock the door with Mom, Gus, and Mr. Butters in tow. Gus has a late start at school today, so he's tagging along with us for part of the morning. Mom sees Walt and steps back as he comes through the door, hitching up his baggy jeans. He nods to her and touches the brim of his ever-present Cubs baseball cap.

"Gwen," he says gruffly, and she nods back stiffly.

"Walt." She has the pinched look of someone smelling something unpleasant, although Walt smells very faintly and really quite pleasantly of pipe tobacco smoke. I catch a whiff as he walks by me into the shop. What is her problem with the man?

Walt Perkins is not tall. He's compact with a little potbelly from the beer he has a fondness for. I've never seen him without a Cubs baseball cap. He's got bright eyes that peek out sharply over a bushy gray beard, giving him a slightly grizzled appearance, like a blue-collar Santa Claus. He projects a curmudgeonly air of absolute indifference, as though he's spent years giving the world the middle finger. He lives life on his terms and simply does not care what others think. He nods to me, then turns to Gus and Mr. Butters, who are standing behind me watching the newcomer.

"Hello, youngster," Walt says, nodding to Gus.

"Hi," Gus murmurs, eyeing Walt in fascination.

Walt catches sight of Mr. Butters, who is wearing a tweed vest and a tiny matching English driving cap. "That is the most absurd thing I've ever seen," he announces. "Gwen, what have you done to that animal?"

Mom bristles. Mr. Butters is her baby and she takes great pride in his outfits. "Martha Stewart buys outfits for her dogs from the same company," she tells him, looking offended. Walt eyes the dog skeptically again.

"Some people have too much time on their hands." He turns to me, getting down to business. Behind him, Mom is puffed up indignantly. Walt is blunt, but he's not wrong. Mr. Butters scratches his head against a shelf of gummy candies, trying to dislodge the hat.

"Heard you all had a flood?" He looks around, noting the soggy, water-stained carpet.

"Yes, in the bathroom. Let me show you the damage."

Mom and Mr. Butters disappear into the kitchen with Gus in tow while I show Walt the burst pipe and the extent of the water damage.

"Well, shoot, how did I miss that?" he says, frowning.

"Miss it? What do you mean?" I ask, confused by the odd statement.

"Nothing." He waves away the question but stares at the pipe as if he's annoyed with it.

"How soon do you think you can fix all the damage?" I ask anxiously. I'm seeing dollar signs everywhere I look. Walt takes off his baseball cap and scratches his head.

"Depends on a couple of things. We won't know till we can get this bathroom flooring peeled up and see how much damage there is. Looks like you've had a leak for a while now, a slow one, and I'm going to guess it's probably rotted part of the floor under here." He kicks at the vinyl flooring under the sink. I notice it's bubbled up a little. Has it always been like that? For years there's been a faint odor of mildew in this bathroom, but I always attributed it to being so near the bay and our wet climate. Looks like a slow plumbing leak didn't help matters.

"But you can fix it?" I clarify.

"Oh, sure." Walt nods. "Just about anything is fixable if you throw enough time and money at it."

The two things we don't have. I called our insurance agent yesterday and was informed that the water damage won't be covered under our policy because the flood was caused by poorly maintained plumbing that wore out over time. The fact that the pipe had been leaking a little for years means we are on our own to cover the cost of repairs. I worry my lower lip between my teeth, thinking. "Any idea how much it will cost?" I ask tentatively.

Walt grunts and shakes his head. "Not till we get in there and see what's going on. Might be just a couple of thousand for the pipes and new carpet and such. Might be more depending on what we find."

"Okay," I sigh. I guess we don't really have a choice. "Do what you have to do."

"Now, I can speed things up if I hire someone to help me," Walt offers. "I've got a guy—good worker and not too pricey. Pay him the same as me, and we can get it done quicker."

Quicker is good. "That sounds great," I tell him. "As long as we can try to keep the cost down and do it as quickly as possible."

Walt nods. "Okey dokey," he agrees, hitching up his jeans and following me from the bathroom. "I'll give my guy a call. Plan on us starting this afternoon."

He pauses by the fudge display case near the register and gives me a sly look. "How about I take that first quarter pound of fudge in advance?" he asks. "Go ahead and make it that vanilla walnut stuff."

"Coming right up." I measure out a generous quarter pound of fudge. I see him eyeing the scale, making sure I'm not shorting him. I hand him the wrapped package just as Mom returns from the kitchen, walking slowly with the help of her cane, Mr. Butters waddling behind her. In his tweed outfit, he resembles a portly member of the English landed gentry, like he belongs in a doggy version of *Downton Abbey*.

"Gus is having a granola bar and an apple before school," she tells me.

"See you later, Emmie. Gwen." Walt gives a little salute to me and an elaborate sort of half bow to Mom on his way out. He looks at Mr. Butters again and shakes his head, guffawing as he goes. I lock the door behind him, and turn to find Mom wrinkling her nose in distaste.

"I hope you know what you're doing, hiring that man," Mom says with a little disapproving frown, gazing out the window in the direction Walt walked away from the store. "And I hope he doesn't come to work pickled as a herring. He used to drink like a fish."

"I'm sure it will be fine," I tell her. "Walt says it's probably a pretty straightforward plumbing fix and water remediation. What have you got against Walt, anyway?" I ask curiously.

Mom crosses her arms and her lips thin with displeasure. "We have a lot of history, Walt and I. He was a friend of your father's when they were young men. Walt was always wild, always getting Bert into trouble." She shakes her head at the memory. "After we had you, I had to put my foot down. There was an . . . incident. Walt took your dad fishing out by Blake Island, but they capsized and had to be rescued by the coast guard. They were both almost hypothermic by the time they were rescued from the cold water, and also both three sheets to the wind. There were empty beer cans floating all around them when the coast guard pulled them to safety. That was the last straw. I told your father he needed to find new friends. And yet here Walt Perkins is again, turned up like a bad penny."

I'm fascinated by this glimpse of my family's history. The dad I knew was a quiet family man. I had no idea about his wild younger days. The thought of him speeding around in a boat with Walt, getting tipsy on cheap beer and needing to be rescued by the coast guard, is actually really entertaining. I make a mental note to ask Walt to tell me more about him and my dad when Mom isn't around.

"Well, this job does not involve boats or beer, so hopefully we should be okay," I reassure Mom, ever so slightly tongue in cheek. I'm trying to cover up my niggling concerns about this whole process. What if it's a bigger job than Walt thinks it is? What if there isn't enough money after the repair to start my chocolate shop? How will I help bring about my vision if I can't open my shop before Henry leaves? Speaking of Henry, he hasn't contacted me since the tea at his place, which is also really bothering me. I feel very stuck. I can't seem to move forward on anything. I check my watch. Time to head to school.

"Gus?" I call back to the kitchen, then turn and find my son standing silently directly behind me. I jump a little and squeak in surprise. He has a quietly disconcerting way of sneaking up behind people like a ninja.

"Who was that guy?" Gus is chewing the last of his apple. He's got his little navy blue sweater on, the one Mom knitted for him. It has a colorful depiction of the solar system on it, and it says in felt letters, "Give me some space."

"A man we're hiring to fix the leak," I tell him. "Walt is helping us get the store ready to open again as soon as possible."

Gus looks from Mom to me doubtfully. He really doesn't like change, and he's sensitive to anything that feels threatening or stressful. He's picking up on my stress and it's making him anxious. I should have prepped him better about the flood and us having to close the store.

"It'll be okay, buddy," I assure him. "Walt is going to get the store open again as soon as he can."

"Mommy, did you know astronauts have vacuum toilets in space?" Gus asks, seeming to forget about Walt Perkins. He picks up his backpack by the door. "Because they don't have gravity. And they have to drink their own pee in space. The scientists recycle it into water you can drink. Isn't that cool?"

"Super cool." I grimace. I check the time again. "Okay, buddy. Let's head for school."

Gus hugs Mom and pats Mr. Butters, then follows me out the door. I cast a last glance back at the building, at the **CLOSED** sign, and Mom's small, bent figure standing at the window. She's going to go visit with Dot at her shop for the morning.

Pausing for one second, I offer a brief prayer that the remediation will go smoothly, that our money will hold out, and that I'll be able to move one step closer to that moment I am aiming for, the vision of my life's purpose. Then I turn and grab Gus's hand and hurry to the parking lot, hoping we're not going to be tardy, hoping this hard day takes a turn for the better soon.

CHAPTER 12

"I just have to stop by the shop for a minute," I tell Gus later that afternoon after I pick him up from school. "I have to grab some papers from the office."

"Okay." He trails me into the store reluctantly. "But then can we go home and keep building the LEGO spaceship?"

I ruffle his hair. "Absolutely. Just give me a minute."

The storefront is empty, but I hear noise from the bathroom. Someone is playing Nirvana turned down low. I poke my head in the open bathroom door, expecting Walt, and get an eyeful. The bottom half of a long, lean, blue jean–clad male is sticking out from under the sink. That's a view I could get used to. I appreciate it for a half second before I clear my throat, not wanting to startle him. This must be Walt's helper. "Hello?" I call over the sound of Kurt Cobain's raspy vocals.

The man stands up so abruptly he hits his head on the sink, utters a mild swear, and turns to me. When I glimpse his face, my stomach drops. It's Jakob Kristensen. He's wearing a T-shirt and blue jeans and holding a large metal wrench. He rubs his head and winces.

"You!" I blurt out, staring up at Jakob. He looks down on me with a vaguely amused expression. "What . . . what are you doing here?" I ask, feeling off-kilter.

"I'm fixing your leak." He punches a button on his phone and the music goes silent.

For some reason, the whole scene is disconcerting. I'm pretty sure I've had spicy dreams about this exact scenario, although Jakob has never been the romantic lead. I blush bright red thinking of how I just ogled his backside in those snug jeans. I notice Jakob's shirt, a tight, faded blue tee with our high school mascot, a heavily bearded and mustachioed Viking wearing a purple helmet with horns on it. That shirt takes me back a few years.

Gus is peering around me, staring at Jakob with wide eyes. "Who are you?" he asks cautiously, looking at Jakob like he's trying to determine if this stranger is the coolest guy he's ever seen or one of the tricky people who lure children into vans, the ones I'm always warning him about.

"I'm Jakob." Jakob squats so he's at eye level with Gus. "Who are you?"

"Gus."

"Nice to meet you, Gus." Jakob sticks out his hand. Gus looks at it in surprise, considers for a moment, then shakes it hesitantly.

"You need to put a quarter in the swear-word jar," he informs Jakob.

Jakob's mouth twitches upward, and he pulls out a battered wallet and hands Gus a dollar. "Consider this a prepayment for my next three citations," he says.

Gus narrows his eyes and thinks for a moment, then nods and

pockets the dollar. He seems to have decided that Jakob is okay, because he leans in a little and asks confidentially, "Did you know there are more stars in the universe than grains of sand on all the beaches on earth?"

Oh boy. We've gone straight to weird space facts. Curious, I watch to see how Jakob handles it.

Without skipping a beat, Jakob nods solemnly. "Actually, I did know that. Pretty wild, huh," he says. He raises an eyebrow. "Did you know that humans are made up of elements that were formed inside stars and released into the universe when they died?"

Gus looks intrigued. "Really?"

"Really. Do you know what that means?" Jakob asks.

Slowly Gus shakes his head. Jakob leans closer. "That means you and I, all of us, are made of stardust." He watches Gus digest this information.

Gus looks awestruck at the thought. "I'm really made of stars?" he asks, eyes wide. "Is that true?"

Jakob nods. "You, buddy, are a living part of a star. We all are. Cool, huh?"

Gus stares at Jakob, his mouth slightly open, as though he's just received some sort of divine, esoteric secret.

"That's so cool," he breathes, clearly impressed.

I'm impressed too. Most adults chuckle at Gus's science facts and think his obsession with space is kind of cute, but few actually engage with him on his level. Jakob isn't patronizing him, just meeting him where he is. And how does he know such weird facts about space? I guess it's no surprise. Jakob was always like a lint roller for information, picking up trivia everywhere he went. I look at him, the tattoos and muscles and little baby man bun, and wonder what has happened to him to turn him from the sweet, awkward boy I knew in high school to this sexy, space trivia–spouting ex-Marine. I still see him in there, the Jakob who was my friend, but he's so much more confident now. I wonder what the years have held for him.

Gus is eyeing Jakob's wrench and the broken plumbing under the sink with an interest usually reserved for outer space.

"What are you doing?" he asks.

"Fixing a leak so your mom can get your store open again," Jakob tells him.

"Oh, cool," Gus says. Then he turns to me. "Mom, can I have a snack?"

"Sure, honey. There are pretzels and a cheese stick and an apple that Grammy packed for you in the front pocket of your backpack. Do you want to go grab it from the car? Remember we parked right in front of the shop."

"Sure!" Gus trots off toward the entrance, motivated by the promise of a snack. He gets hangry if he doesn't have protein every few hours. Cheese sticks and those little cups of peanut butter often save us from a meltdown.

I'm aware that Jakob is watching our interaction with interest.

"How old is he?" Jakob asks.

"He was six in November," I explain, watching Gus as he heads out the door. "He's six going on sixty."

"Smart kid," Jakob says mildly. I sense he wants to ask more, but he doesn't.

"He's obsessed with space," I tell him. "Be forewarned, he'll pepper you with more odd facts about space than you even knew existed."

"I'll look forward to that," Jakob says with a wry smile. He glances back at the sink. I should let him get back to work. Gus grabs his backpack and slams the car door shut.

"His father and I aren't together," I blurt out instead, not sure why I feel I need to explain. "His dad lives in Belgium now with his wife and baby."

Jakob tilts his head and eyes me. Even though I'm wearing wedges, he still towers over me by a foot. "Single parenting and running a business? That's a lot to handle. And your mom's health isn't great either, right?" He's looking at me intently with those arctic eyes and a little frown. I feel like he's peeling back the layers of competency and cheerfulness that I try to wear every waking moment, like he is catching a glimpse of the raw exhaustion and grinding worry lurking at the back of my mind all the time. Uncomfortable under the scrutiny, I ask, "What are you doing under my sink?"

He chuckles. "Helping Walt. I'm done at the bakery by noon every day, so Walt hires me on projects if he needs another set of hands. Frankly, I like it a lot more than making bread."

I sense there's a story behind his comment about the bread, but I don't ask. I'm too caught off guard by the fact that it seems like Jakob Kristensen is going to be around . . . a lot.

"I got my snack, Mom!" Gus comes in the front door, holding up his backpack. "I'm gonna eat it in the kitchen and read my space book, okay?"

"Sounds good, bud." I give him a thumbs-up, then turn back to Jakob as Gus disappears down the hall. When I told Walt he could hire someone, I had no idea he'd hire Jakob. I don't quite know how I feel about it. Jakob makes me self-conscious and flustered, but there's no denying he's fascinating too.

"You're a man of many talents," I observe. "Where did you pick up plumbing skills?" The Jakob I knew was a nerd who was on the debate team and president of the robotics club but who suffered from two left feet and poor hand-eye coordination. When he left town right after graduation to join the Marines, no one was more shocked than me.

"After I got out of the Marines, I bummed around for a while and ended up with a buddy of mine in Alaska. I did some commercial fishing and helped him build houses near Sitka for a few summers." Jakob leans against the bathroom wall, arms crossed. I try not to stare at his rounded biceps. Shaping loaves of bread. Swinging a hammer. Clearly he must have gotten better at the hand-eye coordination thing. I swallow and look away, feeling a little out of my depth. I can't ignore the thing that sits between us, what happened the last time I saw him on graduation day. It's haunted me for years, the unanswered questions and the remorse. I wonder if I should just address the elephant in the room. Maybe it's time.

"Jakob, I . . ."

At that moment the bell over the front door jingles wildly.

"Yoo-hoo!" It's Dani. "Emmie, where are you hiding, girl? I saw your car out front. Are you in here?"

"Coming!" I call out to her. "Sorry," I tell Jakob. "One minute."

I hurry out of the bathroom to find Dani standing in the middle of the shop. She's not alone.

"Look who I found!" she exclaims, turning proudly to reveal none other than Henry Summers, who is standing behind her, looking around him at the waterlogged damage.

"Hello, Emmie," Henry says, meeting my eyes and giving me a heartwarming, lopsided smile. "I do hope I'm not intruding." He looks adorable in a navy blue swazer and jeans with a simple gray T-shirt underneath. His hair is falling over his forehead. He's giving off very Hugh Grant in *Notting Hill* vibes. I love *Notting Hill.*

"Henry!" I'm surprised and delighted to see him, though I suddenly wish Dani had given me a little heads-up so I could brush the lunchtime grit from my teeth and smooth down my flyaways. At least I'm wearing my sexy new bra. "Good to see you again." I give Henry my brightest, warmest smile. I wonder why he hasn't called or texted. I wish I had a mint.

Out of the corner of my eye I see Jakob appear in the bathroom doorway with a wrench in one hand. He stands there silently, watching us. He's always been a quiet observer, not saying much but missing absolutely nothing. Behind that wall of muscle and taciturn façade is a lightning-fast brain. He was always one of the smartest boys I knew.

"Hullo." Henry spots him and crosses the room to Jakob, holding out his hand. "Henry Summers," he says cordially in that plummy accent of his. It's a little Benedict Cumberbatch and a little Hugh Grant.

"Jakob Kristensen." They shake in a firm, manly way. I get the feeling they're sizing each other up. Dani looks from one to the other, then catches my eye and grins, wiggling her eyebrows dramatically. She goes to where Jakob and Henry are standing. I roll my eyes at her and join the group.

"Henry Summers . . ." Jakob's eyes narrow. "As in the guy on TV?"

"Ah yes, yes I am. Guilty as charged," Henry admits. "But please don't hold it against me." His smile is self-deprecating. He seems to have no ego when it comes to his fame. In fact, he seems a little uncomfortable with it. It's endearing.

Jakob smiles thinly in return but doesn't say anything. Henry clears his throat and turns to me. "Emmie, Dani filled me in on your unfortunate plumbing situation. I'm so sorry. I hope all is set to rights soon. Is there any way I can help?"

I swear I hear a faint snort from where Jakob is standing in the doorway to the bathroom. "How handy are you with a wrench?" Jakob mutters so low I think I'm the only one to catch his words.

"That's kind of you to offer, Henry," I tell him, ignoring Jakob. "Actually, there is something you could do for me. I want your opinion on something. All of you, actually. Just a minute."

I run into the kitchen and return with a Tupperware container of my newest creations.

"These are Rainier cherry and vanilla buttercream truffles," I explain. "The cherries are locally grown. It's my first new recipe in a long time." I nervously dole them out, one to each person. "I want your honest opinion."

I'm nervous as they each take a truffle. What if they don't like them? What if I've lost my touch? It feels strangely vulnerable to be standing here waiting for others to test and pass judgment on my creation.

"Ooh, look at the fancy sprinkles," Dani coos, admiring her truffle. "I like the bling."

I dusted each truffle generously with the mysterious gold sprinkles. For courage. I pop a truffle into my mouth and lift my chin, waiting for feedback from the others, waiting for the courage to zip through me. There is a moment of silence, and then a chorus of approval. I feel a zing of excitement in my belly, and it's not just from the truffle.

"That is one of the best things I've ever put in my mouth," Dani exclaims, putting her hand to her chest as though she's about to swoon.

"Wow," Jakob acknowledges. "That's . . . really good."

But it's Henry I'm really waiting on. He rolls the truffle around in his mouth contemplatively. I watch his face closely.

"Emmie, this is . . . absolutely delicious," he says finally, a note of wonder in his voice. "I can't even quite put my finger on what it is that makes it so special . . ." he trails off as though puzzled.

"Does anyone else feel sort of warm and tingly?" Dani asks, looking bewildered. "Do these chocolates have booze in them, Emmie?"

"No booze, just a little magic," I tell her with a smile.

Dani shoots me a quizzical look, and I hand her another truffle.

"Well, whatever they've got in them, you should definitely carry these in the new shop," Dani says, popping the second one into her mouth.

"New shop?" Henry asks. I see Jakob's head come up as well. All eyes are on me.

I close the lid on the Tupperware container and burp the air from it. "I'm opening my own chocolate shop," I confirm. "I've dreamed of doing it for years, and now seems like the right time, so I'm going to give it a go." I don't add anything about the vision being the impetus, about how I'm hoping one day to see Henry proposing to me in that very chocolate shop.

"Emmie, that's wonderful news!" Henry says, looking pleased. "Where are you going to open it? Are you thinking a culinary hot spot? Paris? Or closer to home? Perhaps New York or LA?"

"What's wrong with Poulsbo?" Jakob almost growls from the doorway, frowning at Henry.

Henry looks a little surprised. "Of course," he hastens to add, smoothing over the awkward moment. "I'm sure wherever you choose to open a shop, Emmie, it will be a success."

Jakob narrows his eyes at Henry like he's trying to take his measure.

Henry clears his throat. "Emmie, could I trouble you for a few minutes? There's something I'd like to discuss with you. I've had a thought after our last conversation."

Henry's been thinking about me? I like the sound of that. Next to me Dani elbows me in a very unsubtle manner. "Say yes," she hisses under her breath.

Jakob clears his throat. He's standing in the doorway to the bathroom, arms crossed, looking a little annoyed. He raises a brow at me and holds up the wrench. "I'll get back to work if you don't need me for anything else?"

I flush, feeling the weight of his assessing gaze on me. Why do I feel like he's judging me, or that somehow he's disapproving? My life is none of his business.

"Of course, go for it," I tell him briskly, then turn apologetically to Henry. "I'd love to chat now, but I've got Gus with me. He's having a snack in the kitchen. Could we find another time soon?"

Dani jumps in. "I'll take Gus home and make sure his homework's all done. You stay and talk to Henry, Emmie." She shoots a pointed look at me behind Henry's back and mouths, *"Go with him!"* jabbing a finger toward the door.

"Are you sure?" I ask her.

"Stay out as late as you want," she calls over her shoulder, already heading toward the kitchen to get Gus.

"Tell Gus we'll finish the LEGO spaceship as soon as I get home," I instruct her. She gives me a thumbs-up over her shoulder. Gus won't be disappointed by this turn of events. He adores Dani and is always begging to have more time with her.

"Well then." Henry gestures toward the door. "Shall we?"

I can still taste the sprinkles from the truffle, a sliver of gold dissolving slowly on my tongue. Looking at Henry, I feel something new rising in my heart, the courage to take risks and reach for the stars.

"I'd love that."

I follow Henry out the door.

Chapter 13

It's late afternoon, the clouds low and gray and the air smelling like ocean brine and impending rain as Henry and I walk side by side through historic downtown Poulsbo. I'm giddy and eager to hear what he has to say. Being with him feels like drinking a triple shot of espresso. I can feel my heart beating fast in my chest. I can't believe I'm just walking around my hometown with Henry Summers like it's the most normal thing in the world. This late in the day, the sidewalk is almost empty. Henry sets a very leisurely pace, hands in his pockets. I picture him at eighty, wearing a cardigan and doing the same thing, with salt-and-pepper hair and those same clear hazel eyes. I wonder where we will both be at that age. Will we grow old together? Will we still be in love? It's a strange yet lovely thought. Every moment with Henry feels like it has a subtext of destiny running below the surface. Every word has extra meaning, every second feels like it's leading up to something good. I shiver in anticipation.

"So you've decided to open your own shop?" Henry says, turning to me, his gaze warm and open. "That's excellent news. When we spoke about it over tea, you seemed to have some serious reservations. What changed your mind?"

"I'm doing it partly because of something you said," I admit. "You said I have a talent and that you hoped someday I could find a way to share it with the world again. I couldn't stop thinking about it." I glance at Henry, then muster my courage. "The truth is that I've been too scared to take the step I've dreamed of taking for years. But your words inspired me, and then my mom generously offered to help make it a reality. I'm still not sure I can really pull it off, but it's like I found enough courage to take the risk. All I needed was a little push."

A little push in the form of my birthday vision, Henry showing up in town, and a glass cylinder of mysterious but seemingly potent magical sprinkles. I think of the sprinkles. They appear to be working because somehow I'm here with Henry, telling him about my dream and reaching for that vision with a boldness I didn't know I had. It feels terrifying and exhilarating all at the same time.

"I'm so glad to hear that." Henry smiles. He peers at me from under the hank of hair falling over his forehead. He's concentrating on me like I'm the most important person in the world. I love it. Even though it's chilly, I'm warmed by his attention.

"Emmie, I've been thinking about you since we talked—about your family's fudge shop and the challenges you're facing right now. And I'd like to help." He clears his throat. "I hope this isn't too forward, but how would you feel about me featuring your family on an episode of *Savor*?"

I stop dead still on the sidewalk. "Are you serious?" I stare at him wide-eyed. In my wildest dreams I've imagined Henry saying these very words. Now he's saying them for real. Mom is going to lose her mind when she hears about his offer. She's wanted us to be on *Savor* for years.

"I'm quite serious." Henry nods. "And now that you're opening your own chocolate shop, we could feature that too. I want to focus on the generational family aspect, how you're carrying on your family's legacy in a new way for a modern time. I think it will be a great fit for *Savor*."

What he's not saying, but what I know to be true from doing my own internet research, is that being featured on *Savor* is a huge marketing boost for any business. The high-profile exposure leads to a big jump in sales, visitors, and visibility. It would be a tremendous benefit for my fledgling chocolate shop as well as for the Happy Viking. And I'd get to spend more time with Henry. It feels like Christmas and my birthday came early this year.

"Eek, thank you!" I squeal and impulsively throw my arms around Henry and hug him. He laughs, a puff of air against my hair, and returns the hug. He is warm, lean muscle underneath his soft swazer, and he smells as delicious as he did before, like steeping Earl Grey tea, an elegant, pleasant aroma.

"You're very welcome, Emmie," he tells me, pulling back to peer into my face. "This is why I host *Savor*, to showcase local families and businesses who are pillars of their communities, who are contributing in some way toward making the world a kinder, happier place. Everywhere I've gone in this town, people have spoken highly of you and your family. You've made a big impact on this community with your kindness and your generosity, and that's exactly the kind of folks I want to highlight in my show."

"This is a dream come true," I tell him, beaming. I mean that in more ways than one. I step back, but I'm still clasping his arm. I don't want to let him go.

"It's my pleasure. I'm glad to be of service," Henry says with a smile. We stand there for a moment, not saying anything, just sharing a look. "And I'm glad you're saying yes," Henry says softly. I blush pink.

"Me too."

We don't say anything more. We don't have to. As we head back to the shop, I am almost skipping with glee. I see it now. This is how it happens. This is how my vision is going to come true.

"What are you all still doing here?" I ask in surprise as we walk into the fudge shop after our stroll to find Dani and Gus standing with Mom and Dot, peering into several open cardboard boxes of candy. Mom sighs wearily as we approach. She looks tired and is leaning heavily on her cane.

"The leak went through the back wall of the bathroom and soaked some of the inventory in the storage closet," she explains. "We're sorting through it now. I think most of it's going to have to be thrown away."

"Oh no." This is not good news. Damaged inventory means more lost money. I wince at the thought. I hear metallic clanking coming from the bathroom and glimpse a pair of long, blue jean–clad legs through the doorway. Jakob appears to be still hard at work on the plumbing. Nearby, Mr. Butters is snoozing in his bed wearing a doggy-sized bumblebee costume complete with antennae on springs, oblivious to the chaos around him.

"More bad ones, Grammy." Gus holds up a handful of waterlogged M&M packets to show my mom, the rainbow colors from the candies seeping through the brown wrapper and staining his hands with red and blue and orange dots. He throws them into an industrial-sized garbage bag on the floor. The bag already looks half-full. "Mom, did you know that M&M's were the first candies to go to space?" he asks.

"I did not know that, honey." I glance around at the carnage in dismay.

"This whole box is bad," Dot announces, squatting over a box filled with a variety of old-fashioned candies in waxed white paper bags. She opens a bag of lemon drops that have melded together into one solid clump. "It's not looking good for the other boxes either." She shakes her head and pitches the entire contents of the box into the garbage bag.

Henry takes off his swazer and lays it aside. "What can I do?" he asks.

"Are you sure?" I look at him doubtfully. Is a famous TV host really going to sort through our flood debris?

"Absolutely. Put me to work," he says firmly.

I eye Mom in concern and send Henry to get a chair from the office for her. Then we give him the task of hauling trash to the dumpster while I check unopened boxes of candy for water damage. With two extra sets of hands, we get a lot done. After a half hour though, Henry checks his watch, an expensive-looking Omega. "I'm so sorry," he says in a low tone to me. "I've got a work call with my producer in fifteen minutes. I've got to go, unfortunately. I hate to not stay and finish."

"You're being plenty helpful with *Savor*," I tell him. "And thanks for staying to help out. That was very kind."

"I'll call you after I talk with my production team and work out the details," he tells me, checking his watch again. He says goodbye to everyone, but his smile is just for me. I walk him to the door and he clasps my hand briefly. "I'll be in touch soon," he promises. And then he is gone.

As soon as he's out the door, Dani whirls on me. "So?" she demands. "Tell us everything."

I glance around the circle of expectant faces. Only Gus is going about his business, focusing on finding more ruined candy and clearly not interested in adult conversation. The clanking from the bathroom stops. I wonder if Jakob is eavesdropping.

"Well, I have big news." I look around at their eager faces. "Henry wants to feature our family in an episode of *Savor*."

Dani screams, Mom gasps, and Dot whoops and high-fives me.

"Attagirl!" she says.

I tell them all about Henry's idea to feature both the Happy Viking and my new shop.

Mom puts her hand to her heart when I finish. "Oh, Emmie, this is such wonderful news."

"And of course you'll have to spend lots of time together," Dani says slyly.

I glance up to find Jakob standing in the bathroom doorway, one toned arm gripping the doorframe, a length of pipe in his other hand. He's staring at me with an expression I can't quite place. It looks a little like annoyance. I get the feeling he's heard everything we've said. He turns and goes back into the bathroom without a word.

"I hear wedding bells in your future!" Dani predicts as she flings handfuls of ruined boxes of Mike and Ikes and Good & Plenty into a trash bag. "Dibs on being maid of honor."

"Way too soon for all of that," I scold her. Yet as I grab a big box of waterlogged Skittles, I'm smiling from ear to ear. We are on the cusp of something new. I can feel it. Somehow I can't shake the most nervous, delicious feeling that everything is about to change.

Chapter 14

"This place looks like a crime scene," Dani hisses in my ear, wrinkling her nose in disgust as we wander through one of only two available storefronts for rent in Kingston. It's a few days after my spontaneous walk with Henry, and we're searching for the perfect location for my chocolate shop. This is clearly not it. So far we've seen a handful of places, all of them very underwhelming.

Across the room, our real estate agent Dawn is extolling the virtues of the plastic louvered blinds to block out light. She's really scraping the bottom of the barrel here, though to be fair, it's not her fault. As she explained to us, there are very few storefronts available at any given time. When I shared my list of specifications and the amount of rent I could afford, she looked alarmed.

"If you can wait a year or two, something might pop up that's more in your range," she told me, trying to be tactful. "As it is, you're going to probably have to budge on price or your requirements to get something soon."

I'm holding out hope for a miracle, but frankly I'm starting to panic a little. What am I going to do if I can't find a space that will work?

"At least that last one had big windows, even if they looked out on an alley with dumpsters," Dani mutters, looking around critically. "And we only saw the one rat."

This one is in a basement and the windows are only about a foot tall. There's not really any natural light, and the damp, musty smell is unpleasant. It's right on the main street in Kingston and would get lots of ferry traffic and tourist traffic, but still . . . there is no way I can even remotely make this into the shop I saw in my vision. It just feels . . . wrong.

"I don't think this is going to work for us, Dawn," I admit reluctantly.

She looks disappointed but nods. "Okay, we'll keep looking. Maybe something will pop up." But her tone lacks conviction. I have a feeling I'm looking for a unicorn—a shop on the main street of a small, touristy town with loads of charm and a rental price tag I can afford. I say a little prayer and try not to feel discouraged. I believe my vision will come true. If I have faith and the courage to work hard, I'm sure everything is going to turn out the way it's supposed to. Right?

"Bad news, kid. Your pipe caused more damage than we thought."

Walt greets me with these ominous words when I step in the door of the shop after getting back from the disappointing trip to

Kingston with Dani. He's wearing a Chicago Cubs cap backward and chewing gum. His face is grim.

"Oh no." I massage my forehead. This is not my favorite day. "Lay it on me. How bad is it?"

"We're gonna need to replace the carpet like we talked about, but also part of the subfloor underneath, at least around the bathroom," Walt tells me. "It's rotted out." I shudder. All I can see are dollar signs, but we have no choice. We have to repair the damage.

"Okay, do what you need to do," I tell him wearily. I'm tired from staying up all hours of the night juggling paperwork and bills and the details of life along with my chocolate-making experiments. Ideas are coming to me thick and fast, and I'm flying through my duties after Gus goes to bed, eager to get back into the kitchen and create new flavor combinations. Currently I'm working on a peach ginger bonbon that is particularly promising. It's exhilarating, but I'm sleeping fewer hours than ever. I've been staying up until at least one a.m. every night, experimenting and watching reruns of *Savor*, with only Henry on the screen for company.

Now staring down at the rotted wood, I'm struck with a horrible thought. "If we tear up the carpeting, does that mean we have to empty out the entire store?" I glance around the cluttered space with alarm. Walt follows my eyes.

"Yup," he confirms. "You're gonna have to pack up everything, clear out all the shelves. This place has got to be empty."

I bite back a groan. So much work. So much time with the shop closed, which means even more lost income. Then another thought comes to me. Henry. Specifically, Henry's desire to film an episode for *Savor* about our shop. Henry is lining up everything with his production team and hasn't yet gotten back to me about when we will film the episode, but he's definitely going to shoot some footage inside the store, and we can't have it all torn up. Right now, except for the bathroom, everything looks pretty normal, if a little soggy underfoot. But for Walt and Jakob to fix the floor, it's going to be a huge pain to empty the space, replace the rotted part of the subfloor, lay carpet, and then put everything back the way it was.

I heave a sigh, looking around. This was once a cute space, years ago before it got shabby. It's got huge windows and great light, high ceilings, and actually a lot of good vintage character hidden under layers of white paint. With a little effort and elbow grease, I bet this place could look adorable again. I try to envision it with different flooring and better décor, but I find it's hard to think of it as anything other than the fudge shop where I grew up.

"Can you focus on the bathroom for now?" I ask. "I'll talk to Henry and get back to you about how soon we can start emptying the store to replace the flooring." I need to know what he's thinking about filming footage of store for *Savor.*

"Sure thing, boss." Walt snaps his gum. "We're already working on replacing all the old pipes, and we'll put in a new toilet tomorrow. Just say the word and we can get this floor repair going."

I call Henry as soon as I step out the door. When I explain the situation, he promptly offers to start filming in a few days. He has a friend, a former cameraman, who lives on Bainbridge Island and has agreed to film the episode for us. Apparently Henry's friend is the one who told him about Poulsbo in the first place. And Henry's producer is going to fly in from LA for the few days we will film to help everything go smoothly.

"If you're ready, we can plan to start filming on Monday," Henry tells me. "We can get all the inside shots we need of the fudge shop and do most of the interviews that day. We'll get the shots of the chocolate shop once you find the space you want to rent. No rush there. When you are ready, we can get some footage as you prepare to open your new shop, and we'll finish the segment with some footage of your grand opening day. How does that sound?"

It sounds amazing. It also sounds like a lot. Thinking of being filmed, shooting this episode knowing millions of people will see it, is a little daunting. And the fact that I haven't yet found the right space feels like extra pressure.

"Perfect!" I tell Henry, masking my nerves with chipper energy. I reach my car and linger outside, looking across the parking lot at Liberty Bay. There's a strong breeze, and a few sailboats are gliding across the water.

"Excellent. I'll be in touch once I've had a chance to chat with my producer about the specifics," Henry tells me. "This is going to be great, Emmie. I'm very much looking forward to it."

"Me too! See you Monday." I disconnect the call and lean back against my car, trying to breathe deeply. I don't have time to be nervous. There's a lot to do. Monday is coming soon.

"What in the world is he doing here so early?" I blink, a little bleary-eyed as I reach the front door of the store and see the lights on inside and Jakob Kristensen vacuuming the carpet while Metallica blares from a radio by the door. It's a little after eight on Monday morning. We are supposed to start filming in an hour, and I came in early hoping to find a little peace and quiet before what promises to be a very full day. So much for that idea.

I sigh, sipping my usual double-shot hometown honey latte from Byrdie's, and linger on the sidewalk for a moment, taking my peace and quiet where I can find it. The town is just stirring to life. It's a sunny day (hallelujah!) and a few early-morning folks are walking dogs or exercising in our adorably scenic downtown. Two silver-haired ladies pass by, jogging very slowly. I'd bet a dollar they're headed to the senior center just a few blocks away. It's housed in a cream building with gingerbread trim and a steeply pitched gable with a charming antique clockface embedded in it. The senior citizens of Poulsbo are a timely lot, apparently.

I take another sip of my latte and check the time on my phone. Henry and the cameraman are coming at nine, and we will be filming footage of the candy shop and downtown Poulsbo until the early afternoon. Then we'll jump right in to packing up the store around dinnertime, readying the space to start replacing the subfloor tomorrow. It's going to be a huge amount of work to pack up the entire store tonight, but Walt is eager to get going so we can open as soon as possible. For now though, I need to focus on the filming.

Everything is in motion, but I'm feeling jangly with nerves, equal parts eager and apprehensive. My Honda is packed with outfit changes, hair spray, and my makeup kit. Mom will come as soon as she and Dot drop Gus off at school. Deciding I've loitered on the sidewalk long enough, I head inside.

"Good morning!" I yell to Jakob.

He looks up, surprised, and turns off the vacuum. I switch off the radio and enjoy the blissful moment of peace.

"What are you doing here so early? Aren't you supposed to be at the bakery?" I take a sip of my latte.

Jakob shrugs. "I got done early, and my mom is handling the register. Figured I'd make sure everything was prepped for the big day." He wraps the cord around the vacuum cleaner. I'm touched that Jakob came in early just to make sure the shop was cleaned up. It's a considerate gesture.

"You ready for today?" Jakob asks.

"No, I'm totally panicking," I admit. "This is such an amazing opportunity, but I feel unprepared. You know what it reminds me of? A debate tournament. This feels like a debate tournament all over again, but the stakes are higher." I sneak a glance at Jakob. If anyone understands that feeling, it's him. We used to be nervous together.

He stops and looks at me questioningly. "How so?"

"Oh, I guess it just feels like I have to perform at a high level, you know—like I can't slip up or make a mistake. There's a lot riding on this opportunity, and I don't want to blow it. And as you may remember, pressure always makes me nervous." I laugh uncomfortably and smooth the skirt of my spring-green-and-white-checked gingham dress. It's a Hill House knockoff I got at Target for twenty dollars. I love it. It makes me feel pretty and feminine, which are not things I think about enough anymore. Faced with motherhood and managing a small business, my wardrobe has crept slowly into a sort of functional, utilitarian style that, when I think about it much, makes me feel about as sexy as a pair of khaki pants. I used to have a sleek capsule wardrobe, Parisian cool with blazers and trench coats and loafers and cigarette pants. That was another life—pre-baby, pre-return to my small Pacific Northwest town. I left all that behind long ago. I smooth my hair, which I curled with a flat iron this morning. I think I look cute, but I still feel nervous to be on camera.

Jakob scrutinizes me, seeing my discomfort. "You look good," he says gruffly. "You'll do great. And feeling anxious isn't a bad thing. We think it is, but we've got it all wrong." He stashes the vacuum away in the torn-up bathroom where it can't be seen on camera. "It just means your body's sympathetic nervous system is releasing adrenaline to meet a challenge. It's a good thing, actually. It means your body's giving you what you need to fight a bear or run for your life—or in this case be interviewed about candy by a Brit in a cardigan." His mouth twists ironically.

"It's a swazer," I tell him, sticking my tongue out at his sarcastic last remark.

"That's not a real clothing item worn by men," Jakob counters with a half smirk. I get the feeling he's not the biggest fan of Henry.

"I've never been on a TV show before," I admit.

"It's no big deal," Jakob says. "Just relax and you'll be fine."

"How do you know?" I challenge with a touch of amusement. "Besides being a baker, a Marine, and a plumber, are you also secretly a movie star?"

"I've been a lot of things," he says calmly as he packs up his toolbox. "I did a little modeling for a while for a few companies that made outerwear. I went on some photo shoots in Alaska, Canada, and Iceland. Basically I learned to fake confidence. If you look confident, you can pull off just about anything."

So that's his secret? Is he just going around faking confidence all the time? Somehow I don't think he's faking. I think he really is comfortable in his skin. "Sounds like you've lived quite the life since our high school days," I observe, sipping my latte. "Alaska, Canada, Iceland. Makes mine look boring by comparison."

He casts a wry look in my direction. "From what I've heard, you didn't do too badly yourself. You studied in Europe, right? Just like you always planned."

I clear my throat. "I studied in Switzerland and then I interned in Paris." I cock my head, curious. "How do you know that?"

He chuckles dryly. "You remember my grandma Grethe? She wrote me letters every week I was away." He stops and surveys the store critically. It looks tidy, no trace of the damage except for the carpet, which is still damp and squishy, but there's nothing we can do about that. "That woman loves a good, juicy piece of gossip. She spent pages of each letter keeping me updated about everyone in town." He cracks a small smile. "I probably know more than anyone suspects. Who had bunion surgery, who had an affair, which city council member was caught cooking the books."

"Wow." I laugh. "That's . . . a lot of information."

He shrugs. "I didn't mind it. It made me feel close to home when I was so far away."

I study him for a moment, trying to imagine what his life has been like since high school graduation, the day I wrecked our friendship, the day I'll regret for the rest of my life. By the next morning, he was gone. He enlisted with the Marines and never came back. Until now.

"And now here you are, home again," I say, and there's a question in my words.

He glances away and rubs the back of his neck. "Here I am," he says, and there's an edge to his reply. I can't read his tone. Is he happy? Disappointed?

"Home for good?" I ask lightly.

"For now. Probably for good. My dad is getting older. He wants me to take over the bakery. That was always the plan." He sounds so resigned.

"Is that what you want?"

He thinks about it. "I've seen the world, and now it's time to come home. This town, these people. I can't imagine settling down anywhere else. But being a baker for the rest of my life? That, I'm not so keen on. I like working with Walt way more. I'm happier swinging a hammer than making kringles. But I'm kind of stuck in the family business now." He blows out a breath and then glances at me. I get the feeling he's not used to sharing this with anyone. "What about you? Are you happy to be back here?"

I nibble the lip of my paper coffee cup. "I never thought I'd come back," I admit. "I loved Europe. Right before I came home I was offered a permanent position with the chocolatier I was apprenticing with. It was a life I thought I wanted, my dream to stay in Paris."

"And then your dad got sick?" He leans back against the counter where the register is and crosses his legs, once more in command and at ease in the world. "Grandma Grethe's letters," he adds. "She told me you'd come home and had a kid. And then she told me about your dad's cancer. I'm sorry."

I look down at my cup and nod. "It was long and slow and brutal, but he fought hard to stay with us as long as he could." I feel my throat tighten with sorrow. "I still miss him every day."

Chapter 15

"Your dad was a good man," Jakob says gently. I nod, closing my eyes against the familiar feeling of loss.

"Dad held out longer than anyone thought he would though," I reply. "We had more than four years with him. He was sick a lot of the time, and in treatment, but he fought so hard for more days with us. And by the end, he'd gotten really close with Gus and gotten more time than we and the doctors ever expected." My voice breaks a little. "After he died, there was no way I could leave. Not with Mom's condition worsening. Not with Gus so little. I couldn't abandon Mom and the store, and I couldn't imagine being a single parent in Paris." I turn the coffee cup around in my hands, rubbing away the lipstick mark on the rim. "So I gave up the dream. This is our home now, for better or worse. Some things just are what they are, right?"

"Gravity problems," Jakob says.

"That sounds like a Gus term." I smile. "What's a gravity problem?"

"The things in life you can't change, even though you wish you could," Jakob explains. "The trick is knowing which things in life are gravity problems and which aren't. Usually we have more choices than we think we do. But some things you just have to learn to live with the best you can."

I sip my latte and mull over his words. What things in my life are gravity problems? Mom's health. The store. What does that leave? What are my choices? I think of the vision, of the guidance it provides. Not a gravity problem, but certainly it has a lot of sway. It doesn't feel limiting though. It feels bright and shiny and full of promise and potential. If only I can help it come true. That's my job now, to help it come true. The next step is not to mess up filming the episode of *Savor* today.

"Even after your pep talk, I'm still nervous about today," I admit. There is so much I want to get right, starting with not making a fool of myself on camera. I want to impress Henry. I want to help put my chocolate shop in the best possible position to succeed.

"Well, it sounds like there's only one thing left to do," Jakob says. He grabs a KitKat bar from one of the candy racks and pulls two dollars from his wallet.

I wave away the payment, curious to see what he's doing. "It's on the house."

"Okay then. Ready?" He tears open the shiny red wrapper and holds out the square of chocolate to me. I stare at it a moment before realizing what he's doing.

"Our good luck ritual," I say, a smile breaking across my face. He remembered. It's how we started every debate meet in high school. I'd bring a KitKat bar, and we'd each hold a side and break it on the count of three. If it broke cleanly, separating the fingers of chocolate without cracking the wafers in half, we believed we would win our debate. If we snapped the wafer unevenly though, it was a bad omen and we would lose our debate. I gingerly grab hold of the bar.

"One, two . . ." he counts, and on three we both exert a little pressure. With a snap the bar breaks in half the wrong way.

"Oh no!" I groan, staring at the jagged shards of crisp wafer. "Bad luck!"

"You know there's no such thing as luck," Jakob says calmly. He stares at the broken edge of wafer, then takes a big bite. "Just opportunity and what we do with it. A broken KitKat is not a gravity problem. You can rise above this. Use your adrenaline."

We eat our chocolate in companionable silence. "Do you ever miss debate?" I ask suddenly.

Jakob glances at me. "I miss some things about it," he says opaquely. "I liked the studying, not the debate part as much." He casts a look in my direction, and I catch what he's not saying. He liked spending time with me. I liked spending time with him too. Jakob was the most interesting boy I knew in high school. He was curious about everything and had a unique perspective on life, like he could see the world clearly, like he had a thousand-foot view. He'd weave together things he'd read about physics, mathematics, music, history, social theories, philosophy. He was constantly reading, constantly absorbing knowledge. There was always something going on in his head. There still is, and as always, I want to take a peek inside. His mind has always fascinated me.

"Those were good days," I say with a sigh, almost thoughtlessly, then realize where I am—a grown woman eating KitKats early in the morning with a former best buddy whose heart she accidentally broke. I need to shut this down fast and get on with the day I'm supposed to be having. But Jakob is standing there watching me, and my heart thuds in my chest. The words I've wanted to say for sixteen years bubble up in my mouth. I want to set right whatever went awry between us.

"Jakob, what happened . . ."

Just then the door jingles. "Hullo, Emmie. Jakob." It's Henry, followed by a petite woman in heeled boots, her long dark hair caught up in a bun, and a slight young man lugging a camera bag. As they come into the shop, Jakob crumples the KitKat wrapper and straightens from against the counter. The moment is over.

"That's my cue to wrap this up," he says. As he grabs his toolbox, I notice a dog-eared copy of *Atlas Shrugged* sticking out amid the screwdrivers and nails. Seems he hasn't changed his reading habits. "I'll just finish up a few little things and get out of your hair. Good luck, Emmie," he tosses back to me as he heads toward the bathroom with his toolbox in hand.

"Thanks for the bad luck," I call to him with a smile.

He waves dismissively without looking back. "Remember, there's no such thing as luck." But I can hear the answering smile in his voice.

Henry comes up to the counter where I'm standing. "Emmie, I'd like to introduce you to our brilliant team for the day—my producer, Azra Kaya, and Crisanto Tan, our fantastic cameraman."

I shake Azra's and Crisanto's hands. "Thank you so much for helping on short notice." I like both of them immediately. Crisanto gives off an air of affability that puts me at ease, and he looks effortlessly cool with green designer glasses and a fauxhawk. Azra is warm but very no-nonsense and exudes capability. I feel reassured that in her hands all will go smoothly. Henry is looking dapper and polished in one of his many swazers. This one is herringbone. He's paired it with camel-colored trousers, a black T-shirt, and leather loafers. He looks camera ready.

"You look beautiful," Henry tells me, giving me a hug. "The camera is going to love you." We've gone from handshakes to hugs now. Good progress. Henry looks around the shop as Azra and Crisanto walk around discussing camera shots and angles and lighting. "I feel as though I've jumped into a time capsule, a true bit of Americana," Henry muses, wandering over to examine an endcap of classic American penny candies in open bins. He seems genuinely fascinated by everything. It's one of his best qualities and part of what makes him so watchable, that affable curiosity.

"I want you to try something before we get started," I say spontaneously. "Stay right there." I race to the kitchen. I don't know where I found the time to make a new variety of truffle. No, that's a lie. I do know where I found the time. Two a.m. yesterday. I sacrificed sleep to make something I'm proud to share with Henry. I was too nervous and excited to sleep anyway, so I got up and did something productive. Television Henry kept me company. It was the episode where he's in Thailand, up in the mountains, shadowing a family in their restaurant on a remote hiking path.

I come back with a Tupperware container and give Henry one of my new creations. It's a pink truffle flecked with the special gold sprinkles. These turned out perfectly—the color and texture and flavor are all gorgeous, complex, and unexpected. I take one for myself too, the one with the most sprinkles. I need a big dose of courage before we film.

I offer a truffle to Crisanto, who declines as he's on Whole30 for the month and can't eat sugar. Azra takes one though, and her eyebrows lift to her hairline when she tries it.

"Oh wow, where can I get more of whatever this is?" she asks in genuine amazement. "It reminds me of a special sweet I had growing up in Istanbul. Delicious." I laugh and give her another one. I eat another too. I need the extra dose of courage today. Just like before, I feel the familiar zip of energy and a lift in my spirits. I square my shoulders. I can do this. With adrenaline and a good lipstick, I might just manage to rock today. I take the container to Jakob. He's in the bathroom doing something to the new toilet with a screwdriver.

"What's this?" he asks in surprise, looking at the rich pink tone of the ruby chocolate I used to coat the truffle.

"It's a truffle," I explain. "I made them."

He takes one and examines it. "Why is it pink?"

"I used ruby chocolate. It's naturally pink," I explain. "Most cocoa beans are fermented, but these are left unfermented and then combined with natural acids to produce the pink color. Also a very pleasant creamy texture. Try it."

"Emmie, is this rose I taste in the filling"—Henry pokes his head into the bathroom where we're standing—"and . . . cardamom, perhaps?"

"Exactly!" I beam at him. "You win a prize." I offer him another truffle. "Those are rose petals from our own garden."

"These, my dear, take the biscuit." Henry examines the truffle, clearly intrigued. "What you've done with the combination of flavors. I've never had anything quite like it. It's like a little bite of pure happiness." He looks at me in open admiration.

Jakob bites into his truffle hard and shoots Henry a dark look. I beam at the praise. This is why I'm opening my own store, I remind myself. Not just because I saw a vision or because of Henry's encouragement, but because I love making chocolates that spread a little joy. The world is full of grief and hardness, and I love the idea of something I made being given as a gift, a consolation, or a celebration. Each truffle can brighten a moment, make it special and sweet, and then it's gone, leaving only a lovely memory. I love making something that helps people make memories out of moments.

"It's really good," Jakob tells me quietly. "I was skeptical about the pink chocolate."

"I know it's unique, but I love making something that's both delicious and surprising," I explain. "In Paris I was just starting to experiment with flavor combinations like this when I had to come home. Now that I'm making chocolates again, I'm starting to experiment with ingredients that grow in the Pacific Northwest. I've got a smoked salted caramel with salt from San Juan Island that will knock your socks off." I say it confidently, and it comes out a little flirty too. Jakob looks up sharply. Our eyes catch. One corner of his mouth ticks up in amusement.

"I'd like to try one of those," he says huskily, but I almost can't hear him.

Something is happening to my knees under that silver gaze. His eyes don't seem icy cold. I was wrong. They're not glacial-milk blue. They're the color of the hottest August afternoon sky, when the heat burns away the blue and leaves only a pale haze.

Henry clears his throat. "Emmie, I think Azra and Crisanto have everything squared away. Shall we get started?" He looks between me and Jakob, a tiny frown furrowing his brow.

In an instant I'm jerked back to reality. I glance from Jakob to Henry and clutch my Tupperware container against my chest like armor. What is happening? I'm supposed to be falling for Henry Summers, not getting caught up in the unreadable gaze of my greatest friendship failure.

"Yes, of course. I'm ready," I tell Henry firmly, turning away from Jakob. *Stop looking back*, I scold myself, marching out of the bathroom and away from temptation. Jakob is my past, but Henry holds the keys to my future. Resolutely, I follow Henry without a backward glance, but I can feel Jakob's eyes on me every step of the way.

Chapter 16

"Emmie." Henry's voice is low and warm in my ear, making the fine hairs on my arms stand up. I shiver even though we're standing in the sun in front of the store and it's turning out to be a very pleasant morning.

"Yes?" I whisper, keeping the stilted grin plastered to my face as Crisanto slowly walks forward a few steps, filming the opening shot. I've been dreading this moment, when the camera starts rolling. I don't love being the center of attention. I get stiff and awkward and wooden, and my mind goes blank. But I have to do this. It's important and it's going to be worth it.

"It's natural to be a little nervous," Henry observes gently. That's being generous. I can feel that the smile stretching my face is more of a rictus, a horribly frozen fake grin I can't seem to stop. I look like I'm being held at gunpoint and commanded to smile.

But then Henry's hand is touching my bare arm, steady and reassuring. He seems perfectly comfortable in the eye of the camera. "This is very informal. Just relax and be yourself," Henry tells me with an encouraging smile. "Let's see if we can make this fun, shall we?" He gives my arm a little squeeze and peers into my eyes. "I'm right here," he tells me. I swallow and feel my smile slip into something that feels more natural.

After that, I loosen up. Having Henry with me helps a lot. He's so at ease in front of the camera, so genuine and relaxed, that within a few moments I forget about my nerves and start having fun with him. We banter. We walk through Poulsbo, Crisanto trailing after us getting footage of the town—the shops, the harbor, the bay. Back at the Happy Viking, I show Henry around our shop, telling a few cute anecdotes about growing up in a candy store. Mom pops on camera midmorning to share about how she and Dad ran it for so many years together. It's a sweet moment. She even shows their wedding photo, and a picture of the day they opened the store. They're standing with their arms wrapped around each other, looking exhausted and so hopeful and in love. I feel a twist of longing in my belly when I see that photo. I want that kind of love. It's what I've been waiting for, what I hoped my vision would finally show me. I cross my fingers and concentrate on Henry. Maybe my someday isn't far away.

The hours fly by as we film different parts of the episode. Henry goes over each segment beforehand with me. I refresh my lipstick and smooth my hair a dozen times. By midmorning I've found a rhythm and rapport with Henry that feels natural and flirty and really quite enjoyable.

We take a break for lunch, sitting on a bench outside the shop in the sunshine, eating sandwiches from Britt's Delish Café and washing it down with more coffee for me and tea for Henry. I'm buzzed and energized and a little giddy. I haven't felt this alive in . . . I can't remember when. This is actually really fun!

"Azra says the footage we're getting is great. This is going to be a really engaging episode. You're a natural," Henry tells me, taking a bite of his turkey and Swiss sandwich.

"I'm really not," I assure him. "You just make it feel easy." I unwrap my turkey pesto and take a big, unselfconscious bite.

Henry smiles, looking pleased. "I'm glad to hear you think so."

"What do you like about this work?" I ask, taking a sip of coffee.

Henry chews and considers. "I enjoy the travel," he says. "New places, new food. All of that intrigues me. But I love the stories the most, the human aspect of the job. The world is full of sad and difficult things, and I get to highlight some of the unsung heroes, the people who help make their communities better places to live. I like spreading that hope around. I like getting to meet and champion people like you, Emmie."

"Oh." I wave away the compliment. "I'm not a hero. I'm just a tired mom trying to keep all the pieces from falling apart." I give a self-deprecating little chuckle.

Henry looks at me gravely. "Emmie, anyone who can run a business, raise a child, and take care of a parent in poor health, not to mention be involved in the community like you are, is an unsung hero. Everyone knows you here, everyone loves you. I don't think you see how remarkable you are."

I blush beet red and have to look away, concentrating on my sandwich. It flusters me when Henry looks at me like that, like I'm worthy of admiration. I haven't felt this admired in . . . well, since Romaine. And what a disaster that was. But this is different, I remind myself. This is Henry. The man I am supposed to fall in love with. The man who, according to my vision, is going to get down on one knee and ask me to marry him one day. The thought boggles my mind. How lucky am I?

In the afternoon, Crisanto films while Mom and I reenact the scene in the kitchen where she tells me about the nest egg and we decide to move forward with me opening my own shop. Of course we don't mention the vision, but Dani does get to make an appearance, playing the role of supportive friend, which she hams up. She wears her red romper and has big hair and an even bigger personality on camera. She's a force of nature. Mr. Butters makes an appearance too, wearing his best bow tie and uttering several long-suffering grunts and snuffles on camera. I make fudge as Mom, Dani, and I chat. It feels a little stiff, but when Mom offers me the money to open the shop, we both tear up again for real. Looking at her, I'm overwhelmed with gratitude. She lives with daily pain but never stops loving those around her as best she can. She's a true hero, and I'm so glad Henry is highlighting her generosity and the legacy she and my dad built together.

After our fudge-making scene is over, Dani heads out to finish her last hour of her shift. She'll come back later. Mom bids us farewell too. She and Dot and Mr. Butters are going to pick up Gus from school and then come back to the shop after the filming is done to help pack up the store.

Henry and I shoot our next scene in the kitchen as we discuss my vision to open my own shop.

"What is your dream, Emmie?" Henry asks me. "What draws you to making chocolates?"

This part is where I truly shine. I'm not nervous. I'm bright and articulate and vivacious as I share my genuine enthusiasm for chocolate making and describe the storefront I've dreamed of for years. I talk about how a chocolate can make a moment into a special memory, how it can console, or show love, or bring a little spot of happiness.

"I love that something I make can brighten someone's day," I explain. Then I look up at Henry and stumble over my words. There's an expression on his face I can't quite place. It's almost tender, a dash of astonishment mixed with a healthy dose of admiration. It catches me off guard. When I finish my answer, fumbling over the last bit, Henry just keeps looking at me that way for a moment until Crisanto clears his throat meaningfully. Henry blinks hard and then seems to snap back into reality to focus on the show. Somehow we finish the scene. My heart is beating a little more quickly than normal, as though I've been running up a flight of stairs. This is happening fast and it feels intense. I don't know how to handle it all. My insides are like half-set fudge, smooth and creamy and so thoroughly agitated I can't quite seem to catch my breath. Adrenaline is good, I remind myself, thinking of Jakob's explanation. I need to channel this feeling to help me do my best.

We have just finished filming the last sequence and are debriefing the day when Mom and Dot walk back in the door with Gus and Mr. Butters in tow.

"Mommy!" Gus cries, flinging himself at me. I catch him in a tight hug.

"How'd your science project presentation go, buddy?" I nuzzle the top of his head where his hair is still downy-chick soft.

He disengages and says nonchalantly, "Easy. It was about the moon." Then he catches sight of Henry and stops short, eyes round and mouth open. This is the first time they're meeting in person.

"Hello," says Henry, sticking his hand out. "You must be Gus. I'm Henry."

Gus shoots a sideways look at me, dumbfounded. He's grown up with *Savor.* I used to nurse him late at night while watching the show to keep myself awake. Henry Summers has been a fixture in our lives since the beginning of Gus's life. Gus has never known a world without Henry Summers in it. Tentatively, Gus extends his hand and gives Henry a solemn look and a firm handshake. "Did you know that there's such a thing as vampire stars that suck the life out of other stars?" he asks conversationally.

Henry looks startled by this information. "I did not know that," he says, casting a quick, cautious look at me. "That sounds quite violent."

Gus cocks his head and considers this. "Maybe," he says confidently, "but once the vampire star eats another smaller star, it explodes." He shrugs at the casual brutality of the universe.

"Sounds like poetic justice," Henry says diplomatically. He looks like he doesn't quite know what to do with this conversation, but he's bravely forging ahead anyway.

Gus wrinkles his brow. "It's not poetry," he says in confusion. "It's just the laws of space."

"Right." Henry nods quickly. "You're a very clever boy, aren't you, Gus?"

Gus heaves a sigh and nods sagely. "Yes, I guess I am, but thinking about space can make a guy feel really small."

That's my cue to step in before this conversation derails further. "I think Grammy's got a special job for you, bud," I tell him, kissing the top of his head. "Why don't you go find her? She's in the kitchen. I brought some of my sprinkle sugar cookies. You can have one." I brought them for the shoot and set some aside for Gus. It's my mom's tried-and-true recipe and Gus's favorite cookie. We cover them with sprinkles and he takes them to school on hard days. Gus scampers off to find Mom and the promised cookies.

Henry looks after him thoughtfully. "What a singular child," he says. "As a boy all I remember thinking about was trains. I'm not sure the universe ever crossed my mind."

"Gus has gotten very interested in space since my dad passed away," I explain. "They were very close, and I think it's Gus's way of trying to make sense of Dad's death, of mortality in general. He's become obsessed with space catastrophes and weird facts. I'm not sure if I should encourage it or not." I spread my hands, a gesture of helplessness. I don't know how to help my son with his fears and fixations, other than to keep showing him constancy and care. A lot of parenting is just showing up and doing your best, Mom tells me all the time. So that's what I try to do. I hope it's enough. I fear it might not be.

"Gus is lucky to have you," Henry says.

"Do you like kids?" I ask, unsubtly prying. It's an important question to ask if we are going to have a future together.

Henry hesitates. "I do. I haven't been around them much though, to be honest. I never quite feel like I know the right things to say to them. It's funny. I can be in front of an audience of millions with no trouble, but one primary school child makes me feel tongue-tied." He gives me a rueful smile. "I have a niece who's nine though, so I'm not wholly unskilled when it comes to children."

I don't know why, but I feel a little disappointed and unsettled by his answer. Gus is the most important person to me, and I always imagined my partner, when I found the right one, would be an excellent mentor to my son. I guess Henry could grow into it. People learn and grow, right? I push the niggling worry aside. It will all work out. It has to.

Chapter 17

Right before dinnertime, Henry confirms that we are done filming. We have everything we need for the day. Crisanto is packing up his equipment, and Azra is standing in front of the store texting on her phone. I feel light and a little giddy. I did it! We did it! And now it's over. We'll get footage of the new store whenever I find the location and footage of the grand opening whenever that happens. I head back to the kitchen, intent on a snack. I'm starving. That sandwich was a long time ago.

"How's it coming with finding a storefront?" Henry asks as I find the plate of sugar cookies I brought to share. They're a recipe Mom used to make all the time when I was young, so buttery and soft and rich they're almost like shortbread. Now I make them for Gus. This batch I've rolled in a mixture of colorful and gold sprinkles. I offer Henry a cookie and take one for myself.

"Not good," I admit with a sigh. "We've looked at all the inventory in the surrounding small towns, and there's nothing that's a good fit."

Dawn found a beautiful storefront in downtown Winslow on Bainbridge Island, but the rent was more than twice what I can afford to pay. I'm beginning to get really worried I won't find a place.

"I'm sure something will turn up," Henry says comfortingly. "Have you considered something farther afield? I'd be happy to put in a good word for you if you want to try a city with a strong food scene." He looks at me expectantly.

"Thanks," I murmur. "I'll think about it." It feels impossible to consider moving, but maybe I need to widen my geographic search area since nothing is turning up in Winslow or Kingston.

Henry is just heading out with Azra and Crisanto when Dani shows up, ready to help pack up the store. She's changed into a denim jumpsuit like auto mechanics wear, and it's giving big Rosie the Riveter vibes. I check the time. Dot, Mom, and Gus are due back any moment to help. I look around the shop. I need to change clothes and eat something more than a sugar cookie. It's going to be a long night with just the five of us to pack everything up.

Now that the filming is over, I realize I'm exhausted and wired at the same time. I glance around in discouragement. How are four women and a little boy going to get all this cleaned out tonight?

Dani is standing at one of the big front windows craning her neck and texting on her phone when I come out of the bathroom wearing leggings and a Mariners sweatshirt. My dad was a big baseball fan, and we used to go see a game every summer in Seattle.

"Finally!" Dani exclaims as I join her at the window. I see Dot and Mom and Gus coming down the sidewalk. Dot is holding a big stack of pizza boxes.

"What on earth are we going to do with that much pizza?" I ask in astonishment.

"Don't worry. You'll see," Dani murmurs distractedly. "Oh, here they are! Finally!"

And then I see them . . . little clusters of people coming down the sidewalk toward us. I recognize our postal worker, George, and several of the small-business owners in town. Mary Beth and a few of her nail salon employees from the Nail Boat are crossing the street and headed our way. Sebastian and Hilda, the two other owners of the shops in our building, pop out onto the sidewalk. Sebastian owns Seasonings, an infused olive oil and spice shop, and Hilda is the owner of Retro Runway, a vintage clothing store.

"What are they all doing here?" I ask in bewilderment as Dani pulls the door open and people start to pour into the shop.

"They've come to help," Dani says matter-of-factly.

I stare at the folks filing in the door, suddenly at a loss for words. I spot the owners of Away with Words, my favorite store in Poulsbo to buy gifts, handmade beauty products, and books from local authors. Justin, the gangly young barista from Byrdie's, follows them in, holding an armful of bottles of wine and a stack of disposable wineglasses. He's accompanied by one of the booksellers from Liberty Bay Books. One by one they come through the door. More than a dozen people in total. Each one gives me a hug or a high five or calls out a greeting. Even Walt is here, grumbling about the crowd but carrying his big toolbox.

"Why would everyone do this?" I ask Dani, astonished and touched.

"Because you always help everyone else," Sebastian says, overhearing my question. He joins Dani and me at the window and presses a glass of crisp, fruity local Washington Riesling into my hand. "You look like you need this, honey," he says. He's impeccably dressed as always.

"There's not a person in this room you haven't helped somehow," Hilda says, popping into the conversation. "You're always doing someone a favor, dropping off a container of soup during flu season, babysitting somebody's kid."

"You agreed to be a cat sitter for Cinnamon for two weeks so I could go on that spice tour in Indonesia last year," Sebastian chimes in. "Think of this as our way of giving back to you." He looks at me fondly and clinks his wineglass to mine.

"Sebastian's right," Dot says as she walks by, carrying the stack of pizza boxes. "These are your people, Emmie. We've got your back." Her answer warms my heart. She sets the pizzas by the register next to the wine.

"Remind me to pay you for the pizza," I tell Dot, following her to the register.

"No need. Henry ordered these," Dot tells me casually, hooking a thumb over her shoulder at the stack of pizza boxes. "Said to tell you he's sorry he can't be here in person to help. He's got a production meeting tonight with some studio head of something or other, but he heard that pizza is an American moving tradition and he hopes it helps."

I'm touched by the thoughtful gesture. A man who hauls trash without complaint and sends pizza when he can't be there himself? That's a keeper right there.

"Okay, everybody," Dani yells, getting the room's attention by using her police officer voice. "Let's get this party started! Thank you all for coming. I know we all love Gwen and Emmie and want to help them pack up the store tonight. So here's what we're going to do." She has a clipboard and has divvied up the volunteers into teams. She starts assigning tasks to each team, then turns them loose to get to work. Someone puts on a playlist of '90s pop hits, and Madonna starts pulsing through the store. People are dancing by, carrying cardboard boxes and big plastic trash bags. Someone is dispensing wine, and people are grabbing slices of pizza as they work. I feel myself tear up as I look around. What a beautiful show of support. All these people have given up their evening to help us pack up the store. I don't know what to say, but I'm profoundly grateful.

Suddenly Dani is there, slinging her arm around me. She squeezes my shoulder and holds out a little plastic packet of tissues she keeps in her bountiful purse.

"How did you get so many people here on such short notice?" I ask, dabbing at my eyes.

"Dot invited everyone and I threatened to issue parking tickets for anyone who didn't show up." Dani grins. "Just kidding. Everyone loves you guys. They want to help. We had to turn people away because we were worried it would get too crowded in the store and make it harder to pack."

"Thank you for this," I say thickly. Mr. Butters comes up to Dani for a head scratch, then makes the rounds of the room, going to everyone, wagging his stubby tail, and grinning at all the commotion. He loves a good crowd. Tonight Mom has dressed him in a doggy-proportioned Mariners baseball jersey. He looks absurd, happy, and squat in his navy blue jersey that buttons around his thick tummy.

"Isn't this amazing?" Mom asks, coming up to me. She looks teary too. I give her one of Dani's tissues from the pack. "We're so blessed to live in a place like this," she says, wiping her eyes and looking around.

"We are," I agree.

Just then I catch sight of Jakob coming through the front door with a huge pastry box. I'm surprised to see him after his early morning here. He's already helped so much. He comes over to us and sets it between the pizza and the wine.

"Thought you could use some pastries," he says, opening the box, which is stuffed with delectable-looking baked goods. He must have brought half the bakery. Gus runs up to him wide-eyed, peers in the box, and grabs a bear claw.

"Hey, Gus," Jakob says easily. "Want to help Walt and me unscrew some shelves, if it's okay with your mom?"

Gus nods mutely, cheeks bulging with bear claw.

"Fine with me," I tell Jakob. His eyes catch mine. "Thank you," I say, so low he has to lean in to hear me.

"For what?" he asks.

I glance at the pastries and at Gus, who is enthusiastically stuffing the rest of the bear claw into his mouth as he waits to help Jakob. "For all of it," I tell him.

He nods once, then motions to Gus. "Come on, pal. Let's get the toolbox."

The entire store is a beehive of activity—packing, labeling, dismantling shelves when they are empty. Hilda is unfolding cardboard boxes and taping them. Sebastian is delivering empty boxes for the teams who are packing up various areas of the store. Barista Justin and our mailman George are filling boxes of candy in a flurry of activity. Mary Beth and a few of her nail salon employees from the Nail Boat are tackling packing up the wall of bubble gum. We have over a hundred types of chewing gum. Walt, Jakob, and Gus are taking apart the shelves as they are emptied.

The whole shop is humming with happy energy, and people are working fast. I thought this might take us all night, but at this rate, the room will be cleared within a couple of hours.

I look around me, overwhelmed with a feeling of humble gratitude for this community that turned up tonight to help us when we needed it most. Spontaneously, I slide open the glass display case of fudge.

"Free fudge for everyone!" I call out. "Come and get it!"

A cheer goes up from the crowd and people peel off from their work groups to come grab their favorite flavor. I talk to each of them, thanking them and doling out generous portions of fudge. Walt comes up to get his fudge, and I give him the biggest slice. He takes a look at Mr. Butters's Mariners jersey and breaks into a disbelieving guffaw.

"That dog is ridiculous," he states matter-of-factly. "At least dress him in a good baseball team's jersey."

Mom overhears him and bristles. "Bert loved the Mariners."

Walt shrugs. "Bert didn't know squat about good baseball. You come with me and I'll take you to a real baseball game. Wrigley Field, now that's baseball. I'll even buy you a hot dog."

"Is Walt asking your mom on a date?" Dani asks in a stage whisper, sidling up to me.

"I think it's more taunting than asking," I reply, watching with interest.

Mom's color is high and she lifts her chin. "No, thank you," she says politely, her tone chilly.

Walt shrugs. "Suit yourself. But it's a shame for a fine woman like you to waste her life dressing up a dog like that. Bert would have wanted more for you, Gwen, and you know it."

Mom looks stunned. Her mouth opens and closes. "Well, I never . . ." she says finally.

Walt eyes Mr. Butters again and shakes his head. "You let me know if you ever change your mind. The offer still stands," he says, and then he goes back to dismantling shelves.

Chapter 18

I'm sitting on the worn carpet in the middle of the empty storefront the next morning, feeling tired but peaceful and like I really need another cup of coffee. I'm not doing anything, just sitting in the room, feeling the emptiness of the space, reliving the echoes of so many days and years of life here. Last night was a whirlwind. We laughed, yelled, packed, and sang along to Britney and Madonna and ate all the Danishes and pizza and fudge. By ten the store was empty, the last shelf taken apart, the last box of Root Beer Barrels and Mike and Ikes carried out to Dani's giant Suburban to be stashed in the storage space we rented temporarily until the store is ready to reopen.

I look around the storefront now. Uncluttered, it really is spacious. Unfortunately, when we put all the shelves and candy back in, it will go back to feeling cluttered and a little claustrophobic. For a brief instant I wonder if we should take this opportunity to renovate it, to try to modernize the shop, but in the next instant

I dismiss the idea. If we do that, I won't have enough capital to open my chocolate shop.

Already I'm nervous about how much the repairs are going to eat into the money Mom offered me. Every day I'm watching it drain away a little more. I sigh and rub my temples. I really need some more coffee. I think of Henry's offer to help me if I want to relocate farther afield. It's tempting, but something holds me back. I just don't think it would work.

A knock on the big plate glass window startles me, and I shriek and jump to my feet. Jakob is peering in the window, two cups of coffee from Byrdie's in his hands. I open the door for him, and he comes in.

"It's weird to see this place so empty," he comments, handing me a cup of coffee. I take a sip. It's a hometown honey latte, made extra sweet the way I like it.

"How did you know?" I ask, lifting the cup in a question. "And thanks. I needed this today."

He waves away the gratitude. "I asked Justin what you normally get. Extra pump of honey, huh?"

"Hazard of growing up in a candy store. I was born with a sweet tooth," I tell him dryly.

He nods and looks around. He's wearing a pale blue thermal shirt that brings out the ice in his eyes, and a pair of dark jeans. His hair is pulled back in a stubby ponytail that serves to highlight his sharp cheekbones. As a teen he was all sharp planes and angles, jaw too angular, eyes a little too wide for his face. Now those angles are sculpted by muscle and sinew into a thing of beauty.

"I've got Mom running the store for me today. I was planning to head outside, get a little fresh air," he says. "You want to come along?"

I look around. There's nothing I absolutely need to do for the next little while. Mom is at water aerobics this morning, and Gus is at school. For once, no one needs me for anything.

"Sure." I don't ask where we're headed. Instead, I just walk out the door after him. I don't even lock it. What is there left to steal?

Five minutes later I'm having second thoughts as we reach the marina next to Liberty Bay Waterfront Park and Jakob pulls a tandem kayak from a rack.

"Wait, we're going kayaking?" I hesitate. I haven't been in years. Not since middle school, probably.

Jakob glances back, hefting the double-seat kayak like it weighs nothing. "Sure. Ed lets me use a kayak whenever I want to in exchange for free pastries." He shrugs. "Good deal for both of us. Grab two paddles, will you? And life jackets are just there."

At the end of the dock we slip into our life jackets and he steadies the kayak while I clamber into the front seat. I'm not graceful, but I don't tip out. Once I'm settled, Jakob hands me the paddles and gets in the seat at the back with considerably more ease. Those panther-like reflexes must be nice. I'm not uncoordinated, but I was never chosen first for sports in school. I pass a paddle back to him and find a cup holder in front of me for my latte. We don't talk as we paddle out into the bay. It's a beautiful morning, clear and gray, with the promise of sun when the clouds burn off later. There's only a little activity this morning at the marina—a sailboat heading out on the bay, a fishing vessel coming back from an early morning on the water. We pass the waterfront park with its wide lush lawn and large wooden gazebo in a Scandinavian style, around which flags from different Scandinavian countries flutter in the slight breeze. Gulls wheel and cry overhead, and the rhythmic dip of our paddles is almost hypnotic. The silence doesn't feel unnatural, but it doesn't feel easy either. I can sense him behind me . . . looming with his ice-blue eyes and his perceptive quiet and his . . . muscles.

"How did filming go yesterday?" he asks, breaking the silence.

"Oh, it was actually really fun. I don't like being in front of the camera, but Henry made it easy."

"Did he now." There's a dry inflection to the comment that I don't appreciate.

"He's being really nice helping us out," I say, a touch defensively. "It could be a big boost to the store and to my new business."

"Sure, Henry seems like a nice guy," Jakob says, and somehow it doesn't sound like a compliment.

I turn in my seat, feeling indignant. What right does Jakob have to judge Henry? He doesn't even know him.

Neither do you, a little voice in my head whispers. I ignore it.

"What do you mean by that?" I demand of Jakob. "What's wrong with someone helping us out with some free publicity?"

"Nothing at all," he says, meeting my eyes calmly. "But for the record, I don't think Henry is just being nice."

"Why?" I narrow my eyes at him.

He looks at me steadily. "How he looks at you for starters."

"How he looks at me?" I ask, suddenly flustered. "What do you mean?" I really want him to elaborate.

"I don't think it's escaped Henry's attention that you're a very pretty, single woman," Jakob remarks evenly.

"Oh." I feel my cheeks flush scarlet and turn back to face front. I don't know how to respond to that observation, but secretly I'm pleased. Maybe Henry's just a nice guy who likes to look for good human interest stories. Or maybe Jakob is right and he's noticed me as a woman. I hope so. That's exactly what I want. Also, Jakob thinks I'm pretty? "So what if he's noticed me?" I ask. "We're both unattached. It's not a crime."

There's a long silence. "Just be careful, Emmie," Jakob says at last. "Guys like Henry, they're used to getting whatever they want. I don't want to see you get hurt."

"Henry isn't like that," I counter.

"How do you know what Henry's like?" Jakob challenges softly.

He's right, but I'm not about to admit it. I'm a pretty good judge of character, and I'm positive Henry is one of the good ones. But still, I don't know him well, not yet anyway.

"Maybe I'm trying to take advantage of him," I say tartly.

Jakob chuckles. "Are you?" he says, paddling smoothly. I catch the faintest edge to his question. I think he genuinely wants to know.

I ignore the question. "I'm not some novice at relationships, you know," I say finally. "I'm a mother. I've had a partner. I've dated my share of men." I dig my paddle into the water, straining to propel the kayak forward for a few seconds until my arms get tired. I really need to get more exercise than just hauling trays of fudge from the kitchen.

"And how do you know I'm single?" I demand. "I could have a boyfriend."

I hear rather than see his smirk. "Emmie, you're forgetting where we live. I can find out everything if I ask around. Sometimes, I don't even have to ask. People just tell me things. And on your birthday, when you and Dani came into the store, she offered a lot of information. Something about you needing a Danish because your love life wasn't so hot?"

Ugh. Dani and her big mouth. My cheeks flame. She basically told Jakob my love life was gathering dust on a shelf. He's right. It's not his fault we live in a town that loves nothing more than minding other people's business.

"It *was* a really good Danish," I mutter grudgingly.

He chuckles. "Not *that* good," he says.

I flush brighter pink at his words and concentrate on paddling for a few moments, trying to regain my composure and my dignity.

"It's been sixteen years since we've seen each other," I tell him finally. "I've had a lot of life experiences in that time."

"I'm sure you have," he agrees. "And I have too. And yet here we are, back where we started."

I don't say anything for a long minute. "I never thought I'd come back," I confess softly. "I always swore I'd leave one day and do something big."

He blows out a breath. "Yeah, if you asked me the one person I thought would be least likely to be here sixteen years later, you'd have been who I picked."

"And you would be who I picked as the person least likely to leave," I say without thinking.

Jakob snorts, a humorless puff of air. "Before graduation, I thought so too," he says.

And there it is. The thing between us, the thing we haven't talked about. Are we doing this? Are we going to finally talk about what happened that day?

"I couldn't believe it when I found out you'd left and joined the Marines," I admit hesitantly. "You always told me you intended to stay in Poulsbo."

"I did. Things change," Jakob says flatly.

"What made you leave?" I ask, holding my breath. I'm treading on dangerous history right now. I stop paddling, poised for his answer. I don't turn around, but I can feel his gaze boring into the back of my head.

"I think you know."

His words send a shiver through me. It's what I've suspected for years. We fall silent, paddling at a brisk pace for a few minutes. A harbor seal pops up ahead of us, eyeing us curiously. I want to clear the air, and I've started to broach the topic more than once, but I keep getting interrupted. This time there is no one to interrupt us. We're going to be seeing a lot of each other as he helps Walt with the repairs, and I don't want to keep feeling like there's something big and historical lingering between us. He was my best guy friend. When he left town without saying goodbye, I felt an empty ache in my chest, right in the center of my rib cage. There's been a hollow space there for so long I've gotten used to it. Longing. Regret. I can't tell them apart anymore. I stare out at the water, at the sleek head of the seal who looks at us with liquid puppy dog eyes. I summon my courage. Words rise in my throat, words I've wanted to say for so long.

"Jakob, I'm so sorry about what happened before you left."

"You really don't have to do this," he interrupts me curtly.

But I want to. I need to. I've been sitting on the regret for sixteen years.

"I think I do," I say quietly. I turn in my seat, craning my neck to look up at him. The sun is limning him in gold. There's a fine dusting of flour on the crescent of skin between his neck and his T-shirt. I have a sudden urge to pull him to me, to hold him tight and murmur apologies into his skin until he forgives me. "I didn't mean to hurt you, but I know I did. I'm so sorry," I say finally.

I don't move. He's staring at me with an unreadable expression. He swallows once, hard, and then gives a tired sigh. "Emmie, it's fine. It was years ago. We were kids. I was dumb to say what I did, to wait until graduation to tell you how I felt . . ." He looks away. "I was just a kid with a crush who waited too long and chose a bad moment to spill his heart out. But I just hoped, dared to hope, stupidly, that you felt the same way about me. After what happened at the debate tournament, I thought . . ."

"I know."

I haven't thought of that night in years. His words take me back instantly.

Chapter 19

It was the end of May of our senior year and we had qualified for the state debate championships. A mere week before graduation, we found ourselves at a huge Hilton near the airport in Seattle with debate teams from around the state. It was an exhilarating weekend, made all the more poignant by the fact that it would be our last. We'd been debate partners for three years, and now it was just . . . over.

Everything that weekend felt monumental and bittersweet—meeting in my hotel room to review our talking points, huddling together over pancakes in the morning to strategize. I was headed off to Switzerland in a month for my program. Jakob would be staying in Poulsbo and attending community college for two years before he transferred to a state school. His plan was to stay in Poulsbo permanently. Mine was to leave as soon as possible. But in leaving my hometown, I was leaving everything familiar, everything I loved, including Jakob.

Watching his close-cropped blond head bent over his notes as he munched an enormous pile of bacon from the breakfast buffet, I couldn't wrap my mind around the idea that everything was changing so fast. I felt like I was on a speeding train, zipping away from everything I had ever known.

We were brilliant that weekend, working effortlessly in unison. He'd glance at me and I'd read his mind. He remembered a key fact about an obscure legal ruling from the 1800s that bolstered our position significantly. I gave a brilliant closing speech. I'd never felt prouder of us, and when they held the awards ceremony on the last night and announced our names as the team who took second place, it felt like a dream. We knew from the start we wouldn't win. The Bellevue prep school kids had won the championship each year for as long as anyone could remember. But no one in our school district had ever even placed in the top three.

We jumped to our feet in that cold auditorium, screaming in shock and excitement to the sound of wild applause. I threw my arms around Jakob, jumping up and down and squealing in glee. He clasped me in a tight hug. He smelled like his dad's cologne, and his good suit was a little too short at the cuffs. He just kept growing like a beanpole.

"We did it, we did it," we both kept exclaiming, words overlapping, flush with victory. I pulled back and looked at him, that familiar, dear face. His hair was cropped so close to his head that it made his eyes look too big and icy bright. I took him in. The lean, hungry look of him. His kindness and quiet steadiness, that lightning-fast brain. What would I do without Jakob? Our eyes locked, and something shifted in his. He glanced down at my mouth, and then an instant later he bent down and pressed his lips to mine.

My mind went blank from surprise. He tasted like Wrigley's

gum, and his arms around me were surprisingly strong. His mouth was warm and tender amid the cheers and shouts of the crowd of debaters celebrating or voicing their disappointment. Somewhere in the back of my mind, I knew he had been wanting to do this for a long time. This was not a casual kiss.

I regained my senses and pulled back after a moment, and we gazed at each other in astonishment. His expression was shyly hopeful, longing stamped across his features. I didn't know what to think. I'd never thought of Jakob in a romantic way. He was just my best friend.

"Emmie," he said, reaching out to touch my cheek. But then our names were called from the podium, and we had to go up to the front to get our medals. I walked up the steps in confusion. What had just happened? My best friend had kissed me, and I had sort of kissed him back. I didn't know what to think about it. Did I like it? Did I like *him* that way? I didn't know.

We didn't have a chance to be alone in the aftermath of our win. The other teams from our school surrounded us, and we were separated in the chatter and hubbub. We didn't get a chance to be alone that final week of school either. We saw each other every day, but always in class or at lunch, surrounded by friends and classmates. Every time I glanced in his direction, he was looking at me. He didn't seek me out, and I didn't approach him either. But I thought of that kiss often, still surprised by the way he'd held me, the firm joy of his mouth on mine. What did it mean? What could it mean? I was leaving. He was staying. There was nothing more to talk about.

And then came graduation day.

I shake my head, pained by the memory of him running up to me after the graduation ceremony, looking like a black crow with his graduation gown flapping around his wiry frame. He was holding a dozen red roses, still in cellophane from the grocery store. He grabbed me in a hug and held tight, in full view of my mom and dad and Dani. I was eye level with his Adam's apple. I remember looking at a little patch of skin he'd scraped raw while shaving. I was confused. What was he doing?

And then he held me at arm's length and spilled his heart out to me . . . publicly, bravely. He told me I was beautiful and so smart, that he'd never met a girl like me. He offered me the roses and asked me shyly to be his girlfriend. He told me he loved me. I was dumbfounded. I didn't say it back. I didn't say anything at all. What could I say?

"You broke my heart, Emmie," Jakob says quietly from behind me. "That day when I gave my heart to you and you handed it right back." I can still hear the sharp note of pain in his voice. Old hurts can still sting, even after all these years.

I didn't mean to hurt him, though I know I did. I remember stepping back from his embrace on graduation day, feeling a mixture of shock and embarrassment, aware of the eyes all around us, watching with curiosity. That guileless look of heartbreak on his face when I handed back the roses has haunted me for years.

"Jakob, I can't. I'm sorry." That's what I'd whispered to him, feeling awful but also sure of my decision.

I hadn't known what to say until I was faced with his feelings for me, and then it all became clear, standing there on the high school lawn. There was no future for us. So I told him how much I cared about him, but that I saw him as a friend and nothing more. And that had been true. I had made it true. Because I was leaving Poulsbo, ready to embrace a whole new life, and I couldn't let anything stand in my way. Not even Jakob.

There was another reason too, one I couldn't tell him about, one I still can't talk about. Jakob doesn't know about the visions in our family, about how much sway they hold over our decisions and our future. And I can't tell him the whole truth. It's a secret, passed down from generation to generation, held tight by the women and only shared with a select, trusted few. However, that secret has affected my relationship with every man I've ever cared for. Because the truth is that somewhere in my heart of hearts, I've been afraid to fall in love with someone before receiving my vision. What if I fell for someone, and then my vision showed me a different purpose for my life? A different person who is my destiny? What then?

For years I've kept a little part of my heart reserved until I saw my future and knew it was safe to love the right person, the person I am supposed to be with. I didn't give my whole heart to Jakob or Romaine or the other guys I dated. I couldn't risk falling in love and then finding out it couldn't last.

It's felt a little like holding my breath, waiting to see who I can wholeheartedly love. And now I know. I've seen my future, and it isn't Jakob Kristensen. I was right to hold myself back from him, even though I regret that I hurt him. I've waited years to try to make amends. Now I have that chance.

I twist in my kayak seat so I can see him. "I'm really sorry I hurt you, Jakob," I tell him, meeting his gaze. "I never meant to hurt you. I just couldn't see how our lives could fit. I was going to Europe. I was going to have a life that wasn't in Poulsbo. I'd already gotten accepted into the chocolatier program in Switzerland. I knew I wanted to take an apprenticeship in Paris. And you wanted to stay."

Jakob sighs and scrubs a hand down his face. "I'm not blaming you," he clarifies. "It just hurt. I was head over heels for you, and after we kissed, I thought you felt the same way about me."

"I didn't know how I felt," I tell him. "I was confused, but I had a different life waiting for me."

He considers me, then nods, accepting the answer.

"Did you really join the Marines because of me?" I toy with the handle of my paddle. I've wondered this for years.

"Yes," Jakob says flatly. "After you said no to me, I couldn't see a future in Poulsbo anymore. I couldn't imagine waking up every day and being seen as the boy Emmie Wynne rejected, and I couldn't imagine a life here without you. So I left. The Marines seemed like the farthest thing from my old life. I enlisted, and it turned out to be a pretty good fit for me. I learned discipline and endurance, how to keep going when you think you're one step away from dying." He shrugs. "All in all, it worked out for the best."

I stare at him. He's right. Becoming a Marine was good for him. He's centered and self-assured without being cocky. He seems at ease in his own skin. Still thoughtful—as evidenced by my extra-sweet latte this morning—still watchful and astute, but tempered by a laid-back sort of confidence that is really extremely sexy. Not to mention the body the Marines has given him. It's like he's still got the mind of a debate squad captain, but now it's housed in the body of a Norse demigod. I realize I'm staring at his abs through that tight, faded shirt, craning my neck so far around I look like an owl. And what's worse is that he's just watching me stare at his abs and smirking. Gaah! I flick a little water on him with my paddle.

"Oh no you don't," he growls, purposefully rocking the kayak and making a grab for my paddle.

I shriek. He laughs and lunges for my paddle again, which I snatch out of his grasp at the last second. And the tension of the moment is broken.

"I really am sorry," I tell him sincerely. "I didn't mean to hurt you. You were one of my best friends, and I've regretted how I handled things all these years. If I could do it differently, I would."

"Oh yeah? What would you do differently?" he asks, tilting his head and eyeing me.

I consider this. "I would still have said no," I tell him. "I had a lot of growing up to do, and I needed to do it outside of Poulsbo. I loved my training in Switzerland and my time apprenticing in Paris. I don't regret my choice—I got to do what I love—but I do regret how publicly I rejected you.

"If I were to do it over, I'd take the roses and I'd loudly say thank you. I'd give you a kiss on the cheek and tell you that you were the best guy I knew. Then I'd quietly tell you that I wasn't ready for a relationship but that I cared a lot about you. And then as I was leaving I'd yell really, really loudly so everyone could hear, 'Some girl is going to be so lucky to have you.'"

He smiles at this, a flicker of amusement. "That would have eased the sting a bit," he admits. "But then I might not have gotten the push to leave town and join the Marines. It all worked out for the best in the end, I guess. I got a pension and killer abs and you got . . ."

"Tired and chubby?" I supply.

He shoots me a disbelieving look. "Emmie, are you fishing for compliments?" His tone is slightly reproving.

"No. Maybe," I mumble, feeling my face flush red. I swear, I've blushed more in the last week than in the past sixteen years combined. What is wrong with me?

"You'll always be the prettiest girl in school to me," Jakob says with a little wry grin.

I feel myself pink at the unexpected compliment. Jakob

doesn't hand them out often. "Well, you kind of ruined other guys for me," I blurt out before I think about it. "You're why I left Gus's dad."

His eyebrows fly up at this revelation. "What?"

I hasten to explain. "While I was dating Romaine, I kept comparing him to you. All the guys I've ever dated, I've compared to you. You were the kindest, sweetest guy I'd ever met. You were so smart, and so perceptive, and your only flaw was that you couldn't see yourself as worthy, as valuable." I sneak a peek at him. He's focused on me intently, those icy eyes boring into me. I press on.

"After a while I realized that while Romaine was worldly and cool and smart, he was also sort of a jerk. He wasn't kind to people the way you were. He wasn't thoughtful. He took me a little bit for granted, and I think he looked down on me a little too, because I didn't speak four languages and didn't know much about wine and didn't understand a lot about European politics. It wasn't just me. Romaine looked down on a lot of people. He was a snob. I broke up with him even before my dad got his diagnosis. When I came home and found out I was pregnant, it was already over with Romaine. And I didn't try to get back together with him. You know why?"

Jakob shakes his head. His expression is closed and wary, but I soldier on. "Because I knew my baby needed someone else to be a father to him, someone less like Romaine and more like you."

He looks up sharply at that, but I hold his gaze, trying to convey the truth of what I'm saying. "And for four years, Gus had my dad. My dad was the only other man in the world who was as kind and caring and thoughtful as you were. You and Dad made it really hard for any other men to meet those standards. Quite frankly, no one else ever has."

Jakob just stares at me wordlessly for a long minute. He looks a little stunned. Then he clears his throat. "We should get back," he says. "I've got a lot of work to do to get your store up and running again."

I nod and turn around, facing front. Maybe I've said too much, but I don't regret it. It feels good to clear the air. We paddle briskly back across the bay. The silence is easy now between us. I feel lighter, like the words that have been sitting in my chest, waiting to be spoken, have finally been released, floating away like helium balloons. I've done what I could to right the wrong I did to Jakob, and that feels pretty amazing. I paddle hard, feeling lighter than air.

We're almost to the boathouse when Jakob breaks the silence. "How are things coming with your chocolate shop idea?" he asks.

I heave a sigh. "It's run into a bit of a snag, actually." I tell him about the lack of good storefront space in Kingston and Winslow. "I'm stuck until I can find a space that will work."

Jakob is quiet for a minute. I can hear him thinking. "How about here in Poulsbo? Is there anything available in downtown?" he asks finally.

I hesitate. "I haven't really been looking in Poulsbo," I admit finally.

"Why not? It has just as much charm as those other towns, and you already have a good network in the business community." Jakob steers us into the marina. "It would save you a lot of time and trouble to not have to build a name somewhere else and get connected. It's already here for you. It'd take you years to build up somewhere else what you already have here."

He has a good point. I hadn't thought of it that way. I've been too busy dreaming of other places to really think about the value of what I have right in front of me. I consider the idea for a moment, thinking of all the help we had last night. People know us and love us and are willing to sacrifice for us in this town. This sense of community is precious. So why am I trying to start over somewhere where I'll have to build all of this relationship and goodwill all over again? Why am I not locating my shop in Poulsbo? It's a very good question.

I think of the dream—Paris, New York—and I think of the reality. If I were a single woman, younger and free, perhaps that would have made sense. But I am me, and I have Gus and Mom and the Happy Viking to consider. I think of my vision again. There was nothing that gave me a sense of the shop's exact location. Maybe I should consider Poulsbo more carefully, at least be open to the idea and see what's available. Jakob has given me a lot to think about.

Chapter 20

Just as we pull up to the dock, I get a call from the school nurse asking me to come get Gus. Apparently he is complaining about a tummy ache. With a sigh, I tell her I'll be there in ten minutes.

"Everything all right?" Jakob asks when I hang up.

"Yeah, ever since Dad died, Gus has had lots of big feelings, and sometimes those come out as tummy aches," I explain. "I make him chamomile tea with honey, but honestly I think he just needs some cuddles and reassurance." I set my empty coffee cup on the dock and struggle to get out of the kayak gracefully. Jakob leaps from the kayak and is there by my side instantly, his strong grip closing over my upper arms. He steadies me but lets me find my footing and clamber out onto the dock myself.

"Thanks." I tug down the crumpled hem of my cute Poulsbo sweatshirt with "Visit Little Norway" embroidered on it with fuzzy thread in retro colors.

"Anything I can do?" Jakob asks.

I shake my head. "I'll just drive over and get him. I'll have to bring him with me to the shop today, but I'll try to keep him out of your way." I was planning on experimenting with some new chocolate flavors this afternoon. I also have some paperwork I need to do at the store. Maybe Gus will be okay playing with LEGOs or reading a book so I can at least get a little work done.

"I'm sure it will be fine," Jakob says. "He's a cool kid."

"He is." I smile and look up at him. "He's a great kid, but . . ." I worry my lip, and Jakob notices.

"But what?" he asks, hefting the kayak out of the water and carrying it to the rack of kayaks. I grab the paddles and hurry after him.

"I'm always afraid I'm not handling all of this right—his anxiety and the grief over my dad and the stomachaches. It's just . . . it's the thing no one tells you about being a single parent. There's no one else to help carry the mental load. It's just me. And I'm never quite sure if I'm doing it right or doing enough. I mean, Mom and Dot and Dani help out a lot, and they love Gus, but at the end of the day, I'm his only parent. And I worry sometimes that I'm messing it up, messing him up." I put the paddles upright in a rack next to the kayaks and unbuckle my life jacket.

"Nah." Jakob shakes his head. "You're doing great." He stows the kayak, lifting it onto the rack like it weighs nothing. "Look at my family. We boys were raised on Coca-Cola and day-old pastries. We didn't ever go to the doctor, even when Soren broke his arm. And look how we turned out. Lars is a district attorney now for Kitsap County." He shrugs. "I think you're doing just fine, Emmie. He's a good kid who lost a big person in his life. That takes time to find a new normal."

I nod, relieved by his words. It's a good reminder to go slow and let grief take whatever form it needs to take. For Gus, evidently, that's tea and time with me today. I have a thousand things to do, but I'll make the time somehow. I always do.

"Thanks for the paddle around the bay," I say lightly as we walk down the dock and head toward the public parking lot next to the waterfront pavilion. It's the most convenient parking for downtown businesses and my Honda is there. "And thanks for clearing the air." I glance at him sideways, gauging his reaction.

"Anytime," he says. We reach my car.

"This is me." I fish my keys from my pocket. Jakob looks at me for a moment, eyes searching my face, then turns away.

"See you later, Emmie," he calls over his shoulder. I stand for a moment watching him walk away. Long strides eating up the ground beneath his leather work boots. He could be an ad for men in jeans everywhere. I watch him till he's out of sight, then go pick up my kid.

"MOM, DID YOU know that about five hundred meteors reach the earth's surface every year?" Gus looks up at me expectantly. We're in the kitchen of the Happy Viking and I'm fighting with a new bonbon technique that is giving me trouble. The dark chocolate and lilac-purple-swirled bonbon coating keeps cracking, and then the huckleberry gelée shows through. It would be a gorgeous and tasty combination if I could just get it right. Gus is perched on a stool next to me. He's sipping chamomile tea from a mug, reading his book, and peppering me with alarming facts about space. His tummy ache, as I predicted, seems to have all but disappeared.

"Five hundred meteors a year? I didn't know that, buddy. Wow, that sounds like a lot of meteors," I comment, carefully drying my bonbon molds and preparing to begin again. The last ruined batch of bonbons is sitting next to me accusingly, huckleberry gelée shining like little jewels through the cracked chocolate.

I swear silently under my breath and start over. Out front I can hear Walt and Jakob working. They're tearing up the old carpeting and cutting it into strips. I am not sorry to see that gross gray carpet go.

"And did you know there's an enormous rogue black hole that zooms around space going three million miles an hour?" Gus peers up at me, the expression on his face a mixture of fear and a sort of ghoulish fascination. "And someday, in millions of years, it might reach us and gobble up our entire galaxy?"

I glance up, mildly alarmed. "What kind of science book are you reading?"

Gus pulls it to himself protectively. "A good one," he says. "Not like the boring ones we have at school that just talk about the life cycles of plants." He rolls his eyes. At that moment, Jakob pokes his head into the kitchen and sees Gus.

"Just who I need," he says. "Can you help us out, Gus? We've got a big job to do out here, and we could use a hand." He glances at me questioningly.

Gus sits up straight and pushes his glasses up his nose. "Um, if my mom says it's okay."

I arch a brow at Jakob, who shoots me a quick, reassuring nod.

"Sure, honey. Just be careful." I mouth a grateful "thank you" to Jakob, then step closer and murmur, "He's not the most coordinated kid, so maybe nothing sharp?"

"He'll do great," Jakob says firmly, and they disappear into the front room. Only after they're gone do I realize he never actually replied to my concern about sharp things. Oh well. I trust Jakob, and I can hear everything that's going on out there.

"Oh cool!" Gus shouts, stomachache now seemingly completely forgotten. I smile, grabbing this moment of alone time and focusing on my technique once more, slowly brushing the molds with the shiny tempered dark chocolate.

Sometime later the bell on the front door jingles and I hear a familiar British voice call out a greeting. A moment later Henry peers into the kitchen. "Emmie?"

"Henry! What are you doing here?" I ask in surprise. He's dressed very casually—boat shoes, linen trousers, and a striped T-shirt that looks comfortable yet expensive.

"I just popped in, thought I'd check and see if you'd made any progress on finding the right location for your shop?" He comes into the room and surveys my bonbon making process with interest.

"I'm going to stick local for now. I don't think at this stage of life I can uproot my mom and Gus." I try to covertly smooth my hair and wonder if I can get a breath mint without him seeing me. I'm so glad he stopped in. He could have texted me to ask about my progress finding a location, but I'm glad he came by instead. "I'm looking at a couple of possibilities this evening here in Poulsbo, actually." I'm not hopeful they'll work out. According to Dawn, the market for store frontage in Poulsbo is even more competitive than in Kingston and Winslow. She scraped up a few options and I know she's doing her best, but the listings she sent me are all depressing. I'm beginning to wonder if I'll ever find the right spot.

"Well, I hope one of them works out," Henry says. "I'm always happy to be of help if I can."

"Thanks, Henry." I take a little ball of huckleberry gelée and drop it into the chocolate mold.

Henry lingers, then clears his throat. "Ah, there is one more thing I wanted to ask you, Emmie. I was wondering . . ." He pauses, looking a little nervous. "Could I take you out for dinner tomorrow evening? I've enjoyed our time together, and I'd love to see you again." He looks hopeful.

I duck my head to hide my huge smile. "I'd love that," I say sincerely.

"Oh good." He looks relieved. "Do you like wine?"

"I lived in Paris for years." I laugh. "I'm pretty sure you can't live in France and not enjoy wine."

We arrange to meet at seven p.m. and I text Mom to let her know about my date. She never minds putting Gus to bed on the rare nights I have something to do. I text Dani too, in all caps with seven exclamation points. I'm over the moon. Henry has asked me on a real date!

After Henry leaves, I'm finishing up the batch of chocolates when Walt marches through the kitchen carrying a large roll of dirty carpet. I poke my head into the storefront to see what's happening. Jakob and Gus are ripping up a large section of carpet in the middle of the store. Gus is making roaring sounds and stomping around. "Look, Mom, I'm a dino in space," he exclaims. "And I get to use a grown-up knife! See?" Clutched in his hand is a box cutter. He waves it around excitedly.

"Hey, Gus, what's in your hand, man?" Jakob says sternly, seeing my alarmed look.

"This is a tool, not a toy," Gus repeats and straightens up, assuming a look of grave responsibility. He calms down immediately.

"Okay, cut this piece just like I showed you," Jakob says, watching as Gus carefully slices through the grungy carpet. I pause to watch them. Jakob's patient instruction reminds me of my dad's. When Gus turned four, Dad gave him a tiny toolbox filled with small, real metal tools. Gus would follow him around the house and yard like a duckling, helping with any small home maintenance tasks my dad felt up to accomplishing that day, depending on his energy level. It's been two years since Gus opened that toolbox. Now he's graduated to (alarmingly sharp) full-sized tools, but it is good to see him looking so happy and productive. I guess it's hard to worry about the vastness of space when you have to concentrate on not slicing your fingers. He looks so grown up and so young at the same time, crouched beside Jakob's tall form, intently listening to instructions. Feeling thankful, I go back to the kitchen to finish my chocolates. I have a date tomorrow with the guy of my dreams, and Gus has a new big buddy. All in all, things are looking up.

Chapter 21

"Emmie!" Henry greets me as I step onto the patio of the nicest date-night spot in town, a wine and tapas bar on the waterfront. I'm five minutes late, which, to be honest, is pretty good for me. I always have the best of intentions to be on time, but you know, life. This time it was because Dani FaceTimed me right before I left and demanded to see what I was wearing. She nixed my cute sundress as too casual and not sexy enough, and I had to go through eight wardrobe changes before she was satisfied with a sky-blue, silky little ruffled number that shows a little more cleavage than I'm generally comfortable baring. But hey, I'm on a real date with my dream crush. Maybe a little cleavage is a good idea.

Henry's eyes light up when he sees me, and I thank Dani for talking me out of the sundress. This is way more fun.

"You look absolutely lovely," Henry says, brushing a kiss across my cheek. "I reserved a table here on the patio. Is that okay?" he asks anxiously.

"It's perfect."

It's a lovely, clear evening and the patio has a panoramic view of the bay. It is the ideal setting for a cozy, casually elegant date. There are vines trailing up trellises, blooming trees in big pots, and strands of café lights strung overhead. The atmosphere feels a little magical with the lights and the water lapping at the shore a few feet beyond our table. Somewhere, background music is seeping low and sultry on the night air, Diana Krall singing the old classics.

"Do you know much about wine, Emmie?" Henry asks as we slide into rattan-backed chairs at a small table overlooking the water. He scans the wine list with a practiced air.

"A little. I picked up some things while living in France. I'm not a connoisseur, but I do like wine." Romaine was a true wine expert, and I learned quite a bit while we were dating, but often Romaine's way of approaching wine felt too uptight. I just wanted to enjoy a glass and a good conversation, not dissect it clinically.

"You can educate me then." Henry laughs, a warm sound that makes my heart crinkle up with delight. "I come from a beer-drinking family. I consider myself a wine enthusiast, not a wine expert," he confesses. "Now, the best place to get chili crab in Singapore—that I can tell you. But the difference between a"—he scans the menu—"Viognier and a Chenin Blanc? I need a bit of help."

That's what I like about Henry. He's so approachable that I forget how famous he is, and how well traveled. We both order the tasting flights—three whites for me and three reds for him—and agree to share them so we can taste them all. We order half a dozen plates of tapas as well. The patio isn't crowded, but buzzy enough on a Wednesday night to feel fun. The last time I was out on a date like this, I met the guy at a wings place in Silverdale. It turned out he wasn't divorced and wasn't even remotely over his ex-wife. He cried into the buffalo sauce. It was a disaster. This evening is going to be so much better, I can tell. It feels like destiny. I am nervous, but it's a good nervous, the kind where you can feel a delightful surprise is in store.

While we wait for our order, Henry keeps up an engaging stream of conversation, peppering in humorous asides about his travels and mishaps, asking me thoughtful questions, and making me feel like I'm the center of the universe tonight. I feel myself opening up under his attention, relishing feeling like a woman again, someone beautiful and desirable and interesting. I'm Emmie of the smoothly shaved legs and sparkling conversation, not the workaday Emmie who keeps forgetting to throw away her old, grayish, stretched-out bra and who can't recall the last book she actually finished.

Our wine flights arrive, and we sample and laugh and pretend we are wine snobs.

I sniff a Pinot Gris from Oregon. "I detect notes of . . . radish, diesel fumes, and a hint of apricot pit."

A passing server catches the last few words and pauses. "You have a good palate," he says gravely. "That wine is very apricot forward, you're right. Lovely notes of ripe stone fruit." As he sails away, we keep straight faces until he is out of earshot and then dissolve into giggles. It's silly and we're having fun, goofing around, being flirty. I love this. I love who I get to be tonight.

The tapas are delivered to the table, and we sample them all—shrimp in garlic sauce, a lovely egg-based vegetable tortilla, patatas bravas with smoky red pepper aioli, fried eggplant drizzled in honey . . . I lose count of the small plates and just eat and enjoy.

We're almost finished with our wine tasting and tapas feast when I remember I brought Henry a gift. I pull the little silver cardboard box out of my tiny purse. I left my serviceable mom purse at home and borrowed this sleek vintage clutch from Mom, who told me she took it to the opera in Seattle once in the '80s.

"This is for you." I slide the box over to him. "A thank-you for filming an episode of *Savor* about our family."

"Emmie, it was my absolute pleasure," Henry says, looking surprised. "No gift is needed."

"I wanted to." I gesture to the box with my chin. "Open it."

He does. Inside are six perfect chocolates. I stayed up late last night making the last couple of flavors, and I'm proud of how they turned out. I point to each one. "Yakima peach ginger bonbon, San Juan Island smoked sea salt and lavender caramel, dark chocolate huckleberry bonbon—finally got that one right—Storyville espresso ganache truffle, Ripple IPA caramel from Echoes Brewing, and Rainier cherry and vanilla buttercream truffle." I ate two of the Rainier cherry truffles, which are dusted in gold sprinkles, before I came tonight, for courage.

Henry looks impressed. "These look amazing, Emmie."

"They're all handcrafted using Pacific Northwest ingredients from local suppliers," I tell him proudly. "Try one."

Henry picks the Ripple IPA caramel made with craft beer brewed locally in Poulsbo. He bites into it, narrowing his eyes assessingly. "I confess, I had my doubts about this one, but it's . . . well, it's delicious."

He samples the espresso ganache truffle, then the peach ginger bonbon. Ten minutes later he's tried all six chocolates and given his opinion about each flavor profile. He loved all of them, even the huckleberry bonbon, although he isn't usually the biggest fan of blueberries, he tells me. Finally he sits back and looks at me in frank admiration.

"Emmie, you continue to astonish me. These are . . . extraordinary. They're unique, they're local, but more than that, each flavor is just really delicious. Where do you get your inspiration?"

I think about it for a moment. "Partly from my chocolatier training in Switzerland, and partly from Jacques Genin. He was an exacting boss who pushed us all not only technically but creatively too. And the rest . . ." I look around. "The rest is a tribute to my home. I think the Pacific Northwest is the most special place on earth. Just like a winemaker, I like to make chocolate that reflects the terroir of a place." I gesture to our empty flights of wine.

Henry is gazing at me speculatively. "You need a bigger platform," he says finally. "This chocolate shop—I know it's your dream, and it's a good dream, but you need a way to break into the global chocolate scene." He looks at the empty box of chocolates and says thoughtfully, "Have you ever thought about entering one of the big, prestigious chocolatier competitions?"

I hesitate. I used to dream of entering the International Chocolatier Awards competition, which is held in Geneva each year. But those days are long gone.

"Once upon a time," I admit. "But then my dad got sick, and I left Paris and became a mom and . . . well, life happened."

"I think you should consider entering one this year," Henry tells me seriously. "It could do so much for your visibility. Of course the cash prize is nice, but it's really all about the publicity. Winning could really rocket you into a much higher level of name recognition. Being featured on *Savor* will do good things for your visibility too, but winning a competition would catch the eye of the chocolate world in a different way."

"That sounds amazing," I say wistfully. "But I don't have the equipment or the clout or frankly the money to travel and enter one of those competitions. And I can't leave my mom and Gus and fly halfway around the world. It's just not practical right now."

Henry nods in understanding. "Maybe not halfway around the world, but what about Canada? What would you say if I could get you into the North American Chocolatier Competition?" He asks the question with a little half smile, like he knows something I don't. "It's in Vancouver this year, in two weeks. I'm hosting the award ceremony for the competition winners, and I'm pretty sure I could get you a spot in the competition. One of the planning committee members owes me a favor from a few years back. I bailed her out of a sticky situation in Rio. I could make a few calls if you're interested, see if they have a spot for you?" He takes a sip of water and waits for my response.

I'm speechless, both because of his generous offer and because of the absolute enormity of what he's suggesting. This competition won't be mom-and-pop chocolate makers. It draws the best of the best. The award money is often a decent sum, which we could definitely use, but as Henry pointed out, the most valuable part of winning is the name recognition, the free publicity. Winning a competition like that can set your business up for success like nothing else. Not even *Savor* would give me that kind of visibility. And Henry is offering me a chance to compete. It's an amazing opportunity. I'm completely terrified.

"I . . . I don't know what to say," I stammer, heart hammering in my chest. Thinking about trying to compete with people at such a high level is daunting. It's been seven years since I made chocolate on a regular basis. I don't have anywhere near the quality of equipment other contestants are sure to have. Or the recent experience. While I have been busy changing diapers and making endless pounds of fudge, my competitors have been honing their craft as some of the best chocolatiers in the world.

Henry sees my panicked expression. "You don't need to decide now," he says gently. "Sleep on it. Think about it, and let me know."

I nod, relieved and grateful. "Thank you for the offer. I appreciate it, I really do. I just need to . . . consider it." I'd be a fool to say no, but the thought of saying yes is making my palms sweat.

"Of course. Let me know when you decide. The offer stands."

The rest of the evening flies by smoothly, and we stay until the restaurant closes. We are the last to leave. Henry walks me to my car. The night is chilly and I shiver in the stiff breeze that's whipping up over the bay. Without a word he takes off his navy swazer and drapes it over my shoulders. It smells deliciously of Earl Grey tea, and the warmth of his body lingers in it. I cuddle into the softness, luxuriating in the feeling of being taken care of. I feel myself melting a little inside. He's cute and intelligent and kind. A true gentleman. He doesn't make me feel like I've got electricity crackling through me like when Jakob looks at me. With Henry it's more comfortable, it's easy. Like a warm sweater. Like a cup of tea.

Easy is good, I tell myself. With everything else feeling so complicated, I need something easy. We pause by the car and I start to hand back his swazer, but he tells me to keep it until the next time he sees me.

"That way I have an excuse to see you again soon," he says with a bashful grin.

"Clever ploy," I tell him, my voice low and amused. We're lingering by the car, neither of us in a hurry to move away.

"Emmie, this has been lovely." Henry puts his hand under my elbow and leans in. "You're lovely," he whispers against my cheek. I instinctively lean forward, and it happens smoothly and naturally, the kiss he presses on my lips. We linger for a long, satisfied second, our mouths coming apart with a pop. It's sweet and perfect, this kiss. The perfect exclamation point at the end of a delightful evening.

"Goodnight, Henry," I tell him, getting into the car. I drive away hugging the swazer to me. On the way home I think about the evening with Henry as Norah Jones croons from my car radio. It's weird to feel like I know the end of our relationship while we're still at the beginning. It feels a little backward, like reading the end of a love story before you get to know the characters and see them fall for each other. I've watched Henry for years on TV and feel like I know him. That, combined with the vision of him down on one knee, makes it easy to jump too far ahead, but I need to keep a clear head about this. I have to remind myself that Henry and I are learning each other. We're getting to know each other for real, and that takes time and effort and careful thought. I don't want to just fall for him because of the vision. I want to fall for him in real life too. Step by step, getting to know the real Henry Summers.

So far I don't have any major qualms though. Henry is genuinely lovely. I have a crush on him, I'll admit it. And I think he might feel the same way about me. It's been years since I was in the butterflies-in-the-tummy stage with a guy. It's fun to feel like I'm falling again, this time for the right guy.

When I pull up in front of the house, I take Dani's napkin list out of my purse, reading it in the faint light of a streetlamp.

To-Do List

- Henry + Emmie fall in love
- Chocolate shop
- Yellow dress
- Engagement ring + proposal

I pull out a pen and make a faint tick by the first two points. They are both now in motion. Everything is going smoothly. It's early days yet. My chocolate shop is more theory than reality at this point, but at least it's in the works. And Henry and I are getting to know one another. I like him. I really like him. I have a good feeling about where all of this is going.

Maybe it's time to start shopping for a dress the color of sunshine.

Chapter 22

The next morning after school drop-off, I park my Honda in the public lot by the waterfront park and walk the few blocks to the shop. On my way, I pass one of the cute little boutiques that dot the downtown, and something in the window catches my eye. I freeze in wonder, staring at the floaty yellow dress on the faceless mannequin. It wasn't there yesterday.

"That's it! That's my dress!" I press my nose to the glass, drinking in the sight of it, heart beating with excitement. It's exactly as I pictured it. The store isn't open for another half hour, but I see a light on inside and rap on the door, hoping the owner, Paula, will make an exception and let me in. I bought a very overpriced tin of popcorn last year for her granddaughter's pep band fundraiser. Paula remembers the popcorn and is delighted to let me try on the dress.

"I only have this one size in yellow, so I hope it fits," she says cheerily, stripping the mannequin with an expert hand. "It just came in yesterday. It also comes in red and navy if you need another size."

I check the tag and frown. It's a size smaller than what I usually wear. It's a size I haven't been since Gus was born. Maybe it runs large? Here's hoping.

"It has to fit," I mutter under my breath. "It's my dress."

In the fitting room I shimmy out of my jeans and flutter-sleeved top and slide into the dress. It's cool and expensive-feeling, light as a feather. I suck in my stomach and try to zip it. No luck. It stops at my bra line. Thwarted, I breathe out and empty my lungs, and then by force of will I inch the zipper up and up until it finally reaches the top. I can't quite draw a full breath, but it fits like a glove. A slightly too-tight glove. Still, the image in the mirror matches my vision exactly. I decide to ignore the slightly suffocating feeling of not being able to draw a full breath. I'll just have to take shallow breaths when Henry proposes to me.

Paula wraps it up for me and runs my card. It's expensive, and I wince at the price tag, but then again, how can I not buy it? It's destiny. I heave a relieved sigh to be back in my normally sized clothes though.

Almost-perfect yellow dress in a bag on my arm, I float into the shop feeling optimistic. That is, until I open the door and am greeted by a grim-faced Walt.

"You've got a problem," he says without preamble.

My heart sinks. I quickly stash my purse and new dress in our tiny office and Walt takes me over to where the bare plywood subfloor is mottled and dark-looking. The carpet is long gone, exposing what is underneath. Jakob is standing there looking sternly down at a large splintered hole in the floor. He glances up at me and nods a greeting.

I nod back worriedly. "What's going on? Why is there a hole in the floor?"

Walt chews his gum. "Subfloor is rotted out more than we thought. Jakob stepped on this patch and his foot went right through. Looks like you've had water damage under there for a long time."

I stare at the patch, realizing that the floor in this part of the store has felt a little spongy for years. It's not near the bathroom though, so does this mean we have another problem and more damage? "How bad is it?" I ask, wincing before he even answers.

Walt takes off his baseball cap and scratches his head. He has a mop of curly white hair that springs up when he removes the cap. "Depends on how much damage is done, and what's underneath. We're gonna have to open up the floor and see what's going on down there."

"Okay." I pinch the bridge of my nose and take a deep breath, trying not to panic, trying to recapture the sense of lightheartedness I was feeling just a few moments ago. "What's the worst-case scenario?"

Jakob frowns. "You could need new pipes. You definitely need a new subfloor. Depending on the extent of the damage, it could be a couple thousand dollars." He meets my eyes, his gaze sympathetic.

A couple thousand we don't have. I nod, trying to keep calm and not fly into a panic. Obviously there is nothing we can do but fix it. We have to have a functional floor that we won't worry about customers falling through.

"Okay." I sigh. "Do what you have to do and let me know what you find. We'll figure out the money somehow." I wonder how in the world I'm going to afford to open my own store at the rate things are going. The repairs are eating into that ten-thousand-dollar seed money at a worrying rate. We're going to have to find the extra money for these repairs somewhere.

The bad news casts a pall of worry over the morning that isn't dispelled even by the arrival of a beautiful bouquet of flowers. A delivery guy from Petal and Pitchfork Flowers comes through the door with a gorgeous arrangement of locally grown dahlias, cosmos, and other blooms. "I'm looking for Emmie Wynne?" he asks, glancing around the construction site in confusion.

"That's me." I take the flowers from him and read the card.

May your day be as lovely as you are.—Henry

Jakob is watching me. When I glance up, he quirks an eyebrow questioningly. I ignore him and take the flowers into the office where I can admire them in peace. I put them next to the bag with my new dress in it to remind me of what is coming, what I'm aiming for. Somehow this will all be okay.

I'm in the middle of composing a thank-you text to Henry when Mom pops into the office. Dot must have brought her over. Mr. Butters waddles into the office too, and I scratch him under his chin. He's wearing a satin bow tie with daisies on it.

"Emmie, why is there a giant hole in the floor out there?" Mom asks worriedly.

I sigh, punch send on the text, and set my phone down. "Because the universe can't let only good things happen, apparently." I tell her about the subfloor and the potential cost.

"Oh dear." She frowns. Her mouth is a little pinched with pain today, and she's massaging her hands covertly. I think I need to take her to see her doctor. Her meds don't seem to be keeping up with her symptoms lately. On the list of things that are not good news . . .

"Can we afford all of these repairs?" she asks quietly.

"We can afford it," I tell her, "but I don't know how I'm going to afford to open my chocolate shop too. We need to cover the repairs plus first month's and last month's rent and a damage deposit on a storefront. And that's provided I can even find a good space for my shop. I need a miracle to find the kind of space I'm hoping for."

Not only that, but I'd still have to outfit the shop, and that takes a lot of money. I could make the chocolates here in our commercial kitchen and would only need to purchase some upgraded equipment, so the costs would not be too high from the chocolate production side. But I still need to find a storefront that looks like the one in my vision and then buy décor and display cases for it. Right now it's feeling like a herculean task.

"Oh, honey." Mom sinks into the single folding chair wedged in the corner of the tiny office. "I wish there was something I could do." She looks concerned and helpless. I hate to see her worry like this. It's not good for her. I try to shield her as much as I can, but even I can't pretend the giant hole in the floor isn't a problem.

"Ask your church ladies to say a prayer for the right space to fall into my lap," I suggest. "The right space at a price I can afford. It feels like it's going to take a miracle."

I've learned never to underestimate the praying power of a group of motivated, retirement-age women. No one can rival them for stamina and sheer force of will.

Mom spies the bouquet on my desk and brightens considerably. "Oh, those are lovely. Are they from Henry?"

I blush and she reaches out and strokes the petals of a peach dahlia. "How thoughtful of him."

We hear the bell on the front door jingle, and then Dot yells for us.

"In the office," we reply in unison. A moment later she sticks her head in the door. Mr. Butters gets up to greet her, wagging his stubby tail.

"Why is there a giant hole in your floor?" Dot asks in alarm. We explain the situation and she listens with a frown.

"Well, I'm afraid I've got more bad news for you," she says. She looks gloomy. My heart sinks. Dot never loses her can-do attitude. This must be really bad. Mom and I exchange a worried glance. "What's going on?" I ask.

Dot heaves a sigh and leans forward confidentially. "I heard this from Mary Beth over at the Nail Boat. Her husband works for the county, and he heard it firsthand. The county finally got around to voting to approve the new water and sewer codes they've been talking about for years." Dot absentmindedly scratches Mr. Butters between his ears. "They go into effect in January. All the affected businesses are going to get a letter in the mail this week about what we're going to have to do to upgrade our buildings to meet the new codes before January."

We stare at her in dismay.

"What rotten timing," I whisper, heart sinking. This is terrible news. "These are the new codes that everyone keeps saying are going to mean huge renovation bills for property owners?" I ask with a sick sense of foreboding in the pit of my stomach. They've been threatening to update the codes for years, requiring all local businesses in the county to comply with the new standards for water and sewer, but so far it hasn't happened. Until now.

Dot nods. "Everyone who owns property in downtown is on the hook for the cost of getting their property up to code."

I lean my head back and shut my eyes. This is turning into a truly awful day, and it's not even noon.

"Oh dear," Mom breathes, hand at her throat.

Dot shakes her head solemnly. "I'm not going to sugarcoat it, girls," she says. "It's bad news. And not just for you and me. There are a lot of folks who are not going to be able to pay. Some of the bigger stores can probably foot the bill, but I'm guessing at least half a dozen are going to have to close up shop and sell their storefronts because they can't afford to upgrade. Maybe more. And I'm worried I'm going to be one of them."

We look at one another in dismay. Just a few minutes ago, yellow dress on my arm, I felt like I was on top of the world. Now we're facing some huge hurdles that threaten everything I'm working toward. And many of our friends and business neighbors are going to be affected too. This is going to be a big blow to our downtown business community. I think of the little shops owned by friends who are fellow small-business owners. The Cat's Meow, Saltwater Vintage . . . Cargo Hold . . . the list is growing longer the more I think about it. This could be a catastrophe for historic downtown Poulsbo. What are we going to do?

Mom places her hand on my shoulder gently. "It'll be okay, Emmie," she says quietly. "Like your dad always said, there's always a path, even if you can't see it yet."

"This path may lead me straight to bankruptcy," Dot grumbles. "I'm just barely breaking even as it is. My mermaid-for-hire gigs are the only thing keeping me afloat, and I can only spend so many hours in the water without getting all pruney."

I think of the napkin in my purse, of the two items I ticked so confidently last night. I glance at the hem of the yellow dress peeking out of the bag on the desk. I need to open my own chocolate shop. Everything hinges on it. If I can't make it happen, how will my vision ever come true? But the mounting cost of repairs is a big stumbling block, and now Dot's news about the codes means our financial position is about to get even worse. How can I possibly make everything work out?

CHAPTER 23

Later that afternoon, after I pick Gus up from school, I swing by the store again to check in with Walt about the extent of the water damage.

"Got any good news for me?" I ask hopefully, standing over a gaping hole in the floor that is now much larger. Walt is beside me, gazing down into the hole. Jakob is actually standing *in* the hole, since Walt has a bum knee and isn't as spry as he once was. Next to me Gus is peering down into the hole with intense interest. He's taken quite a shine to Jakob and has started to follow him around like a duckling. I think he's even trying to copy Jakob's long stride, but on a slightly-less-than-coordinated six-year-old, it looks like an exaggerated swagger. It's making me giggle, which is good because all the other news is bad bad bad.

"Sorry, girlie, but looks like we've got to totally replace the subfloor in this quarter of the store too, which is going to set us back a little bit time- and money-wise." Walt hooks his thumbs in his belt loops and chews his gum loudly.

Standing in the hole, Jakob nods in agreement. He's got a streak of grime running down one cheek and his work shirt, pants, and big leather work gloves are all filthy. Apparently he's been crawling around in the space under the floor, assessing the situation.

"Your galvanized pipes are at the end of their life," Jakob explains, wiping his brow and leaving a new streak of grime across his forehead. "The whole plumbing system needs to be replaced or you're in danger of us doing all this work and another pipe failing at any moment."

"Seems you and the county agree then," I say with a sigh of resignation. "Dot told us the county finally approved the new updated codes they've been threatening forever. Looks like we're going to have to replace the entire plumbing and electrical system in this building."

Walt whistles. "That'll cost a pretty penny."

"Can I get in the hole?" Gus asks, tugging on my arm.

"Not today, champ," Jakob tells him. "But I've got an important job for you."

Gus puffs up his chest. "I can do it," he says confidently.

Jakob nods. "I know you can. That's why I'm counting on you. Can you go to my toolbox and get me a hammer?"

Gus dashes off. Jakob sits down at the edge of the hole with his legs dangling into the void and drinks some water from a stainless steel water bottle.

"Can we still go ahead with the floor repair even if the city is going to demand we upgrade the plumbing in the whole building?" I ask Walt nervously. "I don't want to do work that they'll make us redo to meet the new codes."

And how long of a delay are we talking here? Henry is only here until the end of summer. I have to get the store back up and running and turn my attention to my own shop. It feels like the clock is ticking fast. Not to mention that every day our store is closed is another day of lost business. We're bleeding money at this point.

Walt chews his gum and considers. "I've got a buddy that works over at the county. I'll ask him what the new codes are. We can bring whatever plumbing we do here up to the new code so it's already done for you in here. Then you can worry about the rest of it later when the county tells you exactly what you need to do for the whole building. That's out of my league. You'll have to bring in a real plumbing outfit to handle that big of a project."

"Okay, that's good to know." I sigh. I suppose we will wait to see what the letter from the county says, then start gathering quotes from contractors. "For now I guess just get the floor fixed as quickly as you can then."

"Will do," Walt says. "What kind of flooring are you planning to put in here? You want new carpet, or do you want to go with something like vinyl planks?"

I open my mouth and then stop with a frown. "I have no idea," I confess. "I'll have to ask Mom."

"Let me know in the next day or two so I can order it and have it ready when we need it. Don't wanna lose more time than we have to," Walt tells me.

Jakob screws the top on his water bottle and gets back in the hole just as the bell over the front door jingles and Mom pokes her head into the shop, Mr. Butters at her heels. She was over at Dot's store helping unpack new inventory. "Emmie, honey, is there any way you could run me to the pharmacy for a quick minute? I need to pick up a prescription . . ." She breaks off abruptly when she sees the size of the hole. "Oh dear me."

She comes over and surveys the damage. Mr. Butters follows

along, sitting down and staring into the hole with interest. He is grinning happily, glad to be part of the action. It must be nice to live in his doggy brain. Not a care in the world. Jakob has now disappeared into the hole and is doing something underneath the floor.

Walt nods cordially. "Gwen." He snorts in derision when he sees Mr. Butters's hot-pink polka-dotted bow tie, but he scratches the dog under the chin anyway, and Mr. Butters wiggles his stubby tail enthusiastically.

Mom purses her lips and nods back stiffly. "Walter."

"I got the hammer," Gus yells, racing back toward us with the hammer in his hand. Focused on his task, he doesn't pay attention and runs squarely into Mom, who cries out in alarm as she loses her balance and starts to fall. Her cane clatters to the floor.

In one surprisingly quick motion, Walt grabs her around the waist and pulls her up tight against him, keeping her upright. For a moment they are locked in an embrace, his strong arms clamped around her slight form. Her head comes up and their eyes meet. They're toe to toe and nose to nose. Mom gives a little gasp. Walt immediately releases her and lifts his hands as though he's being held at gunpoint.

"Years of baseball. Good reflexes," he says to no one in particular.

"Oh my goodness." Mom presses her hand to her heart, looking bewildered. I grab her cane from the floor and steady her with a hand under her elbow until she's regained her balance. I study Walt in surprise. That was impressive. Who knew he was that quick on his feet?

"You're like Superman," Gus announces, looking at Walt with a touch of awe. Then he turns to Mom. "I'm sorry, Grammy." His lower lip quivers. "I didn't mean to run into you." He's still holding the hammer. Mom steps back, putting a little more distance between her and Walt. She smooths her shell-pink cashmere sweater.

"It's all right, Gus honey. No harm done." She leans down and pats his cheek.

"You all right, Gwen?" Walt asks gruffly, and there's a note of concern in his voice that takes me by surprise.

"Yes, thank you, Walter," Mom says stiffly. Her cheeks are as pink as her sweater. "I appreciate the rescue." She lifts her chin and doesn't make eye contact with any of us. I think she's embarrassed, but I'm not sure if its because of her near fall or the gasp she made when she was pressed up against Walt.

"I can run you to the pharmacy if we go right now," I tell her.

She looks grateful. "I'll wait in the car," she says and heads for the door, leaning heavily on her cane. "Come on, Mr. Butters." The dog follows her, trotting across the bare wood floor.

"Whoa there, big guy. Watch yourself. We don't need two people in this hole." Jakob pops out of the hole and reaches out one hand to stop Gus, who is teetering on the edge, peering into the hole in fascination. Jakob takes the hammer from Gus's hand. "Thanks, pal. Now let's see. Walt, you got any jobs that need a smart, strong guy like this to help you out?"

Walt is staring after Mom with a far-off look in his eyes. He snaps back to the present. "Sure, I got some things that need hammered. Come on, squirt."

"I can take Gus with me to the pharmacy," I tell them.

Jakob meets my eyes. "He can stay. We'll keep him occupied," he offers. "If you want us to."

I pause. Across the room Gus looks up. He's holding a fistful of nails. "I want to stay," he pleads. "Walt's gonna let me hammer things."

I glance at Jakob. "You sure about this?"

He nods confidently. "We'll keep him safe."

"Okay, I'll be quick. Twenty minutes tops." Still I hesitate.

"Take your time. We've got this. Don't worry," Jakob says easily. He hops out of the hole.

"Hey, Jakob," Gus calls across the room. "Do you know there are dead people floating around in space? Animals too. From failed space missions."

"Cool," Jakob says. "How's that board coming along?"

"Almost done," Gus replies. He starts hammering.

"Okay, I'll be back soon then." I take out my keys and head out the door, struck by how quickly I find myself entrusting my son to Jakob. My support community—Mom, Dot, and Dani—consists only of women. It feels nice to have a guy choose to spend time with Gus, a man I respect and trust. And even though I'm a little leery of leaving Gus on a construction site with so many potential hazards, I haven't seen him this happy since Dad died. I know Jakob will take good care of him.

"NOT TO GIVE in to the whole cop stereotype, but . . ." Dani grabs a donut from the bag as we meet outside the walk-up counter at Byrdie's Coffee the next morning after I drop Gus at school. It's still early, but already the day is sunny and starting to warm. It's going to be glorious. I stopped at Kristensen's on the way over to meet Dani and grabbed a treat for both of us. I did *not* go to Kristensen's to see Jakob, which was good since he wasn't on the counter anyway. He's probably over at the shop right now, fixing the giant hole in the floor. Dani's technically on a shift but is taking a quick break. As we wait for our coffees, I fill her in on my magical date with Henry and the giant hole-in-the-floor fiasco.

"So wait, let me get this straight. Henry offered you a chance to compete in this fancy chocolate show in Vancouver?" she clarifies as we grab our lattes from Justin and go sit at the tiny table for two perched on the busy corner right in front of Byrdie's walk-up window counter. There's just one table, positioned in the middle of the sidewalk. Luckily for us, it's available. "And then you come in yesterday morning and find out the repairs are gonna be super expensive? And you're asking if you should enter the competition?" Dani bites the head off a maple doughboy. It looks like a gingerbread man but is made of donut dough and fried a rich golden color.

"Yes," I confirm, biting into a delicious Danish donut with a pretty twisted design. I imagine Jakob's deft fingers working this dough, and something strange happens low in my belly, a little throb of desire that takes me by surprise. I swallow hard and put the image from my mind. I have no business thinking of Jakob like that. I need to concentrate on Henry.

"Well, duh. Isn't the answer obvious?" Dani says, rolling her eyes at me.

"Is it? Enlighten me." I glance around. The intersection where we are perched is busy, cars waiting to turn in every direction. A handful of pedestrians wander by, gazing in shop windows, eating bakery treats, and walking dogs. A woman with two corgis passes our table. The morning sun is warm on my arms, and the air is perfumed with brine and a hint of something floral and expensive wafting from the spa around the corner.

"You said the competition has prize money for the winner, right?" Dani prods, biting the arm off her donut man.

"That's what Henry said. It's usually a few thousand dollars, sometimes more. But you do it more for the publicity than anything else. Winners get bragging rights, and it's really good for your business if you win." I take a sip of my hometown honey latte, extra sweet and hot and strong, just the way I like it.

"So what's the downside?" Dani asks, ripping off the other donut arm. "If you enter this competition and win, you get prestige, free publicity, and extra money to fix that hole you now have in your floor. Seems like a no-brainer. Say yes and enter." It seems so obvious, except . . .

"The downside is that I'm totally not prepared to compete on that level," I protest. "I don't have the equipment and I'm rusty at techniques. I've been working hard on ideas at night for the past week or so, but I'd be competing against the best of the best in North America. I don't think I'm up to their level. There is no way I'm going to win."

"Henry thinks you can compete at their level," Dani points out.

"Maybe Henry is biased?" I say meekly.

"Biased, maybe, but he's not wrong." Dani shrugs, licking sugar glaze from her fingers. "You make the best chocolates I've ever had. I mean, come on, Emmie. What's the harm in trying? It can't hurt, right? And maybe you'll surprise yourself and win. Then you take that big fat prize check and buy new plumbing and open your dream shop."

I nibble my pastry. "Well, when you put it like that . . ." It's a long shot. A very, very long shot. And I have only two weeks to prepare. It feels daunting, but then again, what are the other options? I already know we don't qualify for a bank loan. I spent a couple frustrating days earlier this year at the credit unions and banks in the area trying to get a loan so we could replace the failing equipment at the fudge shop.

"What else do you have to do in the next two weeks?" Dani asks. "The shop is closed. You've got the time. Why not give it a try? Come on. Be bold."

"But what if I fail somehow—make bad chocolate or come in last place?" I trace my finger over the twists on my pastry. At the intersection a truck honks and waves a waiting car through. Someone is blaring their car radio at full volume, shaking the table with the bass notes of a rap song.

Dani shrugs. "So what? You'll never see those people again. And besides, you'll never know if you don't try. What's that famous quote? You miss one hundred percent of the shots you don't take? Take the shot. What have you got to lose?"

Still, I hesitate. I'm intimidated, plain and simple. I know Dani is right, but I'm scared. I reach into my purse for my lip balm and instead of my tube of Burt's Bees, my hand closes around a glass cylinder. I peer into my purse, surprised to see the jar of gold sprinkles sitting there. How did it get in there? Last I knew, it was sitting on the shelf in the kitchen.

When Dani's radio crackles to life and she is momentarily occupied responding to the dispatcher, I covertly open the container and shake a few sprinkles into my latte.

I take a slow sip, waiting for that familiar sensation of courage to zip through me from tongue to toes. I can taste the faint floral note of the sprinkles against the sweetness of the honey latte. Dani is right. I should at least try. If I don't do this, I'll always wonder if I should have taken the shot. Maybe I'll fail. Maybe I won't. But at least I will have tried my best.

I find my phone.

I'd like a chance to compete if the offer is still open, I text Henry. Then I press send before I can second-guess myself. No turning back now.

CHAPTER 24

"What do you think of this one?" I ask early the next afternoon, popping open a Tupperware container and doling out samples of my newest creation to Dot and Mom, who are holed up in the office with Mr. Butters. Dot has the office door open so she can keep an eye on her own shop entrance in case customers come. I head out into the storefront and give samples to Walt and Jakob, who are continuing to work on the floor. They started laying the new subfloor today. "Do you like it better than the Rainier cherry and vanilla buttercream truffle from last time?"

Today I'm testing out a browned butter hazelnut toffee bonbon with caramelized hazelnut bits sprinkled on top. Since I said yes to the competition yesterday morning, I've been obsessively brainstorming my entries. Every competitor is allowed to enter up to three different original chocolate creations. I've spent all morning putting the finishing touches on this new chocolate creation to the sounds of Walt and Jakob ripping up rotting plywood, the whine of the power tools, and the low drone of a baseball game on Walt's radio.

The shop is a mess with only a partial floor, we're still waiting on the letter from the county, and I'm no closer to finding a suitable place to open my storefront. But instead of worrying fruitlessly about things I can't control, I'm focusing on upping my chocolate game to find my best three entries that are unique, delectable, and showcase local Washington-grown foods. I've got some good options, but I want to get people's opinions of them and narrow it down to the top three.

"Oh, this one is my favorite," Mom says, casting her eyes up to the ceiling contemplatively as she savors the crunchy browned butter hazelnut toffee bits. "It reminds me of English toffee at Christmas."

"I like that first peach ginger one you made better myself, but they're both winners in my book," Dot chimes in.

"Both of 'em are too fancy for my taste," Walt gripes when I ask him. "I'm a simple man. I like peanuts and maybe some nougat if I'm feeling sassy. But if I had to choose?" He takes off his baseball cap and scratches his head, thinking. "Go with the hazelnut one. It tastes real rich and buttery."

"I agree," Jakob says. He's holding a dirty pipe and lying in the hole where the floor used to be. "The flavor is more complex."

"Fancy talk from a man in a hole." Dot pokes her head out of the office and grins.

"I'm a man of many talents," Jakob deadpans.

"Well, let's see if one of those talents is nailing plywood," Walt grouses. "I'm not paying you to lie around and eat sweeties all day."

"You're not paying me at all," Jakob points out. He comes out of the hole and grabs his water bottle. He's sweaty and grimy and still manages to look sexy. It's not fair. It really isn't.

I gape at Jakob. "Wait, what do you mean? You're not getting paid?" I turn to Walt. "What's he talking about? You said you were hiring someone to help you."

Walt raises his hands. "Don't look at me," he says. "I offered to pay him like I usually do, but he won't take a dime for this job."

"You're doing all this work and not getting paid? Why?" I cross my arms and turn to Jakob, demanding an answer. He's been working at the bakery from the crack of dawn until late morning, then he comes over here and works until suppertime or later. I thought he was getting paid. This makes no sense.

Jakob looks like he's been caught doing something naughty. "Uh . . ." He casts his eyes around the torn-up store as though he'll find the answers there. "Just . . . wanted to help an old friend out." He gulps some water and looks shifty.

I don't know what to say. "Thank you," I stammer. He looks uncomfortable.

"It's nothing," he says, waving away the words. But we both know it isn't nothing. It's a big something. He's donating hours of his time every day for no pay. Why would he do that?

"I'd better get back to the kitchen." I snap the lid back on the container, feeling confused and a little uncomfortable. "The filling on this batch was great, but I want to work on the swirls of color in the chocolate shell. I'm rusty on the technique." As I head back to the kitchen, Dot leans out of the office and grabs my arm, pulling me inside. "You want to know the reason he's doing all this for free?" she asks sotto voce. "Look in the mirror, darlin'."

I recoil from her words. "We're friends," I insist in a whisper. "He feels bad for us. He's just trying to help."

Dot snorts. "No, honey. That sweet, good boy has been in love with you since you were teenagers. Looks like some things haven't changed." She raises her eyebrows and looks pointedly at Jakob, who is on his knees nailing new plywood over the gaping hole in our floor.

"That skinny, whip-smart kid has turned into a fine, fine man," she says firmly. "And you could cut granite on that ass." She admires the contours of his jean-clad backside.

"Dot!" Cheeks flaming, I beat a hasty retreat to the kitchen. I try to concentrate on perfecting the swirls of burnt orange through the deep goldenrod-colored bonbon shells, but I am so distracted by Dot's words that I don't temper the cocoa butter correctly and have to start over. Frustrated, I try to forget about anything except the tools and ingredients before me, but it proves impossible. Over and over, I hear Dot's voice in my head.

That sweet, good boy has been in love with you since you were teenagers. Looks like some things haven't changed.

Could Dot be right? Is Jakob still in love with me, even a little bit? It's been years! And I broke his heart once before. The thought that he still might harbor feelings for me makes me squirm. Not because I find his feelings distasteful, and not because I find *him* distasteful either. Quite the opposite, actually. And that is the crux of the problem.

His presence in my life is not part of the plan. He's bringing up inconvenient memories and old feelings, and he looks entirely too good in . . . well, everything, to be honest. I am supposed to be starting my love story with Henry, not letting myself get distracted by another man who is not part of my purpose in life. I need to put Jakob Kristensen out of my head and focus on my future, not the past. And for heaven's sake, I need to stop ogling him in those jeans.

Resolutely, I turn my attention back to the tasks at hand—making competition-worthy chocolates and falling for Henry Summers. There is no room for anything else right now. I need to stick to the plan.

A few hours later Dot and Mom wander into the kitchen as I'm finishing up my second attempt at a strawberry champagne truffle dipped in white chocolate. Dani is sitting on a stool keeping me company, which basically means discussing reruns of *The Golden Bachelor* and sneaking strawberries and white chocolate melting wafers from my ingredients. Dot is carrying a long white envelope in her hand. Both she and Mom are wearing sober expressions. I know instantly what she is holding.

"Is that the letter from the county?" I wipe my hands on a towel. The air is sweet with the smell of ripe strawberries and melted white chocolate. There is strawberry juice everywhere.

Dot nods. "It's not good news, darlin'," she says with a frown.

"Way to harsh the vibe, Kitsap County," Dani grouses, throwing a frown toward the envelope.

We gather around the marble slab fudge table and Dot hands me the letter. Mr. Butters sits at Mom's side, watching us with interest.

"We have until January first to have all the upgrade work completed and inspected by the county." Mom clasps her hands in front of her worriedly. Mr. Butters looks from one to the other and thumps his stumpy tail uncertainly.

"I got the same letter," Dot says grimly. "Everyone in town did."

I skim the letter, reading it aloud, taking in the long string of amended codes and the consequences—citations and fines—if the upgrades are not completed in a timely manner. I fold the letter and put it back into the envelope. I'm so tired of bad news. Why can't a letter ever be good news? A single piece of paper to say we won a house in Ireland or the lottery or even just a lifetime supply of Pop-Tarts or something?

"I'll call some contractors tomorrow," I tell Mom and Dot, setting the letter on the marble slab and rubbing my forehead where a stress headache is starting to bloom. "We need to get an idea of what this might cost. And I suppose we should talk with Sebastian and Hilda as soon as we can because we're going to need to get estimates to upgrade the entire building, and they're going to have to agree to whoever we decide to hire." We each own our own parts of the building, four shops in total.

"That's a good idea." Dot nods approvingly. "I'll check in with them and let you know what they say." She glances over at the batch of truffles I just finished. They're cooling on one end of the marble slab.

"Ooh, those look good. Can I try one?"

"Be my guest." I gesture an invitation.

"And they have those fancy gold sprinkles on them," Dot says approvingly. She chooses the biggest truffle and bites into it. "Oh, that is tasty."

"Want one, Mom?" I offer. "Dani?" Although she's already eaten two I accidentally messed up as I was dipping them.

"I'll stick with eating these yummy little wafers," Dani says, popping a few more into her mouth. "I have to run anyway." She takes a few more wafers, gives me a tight hug, and heads out, calling over her shoulder, "Text me if I miss anything!"

Mom chooses a truffle. "I could use a little courage right now," she admits.

"Me too." I take a lopsided one for myself. The flavor is sweet, but the champagne cuts the sweetness with a crisp note. The strawberry is perfectly ripe, and the crunch of the gold sprinkles adds textural interest. I taste the faint floral note, feel the familiar zing down my spine and through my tummy. We need extra courage to face this daunting letter from the county. We need extra courage to face most of life right now. I should have added more sprinkles. We may need every last sprinkle before we're through with all of this.

"You better go easy on these fancy sprinkles or you'll run out," Dot says. "I'd eat them by the handful."

I glance thoughtfully at the little glass cylinder. It's the oddest thing, but they don't seem to run out. I've been using them a lot, and the glass container is always full. Every time I pour some out, there's the same amount left. Maybe when I have my own shop, I can keep using them, putting them in special chocolates for customers who need an extra dose of courage.

Thinking about my chocolate shop reminds me of something.

"Mom, we need to decide what flooring we want Walt to order for the shop. He needs to know today so he can order it in time to be ready when they have the new subfloor installed." I start transferring cooled truffles to a Tupperware container. "Do we want carpet again, or that vinyl plank flooring might be a nice change?" I'm personally voting for vinyl. I'm not a fan of the carpet.

I look up to see Mom and Dot sharing a long glance. Mom is twisting one of her pearl stud earrings nervously.

"Emmie, I was thinking of something a little different for the floors," she says softly.

"Oh, what do you have in mind?"

Mom glances at Dot again, who nods encouragingly. "It's time, Gwen," Dot says softly.

Time for what? I look from one to the other, feeling like I'm missing something.

"I was thinking of putting in really nice wood floors, dark wood," Mom says.

My heart sinks and I hesitate a long moment. "We could do that," I say at last, "but those are expensive."

How will I ever afford to rent my own shop if we spend a lot of money for wood floors? And yet it's her money. I can't tell her no. "I mean, if that's what you really want . . ." I try to mask my reluctance.

"No," Mom says, and her eyes are sparkling like she has a secret. "It's what *you* want."

I'm confused. "I want dark wood floors in my chocolate shop, Mom," I clarify gently, wondering if somehow she's misunderstood.

"Exactly," she says, looking almost smug.

I glance at Dot, at a loss. Dot rolls her eyes. "Just tell her, Gwen," she says. "The poor thing is completely confused."

Mom takes a deep breath and nods. "You're right. It's time."

I'm officially lost in this conversation.

"Emmie." Mom reaches across the marble slab and takes my hand. Her fingers are fragile and warm against the smooth, cool marble. "I've been thinking about your chocolate shop, and how you're having trouble finding a suitable space anywhere. I'm so glad you decided you were open to finding a place here in Poulsbo. I know how few properties there are to choose from, but I think I've found the perfect place for you."

"Really?" I'm surprised. "Where?"

She takes a deep breath. "Here."

"Here?" I'm so confused. "In Poulsbo?"

"Oh for heaven's sake," Dot interrupts. "Just tell her!"

"Emmie, I want to give you the shop," Mom announces.

I stare at her blankly. "Give me the shop?"

Mom nods. "I want to give you the Happy Viking so you can turn it into your chocolate shop."

"What?" I just stare at her, sure I've misheard.

"I've been thinking about it since you said you wanted to open your own shop. That way you don't have to pay rent and you can afford to renovate it into the storefront you've always dreamed of having," Mom explains.

"But . . . but what about the Happy Viking?" I sputter. "What would we do with the store?"

Mom glances over her shoulder toward the storefront. A brief look of wistfulness flashes across her face. "Emmie, your father and I had such a good life together. We lived my dream for forty years. But everything comes to an end. No vision lasts forever. And I think it's time. I've been thinking about it for a while, wondering if it was time to close the shop for good. It's been such a struggle. I appreciate that you've tried to shield me from how bad things have gotten, but I know it hasn't been good for a long time. I just couldn't bring myself to shut it down, for the dream to be over." Her mouth turns down at the corners.

"After we lost your dad, I knew it was just a matter of time until I needed to move on." She holds up her gnarled hands. "I can't make fudge any longer. And I know it's not your passion in life. Truthfully, Emmie, I think the dream ended a while ago. I just wasn't ready to let go. But now that you have your vision for your future, it feels like the right time. It's right for me to step back and help you achieve your vision. It's what all the women in our family do. When our vision has run its course, it's our joy and our responsibility to help those who come after us. I couldn't be more excited for you. I had many good years living out my vision. It's been a sweet, sweet life with your father and this store. Now it's your turn, my girl. It's your time, and I will do all I can to help you shine."

It's such a tender speech. Her eyes are shimmering with tears, and so are mine. Dot puts her arm around Mom's thin shoulders and shoots me a sympathetic smile. "So what do you say, kid?"

"I don't know what to say," I whisper, touched by Mom's generosity. My mind is whirring. I can't imagine a world without the Happy Viking in it. This place has always felt more like home than the house where I was raised. And yet . . . I think of the tired shelving, the worn carpet, the mounting bills. As Mom said, it's only a matter of time until we have to shut it down. But I hadn't ever considered an option where we transform it from a fading candy store to the chocolate shop from my vision. Would it even work?

I try to picture the space with a makeover—dark wood floors, big windows, gleaming glass display cases. I actually find I can visualize it surprisingly easily. New floors, paint, a bold accent door color, new fixtures . . . And since we own the shop, there would be no rent. It would ease the financial pressure we're facing and lower the risk of overextending ourselves by trying to keep two shops solvent. It actually makes a lot of sense. I'd never thought of it because it had not occurred to me that it was even an option. But now . . .

"Emmie?" Mom presses my hand gently. I don't know how long I've been lost in thought while Dot and Mom patiently waited for me to come back to reality. "What do you think?" Mom asks encouragingly.

I glance from Mom to Dot. It would mean staying in Poulsbo. Do I want to commit to that? I think of Paris and LA and London. And then I think of Jakob's words, of the community my family has built here, that I've built here over the years. I think of all the people who showed up to help us pack the store. This is our circle, our safety net, ready to catch us when we stumble. If I open my store here, they will be the ones cheering me on, choosing to support me, to buy my local chocolates for birthdays and anniversaries. Somehow the thought of staying in Poulsbo doesn't feel like a straitjacket anymore. I'm surprised to find it feels like a warm embrace.

I think about my vision, standing in my own chocolate shop with sunlight pouring in the windows. I think about all the memories this family storefront holds—me toddling between the racks, Dad standing right where I am now as he showed a first-grade me how to make my first batch of fudge. Me wedged beneath the counter, licking a lollipop after school and reading an American Girl book. So many memories, so much of Dad, so much of our family's history in this place. What would it mean to start a new chapter, make new memories in this same space, to transform it for a new vision, for the next generation?

I taste the faint hint of the gold sprinkles on my tongue from the strawberry champagne truffle, feel that familiar zip of energy and optimism race down my spine. *Be bold*, I tell myself. *Have the courage to go after what your heart desires.* I want this, I admit silently. I want to keep our family shop but transform it into my shop from my vision.

"Yes," I whisper, then clear my throat. "Yes." Louder this time. After all my panic and worry over not finding the right storefront, I realize I've been standing in it all along. Life is funny that way sometimes, I guess. What you really want is often right in front of you. It's been here all along, I just couldn't see it until now.

"Oh, honey," Mom says, squeezing my hand and blinking back tears. Her eyes are happy and sad at the same time. This must be so bittersweet for her, I realize. This is the end of her dream but the beginning of something new. What will her life look like now that she is stepping back? I want more for her than picking out dog costumes and accessories for Mr. Butters. I want her to thrive in the afterglow of her vision, but I don't quite know how that would look. I squeeze her hand gently, trying to convey that I understand how hard this must be for her. Yet I know she's proud of me, and excited for me too.

"Let's go tell Walt and pick out your new floor," she says.

I send a quick text to Dani telling her to call me ASAP because I have *news*, then I follow Mom into the storefront. Looking around, I can already see it transformed in my mind's eye. *This is right, this is right*, my heart whispers, and I whisper back, "I know." I can envision it all as I turn in a slow circle, imagining my dream chocolate shop in this space. Now with Mom's generosity and the help of our community, I can finally turn my vision into reality.

Chapter 25

"Okay, folks, listen up!" Sebastian stands on a diner chair and uses his stage voice to get everyone's attention. Before he opened Seasonings he was an opera singer in Seattle, so he has a resonant baritone. He clinks a fork against a water glass for added emphasis. He waits as the hubbub in the Green Light Diner hushes. "We all know why we're gathered here. Everyone got the same letter from the county. We're going to explore our options and pool ideas to help each other. So without further ado, Emmie?"

I stand in the center of the diner, surrounded by tables full of concerned faces. There are no other customers yet. The owner of the diner opened an hour early this morning so we could gather here. It looks like more than half of the downtown small-business owners in Poulsbo have turned out for this emergency meeting to discuss the letter from the county and brainstorm a plan. We're all crowded around laminated tables in the iconic retro diner, drinking coffee and discussing the situation.

I see Hilda and Dot sitting with Mom at one table. It's before school, so Gus is sitting there too, next to Mom, coloring a rocket ship exploding. Mr. Butters, who I am sure is not supposed to be inside the diner, sits next to Mom's chair, wearing a tiny black bowler hat that makes him look like a prosperous English banker from a bygone era. Mary Beth and Paula from the boutique are sitting together at a table for two. Paula waves to me. I give her a nod and a smile. Next to them I spy Jakob's dad Gunnar, and my heart gives a little skip, but then I see that Jakob is not with him. My sense of disappointment takes me by surprise. Gunnar sits by himself, looking grumpy. I don't think I've ever seen the man smile, and he seldom speaks. But his sourdough is unparalleled.

"Good morning, everyone." I clear my throat and try to speak loudly. "We know this letter is a concern to many of us. Most of us aren't flush with money, and the costs for the changes the county is demanding look like they're going to be high. I contacted a few contractors as soon as we got our letter, and two have given me a bid so far." I nod to Dot, who passes out copies of the bids to everyone.

"Of course, every building is going to be different, but this may give you an idea of the kinds of work that will be needed and the approximate costs."

There is a moment of silence as all heads bow over the papers, reading the figures. Then the outcry starts.

"This is going to bankrupt me!" the owner of one of the gift shops protests, waving the paper in the air. "Thirty to forty thousand dollars for the work?"

"Could be less, but it could be more," Dot pipes up. "I know it's a kicker. Most of us don't have that much spare cash lying around, but we thought it was better that we get an idea of what we're facing now, as soon as we can. That way we can share ideas, pool resources, and figure out how to get through this together. Emmie's got a list of local contractors you can contact to get bids."

The room devolves into a dozen high-pitched conversations as people discuss with their tablemates. Things are reaching a fever pitch quickly as panic and indignation set in.

"An equity loan may work for some of us," Mary Beth offers loudly. "I'd talk to Pat down at the credit union and see what they can offer."

I sit at the table with Mom and Gus and write down the ideas. I'll compile a list and make copies for everyone in attendance.

"Some of this work might already be done if you're in one of the newer buildings," the owner of the local tattoo shop observes. "We've got all-new plumbing that's up to code, so it's just electrical for us."

For the next twenty minutes people share ideas, offer encouragement, and voice concerns. I scribble down anything that might be helpful. Mostly people are just venting their frustration and fear.

"I know it seems awful that the county is making us do all this," Hilda comments loudly, but then she turns to Mom. "But it might not be all bad, right, Gwen? You are in the middle of a big repair because of old plumbing."

Mom nods. "The pipes in our building are at the end of their lifespan, so it needed to be done," she agrees. "Otherwise we could have more water damage like we have now."

"What are you doing to the shop?" someone asks.

"Fixing the leak, replacing the flooring . . ." Mom glances at me questioningly. Do I want to tell the town what I'm going to do? I raise my eyebrows at her. It's her decision too. She nods her permission.

"Actually, we're doing a lot more than that," I say, getting to my feet. "We're not just repairing the damage. We're doing something entirely new." I pause, looking around at the expectant faces watching me. This is it. If I say it, then it will be real. No going back. "We're transforming the Happy Viking from a fudge and candy store into a bespoke artisan chocolate shop. My shop."

There is a moment of stunned silence and then everyone starts talking at once, giving congratulations and advice, offering to help in one way or another. I glance over at Mom, who gives me a tremulous smile. She looks equal parts proud and stricken. I understand the feeling.

A few minutes later Dot comes over as the meeting winds to a close. Sebastian is giving final instructions and making plans for the next meeting as people stand, scraping chairs across the floor, the room filling with a low hum of conversation.

"Proud of you, kid," Dot says gruffly, pulling me into a one-armed hug. "I know it's a leap of faith, but look at this community. We've got your back. We'll help you any way we can. You're doing the right thing. It's going to be great. You'll see."

I nod, feeling nervous and excited and relieved.

My phone dings with a text as I'm gathering my purse and getting ready to take Gus to school. It's from Henry.

Can I take you for dinner and dancing in Seattle tomorrow?

I don't even hesitate. After checking with Mom to make sure she can watch Gus, I text back immediately.

I'd love to!

Feeling flirty, I even add a heart emoji at the end. I have so much to tell Henry, particularly about our new plan to turn the Happy Viking into my chocolate shop. And dinner and dancing sounds fancy. Tomorrow is Saturday night and I have a hot date . . . finally. After this whirlwind of a week, I can't wait!

"MOM, DID YOU know that if you're an astronaut and go to space, you actually grow taller?" Gus asks without glancing up from the tiny pieces of his LEGO modular space station. He's sitting on a stool in the kitchen of the Happy Viking, assembling his new LEGO set while I try to finish up a new chocolate I'm creating. Joni Mitchell croons softly from my phone's Apple playlist.

"Wow, sweetie, really? That's cool," I reply a little distractedly. I'm trying to finish these chocolates before my date with Henry this evening. We had a full day. Gus had a playdate with a friend from his class this morning and then a jujitsu exhibition this afternoon. I'm now racing to finish my last truffles before Henry comes. I have to have them done before he gets here. I want to get his opinion.

"It's true, astronauts get taller in space. Also, sometimes they have to wear diapers, like babies do." Gus pulls a face at this tidbit of information.

"Really? Wow." I look up from rolling my final truffle in espresso powder, glance at the clock, and yelp. Henry is coming to pick me up in fifteen minutes. "Can you go find Grammy?" I ask Gus. "She's with Dot. Dot is going to drive you and Grammy home and then Grammy is putting you to bed tonight, remember?"

Gus nods and hops off the stool. "And I can have mac and

cheese for dinner because Grammy is cooking and that's what she gives me," he announces happily. I usually don't let him have the boxed stuff, but it's an easy dish for Mom to make and Gus loves it. I ruffle his hair and press a kiss to his head, holding him close for an extra few seconds, savoring the quick snuggle. I adore this kid. How can a human heart hold so much love and worry and protectiveness for one small human? It feels like my heart should be the size of a house to hold all that inside it. He gives me a squeeze around the middle, then trots off to find Mom. I wash my hands, whip off my apron, and hurry to the bathroom to slip into the dress and heels I brought with me from home. I had a feeling I might not make it back home to change after our busy day, so I brought everything with me. Smart move on my part.

I pull my hair back with a cute silver beaded headband and slick on a flirty coral shade of lipstick I only wear for nights out. There have been precious few of those in recent years. I can't see all of myself in the tiny bathroom mirror, but I think I look good. The dress is one I wore to a wedding a few years ago, a floaty duck-egg-blue cocktail dress that cinches at the waist and has an A-line skirt. I feel glamorous in it, like a starlet from a bygone era. It's the fanciest dress I own and it reminds me of Paris. It gives off definite Dior vibes although I got it at Nordstrom Rack. Henry told me we were going out on the town and that cocktail attire was appropriate. I hope this is good enough. It's been years since I attended anything fancier than a wedding at our local Lutheran church.

Through the bathroom door I hear the bell over the front door jingle. Probably Henry. A moment later I hear Henry's cultured tones and Mom chuckling softly and Gus's high voice, likely sharing another alarming fact about the universe with Henry.

There's also a loud, rhythmic popping sound from the nail gun. Walt and Jakob are finishing up laying the subfloor today.

The last thing I do before I leave the bathroom is shake a few sprinkles into my palm and place them on my tongue. I tuck the glass container in my purse in case I need a boost of courage. Tonight feels momentous. I want it to be perfect, and I need all the courage I can muster. Then I spritz on a little gardenia perfume and float out to meet my date. He's standing by the front door talking to Mom. Gus is over with Walt and Jakob, who appears to be letting Gus operate the nail gun on the last sheet of plywood of the new subfloor. Soon they will start installing the wood floors. I'm excited to see the shop's new look take shape.

I open my mouth to call Gus over to me, or at the very least to urge caution, but then I catch the look on his face—pure glee and determination. Jakob is instructing him, hovering over the tool and demonstrating what to do, guiding my son's small hands with his big ones. And Gus is looking up at Jakob like he's God's own truth. I pull back. I trust Jakob. He'll make sure Gus is safe. I leave them be and walk over to Henry, my heels tapping on the floor. When he sees me, his face lights up.

"Emmie, you look gorgeous," he says, kissing my cheek. The nail gun falls silent. I look over to find Jakob crouched beside Gus, staring right at me. Or rather at Henry and me. His look is fire and ice, sending a prickle of warmth along my skin as he sweeps me from head to heels. The glance he tosses at Henry is pure, chilly animosity. I shiver.

"Before we go, I've got a few more chocolates for you to try, ones I've been working on," I tell Henry. "Do you mind sampling them and telling me which you like best?"

"I'd be honored," he says.

I grab the Tupperware container from the kitchen.

"These are the top contenders for my competition entries," I tell Henry. He is not a judge for the competition—he's just hosting the awards dinner—so it's not cheating to have him give me his opinion. I trust his palate, and he moves in these culinary circles. He'll be able to provide valuable feedback.

Solemnly, he takes a bite of the first one I hand him, the browned butter hazelnut toffee bonbon, and closes his eyes, concentrating on the flavors and texture. "This is superb," he says, "but I wonder if it would be even better as a truffle, with the hazelnut toffee in a browned butter ganache? Perhaps give that a try. The caramelized crumbles on the top are perfection."

I make a note of his suggestion. Henry peruses the other chocolates carefully, and I watch him as he does so. He's looking handsome in a slim navy suit and a bow tie. It would look absurd on most men, but he looks adorable in it. I smooth my dress self-consciously, glad I chose my fanciest outfit. I don't remember the last time I got this dressed up for a date. Maybe Paris? A gala at an art museum with Romaine. It feels like a lifetime ago.

"I like the dark chocolate bonbon with huckleberry gelée, but I do wonder if it needs a bit more complexity?" Henry smiles apologetically. "Another note to give it some added dimension of flavor."

"That's great feedback, thank you!" I jot down a note to figure out how to make that one more complex. Maybe use wild huckleberries and add lavender or lemon?

Henry tastes all of my chocolate creations, offering helpful critiques for each. At last he glances at his watch. "Emmie, we'd better be off if we want to catch our ferry," he says.

I stash the Tupperware in the kitchen and grab my clutch.

"Night, baby. Listen to Jakob and to Grammy," I instruct Gus, walking over to him and bending to press a kiss on his head. "I love you."

He doesn't look up, just gives a grunt of concentration. "Bye, Mommy," he says, his attention one hundred percent on the task before him.

Jakob glances up, his gaze searching. "Be careful, okay?" he says in a low tone, glancing at Henry. He looks unhappy.

"Of course." I step back quickly, brushing away the dart of warmth I feel with his eyes on me. *Not your past, your future*, I remind myself. I cross to Henry and take his proffered arm. I smile up at him.

"Let's go."

I don't look back, but I feel the weight of Jakob's ice-blue gaze following me all the way out the door.

Chapter 26

"I hope you'll enjoy this evening," Henry tells me as he pulls the vintage Volvo he has on loan from Crisanto into the line of cars snaking off the ferry. The ferry crossing was calm and beautiful, the lights of Seattle twinkling and growing closer as we crossed Puget Sound and Elliott Bay.

"I can't wait," I reply. "Where are we going?"

"You'll see." Henry smiles. "I think you'll like it."

He's right. I wasn't aware that Seattle had a fancy dinner-and-dancing venue, but Henry has managed to find one on the waterfront. It's an intimate, posh space with white tablecloths, waitstaff who speak in hushed tones, panoramic views of Elliott Bay, and a full band in white tuxedos playing big band–era jazz. We are shown to a leather banquette in the corner of the room, the most desirable table, and Henry orders local oysters and champagne, salmon tartare, and some sort of complicated dish with smoked corn miso and fish roe. There are no prices on the menu and the food is tiny, each bite superb. I can't imagine how much this all costs, but Henry seems unruffled by any of it.

"Try this. It's delicious." He scoops a generous bite of the fish roe appetizer onto my plate. I nibble it cautiously, surprised to find it *is* delicious. I'm not the most adventurous eater, a fact that always dismayed Romaine, but tonight I'm feeling bold and daring. Henry makes it easy. He tastes everything in a way that does not seem as though he is a critic as much as an admirer of good food. We savor and sip and I feel like I'm in a dream. I can't remember the last time I wore heels. The other dates I've been on since I moved back have felt sloppy compared to this. Henry speaks French to the sommelier, who recognizes him and thaws his snooty tone immediately, bringing us a very good bottle of white wine to go with our main course—sea buckthorn–glazed black cod grilled on a cedar plank.

I recognize the label on the wine. French and very expensive. Henry seems completely at ease in these surroundings, unpretentious but comfortable. It's obvious that rarefied settings like these are familiar to him. As the meal progresses, I want to feel at ease like Henry does, but I'm not sure I do. Not entirely at least. Something feels a little off. I can fake it. I got good at faking it with Romaine, but I never felt entirely like myself. Now I find I feel the same way. I try to tell myself I'm just nervous, that I need to relax. I have another glass of wine. But partway through the main course I have to admit what I know in my heart to be true, that this just doesn't quite feel like me.

It's not that I'm not having a good time. I feel like Cinderella at the ball. It's just that this doesn't feel like me. This isn't my life. I wear jeans on a good day, yoga pants most days. Now I wiggle surreptitiously in my chair, trying to adjust my support panties.

My Spanx are constricting me. This fancy version of me is not that comfortable. I feel just a smidge like a child playing grown-up. When did my urbane Parisian polish wear off? Was it the grind of early motherhood, where even taking a shower felt like a self-care victory? Or the years spent navigating my dad's slow decline? There is nothing glamorous or sexy about the long slog of a drawn-out terminal illness, the medication bottles and side effects, the mouth sores and bedpans. Or was it the seven years of making endless batches of fudge instead of handcrafting gorgeous artisan chocolates? Perhaps all of these have slowly chipped away at the sophisticated confidence I'd managed to acquire after years living in Europe.

Or maybe that was always just a façade. Truthfully, I always felt a little like I was playing dress-up, playing at being a cool girl in Paris. Somewhere in my heart, I am just a small-town Pacific Northwest girl. This evening highlights that to me. The food is gorgeous, Henry's company warm and witty, but I don't feel totally comfortable. A small part of me wishes I were curled up at home with a bowl of Tillamook ice cream, watching *Savor* in my most stretched out pajamas. Ashamed of the thought, I throw myself into enjoying the evening. I laugh, I sparkle, I try to be at ease. I fake it and tell myself this might be the best date I'll ever go on, which is very possibly true.

"How's the book coming along?" I ask Henry as we finish our perfectly grilled fish entrée.

"Slowly," he admits, "but I'm getting there. I already had a good bit of it written before I got here. I think I have about a third of the book left to write, so that's good progress." He spears a bite of black cod, swirling it through the bright orange sea buckthorn glaze. "My goal is to be done with a first draft of the entire manuscript by the end of summer, and I think I'll make it, or at least I'll come close. I can work on polishing it up over the course of the year. I have a lot of time alone on the road to work in the evenings."

The mention of him going back on the road hits me like a punch. I'm reminded that there is a ticking clock hanging above us. I'm nowhere near ready to open my shop. At least I have a storefront and there is a subfloor now, not a gaping hole. Jakob and Walt will be laying the hardwood floors on Monday. Still, time feels short.

"When do you leave town?" I ask lightly, chewing a bite of tender grilled sunchoke, which I just learned from Henry is the edible tuber of a species of sunflower. It's tasty, with a nutty flavor.

"The end of August," Henry says. "And from there I'll head straight to Vietnam. We start filming the next week."

"How long are you usually gone when you're filming?"

"It depends." Henry sighs. "Sometimes it's a few months at a time with a break in the middle. Usually about ten weeks of filming, a break for a week or two, then back at it. I've been asked to do a special project this year that would keep me on the road longer though, a documentary about the migration and spread of popular foods around the world. It sounds interesting, but it would require me to be gone all next summer." He frowns. "I'm not sure I want to do it. I think I'm reaching a place in my life where I'm beginning to wonder just how long I can keep up this pace."

I see the opening and take it. "Do you ever think about a different life?" I ask curiously, sipping my glass of white wine. "Have you ever wanted a family or to settle down someday?"

Henry dabs at his mouth with a napkin and chooses his words carefully. "I very much enjoy my career, but if the right person came along, of course I would be open to settling down. I suppose the opportunity just hasn't ever presented itself to me." He gives me what I think is a meaningful look.

"And how would that work with your current job and travel schedule?" I ask, trying not to sound like I'm interviewing him when that is exactly what I'm doing.

He considers the question. "I don't know. I wouldn't want to give up traveling and filming entirely. I imagine I'd still travel quite a bit. I know others in my profession who manage to juggle family and career if they have a partner who doesn't mind solo parenting, keeping the home fires burning, so to speak. I suppose I've always assumed it would have to be a situation like that."

I'm surprised by my internal reaction to his words. I feel myself recoil slightly. What Henry is describing seems like a bleak picture of a marriage to me. I'm already single parenting. The idea of a partner is appealing precisely because I want someone to share . . . well . . . everything with. I long to wake up next to someone every day, maybe work with them in business or at least come home to them at dinner every night. The image Henry presents feels . . . lonely. I don't know what to do with how much I don't like the idea. This feels like a red flag or at least a yellow one, and that brings me up short. I expected all green flags with Henry, but perhaps that is unrealistic. No one is perfect. Every relationship takes work. I know this, but I guess I just expected that I'd be in the same hemisphere as my partner most of the time.

Henry turns the conversation to other things—asking about my time in Europe, sharing about his childhood in Cornwall, pranks he and his brother played on their strict headmaster, his beloved pet rabbit Crumpet. Before we order dessert he asks me if I'd like to dance, and we join a handful of other couples on the dance floor. Henry is a good dancer (he tells me his mother made him and his brother take dance lessons when they were younger), and he guides me confidently around the space, his hand strong and sure on the small of my back. We sway and glide and turn to a slow jazz song, and everything should feel perfect. I'm living the dream, the fairy tale. What I saw in my vision is starting to come true. I see how Henry looks at me, with care and interest and respect. I wonder if he can see a future together, or the possibility of one. I suspect perhaps he can. Which is why my ambivalent feelings this evening are so unexpected.

He's everything I've ever said I wanted, but there's just one problem. Now that I'm here, in his arms, being wooed and won, I find myself lukewarm. I feel affection for Henry, and respect and admiration, but I am beginning to worry about our compatibility. It seems like perhaps we do not fit in each other's worlds. What if Henry and I aren't actually all that great for each other? This thought shakes me to the core. That would mean my vision is wrong, but how could that be? The vision is always right. It's a core truth I've grown up with all my life. We stake our future happiness on those visions. How could mine be wrong? It's impossible.

I'm just tired and overwhelmed, or I'm getting cold feet, I tell myself. I have to focus on what I saw in my vision. It's all coming true, my purpose in life. How could it not be the best fit for me? But as Henry pulls me a little closer and I rest my head on his shoulder, I can't help but wonder. If this is my destiny, why do my thoughts keep straying to someone else entirely? As I turn and sway in Henry's embrace, why am I wondering what it would feel like to be held in Jakob's arms instead?

CHAPTER 27

It's late when Henry drops me at my car after we catch the ferry home from Seattle. He ends the night with a single sweet kiss, lingering on my lips for a moment before pulling back and thanking me for a wonderful evening. He brushes his thumb down my cheek, gazing at me admiringly in the warm glow from an overhead streetlight. I tell him it was one of the most magical evenings of my entire life. And it's true. It was a magical night that has somehow knocked me off-kilter.

After Henry drives off, I turn and head for the shop. I need to grab the things I left there earlier. As I walk along the quiet, deserted main street of Poulsbo, my mind is whirling. What does it mean that I am doubting if what I saw in my vision is really what I want? How could my traitorous heart play tricks on me like this? The visions always show us our true purpose in life. So how can I have such grave doubts about mine?

Wincing in my pinchy heels, I quietly let myself in the kitchen door of the shop and click on a dim light over the sink. I gather my work clothes and my big mom purse from the office where I stashed them. It's almost midnight, and everything is silent. The town slumbers around me, but I am buzzing with energy and anxiety. Setting my purse on the counter, I take a Tupperware container and start to transfer the chocolates I was working on earlier so I can store them. The espresso ganache truffle is coated in ground espresso beans from a local coffee roaster, and then I finished each one with a few of the gold sprinkles. The result looks and tastes posh and decadent.

I'm so busy with my thoughts that I must not hear the soft knock at the kitchen door. I glance up to find a large, dark figure looming in the doorway in the dim light. With a shriek, I stumble back, knocking my purse and a handful of truffles onto the floor.

"Sorry, Emmie, it's just me." Jakob steps into the room and holds up his hands placatingly. He's dressed in jeans and a flannel shirt with the sleeves rolled up, his hair pulled back in a little man bun.

"What are you doing here? It's late," I chide him, scooping up the chocolates and my clothes and purse, the contents of which are strewn everywhere across the kitchen floor. Jakob crouches down to help. My heart is pounding, and not just from fright. I'm hyperaware of Jakob's nearness as I stuff tampons and lip balm and a pack of tissues back into the purse willy-nilly. I can never find anything in this purse. Everything that goes in it seems to mysteriously vanish, as though my purse is a black hole. Gus would like that analogy. I need compartments. I need to get organized. I need to stop thinking about Jakob Kristensen, which is difficult because he keeps popping up everywhere. Case in point.

"Couldn't sleep, so I figured I'd get some work done at the bakery. I just stopped by to leave these." He straightens and holds out a small green plastic berry basket. "I found them when I was mountain biking today."

I take the basket and get to my feet. "Salmonberries?" It's early in the year for the berries that grow wild in the Pacific Northwest woods. They look like bright orangey-yellow raspberries. They're rare, with a mild, delicate flavor.

"Thought maybe you could use them for your chocolates," Jakob explains, his tone clipped. For some reason he won't meet my eyes.

"Oh." I'm touched by the thoughtful gesture. "Thank you."

I touch the fragile berries gently with a fingertip. What if I replaced the huckleberry gelée with salmonberry in my dark chocolate and huckleberry bonbons? And maybe add ginger? Crystallized ginger for a crunchy little kick? It would be unique, and very Northwestern. I glance up from the salmonberries, and realize we're standing quite close together. Jakob doesn't move. Neither do I.

He clears his throat. "Guess I'd better get going." He seems ill at ease. He still doesn't move.

I nod and set the salmonberries on the marble slab. I'll figure out what to do with them tomorrow. It was kind of him to bring them to me. "I should go too. It's late."

Neither of us leaves.

"Want to try my newest experiment?" I ask him, handing him one of the truffles that did not fall on the floor. I take another one, savoring the rich ganache as it melts on my tongue. I can taste the gold sprinkles too. I watch him roll the truffle around in his mouth and feel the sparks of anticipation and courage and desire low in my belly. Why did I choose to eat courage sprinkles now? What do I need courage to do? The smart thing would be to march out of here and take myself home right now. I don't budge.

Jakob is watching me, his expression difficult to read. He has a little gold sprinkle stuck to his lip. I almost reach out and brush it away, then stop myself. *Cut this short, Emmie*, I instruct myself firmly. It can only lead to trouble. I'm so aware of him in the darkened kitchen space with only the hum of the refrigerator and the dim glow of the light over the sink. I can almost feel the warmth of him radiating toward me.

"I'd better go." I make myself move, grabbing my purse and brushing past him, heading toward the door. He reaches out and grips my elbow.

"Emmie, wait." The words stop me in my tracks.

I turn, looking up, up. He stares down at me with a potent blend of frustration and longing that makes me shiver. I should not be here, with him. This is too tempting. He's too tempting. My eyes stray to that gold sprinkle perched on his lip like a little beacon. My fingers itch to trace the shape of his mouth.

"What are you doing?" he asks gruffly. I can't tell if he means what am I doing to him, or what am I doing here so late at night, or maybe what am I doing with Henry.

"What do you mean?" I whisper. I don't even realize I'm doing it, but I find myself moving closer to him, pulled as if by a magnet. He smells like sawdust and fresh-baked bread, a woody, yeasty scent that makes me hungry for him.

"Emmie," he says again, half groan, half warning. And then his arms close around me and I push myself up on tiptoe, wincing at the blisters on my heels.

"Are you okay?" he asks, noticing the flicker of discomfort. Instantly concerned, he holds me by the biceps, eyes scanning my body for the source of my pain.

I try to nod but I shake my head, unexpected tears pooling in my eyes. I'm not okay. I'm confused and frustrated and drawn to the wrong man. It's all wrong, and I don't know what to do about it.

"I can't do this. I should go." I put a hand to his chest, willing myself to step back. "I'll see you tomorrow." I push away from him and turn for the door, but then his big hand suddenly clasps mine, and instinctively our fingers thread together like two halves of a whole. He spins me back around to face him. There's a desperate sort of confusion in his eyes.

"Don't," he whispers, his voice gravelly with desire. "I can't . . . I can't stop thinking about you," he confesses. "I've tried, God knows I've tried. For years I convinced myself I'd forgotten you, that I was over you, and then I came home and you walked into the bakery and I realized everything I thought I'd forgotten was just waiting under the surface until I saw you again." He stares at me unhappily. He reaches out and brushes a wisp of hair back from my cheek, the calloused pads of his fingers grazing my cheekbone. His other hand is still holding mine, big and warm and so safe feeling. I never want him to let me go.

"Emmie, what are you doing to me?" he groans. His eyes lock with mine. "Tell me you don't think of me." It's a demand, a challenge. "Tell me there's nothing here." He gestures between us. I shake my head and swallow hard. I'm not a liar.

"I can't," I rasp out finally, a confession I don't want to make. It seems we're both finding the courage to tell our truth tonight. I wonder briefly what the consequences will be.

There is a brief flash of relief and victory in his eyes. "Thought so," he says, and then he pulls me flush against his body, his arm banded tightly, protectively across my back. I catch a whiff of him, sawdust and soap and sweet bread dough. I give a little gasp as his mouth comes down over mine. The kiss is not sweet, not gentle. It's pent-up longing and desire and a touch of despair. He tastes of espresso and dark chocolate, with the faintest floral hint from the sprinkle on his lip. I arch into him hungrily.

He gently rakes his fingers through my hair, pulling me closer to him, his mouth devouring, and mine meeting his. I nip his bottom lip and he growls softly, cradling my skull between his hands. My knees buckle and he turns me, walking me back a few steps until I bump into the marble slab table. Effortlessly he hoists me up and sets me on the smooth, cold marble, pressing against me, his fingers big and warm on my thighs, steadying both of us while he kisses me so thoroughly I can't think straight. I can't breathe and I don't care. I never want this kiss to stop. We're pressed so close together, straining to get closer, completely lost in each other. I wrap my legs around his waist and he pulls me closer still. I feel like my veins are filled with sparklers, shooting desire down through my body all the way to my toes. I can't deny this any longer. I want him more than I've ever wanted anyone before.

He breaks the kiss first, stepping back with a groan, dragging himself away from me. I lean back on the table, panting a little, disheveled and weak-kneed. My head is spinning. Who knew Jakob Kristensen could kiss like *that*!

"You want to know why I can't sleep?" he asks, his voice soft and rough at the same time. "That's why. I can't stop thinking about you—all the time. And tonight you came out wearing that dress, looking so beautiful it scrambles my brain." He runs his hands through his hair, messing up his little man bun. "And then you left with him, and all night all I could think about was you with him, what you were doing, if he was touching you, kissing you . . . it's driving me crazy. I'm tired of trying to fight how I feel about you, Emmie. I want you, pure and simple. I always have."

And all of a sudden like a pail of cold water, I realize what I've just done. Henry. This is all wrong.

"No!" I put out a hand, sliding off the table and inching

around him toward the door, feeling panicked. What am I thinking? "No, this is not how it's supposed to go." I am kissing the wrong man. I am falling for the wrong man. "I can't do this." I can sense the temptation to tell him how I feel rising up in me, the words balanced on the tip of my tongue, but I bite them back. I cannot allow myself to open up to him tonight. I should be kissing Henry, opening up to Henry.

I see the hurt and confusion in Jakob's eyes, but I force myself to gather up my purse and clothes again. "I've got the competition coming up and a lot on my plate. I can't . . . I just can't do this right now."

He shakes his head, a look of disbelief replacing the desire and longing. "Really? Why are you fighting this, Emmie? Am I so revolting to you? It sure didn't seem like that a minute ago." He gestures to the marble slab table where sixty seconds ago I was ready to climb him like an apple tree. My face flames. Now I can't get away fast enough.

"It's just not the right time. It's not the right thing," I babble, putting my hand on the doorknob, feeling shame and desire and confusion all rolled into one. I'm tempted to tell him the truth, but he doesn't know about the vision and I can't spill the secret. Besides, how absurd would it sound to him, that I'm trying to orient my life around a vision I had for a few brief seconds? But he doesn't understand the weight these visions carry in my family. They're infallibly true, held up as beacons and road maps and inspirations. My mom and I and generations of women before us have oriented our entire lives around what we see in those brief moments. The visions are our North Star, true and immutable. I cannot go against what I saw after I blew out Signe's birthday candle, not even for Jakob.

He is standing there in the dim light of the kitchen, hands at his sides, looking frustrated and confused, but I can't fix it. I have to keep my distance. It's for the best.

"Jakob, I'm sorry," I tell him earnestly. And then I turn on my heel and slip out the door, almost breaking into a run in my haste to escape temptation as fast as I possibly can.

Chapter 28

"What is going on between you and that fine man out there?" Dot demands, peering out of the office door at Jakob and Walt. She's just dropped by for a minute to check on the renovations during a late-afternoon lull in customers at her shop. It's almost a week after my dancing date with Henry, and in the aftermath of our incendiary late-night kitchen make out session, I've avoided Jakob like the plague. I've buried myself in my work, spending hours in the kitchen perfecting my three chocolate competition entries. I took the salmonberries Jakob foraged for me and turned them into a gelée that, when combined with crystallized ginger, made a unique and delectable filling for a bonbon. I'm hoarding the precious stuff like a dragon guarding treasure. I have just enough to make one final batch for the competition.

All week I've talked only to Walt, spent time with Gus at home as much as possible, taken a couple of walks and had coffee with Henry, and managed not to interact with Jakob at all. Unfortunately, avoiding him is having no impact on my feelings for him. I'm miserable and annoyed and worried I'm messing up my life. Damn that magnificent man who smells like pastries and can kiss like a demigod. I blow a breath out in frustration.

"Jakob's been as touchy as a bear with a sore paw all week," Dot continues with a frown. "And you're no picnic either, girlie. Did something happen between the two of you?"

"What? Why?" I say defensively, looking up from my computer where I'm trying to finalize a decision about light fixtures. Are frosted globes timeless, or are they going to look dated in a few years? I wish I had a crystal ball to tell me the answer.

"Just wondering," Dot says, holding her hands up as though to ward off my ire.

"Sorry, just feeling jumpy about the competition and worried about money with the county upgrades looming," I tell her. Which is not a lie but is not the whole truth either. I'm also struggling hard against my attraction to Jakob, and I'm afraid I'm falling for the wrong man.

"You're gonna knock those judges' socks off," Dot assures me. "You're a shoo-in to win, and then you'll have all the money you need."

I'm touched by her faith in me, but the knot of worry in my stomach does not loosen.

"I hope you're right. If I don't win, I don't know how we are going to get that money," I tell her with a sigh. The estimates from two more contractors have come in, and the news continues to be grim. They all gave similar bids. We're still looking at around thirty-five to forty thousand dollars for our building to be upgraded. That's at least ten thousand dollars apiece for which we all need to budget just for what the county is requiring us to do. "It feels impossible," I say aloud.

Dot shrugs. "You can always find a way forward," she says. "You just gotta knock on every door and have faith that one of them will open in time. We'll figure something out. I'm noodling on ideas too. We all are. I know sometimes you think you're the only one who can save things around here, but no one has to do it alone, Emmie girl. We're all in this together, the whole community." She gives me a reassuring pat on the shoulder. "By the way, that list of contractors you sent out has been really helpful. The whole business owners group is going to meet next week again to compare notes and see what anyone's come up with. Now I've got to get back to the shop."

A minute after Dot leaves, I hear the front door bell jingle, and Mom's voice calls out, "Gus, honey, slow down. Stay with me. This is a construction site." Mom walked Gus back from his jujitsu lesson so I could finish deciding on light fixtures. Gus runs into the office and throws himself into my arms, giving me a crushing hug. Mr. Butters waddles in behind him, wagging his tail. Today he is wearing a tiny top hat attached to his head with an elastic band under his chin.

"Hi, baby. How was class?" I hug Gus, holding tight. These snuggles are not forever, I realize. One day he won't want to throw himself on my lap. I'm determined to savor every day he does.

"Good. Can I have a snack?" he asks. "And can I help Jakob? He says he has a job for me." He puffs his chest out importantly. He's been helping Jakob and Walt every day after school. I don't know that he's actually being helpful. I suspect he might actually be slowing down the entire process, but he feels included, and he's learning some basic construction skills, which are both big pluses in my book. I may be avoiding Jakob, but Gus is with him every chance he gets.

"Sure, sweetie." I ruffle his hair and he squirms off my lap, eager to get on with his day. I guess cuddle time is over. I can hear Mom chatting with Jakob in the front room.

"I have a snack in here somewhere." I rifle through my purse and find a bag with a handful of sprinkle sugar cookies I'd forgotten about. "Share those cookies with Walt and Jakob if they want one too, okay?"

"Okay!" Gus grabs the snacks, yells "Thanks" over his shoulder, and runs out the office door. Mr. Butters follows him, top hat slightly askew. A minute later I hear Jakob showing Gus how to use a measuring tape, patiently instructing him to measure twice and cut once. In the past week he's shown Gus how to do a bunch of small tasks, like use a handsaw, drive a straight nail, and read a level. It brings a lump to my throat to hear his kindness with my son. I think this time with Jakob might be good for Gus's heart. He seems lighter, not so anxious and sad, and he's even returned his book on space to the library and checked out a book about construction projects.

Unfortunately Gus's time with Jakob is having the opposite effect on me. I am trying very hard to pretend Jakob Kristensen doesn't exist, a feat that is almost impossible when I find the two of them adorably tackling a project together every time I poke my head out of the office or kitchen. It's good for Gus but terrible for me. Nothing screams "sexy" to a single mom like a man who gives off great dad vibes. Ugh. It's utterly annoying. My ovaries cannot handle this.

I stand and stretch, then go to the office door to check on Gus. Yep, he's eating sprinkle cookies and helping Jakob sort screws by size. Walt is on the phone arguing with someone about materials. The renovation is coming along slowly, but progress is being made. The wood flooring is installed and looks beautiful.

The space is starting to really take shape. They're painting tomorrow and then installing the display cases and fixtures. I've been picking out fixtures and even started looking for a faux tree on Etsy. I'm still trying to finalize a door color too. I'm wavering between dark blue and goldenrod. And I really need to order the sign, but the problem is that I still have no name for the shop. I'm definitely not going with the Happy Viking. I want a name that really means something, but so far I'm drawing a blank. I need inspiration to strike me, and soon. I can't open a nameless store.

"Emmie, honey? Everything okay?" I glance up to find Mom has slipped into the office. She has a foil-lined plastic container in her hands. Mr. Butters comes in too and settles in his favorite spot by the desk with a heavy sigh. He looks at me dolefully. He really hates the top hat. It's his least favorite.

"What's in there?" I ask curiously, eyeing the container she's holding. There's a delicious smell wafting from it—sugar and blueberries.

"Oh, nothing much." For some reason Mom blushes. "Just some blueberry muffins for Walt. A little thank-you."

"Thank you for what?" Other than stopping her from falling into the construction hole, I'm not aware of anything Walt has done for Mom. And there is certainly no love lost between them, at least from Mom's side.

"Oh, I forgot to tell you in all the busyness with the renovation." She waves a hand dismissively. "The night you were in Seattle with Henry, Dot's car wouldn't start when we went to take Gus home. Walt came out to take a look at it. He gave it a jump with his truck and then insisted on replacing the battery the next time he was in the shop. Did it free of charge too, just to be nice."

"Really?" I sneak a glance at Walt, who is busy in the front room, and then look more closely at my mom. Her cheeks are pink. This is interesting. And she's put her good lipstick on, the one I haven't seen her wear in a couple of years, at least since Dad died . . .

Does this mean she's softening toward Walt? That would be a surprise twist.

"Did you know he likes puzzles?" Mom asks, looking intrigued.

"Walt likes puzzles? He doesn't strike me as a puzzler."

Mom throws me a rueful smile. "There are a lot of things about Walt that might surprise you," she says. "When he dropped off those paint samples at the house last week for you, he saw the puzzle I'm working on, the French café one with the cats? He told me he does a puzzle a week, the one-thousand-piece ones." She sounds impressed.

"Huh, really?" I try to reconcile this image of Walt as a consummate puzzler with the scruffy, blunt troublemaker I know. "That's . . . unexpected."

"I invited Walt to puzzle club," Mom announces. This does astonish me. Mom's puzzle club is composed of five ladies who meet every Thursday to gossip, drink cocktails (or seltzer in Mom's case), and do a puzzle together. It's the highlight of her social calendar. She never misses a meeting.

"I hope he likes gossip and gin and tonics," I comment.

Mom raises her eyebrows. "He told me he's been sober for twelve years. He's a sponsor in AA."

This conversation is getting more and more astounding. "But what about all the beer he drinks down at the Four Corners?" I ask skeptically.

"Apparently it's nonalcoholic. At least that's what he said." She lifts her hands in a gesture of surprise. I peer around the doorway at Walt again. So that means all the times he's gotten into mischief or arguments, he's been stone-cold sober? I don't know whether to be alarmed by that or impressed.

I look from Walt back to Mom speculatively. I haven't seen Mom this engaged in anything in a while. The years of caregiving for my dad, then the grief of his passing and her declining health, have all taken a toll. Her world has shrunk to the size of this store and puzzle club and buying doggy costumes on the internet. What if her world could expand again? What if Walt had a hand in that? It's too early to say, but I do wonder . . .

"Mom." I decide to change the subject. "Can I ask you a . . . personal question?"

"Of course, honey. Ask me anything."

I glance around to make sure neither Jakob nor Walt is nearby, then shut the door just in case. Mom looks mildly alarmed. "Emmie, is everything okay?"

"Yes. No. I mean, maybe. It's about the visions. I need to know something." I take a deep breath and ask the question I've been wrestling with all week. "Are you sure our visions always come true?"

Mom nods emphatically. "Always, yes. Why?"

I fidget with a trinket on my necklace and ask in a small voice, "What if what you see in your vision isn't really what you want? What then?"

"What do you mean?" Mom peers at me cautiously.

"I mean, what if I saw some part of the vision but maybe I'm starting to suspect it's not actually what I want? If I choose something else, will it mess everything up? Will I not get to fulfill my true purpose in life?" I glance at her anxiously.

Mom considers for a moment. "I don't know, honey. I've never had to answer that question before," she says. "I suppose I'd say it this way. The vision is an invitation, not a decree. You are in charge of your own life. The vision is supposed to help us see our purpose; it gives us a glimpse of the life that will give us the most joy and satisfaction. But we have free will. No one can force you to do something you don't want to do." She looks at me with concern. "I'd say you should follow your heart and then trust that the vision will come true in its own way. Maybe it will surprise you."

"Maybe," I murmur, feeling both relieved and doubtful. The vision seems so clear, but my heart seems to be tugging me in another direction. I'm thoroughly confused.

Mom reaches out and pulls me into a hug. She smells faintly of baby powder and a dab of White Diamonds by Elizabeth Taylor, her favorite perfume. "Listen to what your heart is telling you, Emmie," she murmurs in my ear. "Follow your heart and trust that everything will work out as it should."

Chapter 29

"What a perfect afternoon," Henry observes. He's lying propped on one elbow, dripping wet on a beach towel laid out on the wooden swimming platform anchored a little ways from shore in Liberty Bay. He's wearing red swim trunks and a pair of classic aviator sunglasses, salt water streaming from his hair and lean, nicely toned body, making little puddles on the platform.

It's late afternoon on the hottest day of the year so far. Tomorrow I leave for Vancouver for the chocolate competition, and I've taken a break from preparing my entries to have a picnic dinner and a swim with Henry and Gus. Henry invited us. He is flying to Vancouver on the earliest flight from SeaTac Airport tomorrow. He has to be at the competition before I do, and his travel was already arranged before I decided to enter. I'll drive the four hours alone after I drop Gus off at school.

Today I'm trying not to think of tomorrow and instead focus on the present. I'm still feeling conflicted about my vision and my feelings for Jakob, but I want to spend time with Henry, to give our relationship more of a chance. Today is not fancy—no dinner and dancing—just a picnic and a swim in the sunshine. I am curious to see how it feels to do something so normal with him.

We rented a rowboat from Ed, and Henry rowed us out to the floating dock that Ed puts out in the bay every summer for swimmers. It's unusually hot and sunny today, and the chilly waters of Puget Sound feel deliciously cool as I trail my hand in the ripples and keep an eagle eye on Gus, who is wearing a life vest and swimming around and around the platform.

I am trying to relax, but my mind is spinning with anxiety over the competition tomorrow. There is nothing more for me to do, however. My chocolate entries are all packed up and waiting in the shop kitchen. All that remains is for me to drive to Vancouver tomorrow morning.

I slather on a little more sunscreen and try to enjoy the day. Farther out, the bay is busy with sailboats and speedboats and a few Jet Skis. There are even some folks waterskiing, waving as they go by. I'm wearing a bubblegum-pink swimsuit cover-up, a polka-dotted bikini, and big white cat-eye sunglasses. I don't get to wear this outfit very often because ten months out of the year it's too chilly for swimming here. But today is a rare and welcome exception.

We're sharing a bottle of chilled sauvignon blanc, and Henry brought an assortment of nice cheeses. I bought bread from Kristensen's Bakery, trying to ignore the fact that Jakob most likely kneaded this bread by hand himself. That feels weirdly intimate as I slice off thick rounds of it and spread it with goat cheese and layer on smoked salmon. I am trying not to think about Jakob at all. I want to give Henry my full attention today.

"Look at me, Mommy! I'm going so fast, like a shark!" Gus calls as he paddles past the ladder, huffing in exertion. He hasn't eaten lunch yet, too excited by the rare prospect of a swim. I wave to him.

"Good job, buddy. Keep swimming fast!" I tip my head back and briefly close my eyes, just for a moment. *Follow your heart. Follow your heart and trust that everything will work out as it should.*

I've been replaying Mom's words in my head for days. I'm still not sure what exactly they mean, but I've decided to try to be honest with myself, to follow my heart and see where it leads me. At this point, I'm not sure where that is. I like and respect Henry. I'm drawn like a magnet to Jakob. Henry is leaving town in a few weeks, so my chance to figure out my feelings is growing short. I've decided to lean in with Henry, to be honest but also give us a little more time. It would be so tidy if I fell in love with Henry. Everything would make sense, tied up with a bow. But I can't contort my feelings or force myself to love someone. Today is about exploring more of what I feel for Henry. I'm eager to see where this goes.

"Thank you for joining me this afternoon, Emmie," Henry says quietly. My eyes fly open. There's something in his tone that feels laden with meaning. I glance at him, trying to read his non-verbal.

"It sounds like there's a 'but' there," I say lightly.

He shakes his head. "Not a 'but.' It's just that summer is coming to an end sooner than I'd like," he muses, taking a sip of his wine from a stemless wineglass. "I'm going to miss this town. I haven't stayed in one place this long in . . . years, I think. This summer has been unexpectedly wonderful." He rolls the wine around in his glass. "I see now what I've been missing, and I've had a realization."

I feel something important is coming. "What's that?" I pop a grape into my mouth and keep one eye on Gus and one on Henry.

"That I'm going to miss not just this town but you, Emmie." Henry glances up and takes off his sunglasses, his hazel eyes clear and frank. "I know we haven't known each other long. It's early days yet, but I hope you know how special I think you are." He looks at me with such earnestness that my pulse starts to quicken. He keeps talking.

"You're lovely, and talented, and a pillar of your community. Everyone adores you, and I quickly came to understand why. You're an intelligent, kind, creative woman. And beautiful. It's rare to find those qualities in a person, and rarer still to find you can laugh with them and feel at ease with them. I feel all these things with you, Emmie." Henry pauses and gazes out at the bay, a small, thoughtful smile quirking up the corner of his mouth.

"You've made me realize how lonely my life has become. As I've seen you here in your community, seen you being such a good daughter to your mum and a great mother to Gus, I've become aware of . . . a hole in my life . . . a lack. I didn't know it was there until I saw what I didn't have, what your life is full of—love, community, taking care of others and them taking care of you." He shifts and his face falls into a pensive look. "I want that, Emmie. I want to belong somewhere, to come back to someone. I'm tired of being alone, of not having a place to come home to. And if I'm perfectly honest, I don't want to say goodbye to you. I like you very much. I respect you. Dare I say I want you. And I hope we can continue our time together. So I was wondering . . ." Henry pauses, choosing his words carefully, glancing at me a little shyly. "If perhaps you would consider still seeing me even after summer's end? Even when I'm on the road? I'd like to see where this could go."

Where this could go? Henry is asking to explore a relationship with me? Wow. This is big. I take a moment to consider my answer. I should feel elated, but instead I feel unexpectedly cautious. I glance at Gus, who is paddling a few feet away from the platform, on his back and looking at the sky.

"I'm honored, Henry, really," I say. I see his look slide toward disappointment and hasten to assure him. "I'm not saying no. I like you too, a lot. I mean, I've watched *Savor* for years and of course thought you were cute and sweet and kind. But then I met you and you're all those things, but so much more. You're intelligent and thoughtful and a genuinely caring person. It's been such a wonderful surprise to get to know you for real these past weeks. So I'm not saying no. I'm just curious. How could this work? What would it look like?"

Henry looks relieved and twists a few green grapes from a cluster. He sits up, arm slung over his bent leg. He looks like a model for a 1950s swimwear commercial. "Well, my life will still involve a fair bit of travel. I'm contracted for four more years of the show, so the reality is that I'd be away a lot." He frowns regretfully. "You could come meet me now and then though, on location, if you wanted to. You could see a bit of my world. I'd love to take you home to Cornwall and introduce you to my mum someday if all goes well. But when I'm not traveling, I imagine I'd base myself here. I could rent a place when I'm back, just so we could take things as slow as you like. I've grown very fond of this town. I'd like a chance to spend more time with you here, to give us an opportunity to see what we could become, if you're willing." He darts me a quick glance.

"I need to think about it," I tell him slowly. "And I'm honored you would ask."

It is not how I imagined life with a partner. Could it work between us if he's gone so much? I take a bite of Jakob's delicious bread, trying not to think about him kneading this dough, the golden hairs on his bare forearms dusted with flour, those big fingers twisting and kneading the loaf. *Concentrate on Henry*, I tell myself.

"Take all the time you need to think it over. Answer when you're ready," Henry says reasonably. "I'm not asking for any sort of commitment. I'm asking you to consider giving us a chance to explore what this could be between us. But you have to decide if this is right for you and for Gus, of course."

We both look at Gus, who is climbing up the metal ladder to the platform, breathing heavily.

"Here, sweetie." I hand him his insulated water bottle and a towel, and he collapses next to me and drinks thirstily.

"Guess what, Mom?" he says solemnly when he's done. "Big news. I don't want to be an astronaut anymore."

"Oh, really?" I try to hand him a slice of bread with goat cheese and salmon, but he dodges the sandwich and grabs a sugar cookie with sprinkles instead, grinning mischievously. "What do you want to be?"

He squints at me. "A plumber," he announces. "Or a construction guy. Like Jakob." He takes a big bite of the cookie. I put the gold sprinkles on top, just for Gus, for courage.

My heart gives a little kick hearing that name coming from my son's mouth. "That's great, sweetie," I tell him, pulling his wet little body in for a quick hug.

"Those are sensible jobs," Henry interjects with a smile. "I wanted to be a garbageman when I was a kid."

From what he's told me, I know Henry doesn't have a lot of experience with kids, but he's pretty good with them. He treats them like he treats everyone, with civility and kindness. He talks to Gus like he's talking to an adult. Kids respond well to that. Gus nods importantly and puffs up his chest. "Yeah, maybe I won't go to space. Maybe I'll build stuff instead." He crams the rest of the cookie into his mouth. "Thanks for the cookie, Mom. I'm going to go around this platform ten more times," he tells me, and jumps off the platform. "Watch me be brave and strong."

I look at him as his head bobs to the surface of the water and he starts paddling noisily again. He looks like a sleek little seal. What would it mean for Gus if I have a partner who is absent most of the time? Perhaps it wouldn't bother him. After all, he's used to the absence of a father figure by now. Well, not used to it. He still misses my dad fiercely. We all do. But he's adjusted. Kids are so resilient.

However, just because he's adjusted to something doesn't mean it's the best thing for him. I've always dreamed I would find someone who would be present as a husband and a father. Who would be a partner in work and parenting and homelife, who would go to bed with me and wake with me in the morning, who would sit at the dinner table with us, who would stand hand in hand with me in all the little messes and decisions in life. Is it enough to have a partner who is there some of the time but misses much of the day-to-day reality of life? Could I be happy with a relationship over Zoom and text and phone calls for long stretches of time? Could I be happy with Henry and what he's offering? I don't know. I need to think about it.

"When you imagine your life," Henry asks thoughtfully, wrapping a slice of prosciutto around a date, "what is it you really want, Emmie?"

The question surprises me. I consider it for a moment and find myself stymied. On the one hand, I can conjure up my birthday vision and point to it as my North Star. But then I wonder if that is really being honest with myself. I think of the vision—Henry on one knee, the shop flooded with afternoon light, the dress that glows like sunshine itself. Those are all things I want—my own shop, the love of a good man—but that is just a moment in time. A beautiful moment, but just a moment, a snippet of a few seconds. What kind of life is underpinning that moment? What life leads up to that moment? I find I can't quite imagine it.

"I don't know what I want," I admit to Henry in surprise. "I haven't really given it much thought in a long time. I haven't had the space to ask myself the question."

I've spent years waiting for the vision, holding off on planning too much or hoping for too much while I waited to see what my future held. And then when my dad got his diagnosis and I found out I was pregnant with Gus, my life became about serving others, not about what I wanted anymore. It was about what the people I loved needed from me.

I remember the phone call—Mom and Dad were both on the landline in their house, I was just off a long shift at the Genin workshop. Dad's voice was heavy as he shared what the doctors had found in the scan. Since that moment, my life has not really been my own. It's been sacrificed for others—Dad when he was sick, Mom as she faces deteriorating health, Gus as he grows, and the store as it faltered slowly, so slowly. All of these things have been on my shoulders for so long that I don't know how to imagine a life where I am not tied to these responsibilities.

"But surely you have dreams?" Henry asks gently. "Things you hope for?"

I flush and reply quickly, "I mean, yes, of course. I've always wanted to open a chocolate shop, among . . . other things."

But what other things, exactly? The question is flustering me, because honestly, I'm not sure what other things I want. Somewhere inside the demands of being a daughter and a mom, a business owner, a caregiver, an accountant and fudge maker, a driver and home cook, a scheduler, a nurse and organizer, I realize I've lost my sense of just being Emmie. I have been using all my time and resources, brainpower and willpower, to keep our family together as best I can, and somewhere along the way I've lost all sense of what I want, who I am, and the life I dream of.

It happened so gradually, I didn't realize it until now. I've been sandwiched between responsibilities for so long that I cannot quite recall who I am or what I want without all the demands pressing in on me from all sides. What does Emmie want? Much to my chagrin, I have no earthly idea. It's been many years since I had the time or energy or opportunity to ask that question and figure out the answer.

Henry seems to pick up on my inner turmoil. He lays a hand gently on my knee, and the warmth is comforting. "We don't have to figure it all out now," he tells me. "It's okay to see how things go. If you're willing, I'd love to keep seeing you after I leave. Take some time and tell me if that is something you want."

He sits up, checks his watch, and winces. "I'd better get back to the house and pack my suitcase. My flight to Vancouver leaves at five a.m."

"Gus, one more lap, honey, and then we have to go," I call to Gus, who is tirelessly paddling round and round the platform, narrating as he goes. He seems to be pretending he's a superhero of some sort. Aquaman, maybe? Henry helps me repack the picnic supplies—corking the half-full wine bottle, wrapping the cheeses in their white paper. "How are you feeling about the competition?" he asks.

I sigh. "Nervous. Unprepared."

I'm as prepared as I know how to be. Truthfully, I'll probably never feel prepared enough for a competition of this caliber. I've done the best I can, and I have to trust my chocolates and rest in the knowledge that I am presenting my best. Whatever happens during the competition is out of my hands.

"Don't worry," Henry says reassuringly. "The hard part is behind you. You've got three strong entries. You should be proud of your work, and I think the judges will agree."

Picnic hamper packed, he stands and I join him, shaking breadcrumbs from my cover-up.

"Gus, time to go," I call, and Gus paddles toward the ladder, complaining about having to leave the water but obeying.

Back on shore, we return the rowboat to Ed, and Henry walks us to our car. Gus trails behind me, dripping wet and pretending a stick he picked up is a nail gun. He's making rat-a-tat sounds and nailing everything in sight.

"Thank you for a lovely late afternoon," Henry tells me when we get to my old Honda. He puts the hamper in the trunk and reaches to give me a hug. I inhale the elegant tea scent of him, mixed with briny ocean water. He's still a little bit damp. "I'll see you in Vancouver at the awards dinner," he says. "I'll be cheering you on. And afterwards we could grab a drink if you'd like. I know a great little spot for cocktails. The owner is a friend of mine."

"Sounds perfect." I'm so nervous about the competition that I can't enjoy the fact that Henry wants to take me out afterward. I force a smile anyway.

"Good luck and don't worry, Emmie." Henry meets my eyes with an encouraging smile. "You'll be great." He presses a quick kiss on my cheek. "Call me when you get to the hotel, okay?"

"Thanks," I murmur. "I will."

Then I turn and call for Gus to get in the car. It's time to head home. I'm bone-deep weary after pulling too many late nights in the kitchen making variation after variation of my chocolates, making tiny adjustments to technique and temperature, ratios and measurements. Now I need to sleep, wash my hair, and find my most professional outfit. I've done all I can to showcase my skills and creativity. Now it's time to rest and get ready. Tomorrow I will find out if all I have done is enough.

Chapter 30

"Are we drinking consolation or celebration wine?" Dani asks when she finds me sitting on the steps of the pavilion at Liberty Bay Waterfront Park at dusk, drinking the rest of the sauvignon blanc picnic wine straight from the bottle. A light, briny breeze snaps the Scandinavian flags behind us in the fading blue light. The air is cool and brisk enough to raise goose bumps on my arms.

"Don't know yet. Too early to tell." It's growing late and I should be getting home, but Gus is in bed, Mom is curled up with Mr. Butters in front of an episode of *When Calls the Heart*, and I just needed a little space. I drove into town intending to do some work closing out the bookkeeping for the Happy Viking, but after I parked I detoured to the pavilion instead. My mind is jumpy and I can't concentrate on numbers right now. I keep replaying the conversation with Henry in my head. Him asking me what my dreams are. Me having no answer. How sad is that?

I notice Dani is wearing a super-cute short orange dress and high-heeled sandals, and remember she had plans for the evening.

"How was your date?" I ask as she settles herself beside me on the wide steps looking out over the bay and marina. In the twilight I can just see the swimming platform where we picnicked with Henry earlier. I can smell cheeseburgers cooking from a restaurant somewhere downwind, mixed with the scent of the sea. I offer her the bottle of wine and she takes it.

"Lame," she says and tips the bottle to take a swig. "I saw your text asking me to meet you here, so I said I had to go help a friend with an emergency. Asshat didn't even ask what the emergency was or if you were okay, just asked if I wanted to hook up later." She grimaces and hands the bottle to me. "So obviously I'm free for the rest of the evening since I won't be taking him up on his generous offer. Remind me, why are we drinking at dusk in a public park?"

I'm pretty sure we're not supposed to be drinking alcohol in the park, but since a member of the Poulsbo police force is currently sharing the bottle with me, I guess we are okay bending the rules a little tonight.

"Henry asked me if we could keep seeing one another after he leaves," I tell her. I take a swallow of wine and stare out across the bay.

Dani whoops loudly and pumps her fist in the air in victory. "Yes! This is celebration wine then?" she clarifies with a big grin.

I hesitate.

She reads the pause and instantly sobers, pulling back and looking at me. "Whoa, okay. Catch me up. What's going on?"

I tell her about the picnic conversation on the bay today with Henry, and how confused that conversation made me feel.

"But this is exactly what you want, right?" Dani says, wrinkling her brow. "This is your future. The women in your family live for these visions. You've been waiting years, and you finally got yours and it's amazing. So what's the problem?"

"I don't know," I admit.

"Wait, let me get this straight. A super-cute, hot, famous, and probably rich TV star who also happens to be a really nice guy asks you to be his girlfriend and you're sitting in an empty pavilion in the dark drinking leftover wine and not celebrating, because why?" Dani looks exasperated. It sounds ridiculous when she says it that way. Why am I not jumping for joy at Henry asking to date me?

"I know, I should be over the moon, right?" I sigh. "I mean, everything is lining up." I set the bottle aside and take the napkin list from my purse and smooth it over my knee, reading it in the dim light.

Dani cranes her neck and reads it too. "Everything is going great for you, Emmie," she says quietly, "so what's the problem?" Her eyes on me are probing. She knows me so well, maybe too well. I can't hide anything.

"Jakob," I say shortly.

She mutters a swear word. "I knew it! I knew there was something going on. And you didn't tell me?" She turns on me indignantly.

I shrug. "There's not much to tell. We kissed the night I went to Seattle with Henry. When we got back from dinner, Henry dropped me off at my car. I walked to the shop to grab the stuff I'd left. It was late. Jakob came into the kitchen and it just . . . happened."

I think of that kiss, the lightheaded feeling of desire, my knees turning to jelly. His frustration and pent-up longing. How safe and good I feel when I'm with him.

"How was the kiss?" Dani asks, peering at me.

I sigh. "It was the best kiss of my life." Sadly I take a swallow of wine.

"Okaaay." Dani draws the word out. "But, I mean, you guys have always had a strong connection, even when he looked more like a string bean than hot Thor. It's natural you guys would still have a spark, right? Just because he's hot and bakes amazing pastries and gave you the best kiss of your life doesn't mean he's what you want in a life partner. You can want to get in someone's pants and not want to put a ring on it, you know? You've got to keep your eye on the prize." She emphatically taps the list with one fingernail. "You're this close to getting everything you want. Don't get cold feet now."

I squirm uncomfortably. "You're right, you're right." Of course she's right. What am I even thinking? So I'm attracted to Jakob. Who wouldn't be? It's only natural. But what I saw in my vision—that is the best thing for me, right?

I'm trying to convince myself of this until I recall Mom's words when I asked her about the visions, her advice to follow my heart. That's the kicker. I can follow a list. I can follow a vision, but I'm out of practice at following my heart. I've spent years responding to everyone else's needs instead. I have to get back in touch with my own desires again, figure out what I really want. The thought is mystifying. How do I go about doing that? What if I mess up?

I think of Henry today on the dock, shyly asking for a chance with me, to see where our relationship might go. He is everything I've said I wanted. Sure, a life with him would take sacrifice and look different than I expected, but no partnership is perfect. I don't need it to be perfect; I just need it to be right for me. If it is right though, why do I feel so conflicted? How can I reconcile what is in my heart with what I saw? I worry my lower lip in indecision, then sigh.

"Right now everything feels like such a muddle," I confess to Dani. "I'm tired and overwhelmed and nervous . . ."

"And sexually frustrated," Dani offers cheerfully.

"Probably," I admit. "I just don't know how to make things come out right."

"You can't," Dani says bluntly, reaching over me and grabbing the wine bottle. "Stop trying to control everything, Emmie." She elbows me in the ribs affectionately. "You've got to let go a little and see what happens. Take the next right step. See where it takes you."

I know good sense when I hear it. "You're right," I admit. "I'm not going to solve everything tonight. I just need to take the next right step." I tuck the napkin list back into my purse. The next right step tonight is to go home, wash my hair, drink a tall glass of water, and get some sleep. Then, tomorrow, Canada. And after that . . . I'll just have to wait and see.

CHAPTER 31

The day of the competition starts out so promisingly. I drop Gus off at school, car loaded, ready to head north toward the border. In the drop-off line, he unbuckles his seat belt and clambers from his booster seat, wrapping his arms around my neck.

"Good luck, Mommy," he says. This morning he smells like protein waffles and maple syrup. "I hope you do good on your test. You worked hard and that's what matters. I'm proud of you!" I smile hearing my own words parroted back to me. "Here, these are for you," he says, pulling back and unfolding his hand. In his palm are a few slightly grubby gold sprinkles. "I saved them from my cookie yesterday and kept them in my pocket," he tells me. He scrapes them into my waiting palm and kisses my cheek.

"Thanks, buddy," I reply, touched by his thoughtfulness. "Do you want one today too, for school?"

He nods. "We can each have one," he says solemnly. "So we can both be brave today."

We each eat a sprinkle. I try not to grimace at the bits of lint and slightly gray hue of my sprinkle. Who knows what else has been in that pocket.

"Love you, buddy," I tell him. "Go get 'em, tiger." I ruffle his hair and he squirms away, smiling.

"Go get 'em, Mommy," he tells me, pressing a quick, sloppy kiss to my cheek.

Then he grabs his rocket lunch box and his backpack and heads into school. I watch him go, smiling fondly at my little guy trudging up the walkway, being brave in his own way. I'm so proud of him, of all he's weathered, of how he's growing. Then I pop an aspirin and wash it down with coffee, trying to dispel the headache brought on by the wine last night with Dani. That was a mistake.

Gus disappears inside the doors and I take a deep breath and turn my car toward Vancouver. I've got a double-shot latte from Byrdie's, liberally festooned with gold sprinkles from the jar I've wedged in a cup holder in the console, and I've got snacks, my passport, and most important of all, the chocolates, nestled like babies in containers wrapped in thermal packaging in the back seat. I don't have them on ice, as that could negatively affect their texture, so I have to keep the car below seventy degrees to make sure they're not affected by the heat. Because today, uncharacteristically, is going to be a scorcher, even hotter than yesterday. I can already feel the heat and humidity rising.

While the Pacific Northwest enjoys about eleven months of cool, mild weather, we usually get a few weeks of uncomfortably hot weather in the eighties and nineties. On rare occasions the thermostat might even reach one hundred. Folks like us are used to fifty degrees and rain, so we feel like we're being baked alive on days like this.

But I've got air-conditioning in my trusty old Honda, and in three and a half hours, if all goes well, I'll be delivering my chocolates to the hotel in downtown Vancouver where the competition is being held. My entries have to be there by two p.m., which means I've got a little more than an hour of wiggle room. The border can get backed up now and then, but I'll cross midday, so it should be okay.

I slide on my sunglasses, check the air-conditioning temperature and bump it down another degree just to be safe, then put on my girl-power playlist and head north for Canada.

The first few hours of travel are uneventful. I catch a ferry from Bainbridge Island to Seattle almost immediately and sigh with relief at the first hurdle crossed. Traffic in Seattle is light and I breeze northward to the strains of Bonnie Raitt, Carole King, and my beloved Joni Mitchell. I keep an eye on the temperature inside the car. A quick glance at the weather app on my phone shows me it's in the high eighties already outside and climbing. Today Vancouver is supposed to reach a whopping ninety-seven degrees. Nervously, I put gas in the car at a gas station north of Seattle and use the bathroom. As I start to pull away from the gas station, I say a quick prayer for my air-conditioning, which, to be honest, in the last few miles has started to make a strained sort of chirping rattle I've never heard before.

"It will be fine," I tell myself firmly. But just to be safe, I turn around and buy a bag of ice at the gas station and stash it in the trunk. If something happens, it's better to have chocolate that got a little too cold than half-melted chocolates ruined by the heat. I text Dani and let her know how things are looking.

Ask your Abuela Rosa to say a rosary for my air-conditioning! I tell her, then shake a few sprinkles into the last inch of my latte and put my foot on the gas, heading north again, pushing the speed limit, eager to get to the hotel and register my entries. Dani texts back with a thumbs-up and a praying symbol.

Everything okay? she asks.

So far! I tell her.

Everything holds steady as I whiz past Everett and Bellingham. The peculiar sound coming through the vents is getting louder though, and I turn the temperature up a few degrees, hoping that will ease the strain on the cooling system and maybe help a little. Even though it's comfortable in the car, I'm sweating through the underarms of my one professional-looking linen sheath dress from stress. I google "car ventilation is chirping," and the results are varied, though none of them are good. I keep driving.

Mom calls as I near Canada.

"I'm almost to the border," I tell her. "Say a prayer for the air-conditioning though. It's sounding weird and I'm worried."

"Okay, sweetie, I will. I'll get the ladies praying too. Drive safe and don't worry," she tells me. "And remember, Emmie, nothing is really the end of the world, okay, sweetheart? No matter what happens."

I know she means those words to reassure me, but they are not reassuring at all. They feel a little ominous. She's right though—nothing is the end of the world, but the stakes are high for this one. We need the money to pay for the plumbing upgrades and the rest of the renovations. And even more than that, winning this competition would be a tremendous boon to my visibility and reputation in the chocolate world. Although it's just a chocolate competition, it feels weighty with significance.

I put my hand in front of the vent. Is it my imagination, or does it feel like the air coming out now is warmer than it was a few minutes ago? I push the accelerator down further and zoom toward the border as fast as I dare. Ten minutes later, as I slide into an unexpectedly long line at the Canadian border, the air-conditioning goes out entirely. I feel the warm puffs of air blowing against my face.

"Oh no, no no." I glance in the rearview mirror, wondering if I can turn around and make it back to Blaine to buy some more ice, but I'm already trapped by half a dozen cars behind me. I'm stuck in this line until I get through the border. There are an unknown number of cars in front of me. The line is snaking around a bend and I can't see the border checkpoint booths ahead of me yet. This is not good. I check my phone. It's ninety degrees and the car is sitting in full sun. Feeling jittery and starting to panic, I tap my fingers on the steering wheel, praying desperately for the line to move. It doesn't. I turn the cooling system on and off, over and over, to no avail. The air-conditioning has given up the ghost. I can feel the temperature steadily starting to climb as I sit in the sun. The line does not move. Time for the emergency ice.

Jumping out of the car, heart pounding with adrenaline and dread, I open the trunk and grab the bag of ice, which is already partly melted from the heat. Hopefully it will be enough to keep the chocolates cool until I can get to the hotel. Nervously, I make a little nest of ice cubes in a plastic grocery bag and place the containers of chocolates carefully in the bag, surrounded by the ice. I cover the entire thing with the picnic blanket I keep in the back of the car, trying to insulate the cold and keep the ice from melting.

From my phone's playlist, Bonnie is plaintively singing about not being able to find her way home, and it feels so grimly ironic I skip it immediately. Joni comes on, a relief. I shake some sprinkles from the jar into my mouth. They help a little. But as the minutes drag on and the temperature climbs, I find myself panicking by degrees. I'm stuck in this line, completely helpless. I drum my fingers on the steering wheel and try not to scream in sheer frustration. How stupid was I to trust my old Honda's ancient cooling system? Why didn't I think of a better backup than a melting bag of convenience store ice? I text Dani another update, letting her know things are not going well. She texts back a tearful emoji.

Abuela says to tell you she is praying a special rosary for the car right now! she assures me. Unfortunately it doesn't seem to help. The line moves a few cars and my heart leaps, but then we stop again. Twenty more minutes in the sun. The temperature outside is ninety-two now, and I've pulled up my sheath dress as high on my legs as I can, trying to cool down. Now my thighs are sticking to the seat with sweat. I'm panicked, blood pressure probably through the roof. I sneak a peek at the chocolates in their plastic containers. The ice is mostly melted, but the chocolates are okay so far. I blow out a long breath and try to think positively. I pour a few sprinkles into my palm and lick them up. My palm is salty with sweat. I need more courage now than maybe ever before.

Thirty more minutes pass and I've only inched forward a few car lengths. I check my phone. Ninety-three degrees. And now I've got a new worry. If I don't get through the border soon, I'm going to miss the deadline to submit my entries. This entire trip, and the weeks of preparation, will be for nothing if I can't get my entries there in time. I pound the steering wheel, feeling half crazed with stress.

My phone dings with a text. It's from Henry. *How's it going? Looking forward to seeing you*, with a cute heart emoji.

I start to tell him what's happening, then hesitate. For some reason I'm not eager to share the emergency I'm currently facing. I send him a lame yellow thumbs-up and close my eyes in sheer impotent frustration. I put my head on the steering wheel and pray the line moves. It does not. Slowly, I start to despair.

Twenty-two minutes later, I finally get through the border. It's fifty-five minutes to the hotel, and I have exactly one hour until the competition deadline window closes. The car is almost unbearably warm. I reach back and feel inside the plastic bag. The ice is now almost entirely water, seeping out onto the carpeted floor of my car, but the containers holding the chocolates are cool to the touch. I turn around, brace my hands on the steering wheel, and race for Vancouver.

Chapter 32

Exactly fifty-nine minutes later, I push through the revolving door into the lobby of the big corporate hotel in downtown Vancouver and race to the entry table outside the conference room. I'm red-faced, sweaty, and gasping for air, but I am not too late. I have made it just in time. The woman sitting behind the registration table with her hair in a sleek bun looks alarmed by my disheveled appearance, but I simply set the ominously warm and still-wet containers on the table and wheeze out my name. I have one minute to spare. I didn't even stop to check the chocolates when I got here. There was no time. I hope they're okay. It would be the miracle I desperately need today.

She thumbs through a list. "Ah yes, Ms. Wynne. Here you are. And I see you have three different entries today?"

I nod. "That's correct." I'm trying to catch my breath.

"Excellent. Fill out these forms for me and then you can go on in. They'll start the judging in just a few minutes."

I hastily scribble down the necessary information on the forms for each entry, feeling weak with relief. I made it! I really have to pee and I'm a sweaty mess, but I made it in the nick of time.

I hand the completed forms back to the woman. "Can I go to the ladies' room?" I inquire hopefully. "Before I go in?"

She glances at the clock and frowns. "I'm afraid not. They're starting the judging in a minute or two. You need to go find your table now."

With a resigned sigh, I head into the large conference room. Just before I go in, I place a few sprinkles on my tongue, then square my shoulders and head inside. Around the room, long tables are set up with all the entries displayed. Standing behind their entries are my competitors, about two dozen of them. I smooth my crumpled dress and wish I'd had a moment to freshen up somehow. And pee. I really need to pee. I'll just have to hold it. I'm convinced that one of the superpowers moms develop is the ability to hold our bladders for long periods of time. It's not comfortable, but I'll be okay. I made it. I still have a chance.

I find my spot in the middle of a table near the center of the room and set out my Tupperware containers. I'm flanked by two competitors, an intense-looking young man dressed in an immaculate pastry chef uniform, including the double-breasted white jacket and poofy chef's hat, and a woman who looks to be in her fifties with a crew cut and a stern expression. She's wearing a plain flannel shirt and jeans and work boots.

"Hi, I'm Emmie," I murmur to the woman, who nods curtly.

"Darla, from Racine, Wisconsin," she tells me in a loud whisper. I turn to the young man, but he looks away.

The room is cavernous, windowless, and sterile, with industrial gray carpet, bright lighting, and air-conditioning that is making it very chilly. Suddenly the entire room hushes. The three judges have just walked in. Two men and a woman, all three professional-looking and unsmiling.

"Here we go," Darla mutters. The judges start at the table next to ours. The first contestant, a young woman with purple hair, places a chocolate on each of three small white plates on the table in front of her, and the judges sample the chocolate, then take a few minutes to write on clipboards they carry. No one speaks except the contestant, who simply states the name of each entry. She has two more entries, which they sample in turn, writing down comments on a separate piece of paper for each. Then they nod to the contestant and move to the next competitor.

They proceed down the line slowly, taking their time. No one speaks or even moves. It feels like the entire room is holding its breath. I want to pry the lids off my containers and make sure they have fared okay, but everyone is standing completely still behind their tables. It would be distracting if I made a move now. I lick my dry lips and try not to fret. I'm dehydrated and hungry, and almost dizzy with relief that I actually made it in time. The judges come to our table next. Darla snaps to attention. "Judges," she says.

"What do you have for us today"—a judge with an Australian accent checks his list—"Darla?"

"I have a sweet mascarpone and almond truffle with a layer of amaretto," Darla says proudly, setting her truffles on the three plates. The judges try the truffle in silence. One makes a tiny frown as she sets the uneaten half of her truffle back on the plate. They fill out the forms in silence. Darla sets out her second and then third entries—a Moroccan mint tea meltaway and a freeze-dried raspberry chocolate bar with a sweet cream layer. Then it's my turn.

"Hello, Emmie," the lone female judge takes the lead on this one. "What do you have for us today?" she asks crisply.

I try to look calm and in control, though my heart is pounding like I've just sprinted for my life. In a way, I have. I take a big gulp of air and taste the last faint trace of the gold sprinkles on my tongue. They strengthen me. I'm aware that all eyes in the conference room are on me.

"These are browned butter hazelnut toffee . . ." I stop as I pull the lid off the container. My heart sinks in dismay. My beautiful browned butter hazelnut toffee truffles are a soggy, half-melted mess. The caramelized hazelnut crumbles completely slid off the chocolate and are lying at the bottom of the container in a gooey clump. The ice must have leaked into the container, and the heat finished off every one of the truffles. Nothing is worth salvaging.

"Oh no." The female judge peers into the container and looks at me with sympathy. "Maybe the others fared better?"

They did not. I open the container of dark chocolate and salmonberry gelée bonbons to find them melted and unrecognizable, the bright orange swirls smeared across the container. The rose, cardamom, and ruby chocolate truffle with the gold sprinkles is similarly ruined. It's a disaster. Every single one of my chocolates is ruined. I have nothing for the judges to taste.

"I got stuck at the border in the heat," I explain. "I'm so sorry." I try to swallow down a big knot of shame and disappointment lodged in my throat. It's hard to take a full breath. I think I might burst into tears at any moment. I'm so devastated I feel sick.

All around me I hear the murmurs of surprise and speculation rippling through the other contestants. This is the most humiliating moment of my life.

The Australian judge reaches across the table and claps me on the shoulder. "Better luck next year," he says kindly. I nod, face burning. I swallow hard and put the lids back on the containers. The judges have moved on to the young man in the chef's uniform. There is nothing more for me here. I've been dismissed. Quickly I grab my things and slip from the room as fast as possible.

Eyes burning with unshed tears, I empty the containers into the nearest trash can. I feel sick with disappointment. There is nothing left to do but go home. There's no reason now to go to my hotel and put on my fancy dress for the awards dinner. I am not in the running for an award anymore. Better to just head back across the border. This day is a disaster.

I text Henry, Emergency with the chocolates. They all melted. I'm so sorry but I won't be competing today.

Then I finally use the bathroom in the hotel lobby, splash water on my red, sweaty, disappointed face, and head to the parking garage. I need to let Mom and Dani know. Mom has called twice and Dani has texted numerous times to check on me, but I can't face them right now. I'll call them when I'm on the road. All I want to do is sit down and have a good cry. I'm so disappointed. This was a golden opportunity and I blew it.

Unfortunately it only gets worse. When I reach the hotel parking garage, I find my car won't start. It just clicks, and then nothing. This is the final straw. I put my head on the steering wheel and burst into tears. It's all too much. This entire day has been a parade of frustration and disappointment, and now I can't even get home to put on my pajamas, eat ice cream to beat this heat in our un-air-conditioned house, and commiserate with those who love me. Now what do I do?

After I've sobbed out all my disappointment, I wipe my eyes and take a breath. I feel hollowed out with regret and dismay. How could this day have gone so wrong? I suck on a pinch of sprinkles, trying to regain my composure.

When I'm calm, I consider my predicament. I'm stuck in a

broken-down car in the sweltering parking garage of a hotel where I am not staying. The room prices were too expensive at this hotel, so I booked myself a much cheaper room in a less savory part of town. I need to figure out what to do about my car. I need to find a way to get home. I try to think through the problem and come up with solutions, but instead I find myself feeling stymied and confused. I'm Emmie Wynne. I solve everyone's problems. I'm a fixer. It's what I do and who I am. But somehow, sitting sticky and sweaty in a parking garage in another country in a car that won't start, I finally reach my limit. I don't know anything about cars or how to call for a tow truck or where to find a reputable garage. I'm stuck in Canada, all alone and completely overwhelmed. I need help.

I pull out my phone. The obvious person to contact is Henry, as he's somewhere in the hotel right now. But he's busy in meetings, and he has the awards ceremony tonight. I don't want to bother him, and I feel embarrassed by how terribly I've messed this up.

There's only one person I want to turn to. Feeling guilty yet relieved, I punch in the number.

Jakob answers on the first ring. "Emmie?" His voice is deep and oddly reassuring.

"Jakob," I manage to choke out. "I need you."

"Where are you?" His tone is instantly alert. "Are you okay? Are you in danger?"

At the sound of his protective tone, I burst into tears again and tell him through hiccupping sobs what's happened.

"I don't know what to do . . ." I confess, feeling helpless and embarrassed by my helplessness. I want to be calm and cool and in control so Jakob is impressed by me. But somehow I just can't muster the energy.

"Emmie, it's going to be okay," Jakob says calmly. "We can figure this out."

The "we" is infinitely reassuring. "Where are you right now?" he asks.

"On the fifth floor of a parking garage in downtown Vancouver." I sniffle.

"Okay, here's what you're going to do. You're going to leave your car where it is. Leave your keys at the front desk of the hotel and explain the situation. Then get an Uber or a taxi to your hotel room and wait for me. Take a nap, eat a sandwich, take a shower. Whatever you need. I'll take care of the car and then I'll come get you."

"Thank you," I whisper. I lean my head back against the headrest, close my eyes, and exhale with relief. I'm still heartsick over the melted chocolates and my failure at the competition, and worried about my car and how I'll pay for a repair. It's so freakishly hot. I feel like I'm sitting in an oven. My stomach rumbles and I need to pee again. But at least there's a plan, and a helping hand. It feels more manageable now.

I text Jakob the name of the hotel where my car is stuck and the name of the hotel where I'm staying.

"Emmie," Jakob assures me, "I'll get there as soon as I can. Hang on. I'm on my way."

No one has ever said sweeter words to me. In an instant everything feels like it's going to be okay.

Chapter 33

"Emmie, it's Jakob."

I rouse from a fitful nap at the firm knock on my hotel room door. It's been a little over five hours since my panicked phone call to him, which means he basically jumped in the car and drove straight to Vancouver as soon as we hung up. The sight of him through the peephole makes me go limp with relief. When I open the door, he holds up two grease-stained brown paper bags with Fatburger logos on them.

"Thought you might need some comfort food," he says as he comes inside. I'm not sure which I'm happier to see, him or the burger. I'm ravenous after a quick shower and a little sleep. He glances around the room, which is hopelessly dated. It's done in shades of '70s brown and smells like stale cigarette smoke overlaid with some sort of fake lavender plug-in air freshener.

"Cool place," he deadpans, and sets the bags on the brown fake wood laminated table.

"Thank you for coming to help me." I fidget with a strand of my still-damp hair. I'm hesitant about how to approach him after our explosive late-night scene in the kitchen. I kissed him senseless, then begged him to leave me alone, and then called him asking him to drop everything and come all the way to Canada to help me. And he came. That's what amazes me. He came.

He eyes the brown flowered comforter on the king bed, then opts to lean against the wall, leaving the chair for me.

"Sit, sit," I urge him, perching on the foot of the bed. It's been such a disaster of a day that a dubiously clean comforter is the least of my problems. I dive into the greasy paper bag, finding a cheeseburger, fries, and a strawberry milkshake. "Oh, this is amazing." I groan in appreciation, mouth already full of a big bite of burger.

He takes the chair and fishes a fry out of his bag. "I stopped by the hotel and took a look at your car. I think it probably needs a new starter. I called a tow truck, and they're towing it right now to the shop of a buddy of mine from the Marines. He married a Canadian girl, and now he owns a mechanic shop in south Vancouver, pretty close to here. As a favor he's going to take a look at the car tonight even though his shop is closed. He'll let me know what's wrong with it. He's a good guy. I trust him."

"Thank you," I say fervently. I dip a fry in my milkshake, overwhelmed with a feeling of relief at having someone take care of this, take care of me. It feels like such a luxury. Dealing with cars has never been my strong suit. My dad always handled car-related things before he died. Since his decline, Mom and I have muddled through on our own.

"Thank you for coming even after . . . what happened the other night," I say quietly.

He chews a fry and looks at me, assessing. "Why?" he asks.

"Why what?" I'm not sure what he's asking.

"Why are you fighting whatever is between us? Are you really so against the idea of being with me that you won't even give it a chance?" He takes a bite of burger without taking his eyes off me. I see a flicker of hurt in his stare.

I stall for time, dipping fries in the milkshake, trying to formulate a kind but evasive answer. I find it hard to think under his penetrating icy-blue gaze.

"I'm just not sure it's the right thing for us to be together," I finally reply.

"Liar," Jakob says calmly.

I stare at him in surprise. I forgot who I was dealing with. This is Jakob, high school debate champion. He's got a razor-sharp mind, keen instincts, and a habit of tenaciously digging to get to the root of a matter, no matter what.

"What are you not telling me, Emmie?" he asks pointedly.

I hesitate, feeling caught.

He arches a brow. "I've got all night and nowhere to be," he says, leaning back and crossing his legs at the ankle, a mild threat to wait me out. For a moment I waver. Should I tell him? Try to deflect? Claim confusing feelings for Henry, which is not a lie? But Jakob knows me well. He can read me, and I have a feeling there's no way he's going to settle for less than the truth.

He sits there patiently, eating fries like he's got all the time in the world. Eating fries he brought to me in CANADA when he drove three and a half hours to bail me out, even after I'd rejected him for the second time in our lives. If anyone deserves the truth, it's him.

"Okay, you want to know what's really going on?"

"Are you finally going to tell me the truth?" he asks calmly.

So while I eat my burger and finish my fries, I tell him everything, about the gift given to the women in our family, about my great-grandmother Signe's candle. And then I tell him about what I saw in my vision.

When I'm done, he takes a long drink of his soda until the straw makes the loud sputtering sound signaling more air than liquid going through it. Then he puts down the cup and fixes me with a disbelieving stare.

"You've got to be kidding me," he says flatly.

I'm taken aback by his response. "I'm serious."

Jakob frowns at me. "Are you in love with Henry Summers?" His question is blunt and to the point. I hesitate. Is that what he got from my explanation? I thought there was a lot more nuance to it.

"Well . . . not exactly. Not yet."

He raises a skeptical brow. "But you think he's the best choice for you, the man you could see a future with?"

Again, I hesitate. I think of Henry jetting off around the world as Gus and I stay behind, I think of his sweet but awkward way with my son, and those goodnight kisses that always feel . . . nice, but not knees-to-jelly fantastic.

And then I let my gaze drift to Jakob. I picture all the times he's patiently guided Gus to use a tool correctly, his big roughened hand covering my son's small one as he shows him the correct way to measure, cut, or hammer a nail. I see him kneading dough, forearms straining. Those same hands pinning me firmly to the marble table as he kissed me like he was dying of thirst and I was cool, clear water.

"Um . . ."

"Thought so," Jakob says, sounding smug. He picks up his soda and takes another noisy sip that's mostly air, then rattles his ice in the cup. "So let me get this straight. You blew out a candle and saw a vision of what you think your destiny is, and because

Henry walked into the shop and you found a floaty yellow dress, you're going to base all your decisions on that five-second vision, regardless of what you really want?"

It sounds idiotic when he states it like that.

"You don't understand. It's my purpose in life . . ." I start to protest. "It's the best thing for me. It's what I want . . ." It sounds lame even to my ears when I say it.

"Is it though?" Jakob cuts me off. He leans forward, elbows on his knees. He's got his argument face on. I recognize it from our debate tournaments all those years ago. "I mean, if you really want Henry, by all means, go ahead. But can you honestly say you haven't thought about what it would be like between us? You haven't wondered or wanted more when I've kissed you? Because frankly, Emmie, you don't seem like a woman who's in love with someone else. You certainly don't kiss like one."

He sits back and folds his arms across his chest, eyeing me coolly. My cheeks flame hot with embarrassment under his gaze. I feel so agitated I could pop. Not because he's wrong, but because he's so right. He's right, but I'm afraid. If I follow my heart, what will happen? How could the vision possibly come true? What if I mess everything up? It seems too risky, no matter what I feel for Jakob Kristensen. I'm stuck between my fear and my desire.

"I'm not sure what I want," I mutter, a little petulant.

Jakob shakes his head and swears, low and exasperated. "I can't believe this," he says. "At least the last time you broke my heart it was because you were going after something you really wanted. But this?"

He's out of the chair and to the bed in a split second, looming over me. I shrink backward on the scratchy polyester comforter as he leans over me, bracing his arms on either side of my body.

I feel a thrill, not of fear but of anticipation. But he doesn't kiss me. His gaze bores into mine. He's so close I see the silver shot through the ice blue of his irises, the pale blond of his thick lashes. He pins me to the bed with that gaze. He smells like Sprite and french fries and rising bread dough and sawdust. I want to bite into him, into the softness of his lower lip, but the steel of his gaze stops me cold.

"You know we're good together, Emmie," he murmurs. "And I think that scares you. You let everything else be in control of your life but you. Your martyr complex lets you focus on and fix everyone's problems but your own. If you're too scared to admit what you really want, by all means enjoy weak tea and dry kisses with Henry. But just remember what you're throwing away when you do. Because I think we could have been great, if you'd just had the courage to give this a chance."

Then he straightens abruptly, leaving me half prone on the ugly comforter, heart pounding, breathing in shallow bursts. He checks his phone and frowns.

"My buddy found the problem. Looks like it was a bad starter. He's replacing the part and your car will be ready in fifteen minutes." He glances at me, his gaze angry and dismissive. "Come on, I'll drive you to the mechanic shop."

He doesn't look at me as he stalks out the door, nor does he glance my way on the seemingly interminable drive to get my car. At the mechanic shop, he introduces me to his buddy Dave, and they exchange a few words.

"Good to see you, man. Give me a call when you come south of the border again," Jakob says, shaking Dave's hand. "I'll buy you a beer. I owe you one for helping us out."

Then he gives me a curt nod. "Drive safe, Emmie," he says, and then he gets into the cab of his truck and pulls away, disappearing fast around a corner. Miserably, I go inside to pay the repair bill and retrieve my car.

On the long drive home, Jakob's words ricochet in my mind like a pinball in a machine. Against the angsty wails of Bonnie Raitt and Emmylou Harris, I hear his challenge to me. Over and over I picture his face hovering so close above mine, the frustration and the longing in his eyes.

He loves you, a voice in my head whispers, and I know it's true. Jakob has loved me since we were teenagers. He loves faithfully and sacrificially. I hurt him, and rejected him, and still he came for me. I'm afraid of how I feel about him, afraid that I love him too, against my better judgment. What do I do? Go with my heart or trust the process that has guided my family for generations? I think of Mom's admonition to follow my heart and trust that everything will work out, but I don't see how it could. I'm afraid if I take control of my life and follow my heart, I'll mess it all up. I feel trapped and panicky. What if I make the wrong decision?

Windows down and the hot night breeze blowing through the car, I head south toward home. I'm exhausted and disappointed and heartsick. With every mile I can't shake the feeling that I'm letting something amazing slip through my fingers once more.

CHAPTER 34

It's late when I finally reach home, and I feel completely wrung out. I sit in the car for a moment and answer a few texts. The first is from Henry. He called me as soon as I reached my hotel in Vancouver, but I was so distraught and embarrassed that I let it go to voicemail. I texted him right after, letting him know I was okay and telling him not to worry, that I'd be in touch when I got home. He texted right back. He was getting ready to present at the awards dinner but offered to help as soon as it was over. I assured him I was okay, just disappointed. I didn't tell him about the car starter debacle or that I was stuck in Vancouver or that Jakob was coming to get me.

Now I pull my phone out and send Henry a text letting him know I got home okay. There are no texts from Jakob, although to be fair I'm not surprised. I text Dani too, promising to tell her everything tomorrow over lattes. I just don't have the energy to go into it all today.

Mom has left a light on in the living room of our little

bungalow. When I open the door, it smells like Kraft Mac & Cheese, homey and familiar. I drag myself inside and toe off my shoes in the entry, feeling weary and off-kilter. Mr. Butters waddles out of Mom's room to greet me. The sight of his big warm eyes and goofy smile soothes me, and I scratch behind his ears and murmur a greeting to him. Then quietly I tiptoe down the hall and into Gus's room. I need to see my son. He's the center of my universe, and as soon as I spy his little face, eyes closed, glasses off, mouth slack in sleep, it rights me somehow. I take a deep breath and slide into bed next to him, under his Milky Way galaxy comforter, cuddling him for a brief, greedy moment. He stirs and I gaze down at him, overcome with love. This is what matters. Gus, my family—this is what I have given my life for and would gladly give up anything for again. I want to do so right by them. I've given them all I have.

Gus is sleeping on his back, one arm flung over his head in abandon. The other hand is on his chest, with something clutched in his fist. It's a screwdriver. I recognize the orange handle. It belongs to Jakob. Gus must have taken it from his toolbox at the shop. I carefully pry Gus's little fingers from around the tool and slip it into my pocket. I'll return it to Jakob next time I'm at the shop. Then I press a kiss to Gus's forehead, breathing in his toothpaste and pasta scent.

"Sleep tight, baby," I whisper, even though I know if he were awake Gus would instantly and vehemently object to being called a baby. He doesn't yet understand what all of us parents learn eventually—that no matter how big they grow, our children are always our babies.

When I tiptoe into the hall and close the door, Mom is waiting for me like a slender wraith in a floral flannel nightgown. I jump, startled. She gives me a sympathetic look and wordlessly puts her arms around me. I sag against her, feeling the prickle of tears against my eyelids.

"Oh, honey," she says. "I'm so sorry."

I nod against her shoulder. "I'm sorry too. There was nothing I could do," I whimper a little plaintively. "I tried so hard, but everything melted."

"I know, sweetie. You did the best you could," she says comfortingly, rubbing my back like she did when I was little and was sick or had a nightmare. She smells like Ivory soap. I inhale her, choked up with my failure.

"This was our big chance to get enough money to pay for the plumbing upgrades," I murmur against her shoulder. "I don't know what we're going to do now." I am heartsick thinking about how much money we need for the plumbing repairs, the renovations to transform the shop into my vision, and the county upgrades. It feels impossible.

She keeps rubbing my back. "Oh, honey, something will work out. It always does. Dad and I were in more pickles financially than you ever knew about, and somehow we always managed to pull through. I don't know how, but we'll manage this time too." She pulls back and looks at me, holding me by the shoulders. "Are you hungry? Do you want something to eat?"

I shake my head and say before I think, "Jakob brought me dinner."

She frowns, a little V of confusion wrinkling her brow. "Jakob? What do you mean?"

I'd called Mom as soon as I paid the mechanic's bill and headed home, and while I told her about my failure at the competition and the melting chocolates and that I was on my way home, I left out the part about Jakob driving up to help me. Now I sigh, going into the kitchen and filling a glass with water. I'm not hungry, but I am so very thirsty, dehydrated from the hours in the hot car. I drain the glass and refill it. Mom follows me, Mr. Butters bringing up the rear.

"When I left the hotel after I bombed out at the competition, my car wouldn't start," I tell her, leaning against the kitchen counter. "I called Jakob and he drove up and took care of getting it to a mechanic friend of his. They got it fixed quickly so I could drive home. And Jakob brought me a burger before he drove me to the mechanic." I don't look her in the eye during this recitation of events. I try to make it sound like no big deal.

Mom searches my face in confusion. "Jakob drove up and helped you? But why didn't you call Henry?" she asks. "Wasn't he at the hotel where the competition was?"

It's an excellent question, and one I don't quite know how to answer. "Um . . ." I hold the glass to my flushed face. "He was hosting the awards dinner and was out with colleagues. I didn't want to bother him."

Mom studies me. I hazard a glance in her direction. She looks speculative. "Is Jakob the reason you were asking me questions about not wanting what you saw in your vision?" she asks shrewdly.

I just nod.

"Oh, Emmie," she sighs. I look down at the linoleum floor, feeling exposed. There's no hiding from her.

"Jakob is a good man and a good friend," she says gently. "But what about Henry? Is he not what you want?"

"I don't know. I'm afraid maybe not," I admit. "Henry is wonderful, don't get me wrong. But I don't know if he's the one for me. I'm not sure our lives mesh that well. If I were with him, I'd have to give up so much of what I want in a partner. I think we might be better off as friends." I grimace. Saying the words out loud is surprisingly painful, though they ring true.

Mom sighs. "The heart wants what the heart wants," she says, her tone unexpectedly philosophical. She comes over to me and lays her hand over mine on the counter, her eyes soft and concerned. "Don't second-guess your heart, Emmie. Be honest with yourself. Give yourself permission to love fully. You deserve that kind of love, not something you have to talk yourself into." She looks up and her gaze softens as though she's seeing something not in this room.

"I saw your father in my vision, you know, and a year later I fell in love with him the instant I spotted him sitting there at the Green Light Diner. He ordered the Hungry Viking Signature Plate and ate every bite. Lord but that man could eat! I recognized him as soon as he glanced up at me. I knew, I just knew it was him. I scribbled my number on his check and he called the next day. After that, we were never apart. We saw each other every day, worked side by side, did everything together. And we had many, many good years together. That's the kind of love I want for you, Emmie. The kind Bert and I had. That's the kind of love that makes all the troubles and hardship of life bearable."

I swallow hard around the lump in my throat at the mention of Dad. I drain my second glass of water, trying to ease the tightness. "I want that too, Mom," I tell her thickly.

"And you don't think you can have that love with Henry?" she asks me, her gaze searching. Suddenly the kitchen feels too small, her attention too close.

"I just remembered I need to run by the shop and drop something off." I feel for the screwdriver in my pocket. There is absolutely no need for me to return an orange-handled screwdriver at almost midnight, but suddenly I just need to get out and think. "I'll be right back. Don't wait up."

She hesitates, then nods. "Okay, sweetheart. Just remember, I love you, Emmie, and I want what's best for you."

"I know, Mom." I press a kiss to her forehead. "I love you too." And then I practically sprint out the door.

Chapter 35

Downtown is quiet and deserted. I unlock the shop, return the screwdriver to Jakob's toolbox, and lock up again. As I do, I notice a light shining from inside the Salty Mermaid. That's strange this late at night. I peer in the storefront window and am surprised to see Dot rearranging a display of seashell-themed décor on a round table in the middle of the shop. What in the world is she doing up and redecorating at this hour? I tap on the window and she glances up, startled. Then she spots me and hurries over, unlocking the door and throwing it open.

"Baby girl," she says in that throaty voice of hers. "What are you doing here?"

"I could ask you the same question. It's late."

She waves a hand. "I'm old and I listen to too many true crime podcasts. Walt sends them to me. This one was a serial killer in California in the '70s. Gruesome stuff. I couldn't sleep. Did you just get back into town?"

I hesitate and she presses her lips together and puts her hands on her hips. "I heard," she says. "Gwen told me what happened. I'm sorry, Emmie. What a rotten day."

I nod. "Not my best day, for sure." I try to make light of it, but the memory stings. "I'd better head home and let you get on with it."

But Dot has other ideas. "You need a Band-Aid," she announces.

"A what?" I need a lot of things right now, but a Band-Aid is not one of them.

"Stay right here." She disappears into the rear of the shop and comes back with a mostly full bottle of mezcal. "That's what Jude and I always called a shot at the end of a bad day, a Band-Aid. But you can't drink it inside. You have to get outside, clear your head, and take a shot to chase the stink of the day away. Come on, girlie."

Without waiting for my reply, she locks the shop door and heads toward the waterfront park. I follow hesitantly. I really don't want to do shots at midnight in the park with Dot, but she seems determined, so I go along with it. I'm exhausted but I don't think I could sleep right now anyway. I need to unwind a little from this disaster of a day.

Like the town, the park is deserted. Dot sits down on one of the blue painted iron benches facing the bay and uncorks the mezcal.

"You go first," she says as I gingerly perch beside her. I'm still in my rumpled sheath, which is not the most comfortable of outfit choices. I wish I'd thought of that roughly sixteen hours ago when I put it on. Thankfully the heat has broken and the night air is almost chilly. A few yards away, the water laps gently along the shore, and the wind whispers through the evergreen trees. Everything smells lively—freshly cut grass and seaweed and salt water on wet rocks. I shiver a little and tip up the bottle. The mezcal tastes like smoke and leather with a slight fruity note. It bites as it goes down. Dot takes the bottle from me.

"This'll fix what ails ya," she says, throwing her head back and taking a hearty swallow.

"I wish," I say morosely, staring out at the marina, at the sailboats bobbing in the slight breeze. I shiver again.

"Want to tell me what happened?" Dot asks. I don't really want to rehash it, but I do anyway. By the end of the story about the malfunctioning air-conditioner, the border crossing, and my mad dash to beat the clock, she whistles and passes me the bottle again.

"What a mess," she says.

"Yeah, you got that right. Needless to say, I didn't win the competition and don't know what we're going to do now. We really needed that money."

To my surprise, Dot waves away my concern. "Eh, don't worry about the money," she says. "We're all in the same boat. We'll figure something out. This community is a strong one, and you're one of us. We've got each other's backs. We'll make it through somehow."

I think of Jakob, of how he came to my rescue today. I've never been a damsel in distress. I've always been the one riding to the rescue of everyone else. I wonder for a brief moment how it would feel if I wasn't always the one doing the rescuing. What would it be like if I didn't have the weight of my whole little world resting on my shoulders? If someone was standing right beside me so we could carry the weight together? The thought fills me with longing.

"So let me get this straight, you just took your melted chocolates and came home?" Dot asks.

I hesitate. "Um, not exactly. When I came out of the hotel, my car wouldn't start."

"Rotten luck." Dot clicks her tongue sympathetically. "Did Henry help you get your car started again?"

"I . . . didn't call Henry," I admit softly. And then I tell her about how Jakob drove all the way to Canada to come to my aid. I even tell her about the burger and the strawberry milkshake he brought me.

She whistles. "That boy has always been crazy for you," she muses. "I guess some things never change. So then what about Henry?"

It's a great question. What *about* Henry?

I glance over the water. I know it seems strange that I did not ask for help from Henry. I could have just gone to my hotel room and waited for the dinner to be over so Henry could come to my aid. It would have been faster than waiting for Jakob to drive up, for sure. Henry would have helped me, I'm positive. But instead I called Jakob, hours away. Dot is waiting patiently for a reply.

I take a swig of mezcal. "I don't know what to do about Henry," I tell her bluntly. And then, to my surprise, I find myself pouring out the details of my fight with Jakob in the brown hotel room and the dilemma I find myself in now. Dot listens patiently as I spill out all my worries and conflicting emotions.

"I'm really confused and scared that I'm going to mess everything up," I confess finally. "I don't know what to do, and I feel stuck."

Dot purses her lips and *hmmm*s. "Emmie, how old are you?" she asks abruptly.

"Thirty-four," I reply, surprised. "Why?" She was at my birthday dinner after all.

"I'm just wondering how old you think you need to be before

you get to make your own decisions about your life," Dot says frankly. The question sounds innocent, but I feel the sting of it.

"Ouch." I grab the mezcal bottle from her. "I'm just trying to do the right thing," I tell her, a touch defensively. "I want to live the best life I can."

She nods. "And you're doing a great job. I mean it. You've been juggling a full plate for years, carrying way more than anybody should have to handle. But Emmie girl, ever since you came back home from France, it seems like you haven't been in control of your life. You've been living based on what everyone else needs—Bert's cancer, your mom's arthritis, being a single mom to Gus, trying to keep the shop from going under. It's been a lot for you, for anyone. And I'm just wondering what sort of space you've left in your life for yourself—for what you want, for your own dreams? Because you can't live only for other people, Emmie. It'll suck you dry if you don't have something that gives *you* life, that's satisfying and allows you to give to others in your own way. What you carry in your heart is your gift to the world. Are you making space in your own life so you can give it?"

I glance at Dot in astonishment. Beneath her crusty exterior is a deep soul. I've underestimated her.

"I don't think I am making that space," I tell her slowly. "I don't even know if I know what that gift is. What about you?" I ask, curious. "Are *you* making space in your life? Are you giving your gift to the world?"

Dot considers the question, then takes the bottle back from me and takes a sip. "Yeah, I think so. It took a while for me to find my feet again after Jude died. But then I sort of stumbled upon being a mermaid and I created Serene, and life started to make sense again. I know people make fun of my mermaid gig"—Dot shrugs, sounding unperturbed—"but the first time I put on that tail, I felt like a part of myself came alive again. I know some folks think it's silly or embarrassing that a woman in her fifties with saggy boobs is swimming around pretending to be a mermaid, but it brings me joy and it brings other people joy too, and that's all that matters, isn't it? I'm giving what I've got to make this sad old world a little bit better and brighter. That's the gift I give myself and other people, and that's good enough for me. We can all only give what we've got in our hand. This is what I've got, and I'm giving it the best I can." She leans back on the bench comfortably. I wish I could have her ease, that I could just choose to do what feels worthwhile with no constraints.

"That's amazing," I tell her. "But I've got so many things to consider—Mom, Gus, and . . . the birthday vision."

"Ah yes, the vision," Dot muses, and there's an ironic tone in her voice that surprises me.

"Why do you say it like that?" I ask her curiously.

She shrugs. "I guess I've always wondered just how helpful those visions really are," she replies. An owl swoops low over the water in front of us, and I shiver in a cool gust of briny breeze over the bay. "I mean, it's all well and good to see your purpose in life. Great! It worked out well for your mom, obviously. But how much weight do you think you should put on what you see in a few seconds?"

"What do you mean?" I stammer. "The women in my family wait our whole lives for our vision. It's a great gift."

Dot shrugs. "Yeah, maybe, if what you see makes you happy, if it's really what you want. But what if it isn't? Are you really going to let five seconds define your life for you? Who you love, what you do with your time?"

She has a good point.

"What if you see this vision, but you miss something or you think you know what it means but it means something else instead? What then? Or what if you just plain want something different?" She's voicing what I've been wrestling with this whole time.

"I don't know," I admit quietly, feeling uneasy.

Dot scoffs softly. "So what if you don't follow the vision? What's the worst that can happen? Billions of people on the planet don't get to see a vision. They just get on with life, muddling along as best they can, and at least some of us manage to live pretty satisfying lives. Not everyone needs a vision to find their true purpose in life, Emmie. Maybe you don't either. Maybe you just need to find what brings you joy and follow your own heart." She burps gently. "Baby girl, I think it's time for you to stop letting a fancy candle or your mom's expectations or the whole passel of responsibilities on your shoulders dictate your whole purpose in life and let yourself take the lead for a change." Dot stops and blinks at me like a wise owl.

"How do I do that?" I ask quietly.

"What if you stop following other people's ideas of what your life should look like and let yourself choose for once? What if you show up and get a say in your own life?" Dot spreads her hands wide. "I'm not saying you throw everything away. You're right, you have responsibilities you can't just walk away from, like your Mom and Gus, but what about all the other parts of your life? What do you want to fill those with? You have twenty-four hours in a day, same as the rest of us. What do you want to fill those hours with? What gives you life that also allows you to give something good to others? That's the question you need to ask. And then you need to go find the answers for yourself. Don't let anyone else answer that question for you. You get to choose."

I lean my head back on the bench and consider her words. From the time I was tiny, I was trained to wait for my purpose to be revealed through the vision. I was told it was a great gift, and so I waited and waited, but now that I've seen the vision, nothing seems to be fitting neatly into place. The chocolate shop, which is one of the things I've dreamed of for years, is in real danger of not becoming a reality due to financial straits. My feelings for Jakob have thrown a big wrench in my envisioned happily ever after with Henry. And even my dress the color of sunshine is, if I'm perfectly honest, too tight and pretty darn uncomfortable. The vision I saw of my life seems to be, quite simply, not a good fit.

I say a bad word soft and low, then say it louder, making a mental note to put two quarters in the swear jar. Gus is inching ever closer to having his working model of the solar system.

Dot nods. "Yep, there you go," she says and hands me the mezcal, slipping her arm around my shoulders and giving me a comforting squeeze. I take a long, burning swallow. My head is starting to swim. I need to stop or I'll regret this in the morning.

"So what do I do?" I ask Dot.

"First you slow down on the bottle," Dot says, swiping it back from me. "That's enough Band-Aids for today. Then you throw every plan and expectation and limitation someone else has made for you overboard and figure out what you really want from your life. You gotta stop trying to live other people's versions of your best life, Emmie, and figure out what it means for you to live your best life on your own terms. You've spent enough time letting other people define you. You gotta learn to take up space in your own life again, girlie." She taps my chin thoughtfully.

"How?" I've had no practice at it. Not for a long time.

Dot squints into the darkness. "Ask yourself, what do you love? What makes you feel alive? What's worth sacrificing for, working hard for? Who do you love and who loves you back? What do you have to give, no matter how small, that brings you joy and makes this world a better place? Focus on all of that and you'll come out okay." Dot pauses, then adds, "And if I were you, I'd think really hard about how to show that tall blond drink of water just how you feel about him, but that's just my opinion. What do I know? I'm just a part-time mermaid."

It is excellent advice, but I'm intimidated by the enormity of it. I hate how lost I feel, like I have no agency, no ability to take the helm of my own life. How did I let this happen? And how can I fix it? I clear my throat. "Any idea where I should start?"

Dot stands up and corks the bottle. "I can't help you there, Emmie girl. Sounds like it's time to put on your big-girl panties and figure it out," she says pragmatically. "And now I've got a store to rearrange and a series of murders in the redwoods to help solve." She gives me a little salute and then she's gone.

After Dot leaves, I stay on the bench, thinking. I need to make space for myself in my own life. I turn the novel concept over in my mind as I wait to sober up before heading home. I'm chilled and exhausted but strangely wired too. I feel the energy of Dot's questions coursing through my body. What would it look like if I created a purposeful, satisfying life on my own, without ancestral candles and confusing visions and a laundry list of items I am trying to check off to make it all happen?

What do I love? What makes me feel alive? What is worth sacrificing for, working hard for? I pull the napkin list out of my purse and squint at Dani's writing in the pale silver light of a full moon.

To-Do List

- Henry + Emmie fall in love
- Chocolate shop
- Yellow dress
- Engagement ring + proposal

On impulse, I crumple it and stuff it back into my purse, determining right then and there to stop living my life constrained by this list. When I pull my hand from my purse again, I'm clutching the glass bottle of sprinkles. How did that get in there? I was sure I'd left it in the car. I unscrew the cap and shake a few into my hand, then more and more, a teaspoon of them at least, then a tablespoon. I tip my head back and toss them into my mouth, crunching their floral sweetness.

"I'm going to figure out what I really want my life to be," I whisper aloud, feeling the sweet zing of courage hit my bloodstream. From tonight on, I'm taking control of my power to decide—how I spend my time, what I give to the world, who I love, who I sacrifice for. For too long I've delegated the role of decision-maker to others, letting their voices, their opinions, their needs trump everything else. No more. I am going to figure out what I value, what I believe in, and what or who I truly want. Taking control of my life, starting now.

Chapter 36

The first thing I do the next morning after I drop Gus off at school is return the too-tight, uncomfortable, beautiful dress the color of sunshine.

"Oh, honey, are you sure?" Paula looks surprised when I walk into the shop and tell her I want to make a return. "It's such a great color on you."

"I'm sure," I sigh. "I love it in theory, but it just . . . doesn't fit, unfortunately."

Paula taps her acrylic fingernail against her bold purple lipstick. "Just a second, hon. I got a shipment in this morning. I might have something for you."

She disappears into the back room and I pull the napkin list out of my purse. I cross off the dress with a feeling of regret. But as Dani reminded me earlier when we met to catch up with Byrdie's lattes before she went to work, saying no to good things leaves room for the great things.

"I'm saying no to this dress that doesn't fit so I can leave room for something better," I repeat to myself. Dani encouraged me to practice the phrase over and over so I'd be better at saying no and holding firm. When I told her my plan to ignore the vision and why, she was one hundred percent on board. Now, in her enthusiasm and excitement, I'm having to hold her back from planning my new life. I have to do this on my own. I look at the list and frown. What should I keep and what should I replace? I guess I'll figure that out as I go along. I'm making a new list one step at a time.

"You're in luck!" Paula chortles as she bustles back into the room. She's holding a big cardboard box. "Just came in this morning, and I think it's the next size up." She opens the bag and pulls out the exact same yellow dress. I check the tag, feeling momentarily unsure. It's my size. I had resigned myself to giving up on the dress even though I love it. I hesitate. Is this dress what I really want?

"Feel free to try it on," Paula tells me. I hesitate, running the fabric through my fingers. It's a beautiful dress and a great color on me. Even if I hadn't seen it in the vision, I'd still want it. It's the prettiest dress I've ever seen.

"I'd love to try it on," I tell Paula. In the dressing room I peel off my yoga pants and bamboo-fiber tee and slip the dress over my head. It's a perfect fit. The zipper slides up to the top easily and—gloriously—I can breathe!

I twirl in front of the mirror, amazed by how radiant and comfortable I feel in the dress. I love it.

"How is it, hon?" Paula calls.

"Perfect," I answer, beaming at myself in the mirror. It feels perfect for me.

Five minutes later I walk out of the shop with another bag, this time with the right size dress inside. I stop just outside the door and pull out the napkin and a pen. I make a correction to the list and then I put a check mark beside it.

- ~~Yellow dress~~ the right yellow dress that *fits!* ✓

Feeling strangely jubilant, I head for the shop, delighted that at least for this morning, I've figured out one right thing. For now, that is enough.

I'm almost to the shop when I get a text from Dot asking me to come to the Green Light Diner.

Urgent meeting about the county, her texts says. That sounds serious. Alarmed, I change direction and head for the diner, wondering what has happened. Mom, Walt, and Dot are already there at a table in the window. Hilda is there too, which is a surprise. Dot waves to me when I come in. I slide into a seat and set my bag on the ground.

"Morning, everyone. What's so urgent? What's going on?" I look around the table. Everyone is just drinking coffee except Walt, who is tucking into the Hungry Viking Signature Platter, an enormous plate of breakfast foods that includes buttermilk biscuits, hash browns, ham, eggs, bacon, and gravy. It's like a heart attack on a plate, but from the look on Walt's face, at least he'll die happy.

Mr. Butters is there too, of course, but strangely he is not wearing anything on his tubby body. No hats or ties or doggy vests. That's unusual. He looks a little naked but seems very pleased about it.

Dot gives me a wink. "Morning, sunshine," she says. "How're you feeling?"

"Fantastic." I shoot her a warning look and shake my head slightly. I haven't talked to Mom this morning, and I don't want to start a conversation by confessing that I was out drinking mezcal at midnight.

Just then Sebastian comes in the door and slides dramatically into the last remaining seat at the table. "Apologies," he says. "I couldn't find the right pocket square this morning. Such a bother."

Our waiter appears and pours us coffee before we can even ask.

"Thanks, Brody." I smile at the clean-cut young man. He's Mary Beth's youngest son, home for the summer from college in Pullman.

"Did you all have a chance to review the sales offer?" Dot asks, sliding a document across the table to me. Everyone nods. I scan the document in puzzlement.

"What's this?"

"An offer to buy our building," Mom explains. "From a local investor."

Surprised, I read it quickly. My eyes skip to the purchase price. It's a very good offer, even split four ways. More money than I would have expected. But this is all so sudden. I don't know what to think.

"We all have to decide to sell or the deal is off," Dot says. "It's for the whole building."

"What about our businesses?" I ask, alarmed. "Would we have to move? I'm just about to open the store."

"The owner is offering us very good long-term rents," Dot explains. "No need to move if you don't want to."

"Oh, that's a relief," Hilda says. "What would I do with my time if I didn't have the shop?"

"These *are* very good terms," Sebastian agrees, consulting his copy of the sales agreement. He looks thoughtful. "I have visions of expanding my shop hours, offering some cooking classes and bespoke events . . . This offer would certainly make that financially possible."

Taken aback, I scan the letter. The buyer is listed as an LLC.

"Anyone know who the buyer really is?" I ask.

Dot and Walt exchange a look.

"It's me," Walt announces, chewing a large bite of ham.

"You're Rainy Day Real Estate LLC?" I ask, astonished.

Walt nods. "I am."

"Why do you want to buy our building?" Hilda asks.

Walt shrugs. "I like real estate. I own a good half a dozen buildings around town. Figured this one was a good investment, and it would help all of you out at the same time."

That is an unexpected revelation. I had no idea Walt was a real estate magnate in town. This morning is full of surprises.

"If Walt owns the building, he's on the hook for all the repairs," Dot explains, "including all the upgrades to satisfy the new county codes."

Walt nods placidly. I'm struggling to understand the particulars of the offer, however.

"So you'd be our landlord? We would rent from you?" My mind is skipping many steps ahead.

"Sure, you can sign any length of contract you want," Walt says. "I'll give you a real good deal. It might even save you money in the long run, with property taxes and repairs being so high."

"Why would you do this for us?" Mom asks Walt cautiously.

He shrugs. "A man's gotta do his part for his community. And I gotta do right by my sister too. Can't have her shop closing on account of needing some new pipes." He nods toward Dot. "So I figured it was a win-win. I get a good investment and you get peace of mind. Think it over and talk with the others. I'm in no hurry." He goes back to his enormous platter, sopping up gravy with half a fluffy biscuit.

"I need to get back to the store," Sebastian says, standing. "I have a shipment of oils coming in any minute." He taps the document on the table. "I'll have my attorney look this over, and after he's had a chance to discuss it with me, I'll get back to you with my vote."

Hilda stands too. "I'm okay with selling if that's what we decide," she says. "I don't have the money to pay for what the county is making us do. Either we sell, or I'll have to close up shop and sell anyway."

"Or we could come up with another option," I add. "Maybe we don't have to sell at all." Walt's offer is enticing—easy, generous, and it would solve everyone's immediate financial problems. But to sell our shop? I need some time to think about it. At first glance it doesn't sit right with me somehow.

"We need some time to think about it," Mom says, putting her arm around my shoulders and giving me a soft little squeeze. "Since this is Emmie's new shop, I'm going to leave the decision up to her."

"If there's a way to afford the repairs and keep our shops, I'd be all for that," Hilda tells me as she floats out the door after Sebastian in a cloud of patchouli essential oil and a swish of her full hippie skirt. "Let me know if you come up with any other good ideas."

"That's my cue," Dot says, standing and throwing a five-dollar bill on the table for her coffee. Walt is still plowing through his enormous plate. "I gotta get the shop opened. See you all in a few." Dot leaves.

Now it's just Walt, Mom, and me.

Mom stands with difficulty, grabbing her cane. I stand too. "Thank you, Walter. This is a generous offer. We have a lot to think about." She pauses. "I'll see you Thursday." She hobbles out the door, Mr. Butters at her heels. He's almost prancing this morning, blocky head held high. I follow her out, holding the proposal from Walt.

"No doggy costume today?" I observe, glancing at Mr. Butters.

Mom looks down in surprise. "Oh, I just didn't have time. Too much on my social calendar, something has to go." She waves a hand. I smile. Maybe she's finding a path for herself after all.

"What's happening Thursday with Walt?" I ask as we head down the sidewalk toward our store.

Mom hesitates for the briefest of seconds. "Walt is coming with me to puzzle club again this week. You don't need to drive me. He's picking me up."

How interesting . . .

"And he invited me over to his house this weekend to do a new puzzle he just got in the mail. He's part of a puzzle subscription service, where as soon as you complete a puzzle, they send you a new one. Isn't that clever?" Mom's mouth curves into a little smile of anticipation as we walk side by side down Front Street toward our storefront. "This time they sent him a very tricky one, all ferns in shades of green. We're going to sit on his back deck and listen to a true crime podcast and try to complete the puzzle. Apparently that's what he does every Sunday, listens to a podcast and completes a puzzle."

"But you don't like true crime," I point out. "It's too violent for you."

Mom smiles again, a secret little smile. "Well, it's never too late to try new things," she says. "Who knows, you might find out you like something you thought you loathed for years!" And then she breezes into Dot's shop, Mr. Butters in tow, leaving me standing gape-jawed on the sidewalk.

I linger for a moment in front of our shop, creasing the folds of the offer letter in my hands, thinking over the implications. Mom is letting me make this decision, and it's a big one. If we sold, we could afford . . . so much. The repairs on the house that we've been putting off forever. I could afford the proper equipment I've been longing to buy for years. Walt would cover the very steep cost to upgrade the building. It's a very appealing thought. But is it the right one?

I pull out the list and look at the second item.

To-Do List

- Henry + Emmie fall in love
- Chocolate shop
- ~~Yellow dress~~ the right yellow dress that *fits!* ✓
- Engagement ring + proposal

I unlock the door and wander through the store, hearing echoes of my dad's voice. Everywhere I look I can see him. He swings me high in the air, my blonde pigtails twirling, then he passes me a butterscotch candy, his favorite and mine, when my mom isn't looking. He kept them in his pocket and would give one to any kid who came into the store and couldn't afford to buy anything. He went through pounds of them a year because he was always eating them and giving them away.

There are so many decades of memories in this space. Gus took his first steps right there by the window, and promptly crashed into a stand of licorice and burst into tears. I don't look back into the kitchen, but there are thousands of days of memories back there too: Me eating Pop-Tarts on Saturday morning while Dad made batch after batch of fudge as we listened to NPR. Me heavily pregnant with Gus, making fudge while Dad watched me with an eagle eye and gave me pointers. He knew at that point that his prognosis was terminal, and he was trying to pass on as much knowledge as he could while he still had time. Mom holding colicky baby Gus for hours at a time, rocking him in a rocking chair we brought into the office so I could do the books while he finally settled down to sleep in her arms.

"I don't want to sell this place," I say aloud, and I know in my gut that it is true. It belongs to our family. It was Mom and Dad's, and now Mom is passing it to me. Someday I want it to go to Gus to do with as he sees fit. Selling it now would feel like I was giving up something precious—years of our family history, a stake in the ground in our community. I don't want to sell. I know in my heart it is the right thing to keep the store in our family. Somehow I'll have to figure out a way.

But if we don't sell, how are we going to afford to keep it? The financial reality is daunting. With the water damage repair and the renovations and the lost income from having to close the shop, we have burned through almost all the money Mom had set aside. There is no money left to pay for the county-required upgrades. Our portion of the upgrades is going to run as much as ten thousand dollars, maybe more. Where are we going to get that kind of money?

I was hoping the competition prize would help cover the costs, but that obviously didn't happen. And don't even get me started on where I'll find money for updated equipment. I want to sell chocolates that are high-quality. I struggle with the old equipment I have now. It will only get worse as I ramp up my production volume. It is a conundrum—one I don't know how to easily solve.

But I don't want to sell if there is any way in the world to avoid it. That I know for sure.

With a sigh I make a few notes on the list.

To-Do List

- Henry + Emmie fall in love
- Chocolate shop—need more $ and a name!!!
- ~~Yellow dress~~ the right yellow dress that *fits!* ✓
- Engagement ring + proposal

At least I have one thing on the list so far. A dress that fits. And now I have a vision for the chocolate shop that is definitely my own. I don't know how to figure out a solution to our financial problems, but at least I know what I want. That is a good start. I read over the other two items on the list carefully. Then I tuck it back into my purse. I know what I need to do next, and I'm not looking forward to it at all.

CHAPTER 37

"Hello, Emmie," Henry says as he opens the door to his little beachfront cottage. He smiles warmly at me, and my heart falls. He's adorable as always, in bare feet and a linen shirt with the sleeves rolled up, his hair mussed and falling over his brow. He leans in and gives me a peck on the cheek, and I feel a bittersweet dart of regret. What a lovely, sweet man he is.

"I feel terrible about what happened in Vancouver. Come in, come in." He opens the door and gestures me inside. "I wish you'd called me earlier. I could have tried to do . . . well . . . something. But never fear, there are other competitions. There's a good one coming up in Brussels in the fall. Perhaps you'll have more luck there."

He leads me into the kitchen, which is filled with late-morning sunlight and the homey smells of toast and tea. I set a plate of sprinkle sugar cookies on the counter. They're fresh and warm from the oven. I baked them just before coming to see him and used only the gold sprinkles on the tops. I ate two on the way over, for courage.

"Care for a cuppa?" he asks, putting the electric kettle on. "I was hoping to see you soon. I was wondering if you'd thought any more about our conversation the other day during our picnic?" He looks so hopeful it breaks my heart. "I understand if you need more time," he says quickly.

"Henry," I sigh. "I have to admit something to you. I hate tea. And yes, I have been thinking about your sweet and thoughtful offer and about the future. That's why I'm here."

Henry draws back and sees my regretful expression, and his face clears with sudden understanding. "Ah," he says, rubbing his neck a little bashfully. "I see. I'm not going to like the next part, am I?"

I shake my head, giving him a tender, regretful smile. "Can we go sit down?" I ask.

Over a truly terrible cup of instant coffee that he makes me (which I augment with a few sprinkles on the sly to give me an additional boost of courage for what I have to do), we sit in lounge chairs on the deck and chat, the plate of cookies between us. The day is cool and gray, but beautiful. We watch seagulls wheel overhead and blue herons hunt in the shallows near the shore as I explain why I cannot say yes to a relationship with him.

"You are lovely," I tell him honestly. "Absolutely lovely. It's not that I couldn't see a life with you in it. It's more that I can't see how our lives fit together. I don't want a relationship that's a lot of long distance and the occasional weekend or break between filming. Henry, my life is here. I can't jet off to Vietnam or Argentina or Norway like you do. I have an ailing mother and a young child and a small business to take care of. I'm not portable at this stage of my life. And I want to share my life with someone, all the sweet, small, everyday things, right here, together."

Henry stirs milk into his tea and smiles regretfully. "I thought you might say that, Emmie, and in truth I don't blame you. Bad timing, I guess. I was just hoping perhaps I could convince you, but you're right. It isn't fair to you or Gus or Gwen for you to have a partner who is absent so much of the time. I'd miss so much life here. I think we'd end up regretting our choices, but I had to at least try and see what you thought. No hard feelings. I'd like to still be friends, if you're willing?" He looks hopeful.

"Of course!" I reach across the table and we shake hands, a friendship pact.

"Some man is going to be incredibly lucky to get you," Henry says, biting into a cookie. I blush beet red.

"I'm so sorry," I tell him.

Henry smiles. "It's okay," he assures me. He dips the edge of his cookie into his tea. "You're a wonderful woman, Emmie—a caring mother and a devoted daughter, and you have such a creative mind when it comes to chocolate. I have no doubt you'll succeed in whatever you choose to do, and I'm glad to be your friend. I hope we can see each other when next I'm in town?" He bites into the cookie and looks at me hopefully.

It sounds like a question. "Of course, Henry," I reassure him quickly. "I'd love that. And anytime you want to come back, we will welcome you with open arms."

"Ah, good." He looks relieved. "Because, in fact, I'm considering putting a stake in the ground here. I've grown quite fond of this little town and of this cottage. It's been a long time since I considered putting down roots, but I think it's time. And I think I might like those roots to be here. I'm planning to come back next summer, as soon as my shooting schedule wraps up."

"Oh, that would be wonderful!" I smile delightedly. I really will miss Henry when he's gone. "You'll always have a place here with us. We can be your adopted town."

"Deal," he says, and we grin at each other.

I drive home from Henry's feeling like I could float, buoyed by relief and anticipation. The sunshine filters through the evergreen branches above me on both sides of the road, illuminating the ferns and mossy rocks of the forest that flank the pavement in places. On impulse I pull off into a little turnaround and take the napkin from my purse. I look at the list, then smile a little regretfully as I cross off the first and last items.

To-Do List

- ~~Henry + Emmie fall in love~~
- Chocolate shop—need more $ and a name!!!
- ~~Yellow dress~~ the right yellow dress that *fits!* ✓
- ~~Engagement ring + proposal~~

Henry and I will not fall in love, at least not with each other. He will never get down on one knee in front of me. There will never be an engagement ring in a red leather box. It feels a little bittersweet to cross off those items. I hope someday Henry and I can rejoice with each other over both finding love, maybe share photos of weddings, babies, and grandkids, celebrate our separate full and happy lives. But all we will ever be is friends. And although I feel a little dart of regret at what I once dreamed of, it also feels right and good to let that dream go. My heart is not Henry's. It couldn't be. There has always been something between Jakob and me. I was a fool to ignore it and try to twist my heart into a shape it did not want to be in. But now I'm taking my pretzel of a heart and untwisting it. I'm setting it free.

I look at the list again. I am taking my life into my own hands and rewriting everything. It feels like a huge risk. I don't know what happens next, but I know what I want. I'm not sure it's possible, but as my dad told me when I was nervous about trying to get into the elite chocolatier program in Switzerland, "Emmie, girl, you will miss out on one hundred percent of the jobs you don't apply for."

Boy, was he right.

I scrawl another point on the list along with a big fat question mark.

- Jakob?

I screwed up and hurt him . . . again. I'm not sure he'll give me another chance. But I have to tell him the truth. I have to tell him how I feel. So I take a deep breath and head toward town, knowing this is the next right step, regardless of the outcome. I don't know what he'll say, but right now I can't worry about that. That is up to Jakob to decide. Right now I need to locate a taciturn Norse demigod and share my heart with him.

Jakob's phone is off. It's a few minutes till noon when I get to Kristensen's Bakery, hoping to find Jakob behind the counter, but it is his mother Astrid who is standing behind the bakery cases. The air is warm and fragrant with sweet dough, yeast, and sugary glaze.

"Hello, Emmie," she says. Her tone is cool, and she eyes me with a touch of caution. "What can I get for you today?"

Astrid is a tall, curvy woman with graying blonde hair pulled into a tight bun. She has a strong work ethic, a generous, motherly heart, and the same arctic-blue eyes as Jakob. She and Gunnar make an unlikely pair. Once, I loved Astrid like a second mother. She welcomed me with open arms. But when I came back from Europe, I found her polite but distant on the occasional times when we'd run into each other in town. I've always assumed she blamed me for breaking her son's heart. I understand, but I miss the easy way we used to have with one another.

"I'm looking for Jakob?" I'm suddenly very nervous. "He's not answering his phone."

She calmly rearranges a display of loaves of sourdough bread. "That probably means he doesn't want to be reached." Her tone reveals nothing. I can't tell if she means reached by me or reached at all. Does she know what happened between her son and me?

I clear my throat. "Do you know where I can find him? It's . . . um . . . urgent." Not technically, but it feels urgent to me.

Astrid looks up and studies me for a long moment. Then she sighs. "Emmie." Her tone is gentle, but there is a protectiveness to it. I recognize it, one mother to another. "He's finally come home to us. He's taken his rightful place here." She gestures to the bakery. "He's happy. Can you not just let him be?"

I'm taken aback by her words.

"I'm not here to hurt Jakob, Astrid. I promise," I assure her quietly. "I care about him very much." I glance around me, remember what he said about taking over the family bakery, the resignation in his voice. Does Astrid not see it? Does she not know that he is not, in fact, happy here? It's none of my business, and I should just keep my mouth shut, but I add spontaneously, "And I don't think he's as happy working here as you seem to believe."

She raises her eyebrows and looks at me in surprise. "What do you mean?"

I hesitate. Jakob is a grown man. This is his truth to tell, not mine. "I think you should ask Jakob if he's happy," I say gently. "I think he may be afraid to be completely honest with you because he doesn't want to disappoint you."

Astrid scrutinizes me for a long moment. Then she sighs. "Promise me you'll be careful with my son's heart," she asks. There's a note of resignation in her tone.

"I promise," I assure her.

"Jakob has a faithful heart," Astrid tells me, watching me carefully. "He loves wholly and tenaciously. I hope you know what a gift that is." Her gaze holds a touch of worry.

I swallow and nod. "I do," I assure her. "I've been a fool, but I do love him." Saying the words aloud feels so freeing, so good and so right. "Please, Astrid? I'm trying to make it right."

She sighs again and wipes her hands on her apron. "He's out on the bay. Look for the orange kayak."

"Thank you." I'm beyond relieved. I turn to go, then pause. An idea strikes me. "Astrid, could I have two raspberry Danishes to go?"

The marina is quiet at noon, just Ed puttering around with a hose and a scrub brush. He turns off the water when I walk up.

"Hello, Emmie." He looks surprised, which is fair. I'm not the most athletic person and have never gone out on the bay alone. "That for me?" He looks hopefully at the bag in my hand.

"Sorry." I shoot him an apologetic smile, then reconsider. There are two Danishes in the bag, and I don't really need to eat mine. I do, however, need a way to get to Jakob. "Actually, that depends. I have a favor to ask."

Chapter 38

Five minutes later I'm paddling out into the bay in a borrowed blue kayak while Ed munches my raspberry Danish and watches from the dock.

"You're doin' great!" he calls encouragingly, mouth full. "Just remember to steer into the swells."

I scan the bay, looking for Jakob. A few sleek seal heads bob a little ways from shore, and there is a sailboat far out on the water. Then I spot him, a dot of orange. He's far out. I'm not sure I can catch him, but I'm going to try. Before I head in his direction, I wrestle my purse from the dry goods compartment at the front of my kayak, careful not to tip myself out into the water, and pull out the little glass jar of sprinkles. Keeping my eye on the orange dot on the horizon, I shake a few sprinkles into my palm and lick them up, letting them melt on my tongue, reassured by the familiar zip of energy down my spine. The conversation I intend to have with Jakob is going to take all the inner fortitude I possess. Then I open the bakery bag with the remaining Danish, Jakob's

Danish, inside and shake half a dozen sprinkles onto the pastry. No harm in giving him a little extra courage too, right? Mustering my resolve, I dip my paddle deep into the water and head for the orange dot as fast as I can paddle.

It takes longer than I expected to reach Jakob. There's a breeze today, and I have to work against the current and the wind. I'm gasping and sweating by the time I pull within earshot of him. He's just sitting in his kayak, bobbing on the gentle swells, wearing a pair of silver aviators and watching me struggle across the bay to him. When I get close, I suddenly don't know what to say. Nervously, I stop paddling. The noses of our kayaks bump together gently. He just sits watching me impassively. I can't read his expression behind his sunglasses. I decide to take the plunge and say what I came to say. *Courage, Emmie. Courage.* I think of the sprinkles and lick the faintest floral essence from my lips.

"I screwed up," I tell him bluntly. "You were right about what you said in Vancouver. I was scared."

He doesn't say anything. He's wearing his old faded blue Viking mascot T-shirt from high school under his life jacket, and his mouth is set in a firm line. I wish I could see his eyes. I press on.

"For years I've let other people define my life for me. I have responsibilities to the people I love, obviously. Taking care of Mom and Gus isn't going to change, and I don't want it to. They are my family, and it's my privilege and responsibility to care for them, but somehow in all the taking care of everyone, I forgot to save any part of my life for myself. I let everyone else make my choices for me and dictate how I spend my time and energy and even what my life looks like. I let a five-second vision define my future—what I value and who I fall in love with." I pause and then burst out with the truth. "But I don't want to do that anymore. I want to have a say in my own life, to be at the helm of my own ship. I want to make choices for myself about what I do, what makes me happy, who I give my heart to—all the things that give life meaning and purpose. I want to decide what makes my life worthwhile. I want to make my own choices from now on." I pause hopefully, waiting to see what he'll say.

Jakob stirs. He clears his throat. "Why are you out here, Emmie?" he asks. He sounds skeptical. "Why are you telling me this?"

I swallow down my disappointment and keep my focus on him. I've treated him badly. He has every right to be skeptical. "I came to apologize. Jakob, I'm sorry I was a coward, and I'm sorry I hurt you. I wish I could do it over. I want to treat people I care about better than that, and I do care for you. A lot."

He looks at me, motionless and expressionless. I take the silence as an opening, although I'm not sure that's how he's intending it.

"I know what I want now," I tell him earnestly. "I want to be a loving, caring daughter to my mom in her golden years, and I want to be the best mommy to Gus that I can be. I want to open my own boutique chocolate store here in Poulsbo in my parents' shop, and I want to find a way to get enough money that I don't have to sell the store to Walt. I have no idea how I'm going to do that, but I really want to honor my family's history and keep the shop to pass on to Gus. I want to build a business I can be proud of and make delicious chocolates that honor our beautiful part of the world. I want my creations to help people find comfort or celebration, or just brighten their day a little." I take a beat, thinking of my new list, of the things I just said. There is one more thing I want, if I am brave enough to say it.

Jakob tips his head slightly to the side. He's listening. "Okay," he says slowly. There's a question in his tone. Our kayaks keep drifting apart and bumping back together, so he takes his oar and wedges one paddle under the stretchy deck lines on the front of his kayak and the other end of his paddle through the deck lines on the front of mine, keeping us a few feet apart, facing each other.

I pause and fidget with my own paddle in my lap. I think of the yellow dress. "And I want to wear comfortable clothes, not pinchy dresses, even if they are the color of sunshine and seem perfect but are actually not."

Jakob raises an eyebrow. "That seems oddly specific," he observes dryly.

"I think that dress is a metaphor for my life," I admit. "But also I'm done with uncomfortable clothing. Like, for real."

Jakob gives a little wry twist of his mouth, an acquiescence of sorts.

"I have three more things to tell you and then I'll leave you alone if that's what you want," I say, boldly. He frowns but sits back and waits. Apparently I've got a chance to say what I came to say.

"Number one: I am not interested in a romantic relationship with Henry Summers." I dart a quick look at him. His jaw flexes but he says nothing. I really wish I could see his eyes behind the tinted lenses of his sunglasses. It's hard to be vulnerable with this whole stoic vibe he has going on. I feel like I'm baring my soul to a granite boulder. I press on.

"Number two: I can't stop thinking about you, even though I know I've messed up and hurt you. I have always cared for you a lot, Jakob. A lot. I think you're one of the smartest, most interesting, most quietly caring people I've ever known. I was serious when I said I think you and my dad ruined other men for me. You both love people so well." My voice catches on the words and I choke down a lump in my throat at the thought of my dad. "And seeing you with Gus. He's a weird, lovable, scared little kid grappling with a loss he can't control, and you've given him the gift of time and attention and made him feel capable and strong. I can't thank you enough. And number three, I think . . ." I bite the inside of my cheek and look over his shoulder, off across the water as I almost whisper the last honest words. I summon all the courage I have, wishing I'd eaten more sprinkles. Oh well, here goes. "I'm falling in love with you, and I hope you'll give me another chance if there's any part of you that feels the same way."

And then I stop talking and wait nervously for his response. For a long time Jakob doesn't say anything. Then he stirs.

"Why should I trust you?" he asks bluntly.

I stare at him, at a loss for words.

Jakob's jaw ticks. He shakes his head and laughs, but it isn't a happy sound. "Emmie, I've waited years to hear you say those words, to tell me that you feel this way. First in high school, until you made it clear you had no interest in me other than as a friend. And then when I came home last month, I found my feelings for you hadn't gone away. They'd simmered down for a while, but then I saw you and I started to hope again. But Emmie, you've made it pretty evident that you are not interested in me. At some point a man has to get the message. I've gotten it loud and clear." The set of his mouth is grim and determined. That scares me.

"But I didn't mean it," I choke out, feeling a little panicked. "I thought I had no choice. I was afraid."

"You always have a choice," he says calmly. "The first time you said no, I understood. We were young. You were choosing a different life. That was your right, and you took it. Even though it broke my heart, it was your choice to make. But this time around . . . you were running away from something that could have been good, could have been great. So tell me, Emmie, why should I trust you now? What's to say you won't change your mind in a few weeks or months? How can I trust you won't be fickle? Because I'm not, Emmie. My feelings haven't changed. I'd need to know the same about you before I could ever trust you with my heart."

Somehow his words give me hope. He said "could," which means all is not lost.

"Jakob, I'm not a fickle person," I tell him, desperate to make him understand. "I'm dependable. I keep my word. You know me. You know I'm not wishy-washy." It's one of the core parts of my identity. Emmie Wynne is a responsible and steady human being. "I just got scared . . . and confused." I lick my dry lips and taste the last of the sprinkles. I can feel my skin starting to pink in the glare of the sun the longer we sit here bobbing on the water. I'm desperate for him to understand how I feel, free from the constraints of the vision, how liberated I am now to choose my own path.

How can I make him understand that it was a misplaced sense of responsibility, a sense of obligation that was holding me back from what I really want? Him. Us. I feel panicky. I can't lose him, not when I have finally given myself permission to see what the future might hold for us. Not when I've finally been brave enough to admit it.

He shrugs. "I'm not sure how to risk my heart again with you, Emmie," he says, and there's a note of regret and a fine thread of anger in his voice. Crushed, I nod. I don't blame him. I would feel leery to trust me too. It's ironic that when I finally get the courage to take the reins of my life, I find that I can't have what I really want.

"I'm so sorry I hurt you, Jakob," I tell him sincerely. "I know my confusion cost you a lot. I don't expect anything from you, but please know that my feelings are real and they're not going to change. And if you ever have a change of heart, I'd love to see what we could be together."

I want to argue with him, convince him, but it is his choice. I have rejected him and hurt him, and now I'm trying my best to make amends, but he gets to decide what he'll do. I make my choices and he makes his, and we both have to live with that reality. Jakob doesn't say anything, just nods shortly. He wiggles his paddle free of my deck lines and we drift apart a little.

"Is it really over between you and Henry?" he asks abruptly.

"I broke the news to him this morning," I confirm. "We're friends. Nothing more. Honestly, it was never anything more than that. My heart wasn't in it," I tell him frankly.

He looks at me long and hard, his expression unreadable. "I need to go," he says finally.

Just in time I remember the bakery bag.

"Here, wait. I got you something." I paddle a few strokes and pull up flush with his kayak. I want to leap over the side and nestle down on his lap and put my head on his shoulder and have him wrap his strong arms around me and tell me I have another chance. Instead I hand him the bag. I almost drop it in the water, but he grabs it. Marine-quick reflexes.

"What's this?" he asks.

"Open it and see," I tell him.

He opens the bag and peers inside. "You brought me your favorite flavor of Danish?" he asks in bewilderment. Then, "Is this a Danish I made?" and "Why are there gold sprinkles all over it?"

"The sprinkles are a long story. I'll tell you another time." I wave a hand impatiently. "Yes, it's a raspberry Danish you made. Yes, it's my favorite flavor, but it's not just my favorite flavor," I tell him, looking at him steadily. "It's yours too. All those debate study sessions, you always gave me the raspberry Danishes and took the cheese ones for yourself. You don't even like cheese. You're a little lactose intolerant. I know you, Jakob Kristensen, your kind heart and selflessness and quiet care. I hope someday I get the chance to care for you the way you've always cared for me. I want to, and I hope I can earn back your trust so I can show you how much I care for you, how much I love you."

Jakob stares at me over the bag for a long moment. I can't see his eyes, but I feel that icy-blue gaze boring into me. I wait for him to reply but he doesn't say anything. He seems to be struggling within himself.

"I have to get back," he says finally. "Tell Walt I'll be in a little late today." He tucks the Danish under his kayak seat where I'm betting it will get soggy with seawater.

I swallow my disappointment and nod. "Okay."

Then I watch him paddle swiftly away, the defined muscles in his arms flexing with every powerful stroke. He does not turn as he heads back to the marina, slicing through the water with deep strokes. I follow behind at a slower pace, puffing and wincing. My arms are going to be so sore tomorrow.

I make it back to the marina in roughly double the time it takes Jakob. I'm disappointed by how our conversation ended, though not surprised. Jakob is loyal to a fault, but if you hurt him, he finds it hard to trust again. I don't know what he'll decide, but I've done my best to be brave and honest and make amends. Now it's up to Jakob to decide what he wants to do. I don't expect an answer anytime soon. I'll give him all the time he needs. He doesn't owe me anything, and it makes sense that he'd be hesitant. If I were him, I would be leery too. The best thing I can do is show him I'm a woman of my word. I need to keep writing my own list, keep making my own way. I need to prove to him and to myself that I am at the helm of my own life, that I stand by my choices, that I am living honestly and purposefully according to my values.

Back on the dock, I pull my purse from the dry compartment of the kayak and find the list and a pen. I scribble another item on the bottom of the list. There is no sign of Jakob. It looks like he already put his kayak back on the rack and left. Clearly he needs space. I see the empty bakery bag sticking out of the trash can and my heart gives an absurd little bump of hope. He ate the Danish. Somehow I think that is a good sign.

I focus on my list, on what I just wrote, on what I know I need to do next.

To-Do List

- ~~Henry + Emmie fall in love~~
- Chocolate shop—need more $ and a name!!!
- ~~Yellow dress~~ the right yellow dress that *fits!* ✓
- ~~Engagement ring + proposal~~
- Jakob?
- Chart your own course, one step at a time . . .

Chapter 39

"Everyone got their order? Okay, then, let's get started," Dot announces. I glance around the laminated table at the small group of us gathered for an early-morning breakfast meeting at the Green Light Diner. Hilda, Sebastian, Dot, Mom, and I are all crowded around a table drinking diner coffee and discussing Walt's offer and our options for the building. This is the first chance we've had to meet since Sebastian's lawyer got back to him about the contract. It's been two weeks since my disappointing kayak conversation with Jakob. I haven't talked to him since that day, although he's been at the shop every afternoon, finishing up the remodel. It should be done in the next week or even earlier. It's been agony to not approach him, not try to win him back, but I've stayed true to my word and given him space. I'm focusing on my own path right now.

"Okay, let's get down to brass tacks," Dot says, spooning up some biscuit smothered in gravy and taking a huge bite from her

Hungry Viking platter. The woman can eat like a twenty-year-old linebacker and still stay lean as a string bean. It's a mystery. She sits back and wipes her mouth with her napkin. "What do we think? Are we going to sell to Walt?"

We all look around the table at each other. "I could go either way," Sebastian says. "As long as I can keep my store open."

Hilda nods. "Me too."

"Emmie?" They both look at me.

"I don't want to sell. If at all possible, I want to keep the store in our family," I say firmly. Mom smiles and sits back in her chair. She looks relieved.

Dot nods. "That makes two of us. I like owning my place. I don't particularly want to have my brother as my landlord either. Sebastian, Hilda, how do you feel about not selling the building?"

"How will we afford the repairs if we don't sell?" Hilda asks, looking worried.

Sebastian nods. "I'd be happy to not sell if we could find a way . . ."

For the hundredth time I wish I could think of a way to raise the money we need to keep the shop. I couldn't sleep last night, so I stayed up late making pralines and brainstorming. Unfortunately, in the cold light of morning, none of my ideas look promising or realistic. I don't know what we're going to do. The pralines are delicious though.

"Let's brainstorm. Who has any ideas?" Dot asks.

"Maybe a yard sale?" Hilda suggests tentatively. My heart sinks. That is, surprisingly, an even worse idea than the ones I've already come up with. This is not a promising start.

Beside me in a red vinyl chair, Mom is pecking at her buttered toast. I can tell she's not listening. Her eyes keep drifting to a red vinyl booth at the back. I know that booth. It's where she first saw my dad. This place holds a lot of memories for her. The whole town does.

"Do you have any good ideas?" I ask Dot, pouring syrup on my buttermilk pancake. I know I should probably be eating an omelet or oatmeal or something healthier, but my dad brought me to the diner every Sunday morning to eat buttermilk pancakes before church, and I'm missing him fiercely right now. A pancake doesn't take away the feeling of loss, but it salves the ache a bit.

Dot grins. "No, but I know someone who does," she says. "Ask him." She points with her fork toward the front of the restaurant just as the bell over the door jingles. I see who it is and immediately feel a little lightheaded. Jakob strides into the diner with a stern expression and a sheaf of papers in his hand and stalks toward our table. He looks good. Sort of grim, but good. He's in his usual blue jeans and a tight gray Henley with the sleeves rolled up. He meets my eyes and instantly it feels like someone lit a sparkler and it's crackling down my spine. I can't look away. He breaks the connection first.

"Jakob asked to meet with us today and share something he's found," Dot tells us. "Right, Jakob?"

Jakob pulls up a chair and straddles it backward. He's directly across the table from me. "I got the idea after talking to Emmie." He clears his throat and doesn't look in my direction. "I started poking around online. I figured maybe there was money available to help save historic buildings, some foundation or grant or something that could help. Turns out I was right."

"You found something?" Hilda asks eagerly, scooting to the edge of her seat in anticipation.

Jakob nods. "The American Norwegian Heritage Foundation has a fund for historic building preservation," he explains. "So I did a little research on the history of your building and I wrote to them. I just got a reply yesterday."

"What did they say?" Mom asks eagerly. All eyes are trained on Jakob. He distributes the papers he's holding, and I glance at my copy. It looks like a letter of some sort.

Dot holds up the sheet of paper and reads aloud:

Dear Mr. Kristensen,

We received your application and accompanying documentation regarding the urgent repairs needed to the historic Front Street building in Poulsbo, Washington. After conducting our own research, our foundation historian determined that this building does indeed have a strong and proud Norwegian heritage. It was, in its over one-hundred-year history, the site of many Norwegian-owned stores and businesses, as well as the location where Norwegian American potter Lars Aland produced some of his finest pottery pieces celebrating his family's Norwegian heritage.

We at the American Norwegian Heritage Foundation are dedicated to preserving our Norwegian cultural heritage in America. Based on the historical value of this building and its location in Poulsbo's historic downtown, the preservation committee has unanimously voted to award you and your fellow building owners a grant of twenty thousand US dollars to assist in covering the cost of the repairs. We hope this grant will ensure the building can continue to proudly represent Norwegian culture and heritage for many years to come.

Dot stops and lowers the paper, glancing around the table at us.

Sebastian looks astonished. "They're giving us half the money we need for the repairs?" he asks.

Dot nods and keeps reading.

Please call our office during business hours so we can arrange further details regarding the payment of the grant. We at the American Norwegian Heritage Foundation are proud to support the town of "Little Norway," Poulsbo, Washington, and to help preserve this historically significant building.

Med vennlig hilsen,
Per Pettersen
Preservation Committee Chair, The American Norwegian Heritage Foundation

Dot finishes the letter and Hilda whoops in glee, accidentally spilling her fruit cup all over the table. I glance at Jakob only to find him already looking at me. His gaze snags on mine and we stare at one another for an electric second until he looks down at his work boots.

I sit frozen, a forkful of pancake poised over my plate, stunned by the good news. I think Jakob just saved us. The general mood has shifted from despondent to jubilant in the space of two minutes. The relief is palpable.

"Jakob, thank you," Mom whispers, a little misty-eyed, reaching across the table and squeezing Jakob's hand.

Dot claps him on the back firmly. "You're a hero," she says.

Jakob shrugs off the accolades. "Glad I could help all of you," he says, but he glances at me as he says the words. He scrapes his chair back and excuses himself. "I've got to get back to the bakery," he tells us before he heads out the door.

We sit for a moment in blissful silence, absorbing the momentous news. Dot leans over to me.

"You know he did it for you, right, hon?" she murmurs, watching Jakob disappear down the sidewalk.

"He did it for all of us," I counter, but her words sit like a warm little sun in the center of my chest. Maybe he did it for all of us. Maybe it's true and he did it for me. Regardless, Jakob's gift to us via the American Norwegian Heritage Foundation has suddenly made the impossible feel possible.

"So this means we are not selling, right?" Sebastian asks the table. We all exchange glances.

"Not now," Dot says. "That grant just saved our bacon. It won't cover all the upgrades, but it's enough that I can scrape together whatever I owe for the rest of the costs."

"Me too," Hilda agrees.

"God bless the American Norwegian Heritage Foundation, whoever they are," Sebastian says fervently. "I can cover my part of the costs."

Dot looks at me and Mom. "What about you two?"

"We want to keep the shop in the family," I tell her firmly. "We don't want to sell. We'll find the money somehow."

I haven't done the math, but between the cost of the plumbing repair, the cost of the remodel (which I haven't seen a final total for yet), and the cost of our portion of the building upgrades, I'm fairly certain we are going to come up thousands of dollars short. But I'm determined to figure something out. We've got a little time before we have to complete the upgrades. Surely we can figure something out before then, right?

Dot sits back, satisfied. "Great. Looks like we're agreed. Who's going to break the news to my brother that we're not selling?" she asks, a wicked little gleam in her eye.

As I eat the last of my pancakes, I glance around the table, thinking about Dot's admonition. Maybe I don't have to carry everything. Maybe it's okay to let my community carry me now and then. After all, that's the beauty of it, right? When we share a load, it gets lighter. I think it's high time for me to start sharing my load.

But first . . . I down the rest of my coffee and push my chair back. "You all take your time," I tell them. "I'll go break the news to Walt." I leave a twenty-dollar bill with Mom to pay for my breakfast and leave the table first. Before facing Walt with the news, I stop in at Kristensen's Bakery. Half a block before I reach the familiar red storefront, I smooth my hair, pop a breath mint, and slick on some tinted lip balm. My heart is pounding as I open the door. The bell jingles. The store smells heavenly—sugared fruit and cinnamon, butter and yeast.

"Just a minute," calls a familiar deep voice from the back. "What can I . . . Emmie." Jakob comes into the storefront, wiping his hands on a towel. He looks surprised to see me. Not displeased though, which is heartening. He's wearing a flour-streaked apron over his Henley, his hair tied back in the stubby man bun. He's so beautiful he makes my heart ache. He offered himself to me and I rejected him. Twice. I'm an idiot. A regretful idiot who realized too late how much he really means to me, how much he always has.

"Sorry, I just need to pick up some sugar to soften a blow. I've got to break the bad news to Walt."

Jakob stills. "What bad news?" His eyes on me are instantly wary.

I hasten to reassure him. "More like disappointing news . . . for Walt. We're not selling the building. Because of the grant, we can all keep our stores." I meet his eyes. "Because of you," I add. "Thanks to you." The moment stretches long as we stare at one another.

"Good," Jakob says, clearing his throat and breaking the eye contact. "Glad I could help. I know that's what you wanted." His look is guarded, cautious. I hate that look, and hate even more that I put it there. And there is nothing I can do to remove it except show him I'm trustworthy and serious about all of it—the chocolate shop, our community, and him. I order a bear claw for Walt, and Jakob hands me the paper bag with the pastry in it, our fingers brushing.

"Wish me luck," I say with a sigh. "I hope Walt's not too grouchy about this."

"He'll be fine," Jakob predicts, swiping my credit card for the pastry. "He's a soft-boiled egg beneath that crusty shell."

I giggle at the description, thinking of Walt going to puzzle club with my mom. I hope he's a very soft-boiled egg indeed. My dad adored Mom until the day he died, and I know that even though she has me and Gus, she's lonely. She needs someone to coddle her. Maybe that someone will be, in a twist none of us saw coming, gruff, grumbly, heart-of-gold Walt Perkins. I suppose stranger things have happened.

Five minutes later when I reach the shop and give Walt his bear claw, I realize Jakob slipped an extra pastry into the bag. It's a raspberry Danish. I slide it from the bag and look at it, imagining his hands shaping the round of dough, spooning in the raspberry filling. It's a message, I'm sure, but I don't know what it means. Is this absolution, affection, pity? I don't know how to decipher his intention.

Still, as I take a bite, my heart comes alive with a tiny little flicker of anticipation. I may not quite know what it means, but I know it's a good thing somehow. It's the best raspberry Danish I've ever eaten. The buttery, flaky dough and sweet, tart raspberry filling taste like hope, like possibility.

Chapter 40

Walt takes our refusal of his offer surprisingly well.

"Eh, that's okay," he says, tearing off half the bear claw and stuffing it into his mouth. He's standing in the shop, installing the new light fixtures. I went with brass and frosted globes. It's a very Parisian look, which warms my heart. "I got my eye set now on the building where the Four Corners Tavern is," Walt confides to me. "If I own it, they can't throw me out."

I snort in amusement. "Walt, if you're going to be going to puzzle club with my mom, you're going to have to mend your ways. Gwendolyn Wynne is not a lady to associate with a drunken rabble-rouser." I shoot him a warning look.

"I'm a teetotaling rabble-rouser, thank you very much." Walt rolls his eyes but then meets mine, his bright gaze surprisingly direct. "I expect if I had the love of a good woman like Gwen, I'd straighten up and walk the straight and narrow in a hot minute," he says. "Not much a man won't do for a good woman's love."

It's the most sentimental speech I've ever heard from Walt.

"You be careful with her. If you hurt her, I'll turn your life into one of those murder mysteries you're so fond of," I warn him. "You'll be crab bait. They'll never find your body."

He gives me a little salute. "Understood. Message received loud and clear. I think the world of your mom. Always have. I'll take good care of her."

Then he turns his attention to more prosaic matters. "I've got the invoice for the work we've done so far," he says, handing it to me. "It comes out to a little more than we thought it would because of the extent of the water damage and you getting the more expensive flooring. This is for the plumbing repairs and the floors and fixtures and stuff. It doesn't include those fancy display cases you wanted me to order though. I'll invoice you when they come in."

I glance at the total and my stomach drops. Fifteen thousand dollars? That's more than the total amount Mom set aside. And that doesn't include the display cases or the amount we will need to pay for our portion of the building upgrades. I swallow hard, thoughts racing. What are we going to do?

Walt sees my stricken expression. "Hey, Emmie, I want to talk to you about something now that I know you all don't want to sell." He takes off his baseball cap and slaps it against his thigh. "I know you're not flush with cash right now, and I got an idea. Hear me out, okay? I want to invest in your chocolate business, as a silent partner."

I stare at him in confusion. "You want to invest in my chocolate business?" I ask, baffled. "Why?"

He shrugs and scratches his head. "Call it payback. I don't know if you know this, but I was a friend of your daddy's when we were young bucks. We were always getting into some trouble or another. Truth be told, I was usually the one getting us both into trouble." He shoots me a rueful look. "Bert was a good man through and through. There was one time we were gonna go fishing, but well, it's a long story. Ended up having to get rescued by the coast guard and that didn't set too well with Gwen. After that incident, she made him give up his wild ways and any 'bad influences.'" Walt makes air quotes with his stubby fingers. "Meaning me. But your dad never forgot his old buddy Walt, and I always knew I could depend on him to do me a good turn if I needed him to. He once bailed me out of jail in Seattle after a wild weekend. And about fifteen years ago, I was broke and living in my car, and he let me camp out here at the store after-hours for a few months till I got back on my feet. This was way back, before I won that state lottery."

"You what?" I ask in surprise.

"Oh, I don't tell most folks about that. I kept it real quiet. It wasn't a huge sum, but enough to get me on my feet and let me get started in real estate. I used the lotto winnings to buy my first commercial real estate building," Walt says nonchalantly.

I am gobsmacked. In a town as small as Poulsbo, how has Walt managed to keep this quiet all these years?

Walt holds his cap to his chest like he's saying the Pledge of Allegiance. "Emmie, I have to tell you something." He looks so solemn my stomach drops. "When your daddy got sick, right at the end, he asked me to come to the hospital," Walt confides. "It was just him and me, a coupla weeks before he passed. He asked me to keep an eye on you and Gwen, make sure you had all you needed. And I've tried to do right by him ever since." He hesitates, shuffling his feet nervously. "I had a key to this shop from the time when I was camping out here, and ever since he died, well, I've been comin' in once a month or so at night to fix leaks and do little repairs, trying to keep my word to him."

"You what?" I stare at him, mouth agape. "Has it been you this whole time?" I think back on all the times I repaired something by following a YouTube tutorial, and sometimes days or weeks later I'd notice that it seemed like I'd fixed it even better than I remembered. Was it Walt all along?

Walt grins a little bashfully. "You did the best you could, Emmie. I'd just come in and find what you'd tried to repair and fix it a little better, so it would hold up and do what you needed it to do."

It's been Walt all along. Like some slightly grizzled, potbellied elf helper.

"Did you leave the gold sprinkles too?" I ask.

Walt looks puzzled. "The what?" he asks.

"Nothing." I wave away the question. I guess some mysteries will never be solved.

"Thank you," I tell Walt, tearing up at the thought of my dad looking out for his girls, even from beyond the grave. On impulse I throw my arms around Walt and give him a hug. He looks discomfited by this display of emotion. "It was nothing big," he says, patting my back awkwardly. "Just doing right by my old friend."

"It was big to us," I say, stepping back and seeing Walt with new eyes. Is this why Mom is inviting him to puzzle club? Has she caught a glimpse of the soft center beneath his hard-boiled shell? It's starting to make more sense to me now.

"But I still don't understand why you want to invest in my chocolate business," I point out, wiping my eyes.

"Why not?" Walt says, looking surprised. "Seems like a good idea to me. I believe in your product. I've tried most of it already. I'd be honored to invest if it helps you and lets me keep my promise to your dad."

"Hmm . . ." I eye him speculatively. "What do you have in mind then?"

Walt asks for a piece of paper and scribbles a simple contract on it. He hands it over. He's offering me a no-interest twenty-thousand-dollar loan with a repayment term of ten years. I stare at the few scrawled lines in shock. It's a generous offer, an exceedingly generous offer. It would allow us to pay for our portion of the upgrades with enough left over to purchase the new equipment I need, and probably allow us a little cushion for any lean months too. It feels too good to be true.

"Is there a catch?" I ask shrewdly.

"Well now, you got me," Walt confesses with a sheepish grin. "I guess I've got one condition . . . no, make that two conditions, before I'll loan you the money to get you back on your feet."

I raise my eyebrows, waiting. "Keep talking."

"You gotta keep selling your daddy's fudge. Even if it's just a shelf or two and a few flavors. That's my condition. Fudge sells well, and the price point brings in a wider group of folks than people who shop for fancy chocolates. It's good business. This way, there's something for everyone in this shop. And it honors your mama and daddy and carries on the spirit of their shop."

I consider the idea. He has a good point. Artisan chocolates are a whole lot more expensive than fudge. It's not a bad idea to offer a product at a lower price point, and fudge is a popular item. Plus, Walt is right, it feels like a good way to honor and remember my dad, selling the fudge I make from his original recipe, carrying on the tradition and business he spent his life building. I think about making a few batches of fudge a week and find the idea oddly appealing.

"Okay." I nod. "Agreed. We'll keep selling fudge, but just a few flavors. One shelf of fudge." As soon as I say them, the words just feel right. I guess there is still fudge in my future after all. "What's the second condition?"

"I guess you might call it my interest rate on the loan," Walt says with a mischievous grin.

I narrow my eyes at him. "And what would that be?"

"A pound of fudge a week. Of the flavor of my choice."

"You're going to develop diabetes if you eat a pound of fudge a week for ten years," I tell him sternly, though inside I'm feeling a flutter of excitement at the possibilities this unexpected new offer opens up. We can upgrade the shop to the county's specifications, and I can afford those beautiful but pricey glass-and-wood display cases we ordered and the quality equipment I need to do my best work. It feels like a miracle.

"You let me worry about my own pancreas," Walt grumbles. "A man has to have some vices left or his life becomes too virtuous to be any fun."

I grin at the old codger. "I don't think you're in any danger of that," I tell him. Then I stick out my hand. "Walt, I believe we have a deal."

"JAKOB!" GUS SQUEALS and runs in the front door of the shop straight toward the tall figure standing in the middle of the room. After picking Gus up from school, we stopped to collect Mom, who is meeting us here after her book club in the back of Dot's store. She's developing quite the social life all of a sudden. It warms my heart to see her so happy.

As a bonus for picking up Mom, I get to admire the new light fixtures, which are finally all installed.

"Hey, man!" Jakob chuckles as Gus wraps his entire little body around Jakob's leg and holds on tight. "How's the universe treating you?"

Gus peers up at Jakob with a serious expression. "I think I'm going to stick to doing stuff on earth for now," he says confidentially. "There's always time for space later, but right now I think you might need my help. Do you?"

Jakob lifts his head, meeting my eyes over Gus's tousled hair. "Always, little man," he says. For a moment he doesn't look away.

I move closer to them, trying to play it cool, although my heart is melting seeing my son so happy and excited. He feels he has a purpose, and I sense his newfound confidence. "Thanks for the Danish," I say quietly to Jakob when Gus goes to grab a screwdriver.

"No problem," Jakob says, brushing off the gratitude, but I see his eyes slide toward me as Walt comes in the front door talking to Mom. Is Walt in the book club now too? It wouldn't surprise me. Mr. Butters is trotting along behind them sporting a snazzy zebra-striped collar but nothing else.

"So then they find her body in a septic tank, but the crazy thing is . . . no footprints . . . so the question is, who did it?" Walt is saying.

"Ahem." I tilt my head significantly toward Gus, and Walt gets the hint and stops midsentence. Mom sees Gus and goes in for a hug, asking him about his day as he scratches Mr. Butters under the chin and tells her about playing Home Depot at recess.

"What do you think of how it's turned out?" Jakob asks, gesturing around the shop. I look around carefully. The space has been transformed. It's light, bright, airy, and appealing. Other than the display cases, which should arrive soon, it looks exactly like my vision.

"It's perfect," I tell him sincerely.

He looks satisfied.

"Did Walt tell you about his loan offer to me?" I ask.

Jakob nods. "See, soft-boiled at his center," he murmurs, so low I have to lean closer to hear. I inhale him. The yeast of bread dough and a little sawdust. It's magic.

"Something . . . unexpected happened this week," Jakob says, keeping his eyes trained on me while he coils an extension cord. I try to ignore how the coiling makes his biceps flex. "Walt asked me to help him with another project across town when we're done with this one, a pretty big renovation project on a building he owns. He wants me to work as many hours as I can. When I mentioned it to my mom, she suggested we think about hiring another baker at least part-time so I could do more with Walt." He's looking at me steadily. "She said she talked to you and that you gave her the idea."

"I didn't tell her what to do," I hasten to clarify. "I just told her she should ask you if you're happy at the bakery." I shift guiltily, hoping he's not annoyed I meddled.

He is still looking at me like he's trying to decipher a code. "Thank you," he says finally. "We talked, finally. I thought they might feel abandoned, but it turns out one of my cousins really loves baking. She's coming by the shop next week for a trial run to see if she might be a good fit. If she works out, it will free me up to do a lot more of this." He nods toward his toolbox.

"Jakob, that's amazing news!" I beam up at him.

"Yeah, it is," he tells me with an air of nonchalance, but I know him well enough to see that he is very pleased. Mom and Walt have moved to the office. I can hear them in there gossiping about puzzle club. Gus runs up and begs for a snack.

"I gotta eat a lot to keep up my strength for all the hard work around here," he tells me, eyes big and beseeching behind his blue glasses. I pull a Ziploc out of my purse and dole out two sugar cookies.

"Sprinkles!" Gus shouts enthusiastically when he sees the gold sprinkles dotting the tops of the cookies. I've been using the sprinkles liberally in his afternoon treats. I don't know if it's the magical sprinkles or him growing older or Jakob's influence or all three, but Gus seems so much happier and more confident.

"Thanks, Mom!" He darts away, stuffing the cookies into his mouth.

"So are you saying yes to Walt?" I ask Jakob, offering him a cookie from the bag. He takes it.

"I said I'd do it on one condition." Jakob meets my eyes, a faint glint of amusement in his.

"What's the condition?"

"I can hire Gus to be my helper every now and then."

We both turn and look at Gus, who is huffing and puffing as he manfully staggers across the store carrying Walt's entire toolbox. My heart squeezes hard with love for my kid.

Just then, Gus drops a number of items out of the toolbox on his journey across the shop. We both wince at the sound of tools hitting the new wood floors.

"Adds character," Jakob says philosophically.

I watch Gus struggling to get the tools back into the toolbox. He doesn't give up though. It's been a long time since I've seen Gus so filled with purpose and determination.

"When Dad died, I think Gus didn't know how to process it," I tell Jakob. "They were best buddies, and then one day my dad was just . . . gone. We talked about how Granddad was in heaven, but that's a hard concept for a kid to understand. Gus just knew his favorite guy in the world was beyond his reach. Soon after that, he got obsessed with space. I think it was as close to heaven as he could get. I've been worried about him, but when you started letting him help you, it was the first time since Dad died that Gus was more interested in what's here on earth than what's up there among the stars. Thank you for that."

Jakob looks at me, his gaze steady. "You're welcome," he says. "He's a great kid. Whether he's an astronaut or a contractor or decides to carry on the family business and make fudge, he'll be just fine."

"I hope you're right," I murmur, watching my son, whom I love so desperately. So often I feel inadequate for the task of parenting. "It's hard to know if I'm doing enough, if I'm doing it right, or if I'm just screwing up," I sigh.

Jakob touches my elbow. "Probably all three," he says matter-of-factly. "But isn't that true of most things in life? We're not born life-skilled. We don't know how to do the important stuff. We learn by trial and error, we mess up, and finally, hopefully, we get it right."

I sense something more to his words and hazard a glance. He's watching Gus, but his hand is still on my elbow. Never have I been so aware of a few square inches of skin, his against mine.

"Emmie, I'd like to give us another try," he tells me, and my heart somersaults in my chest with joy. "I think we should take it slow and see where this goes. Are you still open to that?" He glances almost shyly at me.

I clear my throat. "Absolutely." I'm trying to be relaxed and nonchalant when really I want to just climb him like a tree and nestle down against his chest and have him hold me safe forever. "So how do we do this?" I ask.

Jakob surveys me closely. "Like this," he says. "Emmie, would you go on a real date with me?"

"Depends," I tell him cheekily. "Will there be Danishes?" Then I look up and meet his eyes. "I'd love that," I reply, beaming. He nods and scuffs the toe of his work boot against the floor, grinning. "Okay then, it's a date." And then he casually loops his arm over my shoulders and pulls me to him. I go willingly, nestling against his side. I fit perfectly.

"It's a date." I turn back to watch Gus, feeling my heart swell with anticipation and relief.

I look around the shop, touched to realize how far everything has come. How far *we* have come. My gaze lands on Gus, who is holding up the orange-handled screwdriver in triumph. He hasn't had a tummy ache in a while, and he's been waking me up by dragging the miniature tool kit he got from my dad into bed in the mornings. Instead of waking to him reading me alarming facts about space, I'm opening my eyes to his earnest little face bent over a piece of wood, hammering or screwing something in, his tongue sticking out the side of his mouth in concentration. He's being brave and bold, and my heart swells with love for my little man.

I glance at Mom, who is nodding as Walt explains something about light fixtures and electrical currents to her. Her cheeks are as pink as her lipstick. I know the road ahead for her will be a tough one as her health continues to slowly decline, but looking at her and Walt, I think that her golden years are already holding some unexpected sweetness.

Then I glance at Jakob, who is standing tall and sure, steady and calm beside me. Now that I've finally stopped fighting it and let myself acknowledge my feelings for him, I can't deny that I am absolutely head over heels for this man. I think of Henry, who will soon be heading out to shoot a new season of *Savor* instead of getting down on one knee to propose to me. It wasn't how I thought my life would go, and it certainly doesn't match the vision I saw for my future, but it feels so right that it has turned out this way. I know I'm doing the right thing.

I picture the comfortable yellow dress hanging in my closet, waiting for the right occasion, waiting for me to decide when to wear it. I don't have a crystal ball to predict the future. I don't know exactly how all of this is going to play out. But I know I'm on the right track, and that I'm at the helm of my own life at last. Confident in this, I am excited for the unknowns and filled with hope for all the good things that lie ahead.

My eyes wander over the shop and I feel a burst of joy and satisfaction. This space, which holds so many years of memories for my family, is safely ours and awaiting its next chapter. I just ordered a whimsical tree on Etsy. Everything is coming together. I just need a name and I'll be all set. None of the names I've thought of, or names Mom and Dot or Dani have suggested, have been right. I'm waiting for inspiration to strike. When it does, I'm sure it will feel just right.

I think of the mysterious glass jar of gold sprinkles that arrived when I needed it most, of the note that simply said *For courage*. How far I have come since the day it arrived. How brave I've learned to be. And just like that, in a flash of inspiration, I know what to name this place.

CHAPTER 41

Two months later

"Welcome to the grand opening of Sprinkle," I announce proudly, holding the door wide for my parade of guests. Dani is first in line, followed by Dot, Mom, and Gus, who is wearing a little bow tie and a three-piece suit for the festivities. He looks adorable and I can't resist giving him a kiss on the cheek, which he squirms away from. He's also got a tape measure and a screwdriver in the pockets of the suit. He carries them everywhere now. He is flanked by Mr. Butters, who is wearing a dapper doggy tuxedo for this happy occasion. Usually these days Mr. Butters wears no accessories, but today is a special day. He waddles into the store and promptly tries to scrape his bow tie off against the corner of a display case.

Hilda and Sebastian come in next, followed by Paula, Mary Beth, and Justin. A few other friends and neighbors crowd in behind them. I keep the sign on the cheery yellow door turned to **CLOSED**, as we are not officially open for another half hour. But I've invited the VIP guests early to sample the confections and to christen the space with a champagne toast. Sprinkle has been open for more than a month already, but this was the first time Henry could get away from his shooting schedule to join us, so we are throwing a belated grand opening now, when he can be here to film.

Everyone wanders around oohing and aahing admiringly, tasting samples of all the chocolates I offer. Soft instrumental music is filtering out from the hidden speakers.

Mom comes up and squeezes my hand. "It's perfect, sweetheart," she says, looking around. "I'm so proud of you." She's been in here many times before, and even runs the register for me when I can't be in the shop, but there's something special about today. We're celebrating the future and remembering and honoring the past.

"Emmie, these are incredible," Paula exclaims from across the room as she bites into an espresso truffle with sweet cream ganache.

"Ooh, so is this dark chocolate huckleberry one," Hilda chimes in, mouth full.

"Utterly divine!" Sebastian agrees, nibbling one of my Rainier cherry and vanilla buttercream truffles.

Everywhere I look there are truffles and bonbons, caramels and pralines artfully arranged in gleaming glass-and-wood cases around the store. Under a glass dome on the counter sits a very special collection of ruby chocolate truffles filled with rose and cardamom cream and adorned with gold sprinkles. Those are not for sale. They're only for guests who come in looking weary or stressed or heartbroken. They're a gift for anyone who looks like they need a little boost of courage.

I gaze around in satisfaction. The shop looks exactly as I dreamed it would, with dark wood floors, big light-filled windows, and a few whimsical decorations. I got my tree at last—painted silver with twinkly lights and chocolate ornaments, and a bird's nest of spun chocolate with colorful chocolate eggs perched in the branches. There's a big, black old-fashioned cash register at the longest counter, and behind it a mural a local artist painted depicting a beautiful meadow of wildflowers sloping down to a whitecapped sea. It's elegant and a touch quirky and exactly what I had in mind. Well, except for the case of fudge prominently displayed in front of one of the big windows. I thought I was done with fudge, but it turns out that making a couple of batches a week actually feels nostalgic. Seeing the fudge now makes me smile and think of Dad. I believe he would have loved how this is turning out.

The bell jingles and Walt saunters into the shop, wearing his nicest pair of denim overalls and a Cubs hat. "Place is looking great," he says, gazing around admiringly. He greets Mom with a swift peck on the cheek, tips his hat to Dani and Dot, then walks over to the case and checks out the fudge flavors.

"Came to collect my weekly fudge allowance," he announces.

"Sure. What can I get for you, Walt?" I unfold one of the little fancy gilt boxes.

"Well now, how about half a pound of chocolate cherry and half a pound of vanilla walnut?" Walt hooks his thumbs in his overall suspenders and looks proudly around the store. "It turned out super, kid," he tells me. "Your dad would have been proud of you. He was always so proud of you."

I swallow around the sudden lump in my throat. "I couldn't have done it without you, Walt," I tell him, adding an extra portion of Oreo fudge to the box. Walt is my grumpy guardian angel. Without him, I never could have completed the store like this. He and Jakob brought my vision for Sprinkle to life.

Speaking of Jakob, he should be here any minute. I glance toward the door, eager to see him. We've been inseparable for the past two months. They've been the happiest months of my life.

"Walt, come tell Dot about that book we just listened to, the crossword puzzle one where the clues pointing to the murderer are hidden in the puzzle." Mom gestures Walt over and he goes willingly. He is a regular now at puzzle night, and one or two evenings a week Mom is over at his little house outside of town, doing a puzzle and listening to audiobooks. Unsurprisingly, Mom was horrified by the true crime podcasts, so they've found a nice compromise in cozy mysteries where someone still dies but in a gentler manner. I confess I don't always understand their relationship, but Walt's gruff kindness is growing on me, and Gus has even taken to calling him Uncle Walt. I just know that Mom has seemed to bloom in the last two months. Her world has expanded, and she is thriving.

"Emmie, this place looks amazing." Dani comes over to me, sucking on one of the lavender gray sea salt caramels I set out among the samples. "And I still love the name. It's perfect."

"It *is* perfect," I agree. I've kept the meaning of the name a secret. Only my mom and Jakob know the full story. I told him all about the glass container of sprinkles the first week we were dating. He was skeptical at first, but now he sprinkles them on his morning oatmeal just like Gus.

I glance around. "It's what I always dreamed of," I tell Dani, feeling so happy I could float.

Everything is how I pictured it, but I am different now. I'm not trying to force myself into anything. I'm letting myself show up in my own life, letting my dreams and desires have a seat at the table. And what I've found is that when I do that, everything feels smoother, easier. Like switching the pinchy yellow dress for the right size, I feel like I can breathe again. Saying no to everyone else dictating the shape of my life has allowed me space to dream again, to desire, to have a say. Now I can focus on the most important things—the people closest to my heart and the work I love.

I glance over at Gus, who is stuffing mini espresso truffles with sweet cream ganache into his mouth as fast as he can while Mr. Butters watches and wags his stubby tail enthusiastically. "Hey, buddy, slow down," I admonish, ruffling his hair. "Those have caffeine." It's going to be a long night tonight depending on how many he ate before I noticed.

Dani snorts. "Here, try this, Gusto." She hands him one of the huckleberry bonbons. "Have you heard from Henry?" she asks me.

"He's on his way from the airport. He texted me," I tell her.

Henry left six weeks ago, memoir mostly completed, but not before signing a contract to purchase the little beach cottage on the bay. He plans to come back next summer to finish the memoir. But right now he's flying in from Iceland for the weekend on a quick break from filming to celebrate the grand opening of the shop. The episode of *Savor* that we filmed will air in a few weeks, and he has warned me to expect a substantial swell of customers. Our online shop is up and running, so we're as ready as we can be. Today he's bringing Crisanto to film our grand opening.

"That dress is super cute on you, by the way," Dani says with an admiring glance at my dress the color of sunshine. "You're giving me real Doris Day vibes."

"Thanks!" I glance down and smooth the skirt happily. I've saved it for today, for the grand opening, and I feel both comfortable and glamorous. I take a deep breath, happy the dress stretches, happy I returned the other one that simply didn't fit.

In a way, this yellow dress is symbolic. I almost let the vision make me keep a dress (and a love and a future) that wasn't the right fit. But when I had the courage to finally be honest with myself, I discovered the best fit for me. I don't think of the vision much anymore. I don't need to. I now have the dress and the life and the man of my dreams, and I don't feel constricted by "shoulds" and "oughts." I feel free.

The door gives a little jingle as it opens. It's Jakob. He's wearing a sky-blue button-down shirt that brings out the ice of his eyes and a bow tie that matches Gus's. His eyes sweep the room until he finds me. He crosses to me in three strides, sweeps me up, and plants a kiss firmly on my mouth.

"You look beautiful," he whispers against my ear. "You're definitely the sexiest small-business owner in Poulsbo." He chuckles as I shiver and grab his shirtfront, tugging him down to me for another kiss. I'm not sure I'll ever get tired of him walking across a room, eyes fixed on me like that. It's only been two months, but we both know where this is going. We've even spoken the M-word, and I feel certain that our love story ends in forever. Gus adores him, Mom adores him, and most important, I think he's the best thing since sliced bread. It took years in Europe, a few false starts, and some wrong turns, but I got here in the end, right where I'm supposed to be.

The door chimes again and a sweet, slightly disheveled Brit tumbles in, trailed by a cameraman. "Hullo, everyone." Henry raises a hand. "Sorry for the delay. The traffic from the airport was dreadful."

Even though he's just come from a long flight, he looks camera-ready as always in a Breton striped shirt and his iconic navy swazer. He goes around the room, kissing cheeks and shaking hands. Then he stops and surveys the shop.

"Emmie, this is extraordinary. The craftsmanship, the tone—elegance meets whimsy. I love it!" He smiles at me in genuine delight. "Can't wait to show our viewers how this all turned out." He turns to the cameraman. "Crisanto, are you ready to film? I think we're just going to do candid shots of this happy occasion. This all looks brilliant."

"Hey everybody, it's time for a toast," Dani announces, breezing by us.

Henry and Crisanto quickly confer, and Crisanto gets his camera set up. "Ready when you are." Henry gives us a thumbs-up.

Dani brings out a tray of champagne coupes from the kitchen, and Jakob pops the cork off the champagne. I splurged on a few good bottles to celebrate. Dani pours the bubbly and Dot hands out the glasses. Even Gus gets a glass bottle of fancy sparkling soda, a thoughtful gesture from Mom. I shudder to think how much sugar he's consumed by now. Oh well, it's a celebration. Rare September sunshine streams through the big plate glass windows, filling the room with cheery, lemony light. I feel like my heart might burst with happiness as I look at those I love crowded around. Everyone holds their champagne at the ready. Jakob slips up next to me and presses a hand to my back, his presence solid and steady.

My eyes glaze with unshed tears as I hold my coupe aloft. "Thank you all for coming today," I say. "I'd like to raise the first toast to my parents for their love and dedication to family and their community, and for making the Happy Viking a place that brought joy to so many for so long. To Gwen and Bert and the Happy Viking. Cheers!"

"Cheers!" everyone calls out, circling the room and clinking their coupes. The champagne is fizzy and cold, as effervescent as my emotions right now. I feel fizzy and full of mingled grief and joy.

"And to another chapter in the history of this town, our family, and this place." I raise my glass again. "To Sprinkle!"

"To Sprinkle!" everyone repeats, clinking glasses again and

taking sips. Crisanto moves around the room, capturing all of this on film.

"Emmie," Henry calls out. He comes over to me. Crisanto is standing nearby, filming everything.

"I have a little surprise for you." Henry pauses dramatically and pulls a familiar-looking red leather box from his pocket. I stare at it in surprise. It looks like a ring box. Jakob moves a hair closer to me.

"She's already spoken for, Summers," he growls in a tone that is ninety-five percent joking and just a smidge not.

"Oh no." Henry laughs self-consciously. "It's nothing like that. Emmie, do you remember the box of chocolates you gave me as a going-away gift?"

"Yes." I nod, unsure where this is going. I'd made a sampler box of all my favorites as a thank-you and a goodbye to Henry when he left.

"Well, I have something to confess." Henry peers at me with a slightly guilty expression. "I took some of them and entered them in that little competition in Brussels I mentioned to you once. It's small but exclusive. I didn't tell you in case nothing came of it, but something did." He steps forward, tries to open the box, and fumbles with it. Something falls out onto the floor. It looks like a silver medal of some kind, on a silk ribbon.

"How clumsy of me." Henry kneels on the floor, puts the medal back into the open box, and lifts it toward me. It looks for all the world like he's about to propose.

Beside me, I hear Dani draw in a sharp breath. "Emmie," she hisses, elbowing me. "Look. It's just like your vision."

I glance around in surprise, and for a moment time hovers and halts. She's right. I am standing in the shop of my dreams, surrounded by my family and friends. Henry is kneeling in front of me in a shaft of golden sunshine, holding out a red leather box, and I am wearing a dress the color of sunshine.

"Oh," I breathe, stunned. "Oh!" It's come true. The vision has come true, and yet nothing is quite how I imagined it. Henry is not proposing. Everything I saw is here, but different than I thought. It's not what I expected. It's better.

I take the box from Henry and stare at the silver medal. The inscription says my browned butter hazelnut toffee truffles took second place at the European Chocolatier Awards. Reverently, I touch the inscription with a finger. "For real?" I whisper.

"Jacques Genin was one of the judges, and he was very pleased to hear you were the creator of this award-winning entry," Henry tells me, beaming as he gets to his feet. "Of course he judged it blind, so only afterwards did he learn it was you. He said to give you this." He leans toward me and presses a quick, chaste kiss to my cheek. "Congratulations, Emmie," he says, pulling back and grinning at me. "It is very well deserved."

"This is amazing. Thank you," I tell Henry, blinking away happy tears. I press my hand to my chest, overcome with emotion. I glance at Mom and Dot and Dani in turn. Mom is sniffling and smiling. Dot is giving me two thumbs-up. Dani is, for once, speechless. Jakob slips an arm around my waist, steadying me.

"Well, since we're pulling out ring boxes," he says with a pointed look at Henry. He moves around until he's standing in front of me. "I was planning to do this before Henry stole my thunder," he explains. He looks nervous.

"Going to do what?" I ask, confused. This wasn't part of the vision. I don't know what's coming next. And then suddenly Jakob is on one knee in front of me, gazing up at me with those glacial-blue eyes, now filled with warmth and tenderness. He looks so handsome in his button-down shirt and bow tie. Suddenly I can't breathe. Is he . . .

"Emmie Wynne, I've loved you from the start," he says softly. "And I have a question for you."

I press a hand to my chest. "What is happening?" I whisper in shock.

"I think you're getting proposed to for real," Dani calls out. "On camera. By hot bread-baking Thor. Just go with it."

"Bread-baking Thor?" Jakob looks confused.

I'm vaguely aware of Crisanto in the background, filming the interaction. Everyone in the shop is watching with rapt attention.

"Gus, that's your cue, buddy." Jakob looks around and Gus springs into action. He hurries over and pulls a little blue velvet ring box from the pocket of his suit. A few sprinkles fall out onto the floor when he does so. I had a feeling he was stashing them somewhere.

"Here you go," Gus says, handing the box to Jakob. Then he peers up at me. "Mommy, say yes," he says, then runs back to his place beside Mom, job done.

I stare down at Jakob in shock. He's on one knee, waiting patiently for me. "Ready?" he asks. I nod dumbly.

"I'm crazy about you, Emmie," Jakob says, "and I've grown pretty attached to this guy too." Jakob nods to Gus, who is noisily slurping his fancy soda through a straw. "You would make me the happiest man in the world if you'd do me the honor of marrying me."

It's so like Jakob, brief and to the point and filled with candor. I gaze at him for a moment, at the winking little diamond of the vintage ring he's holding out to me.

"I'd love to," I whisper.

The room erupts into whoops and applause. Mom is outright happy-sobbing while Walt offers her a hanky, his arm around her protectively. Gus thrusts his fist into the air and shouts, "Yippee!" Dot finds another bottle of champagne and splashes more into everyone's glasses. But in the middle of the joyful chaos, all I see is Jakob in front of me. He slowly gets to his feet, takes my hand, and slips the ring onto my finger.

"It was my grandma's," he says, his voice low and gravelly with emotion. "If you don't like it, we can get another." I see a flash of uncertainty in his eyes.

"Don't you dare. I love it." I look up, up at him, and he bends to kiss me long and deep. Someone wolf whistles, probably Dani, but we ignore them. We break the kiss, but Jakob pulls me against his chest and holds me. From the safe circle of his arms, I look around me at the celebration, misty-eyed. This is going to make great television for our episode of *Savor*, but even more than that, it is going to make a great story to tell my grandchildren and great-grandchildren.

I'll tell them all about how I almost gave all the pieces of myself away to make others happy, to fulfill others' dreams and expectations, but just in time I learned to listen to my own heart, to make space for myself and my dreams too. I learned to stop trying to control what I cannot control and instead found peace and plenty in charting my own course, in learning to listen to that little voice inside me that guided me toward those true and beautiful things in life that bring me joy and purpose and plenty. I followed my heart, and just as Mom predicted, the vision for my purpose in life has come true in its own unexpected way.

"I have one more toast," I announce, disentangling myself from Jakob's arms. I raise my glass. "To life in all its perfect imperfections," I say, choking up a little with wonder and tears of joy and gratitude. "And to unexpectedly happy endings. And finally, to sweet serendipity."

I glance around the room, at Hilda and Sebastian and the others, at Walt and Dot and Dani, who is surreptitiously feeding Mr. Butters a doggy pot pie, and at Henry, who has turned out to be my guardian angel in a different way than I ever anticipated. Across the room Mom is beaming at me. Beside her, Gus stands tall and proud, sipping his fancy soda and watching Jakob to see how he should act on this festive occasion. Seeing their growing relationship warms my heart.

Finally I turn to Jakob. He's standing right next to me, tall and steady, his blue eyes warm and tender as they focus on me. He pulls me close to his side. I've never felt more loved. Joy rises in my chest like the bubbles in my champagne, languid and golden. I cannot believe this is my life. How perfectly imperfect. What a wonderful surprise.

We toast.

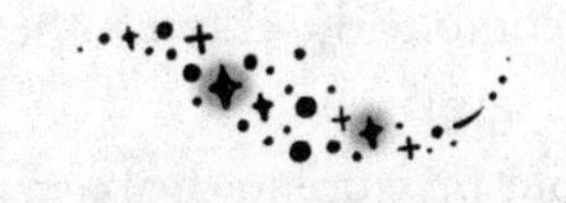

Serendipity Sprinkle Sugar Cookies

2½ cups all-purpose flour
¾ teaspoon salt
2 teaspoons baking powder
2 sticks (1 cup) unsalted butter (at room temperature)
1¼ cups granulated sugar, plus an additional ¼ cup set aside for rolling
1 large egg + 1 egg yolk
1 teaspoon vanilla extract
(optional 1 teaspoon almond extract for a lovely subtle almond flavor.)
Your choice of sprinkles

1. Preheat your oven to 350°F. Line 2 baking sheets with parchment paper.
2. In a medium-sized bowl, whisk together the flour, salt, and baking powder until blended. Set aside.
3. In a larger bowl, use an electric mixer to cream together the butter and 1¼ cups sugar until the mixture is light and fluffy (about 2–3 minutes). If you do not have a hand mixer, you can

simply mix vigorously by hand with a rubber spatula until combined (2–3 minutes).

4. Add the egg, egg yolk, and vanilla (and almond extract if using), and mix until combined, scraping the bowl down once or twice with a rubber spatula.
5. Slowly add the flour mixture to the butter/sugar/egg mixture. Do not overmix. Set aside.
6. Pour the remaining ¼ cup sugar into a shallow dish or bowl. Pour sprinkles into another shallow dish or bowl.
7. Using a spoon, scoop out whatever size portion of the dough you prefer and roll each spoonful of dough into a ball with your hands. Roll the bottom half of each ball in the sugar and the top half in the sprinkles. Place the dough balls (sugar side down) on the baking sheets, spaced a couple of inches apart.
8. Bake for 10–12 minutes, or until the cookies begin to brown very slightly at the edges. Allow the cookies to cool for a few minutes on the baking sheet before carefully transferring them to a wire rack to cool completely. Enjoy!

Fudge Jubilee

Since most of us don't have a marble slab sitting around our house to cream fudge, I've taken the liberty of including my family's special fudge recipe here instead of Emmie's. It's absolutely delicious and takes a whole lot less effort to make!

My mother created this original recipe years ago, and we made it every holiday season when I was growing up, gifting it to everyone from the pastor to my piano teacher to our mailman! This fudge is creamy and decadent, similar to ganache, and so easy to make! If you want to get fancy with your fudge, I've included a list of ideas at the bottom of the recipe.

8 ounces cream cheese
12 ounces semisweet chocolate chips
½ cup butter
1 cup powdered sugar
2 teaspoon vanilla

1. In a medium-sized microwave safe bowl, melt butter and chocolate chips in the microwave, stirring until mixture is smooth and shiny. Or melt in a medium-sized saucepan on medium low, remove from heat once melted, and stir thoroughly. Set aside.
2. In another medium-sized bowl, whip the cream cheese with a hand mixer for a minute or so. Slowly add in the melted chocolate mixture. Add the powdered sugar and vanilla. Cream until smooth.
3. Pour fudge into a buttered 8 x 8 pan and chill in the refrigerator for several hours until firm. This is a softer fudge, so it needs to be refrigerated until eaten.
4. If you want to get fancy with this recipe, you can add any of the following—maraschino cherries, toasted pecans, toasted coconut, cranberries, pistachios, etc. Or you can use peppermint chocolate chips in place of the regular chocolate chips, and sprinkle the top of the fudge with crushed candy canes. You can also swap ½ teaspoon of almond extract for ½ teaspoon of vanilla extract for a delicious almond flavor.

Acknowledgments

An enormous and heartfelt *thank-you* to the following amazing folks who helped make this story better and brighter. My fantastic agent, Kevan Lyon, who is so wise and wonderful. My delightful and insightful editor, Kate Seaver, who strengthens every story with warmth and great instincts for storytelling. The clever and capable Amanda Maurer and the rest of the wonderful team at Berkley, who are all true professionals and lovely humans to boot. The kind and canny Ashley Hayes of Uplit Reads. My lovely and talented book buddies—bestselling authors Marie Bostwick and Katherine Reay, the lively PNW author lunch crew, and the wonderfully supportive brunch bunch, especially Debbie Macomber and Sheila Roberts. The delightful Bookstagram community—true book lovers who celebrate stories with kindness and creativity! All my incredible independent bookstore friends, including but not limited to Away with Words, Watermark Book Co., Invitation Bookshop, Island Books, Magnolia's Bookstore, Third Place Books, Browsers Bookshop, Liberty Bay

Books, Edmonds Bookshop, and Brick & Mortar Books, among other amazing Puget Sound bookshops. A million thanks for supporting local authors. You are the best! Special thanks to the following: Anya, Jen, and Marie, who read this story early and gave great feedback to strengthen it. A and B—you both bring me such joy. It's an honor to be your mom. And Y for being my adventure buddy and constant loving support for seventeen years (even though we both forgot how long we've been married this year and celebrated eighteen years instead by accident! I'll celebrate every anniversary with you, even if we get the number wrong.) And for every reader who feels like they're juggling so much—caregiving, kids, and careers—and yet is still trying to get up each day and make the world a better place in their own way. This story is for you . . . A wise friend once told me, "You can do it all, you just can't do it all at once." I'm still trying to learn the lessons of leaving margin in my life, keeping a gracious, human-speed pace; saying no to distraction; and letting go of lesser things to make space for what I most value. I hope we can each find the space to shine in our own way. We're all in this together.

With love,

Rachel

A Sprinkle of Sweet Serendipity

RACHEL LINDEN

READERS GUIDE

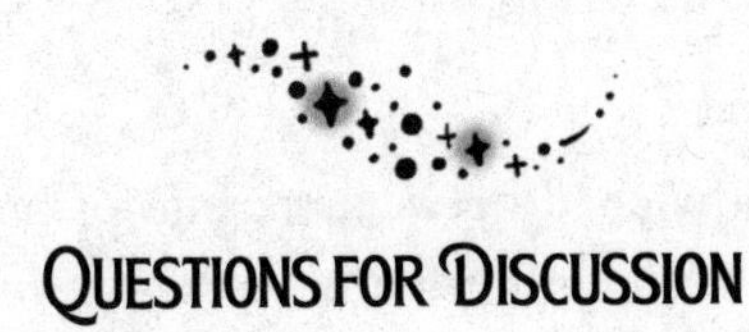

Questions for Discussion

1. If you were given the chance to see a vision of your true purpose in life, how much would you let what you saw affect your life? Would you allow the vision to guide your choices? Why or why not?

2. Emmie's To-Do List changes as the story progresses. How does the list reflect her personal growth?

3. Emmie is torn between her own dreams and desires, and her sense of responsibility to her family, the fudge shop, and her vision of the future. How do the themes of responsibility and dreams play out in the story?

4. What role do sprinkles play in the story? How do they help the characters grow? What gives you courage to face hard things in your life?

5. A core theme in the book is making space in your own life for what you truly value. How does Emmie learn this lesson throughout the story? Is this a lesson you feel is important? Why or why not?

6. Emmie is sandwiched between caring for her mom and her son, and carries a heavy burden of responsibility as a working mom and caregiver. Discuss the emotional labor women often carry as they juggle roles as caregivers, parents, professionals, and household managers. What do you think could or should change to help lessen this burden?

7. Emmie believes she has to single-handedly keep everything together in her life. What does she learn by the end about the strength of community?

8. Mr. Butters is a lovable doggy character, but he serves a greater purpose than just being cute. How does he reflect Gwen's growth throughout the story?

9. Emmie finds herself having to choose between two wonderful men. Is there a time in your life when you've had to choose between two good options? What did you pick, and why?

10. The town and residents' Norwegian heritage plays a role in the story. What aspects of heritage influence your own life?

Rachel Linden is a novelist and international aid worker whose adventures in more than fifty countries around the world provide excellent grist for her writing. She is the author of *The Secret of Orange Blossom Cake*, *Recipe for a Charmed Life*, *The Magic of Lemon Drop Pie*, and several other novels. Currently, Rachel lives with her family on a sweet little island in the Pacific Northwest, where she enjoys creating stories about strong women facing big challenges, food, travel, and second chances at love—all with a touch of whimsy and a happy, hopeful ending.

VISIT RACHEL LINDEN ONLINE

RachelLinden.com